Shakespeare's Invention by W.S. Gent.

Pat Martin

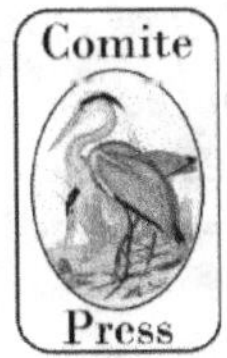

Names: Martin, Pat (Patrick Henry), 1945- .
Title: Shakespeare's invention by W.S. Gent. / Pat Martin.
Description: Clinton, LA : Comite Press, 2026. | Includes 7 b&w illustrations. | Includes index and bibliographic references. | Summary: Examines the theory that William Sterrell, a professor at Oxford, published as William Shakespeare. Two works of Shakespeare are examined closely: Venus and Adonis and All's Well that Ends Well. Sterrell's and his patron's biographies are also traced in relation to other Shakespeare works.
Identifiers: LCCN 2025925951 | ISBN 9781964075136 (hardback) | ISBN 9781964075112 (pbk) | ISBN 9781964075129 (Kindle)
Subjects: LCSH: Shakespeare, William, 1564-1616. | Sterrell, William, 1561-1631. | Worcester, Edward Somerset, Earl of, approximately 1550-1628. | Shakespeare, William, 1564-1616 – Authorship. | Shakespeare, William, 1564-1616. All's well that ends well. | Shakespeare, William, 1564-1616. Venus and Adonis. | Great Britain – History – 16th century. | Great Britain – History – 17th century. | BISAC: LITERARY CRITICISM / Shakespeare. | LITERARY CRITICISM / Modern / 16th Century. | LITERARY CRITICISM / Modern / 17th Century.
Classification: LCC PR2947.S74 M37 2026 | DDC 822.33--dc23
LC record available at https://lccn.loc.gov/2025925951

ISBN (Hardback): 978-1-964075-13-6
ISBN (Paperback): 978-1-964075-11-2
ISBN (ebook): 978-1-964075-12-9

Published by Comite Press, a Louisiana LLC
Clinton, Louisiana
ShakespearesInvention.com
PatMartinauthor.com

To

Tom Galligan and John Costonis

Two Chancellors who, like Leicester and Buckhurst, understood the importance of humanist studies for the development of critical thinking in higher education.

O O O O that Shakespeherian Rag—
It's so elegant
So intelligent.
T. S. Eliot - *The Wasteland*

"Shakespeare is the happy hunting ground of all minds that have lost their balance."
Buck Mulligan

Quanti casus humana rotant!

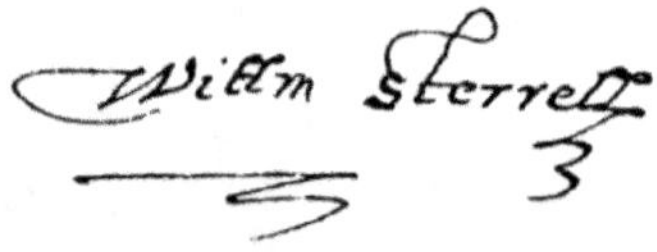

O world, thy slippery turns!
Coriolanus

Contents

Magdalen College, Oxford

Oxford English Dictionary **– Invention**

6.II.6 Something devised; a method of action, etc. contrived by the mind; a device, contrivance, design, plan, scheme.

> 1593 Shakes. *3 Hen. VI*, iv. i. 35 - What, if both Lewis and Warwick be appeas'd, By such invention as I can devise?

7.II.7 A work or writing as produced by exercise of the mind or imagination; a literary composition. Obs.

> 1601 Shakes. *Twel. N.* v. i. 341 - Or say, tis not your seal, not your invention.

8.II.8 A fictitious statement or story; a fabrication, fiction, figment.

> 1601 Shakes. *All's Well* iii. vi. 105 - None in the world, but return with an invention, and clap upon you two or three probable lies.

Chapter 1

Prologue

Does the title of this book intrigue you, or does it discomfort you? If you find it vaguely unsettling because you're not quite sure what it means, read no more. Put it down. Walk away. Save your money and your time. It's not written for you. But if the cover and title make you curious, if they cause you to seek their meaning and to turn over in your mind how the few words and portrait might be interpreted, if they engage you, then take this as your invitation to a journey and a conversation we will have along the way. Consider it an experience.

Let us explore in new ways poetry and plays that are four centuries old. Please, be skeptical. If you are open and patient, you will be rewarded with an enhanced appreciation of great art and insight into how it came to be. If not satisfied, your fare will be cheerfully refunded.

In this first segment of our journey, we will be present at the *invention* of Shakespeare, by whom we mean the author of the first work bearing that name, a "name from hence immortal life shall have." As we travel together, we can have a serious, respectful conversation about Shakespeare and his works during the two decades he was active as a writer. Don't approach this as though you are reading a legal brief. Strict rules of evidence will apply to most assertions of fact, but we will also look to arguments and (informed) speculations that may persuade you about the origins of the named author and his works.

We will focus primarily on one poem and one play, *Venus and Adonis* and *All's Well that Ends Well.* Together, they allow us to discover the origin of Shakespeare - poet and playwright. The poem is admired but unread today. The play is widely known for a catchy title, but it is the least liked play of the Shakespeare canon. So why read a little book about two works that few people now bother with? Because if you read it through, you will never again read

Shakespeare in the same way.

Appearing in June 1593, *Venus and Adonis* is the first work published under the name of William Shakespeare. The lengthy poem about a goddess/queen's failed efforts to seduce a pretty youth is the foundation of the poet's work and early reputation. We will explore the poem and the literary setting of London in which it appeared. Essential to our conversation is why it is highly improbable that an unknown, uneducated native of Stratford could have produced so successful a work. If not Shakespeare-of-Stratford, then who is the poet? To answer the question is the purpose of this extended essay.

All's Well that Ends Well was completely unknown prior to 1623, when it appeared as the fourteenth play among the "Comedies" of the *First Folio.* The play unfolds in two related stories, a young woman's quest to attain the love of a count, paralleled by the failed efforts of a courtier to rise above his station while on a foreign expedition. *All's Well* is the playwright's own account of the events of his life that immediately preceded the publication of *Venus and Adonis.*

A brilliant professor at Oxford University, William Sterrell, found it necessary to assume another identity to publish his work as a means of saving his own life. *All's Well* tells his story. The play has the elements of a *roman à clef* - identifiable people and events appear with invented names and displaced locations. We can read it as a dramatization of the events of the author's life that made him hide his identity as a writer from public view.

Yes, this is a work on the authorship of the Shakespeare poetry and plays. It is the first of a larger project with much greater detail about both the Shakespeare works and the two men behind them. By concentrating here on the one poem and the one play, we can focus on the most compelling aspects of the Shakespeare authorship debate of several centuries duration. Think of it not as viewing the events of 1592-1593 through a microscope, but rather with a prism, redirecting a beam of light.

What does this little book have to offer that is different from all the thousands of books on Shakespeare and the many hundreds of works by traditional Shakespeare scholars? Principally, it builds on transcripts of about three hundred letters of a man completely unknown to Shakespeare scholars. Most of the letters have lain dormant in state archives in Vienna; others in the British archives were under false names difficult to unravel. These letters are accompanied by hundreds of other original documents, and a close examination of known but misinterpreted sources.

The author of the Shakespeare works, William Sterrell, was a highly intelligent lecturer at Oxford University who was associated for most of his adult life with a Catholic nobleman from Wales. In 1591 Sterrell was recruited by two men for dangerous activities overseas on behalf an ambitious earl, the Earl of Essex. His actions led to suspicion of treason at the highest levels of government. Had Sterrell not adopted a pseudonym for his writing, he may have met the same fate as the earl he had served: execution for treason in 1601. Or he may have suffered a sordid murder as did Christopher Marlowe, who was also under scrutiny of the Privy Council.

ഇഇഇഇ--ദദദദ

When we enter Shakespeare studies, we find it is a thick forest with many thousands of trees and countless branches that entangle us and make travel difficult (a dark wood, indeed). Guides will help us through. Dante employed the Roman poet Virgil to assist his readers. Other English writers employed dialogues between characters such as in John Heywood's *Witty and Witless, or, A Dialogue on Wit and Folly* (1479-1580) with characters named to reflect "Wit" and "Folly." John Bunyan's "Christian" receives guidance from Mr. Worldly-Wise and Evangelist as he seeks the Celestial City in *Pilgrim's Progress*. You get the idea.

We'll bring to life our own characters, *Bardophilus* and *Skepticisima,* for exchanges of their views. Let me introduce them and tell you what roles they will play to advance our story. Think of them as fellow readers of this little book who share their thoughts as they react to the author's narrative. They are like the veteran coaches or players who give color commentary during a football or basketball game or tennis match. Their job is to provide analysis, strategy, and background details during a broadcast, adding color or insight to the game that you are observing.

Bardophilus - With trim beard and furrowed brow, he

represents the Shakespeare Industrial Complex, that centuries-old network of professors and intellectuals and progressive thinkers (with the focus of progressivism shifting from nationalist democratic ideals to identity politics). Mark Twain called the members of this coalition the *Stratfordolators* and *Shakespearoids*.

Bardolatry is an industry because the careers and livelihoods of thousands of its members are committed to identification of Shakespeare-the-author with the burgher from Stratford-upon-Avon. They have conjectured a persona and narrative to stitch together the written works with the few known facts of the Stratford man's life. The result is an ill-fitting patchwork. Any serious challenge to that narrative undermines the many works based on that story. Challengers are treated to the ostracism and ridicule that would be leveled by organized Christianity on a person claiming to have found the bones of Christ. *Bardophilus* will try to overwhelm you with his weight and authority. When he speaks, he speaks *ex cathedra,* a superior expression on his lips. He never wishes to sound patronizing as he responds to a question for which he thinks the answer is too obvious. He finishes an answer with upraised chin and taps the desk in triumph. Stratford always wins, for the doubters themselves are insecure. In his opinion, to question the authorship is a "psychological aberration."

The members of the industry, however, often fight among themselves as to detail and arcana. Each generation of Shakespeare scholars has one or two of their tribe rise to the apex of the profession; their Celestial City may be Oxford, Harvard or Yale. The ambition to be the preeminent Shakespeare scholar of one's era has possessed many men and women for three centuries, just as each generation of actors has sought to achieve the definitive Hamlet or Richard the Third or Falstaff or Lady Macbeth. The actors need only a surname: Booth and Kemble; Olivier, McKellen and Branagh.

If a writer and editor cannot match the genius of the incomparable master of English literature, he or she could prove his near-equal by mediating between the demi-god and the millions of his mortal admirers. If one cannot generate the fire of the gods, one can transport it to the masses.

Early editions of the plays merely reproduced the quartos or

First Folio, with minor editing and occasional additions. Over centuries, editors have evolved from scribes into revisers, essentially co-authors, who substitute the words of the original author (or perhaps more accurately compositor) for better words that were surely intended by the genius and now sustained by extensive footnoting that explicate the meanings of the author and his contemporaries. There is a cult-like quality to the Shakespeare industry, with each play being treated as a quasi-religious text. To become the high priest of a cult has been an aspiration of more than a few Shakespeare scholars since the 18th century. And truly, it is a noble goal, and there are true giants of Shakespeare studies whose prodigious efforts are worthy of the greatest admiration. Yet, as with other ambitions, ambition can breed corruption. Charlatans, confidence-artists, thieves and forgers are drawn to or emerge from the desire for eminence, esteem and riches.

Skepticisima – Our second guide is the antistrophe of a Greek chorus, a voice or voices in response to the dominant speaker, often in contradiction. She will challenge the assertions of *Bardophilus.* At times gentle, at times more forceful, *Skepticisima* will offer you a counter-narrative. What she lacks in gravity she hopes to compensate by wit and cleverness. To persuade, she will appeal to your own intelligence and powers of discernment. Do not mistrust her flattery; she knows you share her suspicion of authority and rejection of cant and hyperbole. Look to her especially for exposing factual gaps or caesura in the industrial narratives. Her glasses, an affect not needed, cannot hide a twinkle as she senses an unforced error in the logic of her antagonist. She engages, not haughty but patient, as though dealing with a bright but not-fully-formed student who still can be guided if willing to accept her tutelage. You may wish she had been your English instructor.

There is a separate subculture of alternate candidates for the authorship identity. All of the alternatives as "Shakespeare-the-writer" have two fatal flaws. None of the known facts of their lives can fit the timeline of known, undisputed facts about the writings. Second, everyone proposing an alternative has to find a writer through published writings of their candidate. If that person has an identity as a writer, how do you plausibly explain taking on the name of Shakespeare? How do you find matching quill-prints (as it were) in the two different bodies of works? *Skepticisima* will dispose of those candidates at the outset of consideration of *Venus and Adonis*.

As with any journey or voyage, it is best to plot a course, to map the regions we plan to visit, to prepare our expectations so that we may avoid unpleasant surprises. We begin with the essential elements of the stages we will follow.

The Professor

William Sterrell was an Oxford professor who wrote as Shakespeare

The Shakespeare authorship question: Many have doubted that Shakespeare-of-Stratford had opportunities for acquiring learning or familiarity with the court life of the nobility to enable him to write with the intimate familiarity with history, literature and aristocratic manners that the works display. But if not Stratford, then who wrote as Shakespeare? Why did he need a pseudonym? Scholars have been unaware of a gifted, erudite Oxford professor whose connections were at the highest levels of the Courts of Elizabeth and James throughout the period of the Shakespeare poems and plays, 1593-1612. His name is William Sterrell. An overview of his life and his need for secrecy are set forth.

English Poésie

English literary life in 1593

If the past is a foreign country, we need to examine the literary culture of England when *Venus and Adonis* was published to orient ourselves. This section discusses how and why books came into being and the patronage system within which many writers and their books were supported. We will visit John Harrison's shop at the sign of the White Greyhound in Paul's Churchyard. The poem *Venus and Adonis* will be examined.

The Weary Knight

Why Southampton – Venus and the Weary Knight

The poet of *Venus and Adonis* chose his subject and his dedicatee with care, understanding that his goal was to influence not so much the young Earl of Southampton but others close to him: his mother, the Earl of Essex, and Essex's sister, Penelope. Sterrell knew that these three would have had their own reasons for finding the poem pleasing. If his gambit to appeal indirectly to them worked, it could save him from punishment by the Privy Council. The milieu of the poetry and plays of Shakespeare cannot be understood without examining the Catholic backgrounds of certain persons important to Sterrell's story, going back to the reign of Queen Mary Tudor and her husband, Philip of Spain. Finally, it will be useful to explore the literary setting by a closer look at the *Phoenix Nest* (1593) in which another poem of Sterrell appeared.

The Stratfordian

Shakespeare-of-Stratford to 1594

Sterrell could not publish *Venus and Adonis* in his own name nor could it appear anonymously if he hoped to achieve his purposes. This section explores multiple paths that may have led William Sterrell to connect with William Shakespeare-of-Stratford. It builds upon, but does not depend on, the proposition by Shakespeare scholars that a certain William Shakeshafte named in a Lancashire will of 1581 was the Shakespeare-of-Stratford who by 1594 may have associated with the Earl of Derby's players. These actors form the core of the company that was established as the Lord Chamberlain's Men. The family of the Earls of Derby (in particular Henry Stanley, 4th Earl, and his son Ferdinando Stanley, 5th Earl) is traced, for it is relevant to Sterrell's story.

In Print

The Printer and Publisher; Sterrell's Success

Shakespeare scholars have not adequately explained how an unpublished poet was printed by a printer who had little experience with or interest in vernacular poetry. This part establishes the likely connection between Sterrell and other works by the same printer and publisher contemporaneous with *Venus and Adonis;* they had incentives for taking on an uncertain venture. To bring this into perspective, the existence of extensive surreptitious publication under false names and imprints is examined. Within a year of the poem's publication, Sterrell goes from penury to a worth of £800. Despite the great success of *Venus and Adonis*, the poet (after *Lucrece* a year later) made no further effort to earn money or reputation through poetry. Sterrell reunited with his old patron and did not need to seek other patrons.

The Playwright's Own Tale

The playwright tells the story of his service to a junior earl, his humiliation as an exposed agent, and his return to his senior earl.

All's Well That Ends Well tells the story of the poet/playwright and his two earls. It is a tale of hubris. A man of words thinks he can achieve success by becoming an operative of an ambitious but shallow young lord who seeks military fame abroad. Through humiliation, he realizes he must be "the thing I am [that] shall make me live": a man of words whose selfhood can only be achieved through his skill with words. Thus, he resumes his lifelong service to the senior earl whom he had left. Their successes in entertainment have no equal in history

Shakespeare's Will

The Shakespeare company was formed in 1594; patrons were George Carey (Lord Hunsdon) and his wife Elizabeth Spencer Carey. George Carey died in 1603, leaving his widow a life tenancy in their house in Blackfriars (Lord Hunsdon's House). At her death, the house would pass to their daughter. The overseer of George Carey's will was his brother-in-law, William Spencer. In 1613 when Shakespeare acquired his Blackfriars Gatehouse, used by Catholics for at least 25 years, it was immediately adjacent to Lord Hunsdon's House. Under Shakespeare's will of 1616, his Blackfriars property was given to Susanna, but she could neither use it nor sell it. It was under a lease governed by Shakespeare's trustees of 1613; in 1616 it came under the control of Shakespeare's overseer "Thomas Russell." The father-in-law of Sir Thomas Russell of Strensham was William Spencer who was the overseer of Lord Hundson's will and controlled the Blackfriars house next to Shakespeare's. When 300-400 Catholics crashed through the floors during services in 1623 it was in Lord Hunsdon's House (residence of the French ambassador). The Shakespeare property in Blackfriars was a secret place for priests and other Catholics; it adjoined the house next door owned by his patrons since 1594 so they could get to secret services or escape authorities. The two properties were tied up by control of trustees and overseers to keep them from sale to others.

Chapter 2

William Sterrell and Shakespeare

The Authorship Question

Generations of Shakespeare readers have been skeptical that a son of barely literate parents in Stratford-upon-Avon could have acquired the immense learning and rhetorical skills demonstrated in the plays and poetry. Few respectable Shakespeare scholars in academic posts, however, are willing to accept that a secret author lay behind the Stratfordian. Thus, the authorship field has been occupied by amateurs who are regarded by Shakespeare professionals as eccentrics devoted to conspiracy theories. Please entertain the possibility that this book offers a plausible explanation for the why and how Shakespeare came to be the face of the true author of the poetry and plays and his patron.

Many educated and perfectly reasonable people have entertained the question whether Shakespeare-of-Stratford wrote the plays. What we know about the man of Stratford cannot be reconciled with the characteristics that are displayed by the author of the works: knowledge of Court life; the sports of the elite classes – falconry, fencing, archery, and barriers (jousting); erudition in the classics and philosophy; a familiarity with law and legal terminology. A typical assessment is from the producer of a PBS documentary exploring the authorship question, Michael Rubbo:

> Well, I feel in my gut that Shakespeare was not the author. I don't think the proof against him is conclusive, but he just doesn't feel and smell like the author to me. He's not satisfying. There does seem to be a need to have somebody who's intellectually and emotionally satisfying. And the more I find out about him, the more he fails to come to the party. He just doesn't perform as one expects a great author should. This man who often writes about our theatricality, about how we strut and fret on the stage of life -- he has no strut, no fret

himself. He seems to stand in the wings of life as a gray ghost.

The skeptic of the Stratford authorship appears foolish only upon offering an alternative author (or authors). Prudent writers raise the question and then leave it unanswered.[1]

Any person writing about Shakespeare and the Shakespeare works must deal with two closely related questions: What can we know about the works from the man? What can we know about the man from the works? A third way is possible but perverse: let us dissociate the man from the works – they are independent of one another. This third way is either an interpretive strategy or arises from a belief that intellectual genius rises above personality. It approaches blasphemy, for it makes the writer God-like: creating *ex-nihilo.*

Oh yes, to be sure, a picture of an object can be treated as separate from the photographer and a portrait's subject from the painter. But a work of imaginative literature is precisely that: the work of an imagination, a person's imagination that can no more be separated from their experience than it can be from their language.

This is not to suggest that all fiction or poetry is autobiographical. Yet most literature worthy of the name draws upon the experiences of the author, transfigure them as the artist may, displace them in time or place as he or she sees fit. Those experiences are the stuff of the creative imagination, the foundation and framing of creation. For there to be a tapestry, there must first be loom and thread.

Pop quiz: Name three successful literary writers who did not draw upon their own experiences. All right, for full credit then name just one.

In all of Shakespeare studies there is no work more important than the first writing of Shakespeare-the-author: *Venus and Adonis.* It is the Alpha of Shakespeare scholarship as the *First Folio* is the Omega. *Venus and Adonis* confronts and confounds Stratfordians and non-Stratfordians alike. Stratfordians must account for the sudden appearance of an unknown man of no formal education who produces the most polished poem of a generation, surpassing in learning the most eloquent writers of the period, gentlemen who were Masters of Arts in both universities. And why would he dedicate it to a cash-strapped minor who was under a hardnosed guardian already peeved at his ward? What could the poet hope to gain from so unpromising a patron?

The anti-Stratfordians have no plausible explanation why their favored candidate for the real identity of the author – whether it be the Earl of Oxford or Francis Bacon or Christopher Marlowe – would begin his published career as Shakespeare and dedicate it to Southampton, a neophyte at Court. Nothing known of any of these three men in 1593 and their possible relationship to Southampton can fit into their authorship. The candidacy of the Earl of Oxford in particular as the true author has produced a cult-like following. Of them Buck Mulligan could have been speaking when James Joyce has him say, "Shakespeare is the happy hunting ground of all minds that have lost their balance."

ഈഈ--ഠഠ

Shakespeare-of-Stratford

The known facts of the life of William Shakespeare can be set forth in a couple of pages. Mark Twain did it amusingly in a little book in 1909: *Is Shakespeare Dead?* Samuel Clemens, who knew a thing or two about pen names, was impatient with the Stratfordians, labeling (or libeling) them as *Stratfordolators* and *Shakespearoids.* For the sake of clarity, I will at times refer to William Shakespeare-of-Stratford as *Stratford,* a synecdoche which would surely have been approved by the author of *Hamlet* who referred to "Old Norway" for King Fortinbras (of Norway), to distinguish him from his son Fortinbras.

Before the first publication under the name Shakespeare in 1593, there are only the date of the Stratfordian's baptism, his marriage at 18 to a woman eight years older than himself, the birth of a daughter several months shy of nine months later and the birth of twins in 1585. No document of any sort has ever appeared to evidence that he attended even a day of school. Not one letter by William Shakespeare is known to exist -- if ever he wrote a single letter. What purports to be his signature is found on only six documents, and the spellings are not consistent on those, suggesting that his name may have been signed by a scrivener, trustee or lawyer. During his lifetime, only a handful of documents survive that involve a personal knowledge of or contact with William Shakespeare-of-Stratford, and they have no connection with Shakespeare-the-writer.

A dozen of so contemporary documents do make reference to Shakespeare as the author of poetry (and "sugered sonnets") and plays, but these establish only that works appeared that bore the name of Shakespeare. Two items alone can be cited that link the actor William Shakespeare of Stratford with the plays that appeared as Shakespeare plays, and they were the fruit of one man: Ben Jonson. In his own folio of plays of 1616 (the year of *Stratford's* death), Jonson listed William Shakespeare as a performer in Jonson's play *Every Man In His Humor* in 1598 and in his *Sejanus* in 1603. And in the dedicatory verse of the Shakespeare *First Folio* of 1623 Jonson wrote of the "Sweet Swan of Avon," calling to mind Stratford-upon-Avon, while L. Digges wrote another verse that referred to "thy Stratford Moniment," probably with deliberate ambiguity. Shakespeare wrote no verse to introduce the work of any other writer, and no other writer wrote verse to accompany a single Shakespeare publication prior to his death in 1616.

The one occasion upon which we might have expected the playwright to appear and give testimony about his work, another member of the acting company appeared, Augustine Phillips, and the playwright was allowed to pass in silence. This was in connection with the Essex Rebellion in February 1601. The Earl of Southampton, to whom the Shakespeare poems *Venus and Adonis* (1593) and *Lucrece* (1594) were dedicated, was convicted of treason and sentenced to death along with his friend, the Earl of Essex. Shortly before the attempted uprising, a group of Southampton's men had engaged the company of Shakespeare to perform *Richard II*, a play that puts in mind and perhaps approves the overthrow of a sovereign. "Know you not that I am Richard II?" Queen Elizabeth asked her antiquarian, Lambarde.

Southampton's poet was not called upon to explain himself or the special performance of his play. Much milder work than the brutal plays of Shakespeare had led to imprisonment – such as Ben Jonson for the *Isle of Dogs* in 1597 and for *Eastward Ho* in 1605. Shakespeare's *Julius Caesar* portrays the murderer of a head of state – Brutus – as the noblest Roman of them all. Yet the disgrace and disenfranchisement of his apparent patron (Southampton), the only member of the Queen's Court known to be associated with Shakespeare's writing, caused not a ripple in the appearance of Shakespeare plays as Court entertainment. Who then dispensed favor at Court upon the works of the Shakespeare name? Where are Shakespeare's dedications to a patron post-1594?

♦♦♦ ♦♦♦

Bardophilus: I've given some thought to that problem. It's true that Shakespeare wasn't called on to explain himself for *Richard II.* There is a simple reason. When the play was printed in quarto in 1597, this version appeared with no named author. It did not include the controversial deposition scene in which the monarch surrenders his crown. That scene didn't appear until the 1608 quarto. Shakespeare was never the sole playwright for the Lord Chamberlain's Men. The government officials couldn't know who the author was until someone in the company, such as Augustine Phillips, identified him. Even then, the published book was not offensive in the manner alleged of the performance, so the company was accountable, not the author. Probably Shakespeare was back in Stratford and free of blame for what the actors themselves were doing.

Skepticisima: Thank you, Professor. You make the case perfectly for the author of the plays to find it safer to hide behind the name and identity of another. You establish clearly why the playwright gained nothing (except notoriety) by publishing his plays. But you ignore one other thing. Why wasn't the company's patron held accountable? Weren't they the Lord Chamberlain's Men"?

Bardophilus: They were. But he couldn't be held accountable. If memory serves, the Lord Chamberlain was already quite ill at the time. The pox and mercury poisoning that was used to treat it. He had stopped attending Privy Council meetings.

Skepticisima: Interesting. You seem to be saying the Shakespeare company was leaderless when James came to the throne.

Bardophilus: Patronless.

Anti-Stratfordians have noted the incongruity of the author of

Hamlet and *Lear* bringing suit in 1604 against a Stratford apothecary for the balance of an account for malt and for a debt of two shillings. Surely, they say, the writer who penned *Macbeth* and *Antony & Cleopatra* couldn't be the man who sued for the arrest in December 1608 of another man of Stratford and his surety for a debt of £6 plus damages. Was the author of these great tragedies a tight-fisted litigant? Did the man who explored the depths of the human heart have the soul of a penny-wise shop-keeper? Was his a tiger's heart wrapped in a playwright's hide?

The historical record shows William Shakespeare of Rowington reporting for militia muster in 1605. The militia were organized by manor. The cottage which Shakespeare purchased in 1602 was part of Rowington Manor, as confirmed by a 1604 record of Rowington showing "William Shakespere . . . holdeth one cottage and one garden." How could the playwright of London simultaneously be marching in the local militia in Warwickshire? So, Stratfordians have had to conjure up another William Shakespeare of about the same age to explain away the record of William Shakespeare. Chambers dismisses with no evidence: "That he was a soldier rests on a confusion with one of many William Shakespeares at Rowington."[2] Other Stratfordians have invented a legal clerkship in an unknown lawyer's office for the young Shakespeare to explain his knowledge of legal matters. To account for the apparent influence of a play on Julius Caesar in Latin at Oxford in 1582, scholars have imagined a teen-aged Shakespeare sneaking over to Oxford from Stratford to mingle among the college youth at their learned entertainments.

Most orthodox Shakespeare scholars now acknowledge that the playwright had a working knowledge of Latin, French and Italian and perhaps even Greek. George Steevens, an eighteenth-century editor, said of a portion of *Titus Andronicus*: "This passage alone would sufficiently convince me that the play before us was the work of one who was conversant with the Greek tragedies in their original language. We have here a plain allusion to the Ajax of Sophocles, of which no translation was extant in the time of Shakespeare." Modern explanations of how *Stratford* came by this learning are implausible.

The Stratfordians assert that the grammar school education of

Elizabethan England was exceptional. There is no evidence that Shakespeare even attended grammar school, only that there was a grammar school in Stratford that he could have attended. The names of a few schoolteachers who passed through Stratford are known, and yet nothing directly links them to Shakespeare then or later. As far as can be determined, there were no libraries in Stratford to which Shakespeare would have had access. The writer of the plays had a vocabulary of 15,000+ words. Language skills and knowledge are acquired while a person is young, not when in their 20s or 30s. From whence came then the immense learning that *Venus and Adonis* and even the early plays demonstrate?

Learning (a knowledge base) is like language. It is not innate but must be acquired. Learning is through immersion, as may be found in a university where a person is exposed to diverse disciplines through a number of teachers. Learning requires access to many books, not to single books to be read in one's idle hours. It requires the input of others to bring discipline to subjects such as rhetoric to gain insight into uses of appeals to authority (ethos), emotion (pathos), and logic (logos) or such as Roman history. How can we account for a 29-year-old man without formal education mastering the arcane arts of rhetoric that are on display so ostentatiously in his first published work? Rhetoric is a formal skill that must be learned, just as techniques in painting must be studied and practiced. A painter must know of the mixing of different substances and colors to achieve desired effects, just as the painter must know brushes and strokes to produce a simulacrum of a person or scene upon canvas. Rhetoric is not simply absorbed from reading diverse works that then bursts forth upon a chosen subject. The use of rhetoric is an unnatural use of language with purpose.

It's not too early on our journey to visit *Venus and Adonis.* The poem's first stanza displays the poet's mastery of rhetorical devices and strategies.

Even as the sun with purple-coloured face
Had ta'en his last leave of the weeping morn,
Rose-cheeked Adonis hied him to the chase;
Hunting he loved, but love he laughed to scorn.
  Sick-thoughted Venus makes amain unto him,
  And like a bold-faced suitor 'gins to woo him

The Early Modern English scholar Lucy Gent spells out the mastery of rhetoric this demonstrates:[3] "The stanza includes: *chronographia,* a description of the time of day; quantities of *epitheton* ('weeping', 'purple-colour'd', 'rose-cheek'd', 'sick-thoughted', 'bold-fac'd'), so much admired at the time; *traductio* ('lov'd', 'love'); *prosonomasia,* the play on sound in 'love', 'laugh'd'; *antimetabole,* a pattern taken one way then reversed, in 'Hunting he lov'd, but love he laugh'd to scorn'; brief simile ('like a bold-fac'd suitor')."

Just as the poet's quote of Ovid before the dedication boldly proclaims his ambition, the opening six lines of *Venus and Adonis* are a shout to the world: "Look at what I can do!"

♦♦♦ ♦♦♦

Bardophilus: All Shakespeare scholars know that Shakespeare's education was like that of the Canterbury school attended by Christopher Marlowe. As Gary Wills has told us, "the curriculum stated: 'In the Fifth Form they shall commit to memory the [rhetorical] figures.' These 'figures'—variously called ornaments, schemata, tropes—were signature devices of the ancient orators: *anaphora, polyptoton, khiasmos, ploke, homoioteleuton, isokola,* and on and on. There were scores of them, all mounted like butterflies in book after book." Rhetorical devices and figures were taught to all English school boys.

Skepticisima: You've got to be kidding us. From a single mention of "figures" in an aspirational curriculum you will infer the training of school boys included these highly technical techniques with no mention even of what books or writers they would be derived from? All of the "signature devices of the ancient orators" were distilled into that single mention of "figures." Wills fudged by adding [rhetorical] and omitting the full statement of the "Fifth Form": "In the Fifth Form they shall commit to memory the Figures of Latin Oratory and the rules for making verses; and at the same time shall be practised in making verses and polishing themes then they shall be versed in translating the chasest Poets and the best Historians."

It is as though you and Wills are claiming that a curriculum that provided an introduction to science for junior high school students must have incorporated advanced physics. At most, lads of fourteen had a brief skim of a vast subject, merely tasting of the oratory of Cicero and hearing the odes of Horace. More importantly, the Canterbury school attended by Marlowe was an extraordinary institution: it was the very prestigious King's School administered by the Dean and Chapter of Canterbury Cathedral for which Marlowe had been granted a scholarship. And need I remind you that Marlowe's education did not stop with a brief introduction to "Latin Oratory" in the Fifth Form but was furthered by many years of study and two degrees at Cambridge? The teacher/ministers of Canterbury were well above the itinerant teachers who found themselves stuck at Stratford-upon-Avon for a year or two. What you argue is beyond human capacity. Shakespeare is the Marvel Hero of the 16th century, Schoenbaum's "superhuman."

Shakespeare's works demonstrate deep knowledge of rhetoric and Roman history that cannot arise from occasional casual reading. For Shakespeare-of-Stratford to appear suddenly at age 29 as a multilingual poet and playwright of immense learning and no training whatsoever is to entertain the possibility of an uneducated man of the same age revealing himself as a gifted surgeon, fully knowledgeable of muscle, arteries, veins and tissue. Why and where would a man of such gifts and talents have hidden himself? Why would there be no record of interactions with other men and women with similar interests that show up later in his life?

Shakespeare's will, written first in January of 1616, itemizes a silver-gilt bowl, his clothing, his plate, and leaves his second-best bed to his wife, but it mentions no books or manuscripts. Is it merely a curiosity that the principal items of real estate owned in the name of Shakespeare are set up in such a way that his heirs will realize little value from them for years to come? Or was *Stratford* a holder of title for others? If so, it calls into question his authorship of the poetry and plays.

Despite several centuries of skepticism, the Stratfordians have, thus far, carried the day. This has been due less to the force of their case than the hurdles facing any opponent of the *Stratford* orthodoxy. Anyone trying to overcome the Stratford identity of the author of the plays and poetry must confront a series of challenges.

<> There was a William Shakespeare-of-Stratford. It is the same William Shakespeare who is identified inferentially in 1623 by a few named persons as author of the plays of the *First Folio.* He died in 1616.

<> The name William Shakespeare appears in 1593 on *Venus and Adonis* and in 1594 on *Rape of Lucrece.* It appears in 1601 on the poem known as *The Phoenix and Turtle,* and on the 1609 *Shake-speares Sonnets.* There has to be an explanation why the author of *Venus and Adonis* and *Lucrece* would dedicate these two works to the Earl of Southampton using someone else's name. A poet seeking patronage could hardly use another person's name as the poet, unless Southampton himself were aware of the false presentation.

<> The name William Shakespeare appears in 1595 as receiving payments for theatrical productions. He is a shareholder of the acting company and of the Globe Theater built a few years later.

<> If William Shakespeare is not the true name of the author of the poems and the plays, there has to have been a reason for secrecy about the authorship in 1593. The author and William Shake-speare-of-Stratford most likely would have been in collusion on the matter from 1593 to the death of the latter in 1616.

<> A few others would have had to have been aware of the collusion between the William Shakespeare of the acting company and the author of the poetry and plays. Ben Jonson is one of these. He asserted he knew Shakespeare and that Shakespeare had acted in several of Jonson's plays, but there is no evidence of this before 1616.

A conundrum for both Stratfordians and *Stratford*-skeptics is accounting for the indisputable fact that the Shakespeare plays were at their height at the Court of King James from 1603-1612. The author had a highly placed patron at the Court with whom he must have worked closely. The performances at Court were often plays written for the special entertainment of the King and his Court, just as were the masques performed during the same period. Surely, you would think, the Court official(s) responsible for the royal entertainments would have to have been aware of the author whose plays were being commissioned or revised for command performances. Surely, they would have had to interact with the author to be certain that the entertainments were properly staged and timely completed. *Stratford*-skeptics cannot identify any Court official with ties to any playwright to explain the Shakespeare dominance. Stratfordians have looked to Southampton or Pembroke as earls who might have been able to influence Court entertainment but can provide no evidence of either having such a role at Court.

Court plays were not random offerings by a company's resident writer in coordination with a company producer any more than Court (or private) masques were conceived and produced by the named author of the masque. Unlike a play at the Globe where expenses were covered by box-office receipts from repeated daily performances, a Court play (or masque) depended entirely on finance and management of Court officials guided solely by the anticipated approval and amusement of the King and Queen. The author of the Shakespeare plays of 1603-1612 had to be someone who was intimately familiar with the members of the Court and the royal family. The author of those plays cannot have been someone preoccupied with petty business matters and property questions in a small community one hundred and two miles from London.

Yes, there is an authorship question arising from the disjunction between the known biography of Shakespeare-of Stratford and the qualities we attribute to the author of the poetry and the plays. But there is one person who can speak more directly to the subject. The poet himself. Has anyone examined the poet?

The Poet's Own Words

Poor Shakespeare! No one will take him at his word. His poetry and plays have been pored over for centuries, examined minutely in every detail. Every scrap of paper in records, every reference to him, every rumor has been tracked down. Yet the only times he has spoken directly about himself, using "I" in his poetry (but never in the plays), he has been ignored. Everyone, and I mean everyone, who has ever paid the slightest attention to those words has said the poet cannot have meant exactly what he said.[4] Which of those "I" statements do we mean?

The fixed stars of written Shakespeare are the two long poems of 1593-1594, *Venus and Adonis* and *Lucrece*. Both are dedicated to the Earl of Southampton. Generally accepted as authentic Shakespeare also are the enigmatic *Phoenix and Turtle* (1601) and *Shakespeares Sonnets* (1609), but neither has explicit endorsement by the author. We know nothing directly about any other connection between the writer Shakespeare and a single play or writing of any sort. Shakespeare-of-Stratford, yes. But Shakespeare-the-writer? Only these four works carry authenticity. Yet they are ignored for their hints, their implicit statements, that the name Shakespeare is not the name of the poet/author. Let's listen to him, even if no one else will.

The love epic called *Venus and Adonis* was published in late May 1593. It was dedicated to the Earl of Southampton. It states that the poem is "the first heir of my invention." Is it? The Shakespeare industry insists this can't be true because by 1592 Shakespeare was already known as an "upstart crow" who supposed he was "as well able to bombast out a blank verse as the best" of England's poets and playwrights.[5] He had written, they assert, multiple plays. Never has so much been built on such weak scaffolding.

What a curious way to seek patronage: you tell the potential patron he is the first person to receive your precious gift while others already know you as an author. Surely the patron would be offended. So, Shakespeare scholars dismiss the words of the dedication.

♦♦♦ ♦♦♦

Bardophilus: An exaggeration. Shakespeare was not saying this was the first thing he wrote, only that it was his first long poem. It was his first invention in this form of a love epic. We call it an *epyllion*.

Skepticisima: Now, Bardimus, it is you twisting the quoted words. It is not the "first invention." No, the poem is "the *first heir of my invention*." The name *Shakespeare* is the "invention." Invention is used repeatedly in the Shakespeare plays to mean a fabrication, a lie, a contrivance. And the poem is the "heir." A contrary reading of the author's syntax to make *Venus* both the *heir* and the *invention* would abuse the poet in his command of the language. The poem can have a *godfather* as contemplated by the dedication; it's possible to speak of an *heir* having a *godfather* but implausibly so an *invention.*

Bardophilus: Is that the best you can do? A flimsy start if you are trying to undermine centuries of scholarship.

Skepticisima: The Sonnets are more direct than the dedication of *Venus and Adonis*. Let's hear what Shakespeare has to say in *Sonnet 81*:

Or I shall live your epitaph to make,
Or you survive when I in earth am rotten,
From hence your memory death cannot take,
Although in me each part will be forgotten.
Your name from hence immortal life shall have,
Though I (once gone) to all the world must die,
The earth can yield me but a common grave,
When you entombed in men's eyes shall lie,
Your monument shall be my gentle verse,
Which eyes not yet created shall o'er-read,
And tongues to be, your being shall rehearse,
When all the breathers of this world are dead,
You still shall live (such virtue hath my pen)
Where breath most breathes, even in the mouths of men.

"Your name from hence immortal life shall have." The name *William Shakespeare* has certainly achieved the poet's ambition of immortal life. But let us observe the poet's words in the sonnet: "*Your name,*" he says, will be immortal. That is not the sonneteer himself, is it? Instead, he declares, "***I*** (once gone) to all the world must die." What is that name? Where can it be found?

The same thought is repeated in *Sonnet 107* when the poet says that after he dies, "***I***'ll live in this poor rhyme." He tells the close friend, "thou in this shalt find thy monument," repeating *Sonnet 81*'s notion of the sonnets being a monument.[6] The poet and the "thou" cannot be the same person; one lives by virtue of the rhyme and the other by "this," which is the sonnet or the collection of sonnets that bear only the one name. If it is Shakespeare's name (and there is no other name anywhere in the book) that is to be immortal and to have a monument in the sonnet(s), who is the "***I***" of the sonnets? It must be someone who is not named Shakespeare. How can the poet make someone's name immortal if he is not named in any of his poems?

Bardophilus: Again, you are being far too literal. We all know that the Sonnets were directed to Southampton. He must have meant Southampton to whom two dedications were made, *Venus and Adonis* and *Lucrece*. The Sonnets are love offerings by an older man to his young lover. The poet's saying to Southampton "I'm making you famous" while poor-mouthing himself in false modesty. The real meaning is found in the same-sex relationship, not the words. We have to see what is the overall impression of the sonnets, not the individual words.

Skepticisima: Yes, ignore the words, you say. But we can't accept your argument. The poet is referring to the *verses of the sonnet* as being the monument, not the two Southampton dedications.[7] And what evidence is there of such a personal relationship between the two men in 1593 or 1603 or 1609? There is no evidence of any personal relationship between Southampton and the author of *Venus and Adonis* and *Lucrece* other than these two dedications. Nada. Zip. Zero. Neither before nor after the two were in print. The Sonnets of 1609 have only one name associated with the entire collection of 154 poems: Shakespeare. Your reasoning is circular: Shakespeare and Southampton are lovers because the Sonnets speak to a beautiful young man. We know, you say, that the young man is Southampton because that's the only person he dedicated a single work to. Again, there is no evidence of any identity of that unnamed person or persons.

Bardophilus: Do you have better explanation? Put up or shut up.

Skepticisima: The poet using "I" is speaking to the one person made famous by the Sonnets. That is, of course, Shakespeare. And exactly as the poet declared, the author himself—the "I"—has remained nameless, just as he said he expected. He worked very hard to conceal his identity from the public. If the poet has an arrangement with the man named Shakespeare to use his name, he would address a sonnet to Shakespeare that would indicate that unseen relationship. That would be William Sterrell putting that relationship on display with a wink.

Bardophilus: Are you agreeing with me that they were gay?

How do you explain the love of the young man in the other sonnets?

Skepticisima: No, they weren't gay. And the young man of the sonnets isn't Southampton or Shakespeare. These poems express love, but a pure love, not an erotic one. The young man in multiple sonnets is Sterrell's own younger brother, whom he's encouraging to marry and have children. For example, let's look at *Sonnet 13*:

O that you were your self, but love you are
No longer yours, than you your self here live,
Against this coming end you should prepare,
And your sweet semblance to some other give.
So should that beauty which you hold in lease
Find no determination, then you were
Your self again after your self's decease,
When your sweet issue your sweet form should bear.
Who lets so fair a house fall to decay,
Which husbandry in honour might uphold,
Against the stormy gusts of winter's day
And barren rage of death's eternal cold?
O none but unthrifts, dear my love you know,
You had a father, let your son say so.

This sonnet was written as William Sterrell was encouraging his young brother, a lawyer of the Middle Temple, to marry. He may as well have said "*We* had a father . . ." He even works in his brother's legal training when he speaks of "that beauty which you hold in lease." A lease is a "determinable" property interest of limited duration . . . so if Henry has a child his beauty will not "determine" with his own decease. Or *Sonnet 3*, where the poet seems to speak to a younger brother urging him to procreate recalling their mother: "Thou art thy mother's glass, and she in thee Calls back the lovely April of her prime . . . ." These are the loving words of a brother speaking of their mother. But they are highly inappropriate if a homosexual Shakespeare-of-Stratford is asking his young lover to have a child with a woman and to remember how much he looks like Countess Southampton. It's too yucky to imagine.

Bardophilus: You say the poet was hinting that Shakespeare was not the author. Maybe even that it was made implicit. You can't support that. There's nothing in the plays on which you can make the claim.

Skepticisima: Nope, not the plays. The playwright never speaks as himself in the plays. But he makes playful explicit statements in the *Sonnets*. There's one that your colleagues in the Shakespeare factory have been hard-pressed to explain away. That's *Sonnet 76,* which in part gives us a puzzle:

Why is my verse so barren of new pride?
So far from variation or quick change?
Why with the time do I not glance aside
To new-found methods, and to compounds strange?
Why write I still all one, ever the same,
And keep invention in a noted weed,
That every word doth almost tell my name, [8]

How can *barren* verse, lacking *variation* or *quick change,* tell the poet's name? It is exceptionally difficult to eke an allusion to the name "Shakespeare" by any of these words and phrases. Does he not suggest his name is the same as *barren* – saying "*barren* doth almost say" his name because it is sterile/Sterrell? Does he not make the same suggestion in *Sonnet 16* when he speaks of his "*barren* rhyme"?

Bardophilus: Are you saying the poet is playing word games with us? Why would he do that? Why would some unknown professor hide the fact of his great powers as a writer?

Skepticisima: Now, that's rich! Of course he's playing word games with his readers. That's what Shakespeare-the-author does over and over throughout the entire body of his work. He is mischievous. He is teasing. He is subtle. He is opaque. He wants us to mine his work for meaning. Most of all, he's the world's most gifted punster. Barren-Sterile-Sterrell. A wonderful pun by the punster who provokes us with "lay . . . lie" (*Othello*), with "sun/son of York" (*Richard III*), with "a grave man" (*Romeo and Juliet*), "conception . . . conceive" (*Hamlet*) and on and on. His humor is too bawdy, his puns too naughty for the more squeamish of many in the audiences of history. Too many "Dad jokes."

Poetry is falsehood, as we've been told from Plato to Bentham. Metaphor and simile are falsehood. Think of the witches in *Macbeth.*

They make statements that lead their auditors and us to think one thing, and then they and we see something else. But we were all mistaken: what the witches themselves said was correct. How can "Great Birnam Wood to high Dunsinane Hill . . . come" against Macbeth? They had also told that "none of woman born shall harm Macbeth." Who is not "of woman born? "The murderous king learns the witches told true. The author intends for us to be surprised by his clever word games. He glories in them, and their mastery is his glory.

Bardophilus: Now that is just too far-fetched. You're putting a burden on one sonnet that it cannot bear to establish a relationship between a name and a synonym. You're taking out of context.

Skepticisima: My dear Bardophilus, must we play whack-a-mole? It's you who lacks context. The word games, the puns, are everywhere, including the *Sonnets*. "Barren" and "Sterile" (Sterrell's homonym) are that rare thing of what a linguist would call "total [or absolute] synonymy."[9] The two words are interchangeable. In English dictionaries of 1604 and 1616 "sterile" and "barren" had identical meanings, having come into English usage from two separate routes (linguistic and geographic).[10] The poet didn't use it just in *Sonnet 76*. He made the same wordplay in the dedication of *Venus and Adonis* ("never after ear so *barren* a land"). And Sterrell's poem in 1591 in a friend's publication was anonymous but alluded to his name by saying "Thou with thy Fruits our *barrenness* o'erspread."

Bardophilus: I am underwhelmed. *Barren* was not uncommon in English. So, it's natural there will be coincidences of the sort you are laying out.

Skepticisima: You want a deeper dive? If you realized the source of *Sonnet 76*, you'd have understood the cleverness of the poet. "Sterile" is the English cognate of the Latin "Sterilis." The *Oxford Latin Dictionary* gives as a definition of *sterilis* from antiquity, citing Seneca, Quintilian and Pliny: "Sterilis. 4. *Barren* of ideas or inspiration." This is exactly the usage of "barren" in *Sonnet 76*. When we go to Pliny, we find the source of the conceit of *Sonnet 76*. Read the sonnet's words again. *"Why is my verse so barren of new pride*?" Is the poet not apologizing to the reader for the sterility of his poetry and keeping/hiding his "***invention***"? (again, that word from the dedication of *Venus and Adonis* to mean "identity"). For his conceit (the barren, uninspired nature of his writing) he has chosen to echo the same conceit Pliny the Elder used in the dedication of his *Natural History*. Pliny apologizes to his patron that his material is barren (*blanda sterili materia*). And why Pliny? Sterrell taught "natural philosophy" at Oxford. An authority on the subject as it was studied in Sterrell's time notes: "the scientific text that received the most attention from philologists was Pliny's *Natural History*."[11] We will discover that same passage of Pliny's dedication is the source of the dedication found in Shakespeare's *First Folio* of 1623.

Bardophilus: I've got you there! You can't deny that Shakespeare's dead in 1623. That dedication is by Heminges and Condell, his fellow actors.

Skepticisima: Sure, Shakespeare's dead. But not William Sterrell. The relevant passage of the 1623 dedication in the *First Folio* is virtually a direct translation from Latin of the same part of Pliny's dedication as the source of *Sonnet 76*.[12] No one thinks Heminges and Condell were learned enough to draw on Pliny's Latin. But Sterrell lectured on Pliny in his course of "natural philosophy" at Oxford. Sterrell had every incentive to preserve his work through the *First Folio*. Heminges and Condell did not.

Bardophilus: How can you be sure Sterrell himself knew Pliny or his *Natural History*? Did he publish his lectures?

Skepticisima: Sterrell didn't. But he drew on Pliny in his letters. Under his pseudonym Anthony Rivers in 1602 he wrote to Fr. Persons about the desire for change among members of the Court as Queen Elizabeth declined in her final months: *Mens hominum novitatis avida*, which translates to "The human mind is greedy for novelty" or "The nature of men is desirous of novelty." This maxim is an adaptation of a line by Pliny the Elder in his work *Natural History* (*Naturalis Historia*), specifically found in Book XII, Chapter V, Section 11. The original Latin from Pliny is slightly different: *natura hominum novitatis avida est*. Sterrell's mentor Dr. John Case drew on the same lines from Pliny in his *Sphaera Civitatis* (1588), an Aristotelian treatise on government.

William Sterrell - Oxford Professor

From his earliest appearances in the records of Oxford and the English State Papers, William Sterrell shows himself to be exceptionally intelligent, bold, resourceful and secretive. These were his chief personal characteristics. He must also have been as committed to his Catholic faith as he was to his life-long employer, Edward Somerset. He risked his life repeatedly; his correspondents were Catholic leaders abroad; he had to endure profound loss as his close friends were martyred for their faith. For one special couple whom he tried to save, Anne and Roger Line, he wrote a deeply felt poem in their memory when she was executed at Tyburn, *Phoenix and Turtle*.

What do we know of him? A lot more than many more famous men and women of his time.

William Sterrell was born into the English gentry on May 10, 1561, probably at Gainsborough or its neighboring town Fillingham or the nearby family estate of Redbourne. His father, Henry Sterrell, was a practicing lawyer of some status and influence in the county. Henry Sterrell held the then distinct rank of gentleman, with his own coat of arms (argent a bend gules on a chief of the last three bezants) and the title of "esquire."

At William Sterrell's birth, Henry Sterrell had recently been appointed Undersheriff of Lincolnshire for 1559-60 by the new Queen's first Sheriff of Lincolnshire, Sir Robert Tyrwhitt. Sterrell's mother was Katherine Southill (also spelled Sotehill or Southwell), a family of Lincolnshire distinction. Henry and Katherine Sterrell had one other son, Henry, whose birth may have been as much as nine years after William's. While the Sterrell sons were still young, their father died. When their mother remarried (probably soon after his death), the two boys were sent away: William was at Oxford by 1574, most likely becoming a private student of John Case, a professor who, with his wife, taught private students (often Catholic and as young as eight years).[13] Henry (the younger son) was placed with prominent relatives, the Meres family of Lincolnshire. We can see traces of William Sterrell's boyhood in the plays in references to Lincolnshire not likely to be known to someone from Warwickshire or London.

Sterrell was granted his Bachelor of Arts degree on July 3, 1579, less than a year after he was made a demy (a scholarship student) at Oxford's Magdalen College the previous September 29, 1578. Because he was "suspect in religion," Sterrell's award of the BA was delayed. He then became a Fellow of Magdalen and studied for the Master of Arts; it, too, was delayed because of likely Catholicism. Only with the direct intervention of the University's Chancellor, the Earl of Leicester (backed by the Queen), was Sterrell successful in obtaining his degree. Records of Oxford indicate that Sterrell was probably involved in theatrical productions as a student.[14]

From about 1582 to late September 1585, while a Magdalen Fellow and lecturer, Sterrell met (under assumed names), with the French Ambassador to England, Michel de Castelnau, seigneur de Mauvissière, in London. His purpose in part was to help spirit Catholic English youth to seminaries abroad. Mauvissière shared many letters of the secret correspondence of Mary Queen of Scots with Sterrell, according to a government informant. She was held prisoner by the English government.

Present also at the ambassador's residence was John Florio, a man Sterrell had first known at Magdalen College, Oxford. We will see traces of that relationship in the pages that follow, and understand how this friendship relates to Shakespeare-the-author. They met no later than May 1581 when Florio (age 36) matriculated from Magdalen as servant/tutor to Emmanuel Barnes, son of Robert Barnes, bishop of Durham. Sterrell was already a Fellow of Magdalen. By 1583 Florio had become tutor to the ambassador's daughter. Both Sterrell and Florio were highly trusted by the ambassador, and the fact that both were from the same college at Oxford suggests that they must have interacted in the ambassador's household. The two men's lives would intersect closely for the next thirty-five years. Scholars have noted that it "seems certain that [Florio and Shakespeare-the-author] knew each other."[15]

We know of Sterrell's closeness to the French ambassador because of a government informant who was arrested at Dover on his way overseas. He confessed to government agents that "Kerby" had assisted him and five companions to go overseas to seminary on the French ambassador's boat. Kerby, he said, was actually Sterrell, a scholar he had known at Oxford. The Lord Warden of the

Cinque Ports and Constable of Dover Castle who oversaw criminal activities was Lord Cobham. He passed the confession on to Elizabeth's spymaster, Sir Francis Walsingham, urging him to look into him immediately. No doubt they did; someone must have stalled an investigation. Within a year Sterrell gave up his Fellowship at Magdalen College; he now continued as a praelector/professor. Leaving his Fellowship allowed him to undertake a role as tutor for a patron's family.

When did Sterrell first associate with his life-long patron, Edward Somerset, 4th Earl of Worcester? It was probably around 1583-85 while Sterrell was working through the French ambassador to aid English Catholics. Sterrell's first contacts with the family of the earls of Worcester probably arose from Thomas Somerset's unlawful participation in the correspondence of Mary Queen of Scots, which the French ambassador was facilitating. Thomas was the brother of the 3rd Earl of Worcester and uncle of Edward Somerset (then Lord Herbert, later 4th Earl of Worcester). Sterrell most likely sent Thomas Somerset's son, George, and a nephew to the Catholic seminary at Douay c. 1584, for Sterrell was the man who brought him back a decade later. Thomas had helped found the seminary with William Allen (later Cardinal Allen, an advisor to five Popes on all English matters from 1585-1594). Suspected of complicity with Mary Queen of Scots, Thomas Somerset was imprisoned in the Tower in 1585 where he died the next year.

Edward Somerset, with a castle full of young children in the mid-1580s (Raglan Castle in southeast Wales), was in need of a suitable scholar to prepare his sons for their eventual entry to Oxford University. As the University Chancellor, the Earl of Leicester, had been a protector of Sterrell, so Leicester could have recommended Sterrell to Worcester. Leicester and/or Worcester would likely have been well aware of Sterrell's Catholic activities and work with the French ambassador. For Sterrell to have been a tutor for Worcester's children or interact frequently with the French ambassador while lecturing at Oxford would not have been difficult. It would have taken about a day by horse to reach either Raglan Castle (75 miles) or London (60 miles) from Magdalen College in Oxford.

William Sterrell's course that he taught at Oxford was "natural philosophy." Oxford record entries for 1586 through 1591 for lecturers show Sterrell receiving a stipend for philosophy lectures: *"Mr. Harding et Sterrill lectiones philosophi 13£ 6s 8d."* John Harding would remain a friend; he enjoyed a great career at Oxford (becoming Magdalen College's President), later being named one of the main translators for the King James Bible. The course in natural philosophy focused on Aristotle's science writings; Sterrell would have lectured as well on other works of Aristotle and other authors on science and medicine.[16] As *praelector* in natural philosophy, Sterrell was also authorized to teach moral philosophy. His mentor, Dr. John Case, the best-known Aristotelian of the era, had once taught the same course and authored several books derived from his own lectures.

The counterpart at Cambridge University to Dr. Case and Sterrell in teaching subjects embraced by natural philosophy was Dr. John Caius. He is portrayed by his own name in a Shakespeare play, as noted by his *Oxford Dictionary of National Biography* biographer: "his name, his profession and his oddity were immortalized by Shakespeare in the *Merry Wives of Windsor*."

So, too, is Dr. John Case portrayed as Touchstone in *As You Like It*, down to his physical appearance, mannerisms and personal life with his wife. In this play, Touchstone refers explicitly to his own course in an exchange with the clown Corin. To Touchstone's question "Hast any philosophy in thee?" Corin finishes his answer by referring to someone "that hath learned no wit by Nature nor Art." Touchstone replies to Corin, "Such a one is a natural Philosopher." In his last book, *Lapis Philosophicus,* Case provided an elaborate analysis of grafting as an instance of Nature/Art, which is paralleled in *The Winter's Tale*, Act 4 sc. 4, in a discussion of grafting between Polixenes and Perdita.[17] Polixenes explains that grafting "is an art Which does mend nature--change it, rather; but The art itself is nature." Grafting is also the topic of humorous exchanges between Touchstone and Rosalind in *As You Like It* (Act 3, sc. 2).

Why would the playwright incorporate Caius and Case into multiple plays? The plays in which they appear are plays written for special occasions with the audience made up of former students at Cambridge and Oxford who would recognize these familiar figures from their campus days and from special events in which the two philosophers made appearances.

There are reasons why John Case would be featured or alluded to in Shakespeare plays, especially *As You Like It*. Dr. John Case was very close to the Spencer family. From it came the wives/patrons of Lord Strange's Men (Alice Spencer), the Lord Chamberlain's Men (Elizabeth Spencer), and Sir William Spencer (overseer of the Lord Chamberlain's will and whose son-in-law was effectively the overseer of Shakespeare's will). Dr. Case had treated Ferdinando Stanley (Lord Strange, Earl of Derby) as he lay dying in 1594 and had also treated Stanley's wife. Gifts to Case from both husband (Ferdinando) and wife (Alice Spencer) are specially mentioned in Case's will. Case's biographer says that Ferdinando must have been a student of Case in about 1572.[18] The relationship must have extended to the Spencer family in ways beyond medical treatment for the Case will also provides bequests to Alice Spencer's brother, Sir William Spencer "as a dutiful remembrance for all his kindness" and to Sir William's wife; Sir William was a student at Oxford just after Ferdinando Stanley (who became his brother-in-law). Their sister "the good Lady Mounteagle" was given a jewel and crucifix. This must have been Anne Spencer, whose first husband was William Stanley, 3rd Baron Mounteagle (1527-1581), of the same Stanley family. At the time of the will, she was married to her third husband, Robert Sackville. When Case died and *As You Like It* was written, the sister of Sir William Spencer, Alice Spencer and Anne Spencer was Elizabeth Spencer, patron of Shakespeare's acting company, the Lord Chamberlains Men.

Shakespeare-the-author draws directly upon Aristotle in several plays. In *Troilus and Cressida* Sterrell (Hector) reflects on what it was like to teach Aristotle, treating Paris and Troilus as though they were his students:

Paris and Troilus, you have both said well,
And on the cause and question now in hand
Have glozed [commented on] but superficially, not much
Unlike young men, whom Aristotle thought
Unfit to hear moral philosophy.

As Hector, he then lectures the two on moral decision-making urging Aristotle's own approach of dispassion.

In *Taming of the Shrew* Shakespeare-the-author again, through

Tranio, refers to Aristotle:

Let's be no stoics nor no stocks, I pray,
Or so devote to Aristotle's checks
As Ovid be an outcast quite abjured.

Whether "checks" is a misprint for "Ethics" or not, the meaning is to ignore ethical concerns that might arise as checks from Aristotle's *Ethics*. Other traces of Oxford University and persons associated with it can be found in other Shakespeare plays.

ꙮꙮꙮꙮ--ꙮꙮꙮꙮ

In 1591, Worcester allowed Sterrell leave from his service to go to work as a secret agent abroad for Leicester's stepson, Robert Devereux, the Earl of Essex.[19] Sterrell gave up his lectureship at Oxford for his secret mission to the Spanish Low Countries (now the Netherlands and Belgium) for Essex. Just before leaving on his mission, two of Worcester's sons, William and Henry Somerset, entered Magdalen College in June 26/27, 1591, aged 15 and 14, as did Sterrell's half-brother Clare Frauncis, June 26, 1591; Sterrell surely escorted all three of them. It was not uncommon for a private tutor to accompany his students when they entered Oxford, and Sterrell was still receiving a stipend from Worcester.

Sterrell went abroad on his intelligence mission in August 1591 and met with many English Catholic exiles. He exchanged numerous letters with his handler (on behalf of Essex) Thomas Phelippes, best known as the decipherer of the secret letters of Mary Queen of Scots that had led to her execution.

On his return from the mission in the fall of 1592, Sterrell experienced what has often been the fate of secret agents emerging from their time under cover. He fell into suspicion from his own circle and from others in the government. Essex assigned his close friend and counselor Francis Bacon to debrief Sterrell.

At this time, Sterrell returned to his service with Worcester. Though he probably made trips to London and Oxford, he primarily stayed with Worcester at Worcester's castle (Raglan) in Wales until February 1593 when Worcester, with Sterrell in tow, left to attend the sessions of Parliament. The suspicions about Sterrell having betrayed his mission grew as others learned of it. He was investigated by the government. This period of intense personal danger is explored below as "Sterrell's Mission and Crisis."

Overcoming the crisis, Sterrell was reunited with Worcester by late 1593. Their extraordinary relationship continued until the latter's death in 1628. Worcester was a wealthy lord, patron of an acting company, a high government official with multiple offices, and trusted counselor to two monarchs. Sterrell was more than Worcester's secretary and confidante. He was an alter ego to his master, one who submerged his own personality in deference to his patron. Worcester could always project affability and full conformity to the state religion while his agent worked to maintain England's ties to her Catholic exiles and to counter their domestic dissidents. Sterrell was always close at Worcester's side, so he was always privy to the innermost activities of the government in matters of religion and state after his patron Worcester became Deputy Master of the Horse in January 1598. Worcester and with him Sterrell would be present at Court almost constantly after this appointment and his subsequent higher offices until near the date of Worcester's death in 1628. It was only with Worcester's passing that Sterrell felt he was free to marry (age 68).

Sterrell did not abandon his correspondence and activities with Catholic exiles in 1593; he had the strong, if silent, support of Worcester. Sterrell could work in the interests of English Catholics in ways that Worcester could not directly. He made intelligence trips to the Low Countries and to Spain in the mid-to-late 1590s, some of which activities related to family and friends of Worcester as well as Catholics in exile. He evidently facilitated a trip to Spain for Thomas Thorpe in 1596, the printer who later published *Shake-speares Sonnets* in 1609.

Sterrell associated with the leading Catholic exiles in Europe in correspondence under false names until 1605. Most of these letters were no more than news of political, religious and family matters rather than disclosure of state secrets. But they were forbidden and dangerous.

When James I arrived in London as King of England on May 7, 1603, Sterrell's close association with the royal entertainments began immediately. Within a few days, James took Shakespeare's acting company under his own patronage as the King's Men and simultaneously made William Sterrell the keeper of the Priory of St John of Jerusalem. The title to this magnificent property had been unsettled since John Chamberlain had written to Dudley Carleton in October 1601: "The Quene sells land still, and the house at St. Johns is at sale." The grant of May 1603 to Sterrell was given further legal form and effect by a Crown lease of the Priory (or Palace or Hospital) of St John of Jerusalem to William Sterrell for life, in August 1603.

This palace housed the Office of Revels. It was the primary base and center of activity for the King's players. The Shakespeare plays and Jonson's masques were rehearsed with full dress performances "in the greate chamber" of the Priory until 1608 when the greater part of the priory was sold to Esmé Stuart, Lord Aubigny, cousin to the King. For about five years Sterrell enjoyed the proprietorship (grant, then a lease) of this splendid group of buildings. Revels was one of his tenants.

HOSPITAL OF ST JOHN OF JERUSALEM, ABOUT 1640.
Eastern Side towards St. John's Street.

King James had never met William Sterrell. He had no apparent reason to give him so great a gift immediately upon the new monarch's arrival in London. Surely Worcester himself was behind the grant, just as Worcester was the nobleman who persuaded the new king to make the Lord Chamberlain's Men into the King's Men under royal patronage. Worcester's own company was soon re-formed as the Queen's Men. The property established a substantial income for Sterrell. Although the available records show no payments to the "keeper" or "lessee" for the use of the buildings and lodgings, they do show payments to Revels officials who were lodged there. Property grants and monopolies were sources of revenue for the grantees.

More importantly, the grant to Sterrell placed him in close proximity to the activities for the Court entertainments; he could participate in the supervision of the performances, for himself and for Worcester who was put in charge of the Court's entertainments by the new monarch. Sterrell was able to work with the company personnel on a daily basis. All in the company would have known him not only as the proprietor/landlord but also as the great Earl of Worcester's right hand. All in the company - shareholders, actors, costumers, props, etc. - depended on his favor if they wished to satisfy their patron and his. Worcester was their effective patron even if nominally they were the King's Men.

The transition of the Lord Chamberlain's Men to the King's Men in 1603 was a fundamental change of the company despite the fact that the company remained under ***a*** Lord Chamberlain before and after the adoption of the company by King James. The company went from being ***Lord Hunsdon's*** company to being the ***King's*** company. There was also discontinuity in the immediate period as to who was the Lord Chamberlain, and the new Lord Chamberlain shared responsibilities for Court entertainments with the Master of the Horse.

The 1603 takeover of the company was similar to what had occurred in 1594. At that time, the company known as Lord Strange/Derby's Servants lost its patron when Ferdinando Stanley died suddenly in April 1594. The company was reconstituted under the patronage of Henry Carey, Lord Hunsdon. It became known as the Lord Chamberlain's Men only because the new patron happened to be Lord Chamberlain. The company's name was only coincidental due to his holding that office in the Queen's household.

Henry Carey died on July 23, 1596, and the company came

under the patronage of his son, George Carey, 2nd Baron Hunsdon. The company now became called Lord Hunsdon's Men; it was no longer the Lord Chamberlain's Men. The Queen appointed Lord Cobham as Lord Chamberlain when the office became vacant through Henry Hunsdon's death. But then Lord Cobham died March 6, 1597. The Queen now appointed George Carey to be Lord Chamberlain on March 17, 1597, and the company reverted to its previous name. George Carey's sister was Katherine Carey Howard, wife of the Lord Admiral, Countess of Nottingham (1550 –February 25, 1603).

The relationship of patron, company and office is on display with the title pages of the two quartos of *Romeo and Juliet*. The 1597 quarto gives the play's title and informs the reader, "As it hath been often (with great applause) plaid publiquely, by the right Honourable the L. of Hunsdon his Servants." This puts the date of the printing of the quarto prior to March 17, 1597. The 1599 quarto title says the play has been "newly corrected, augmented, and amended: As it hath bene sundry times publiquely acted, by the right Honourable the Lord Chamberlaine his Servants." Same play, same company, same patron; only the office held by the patron has changed.

It should be added that the same point can be made regarding the "rival company," the Lord Admiral's Men. The patron of the company was Charles Howard, 1st Earl of Nottingham. The company was first known as the Lord Howard's Men, but the name changed when Lord Howard was named Lord High Admiral in 1585. His office as the chief naval official had nothing to do with the acting company *per se*.

George Carey was not active with his company as Lord Chamberlain for very long; he was seriously ill from early 1600 to his death in 1603. He first made his will in May 1599 with a codicil dated April 26, 1601. Nor was his wife in good health. William Sterrell (and Worcester) was keenly observing the Lord Chamberlain. In a letter of March 3, 1602, he wrote:[20]

> The Lord Chamberlain's Lady on Thursday last at supper was suddenly surprised with a strange palsy drawing her head and mouth clean awry, so as she is in as ill case as her husband, some say she amendeth and recovereth speech,

others think the malady incurable.

Lord Thomas Howard, Earl of Suffolk, became acting Lord Chamberlain just a few months before the death of Queen Elizabeth in March 1603. He was appointed to the same office by James while at Theobalds c. May 8, 1603. Suffolk had no involvement in the Shakespeare company before it became the King's Men in May 1603 and had no experience with theatre or acting companies before becoming the nominal head of the Office of Revels.

Worcester, who long had had ties with actors of the Lord Chamberlain's Men, filled the vacuum in leadership and engineered the adoption of the company by the King. Worcester himself became effectively the patron of both the King's Men and the Queen's Men. Suffolk was a weak man, dominated by his wife, and followed the guidance of Worcester on Court entertainments. The 1603 takeover of the "Shakespeare" company by the King meant that the effective control of the company passed to the two men in charge of the King's household: Worcester and Suffolk (with Sterrell always at Worcester's side).

Sterrell's friends and Worcester's family shared the favor of the new king and queen. Worcester's son Thomas Somerset became the Queen's Master of the Horse. Worcester's wife, his daughters and his daughters-in-law were at various times ladies of the Queen's household. As chief assistant to Worcester, William Sterrell had access to the royal Court and household unparalleled by a lesser courtier. Sterrell 's influence (through Worcester) would account for our finding Sterrell and John Florio again working in close proximity, as they had at Magdalen and at the French ambassador's 1583-85. From 1604 to 1619, John Florio served as Groom of the Privy Chamber and private secretary to Queen Anne. He was also a tutor to the royal children.

Although Sterrell received substantial benefits under the new king, secrecy about his activities under false names was still absolutely necessary. At any time, he could be betrayed by someone who knew of his activities as a Catholic agent. Only a year before Elizabeth died, one of Sterrell's classmates from Magdalen reported to Secretary Robert Cecil that a Catholic informant, surely Charles Paget, gave him copies of letters Sterrell had written to Catholic exiles a decade earlier. The classmate was Sir Ralph Winwood, who had taken BA and MA degrees at Magdalen at the same time as Sterrell, and was now (1602) in Paris as an English diplomat. In April 1602, Winwood dispatched a group of letters written under a pseudonym Sterrell had used, together with Sterrell's cipher sheets. Winwood had asked the informant to tell him whether[21]

> in Flanders he knew any now in England which are pensioners to the enemy or any other that holdeth intelligence with him. Now this last week falling into the same discourse he named unto me one William Stirrell, who as he sayeth for many years hath had correspondence, first with Thomas Fitzherbert since with [Hugh] Owen and Sherewood [Richard Sherwood] a priest, and doth receive a pension by their means. I heretofore have known one of that name, sometimes of Magdalen College in Oxford, and since belonging to the Earl of Worcester . . .

Cecil took no action at this time but preserved the letters. Sterrell probably was not aware that Paget had disclosed the old correspondence, which was continuing still under other false names.

Even with the arrival of James, Sterrell did not immediately terminate his dangerous correspondence with the Catholic exiles. This soon got him and his collaborator Thomas Phelippes into deep trouble.

In 1605 more of Sterrell's correspondence under pseudonyms was discovered by the King's principal minister, Robert Cecil, who continued as Secretary of State. Unlike Thomas Phelippes (who lacked a protector), Sterrell escaped prison, but his correspondence apparently ceased for a decade. He claimed the government knew of it and that it was discontinued in 1603. Sterrell told King James's most powerful counselor, Robert Cecil:

> They were acquainted with this correspondence: the Queen Majesty, the Earl of Essex, Mr. Francis Bacon, Mr. William Wade [Waad], and Mr. Phillips [Phelippes].

Sterrell's interrogation was by Cecil himself. As Cecil knew well, the first two were now dead. The Queen had died in March 1603, and the Earl of Essex in March 1601. Although Essex was executed for rebellion against the Queen, his name was once again highly regarded. When he became king, James had publicly praised Essex and had restored his estates to Essex's children. Two of the other three men Sterrell named were living and were highly placed. Francis Bacon was a counselor to the King, while William Waad was now lieutenant of the Tower of London. Sterrell could not mention them as being acquainted with his correspondence unless it were true, for if it were not true and Bacon or Waad testified to the contrary, Sterrell could be put to death for treason. Any testimony of Phelippes would be discounted as he was a collaborator.

Sterrell went on to tell Secretary Cecil, "The three last were acquainted with it, every man in his turn as the Queen or the Earl would employ them." And Sterrell could not resist adding a statement to exculpate himself from deceit in his own dealings with Cecil. To dispel the conclusion that he had cozened Cecil or that he was not worthy of credit, he added: "And I was told by Mr. Phelippes that your lordship was privy to it also, but I never spoke with your lordship about it." The last phrase is a tantalizing indication of familiarity between the two men, for it is implicit that they had spoken upon other matters.

Despite the discovery of forbidden correspondence, Sterrell continued to be involved in the court plays and masques. Had Cecil attempted to punish Sterrell, he would have encountered a fierce reaction from Worcester.

Worcester had authority over and supervision of the masques; his family often participated in these entertainments, some of which were written by Ben Jonson. Though lacking documentation, Worcester likely had the same role for court plays. Sterrell's active role in the masques and his closeness to Jonson is documented in Court records with Jonson's masque, *Love Freed from Ignorance and Folly* (February 1611). Sterrell's role in securing the performance of *Love Freed* was as impresario or supervisor.[22] All told, Sterrell was provided 400 pounds "to be by him employed for the charges of the Queen's Maske" as "authorized by the Right Honorable the Earl of Suffolk, Lord Chamberlain of his Majesty's household and the Earl of Worcester Master of his Majesty's horse." Among the treasury disbursals by Sterrell were "to mr Beniamin Johnson for his Invention, 40 [pounds], to mr Inigo Johnes for his paynes and Invention 40 [pounds], and to mr Alfonso (Ferrabosco) for making the songes,

20 [pounds]."

Was Sterrell merely the disburser of funds, or did he have the larger role of helping plan and stage this masque (and probably others)? Another record would suggest the latter, larger role. In a list of "Free Gifts from the Exchequer in the Eighth Year of the King's Reign, 1610-11" is this item: "William Stirrel - - - 50£." There is no record of Shakespeare-of-Stratford ever being paid for a Court play, despite the fact that six or seven plays were probably written for the Court after James came to the throne. But here is Sterrell, paid even more than Ben Jonson at the height of his career at Court.

Sterrell continued to be active at Court, but he did not resume his intelligence activities for the sovereign heads of the Spanish Low Countries, Archduke Albert and Isabella, until 1616. Between 1616 and September 1626 he wrote hundreds of letters on political and Court developments to them while continuing in the service of Worcester and his family.

Worcester provided well for his confidante. Sterrell acquired lands in Wales (about 60 acres at Lantilio Crossenny, at Llanarth, and a tract or farm of Lantrothy in the parish of Penrhos) and was able to live in fashionable quarters in London (lease of White Horse tenement in Long Ditch, for 40 years on December 4, 1604). At the end of 1615, he apparently moved a short distance, just on the other side of Tothill Street, to a new tenement with a garden adjacent to the Great Almonry. From either residence he was only a few hundred yards from Westminster Abbey, formerly St. Peter's Cathedral, and a short walk to the Parliament buildings and thence to Whitehall where he worked. A few years after Sterrell's move next to the Almonry, Ben Jonson became his neighbor.

We can only speculate about Sterrell's relations with women. Perhaps it was his total commitment to his master Worcester that kept him from marrying before Worcester's death in March 1628. In late 1629, Sterrell increased his household in Westminster by marrying a woman much younger than himself (Anne Belche, Belcher or Belchier). At age 68 he fathered a son (dead within a year). She was probably a daughter of Dabridgcourt Belchier, an attorney at the Middle Temple with Sterrell's brother. Dabridgcourt Belchier was the author of "Hans Beer-Pot, his Invisible Comedy of

See me and See me not." Anne was born in about 1606 and was about 23 or 24 when she and Sterrell married.[23]

William Sterrell made his will on December 14, 1630, in the presence of three witnesses. His executors were his wife Anne and his principal servant, Alexander Choke. He provided generously for his wife and his infant son as well as for the seven children of his brother and sister-in-law, both deceased.

caelo tegitur qui non habet urnam -- From Sterrell's will we have this haunting Latin epigram from Lucan's *Roman Civil Wars*. The poet Lucan imagines himself urging mercy on Caesar, a victor withholding burial from slaughtered losers in civil war: "heaven covers those who have no grave (urn)."[24] Sterrell's will provides: "And upon my funeral my will is that my executors bestow no more than in humanity they need must. *caelo tegitur qui non habet urnam.*"

Shakespeare's works draw on this scene and passage. The opening scene of *Titus Andronicus*, has Titus demanding:

Why suffer'st thou thy sons, unburied yet,
To hover on the dreadful shore of Styx?
Make way to lay them by their brethren.
Titus Andronicus, 1.1

Henry V, Act 1, sc. 2 links "urn" and "tombless" in Henry's opening scene about going to France where they might meet defeat: "Or lay these bones in an unworthy urn, Tombless, with no remembrance over them." In *Julius Caesar,* Act 3 sc. 1, we find Antony paralleling Lucan's *caelo* passage: "That this foul deed shall smell above the earth / With carrion men, groaning for burial." In *Coriolanus*, the protagonist speaks of "the dead carcasses of unburied men that do corrupt my air."

Sterrell's final expression in writing in his will was what he had expressly anticipated in *Sonnet 81*:

I (once gone) to all the world must die,
The earth can yield me but a common grave.

William Sterrell's death occurred on March 10, 1631, two months before he would have turned seventy. Word of his final illness must have reached Raglan Castle at the beginning of February 1631. For twenty years, Walter Powell had been one of Sterrell's tenants in Wales; he was a businessman who also served as deputy-steward and receiver of rents to the Earl of Worcester. Powell's diary records not only the dates on which Sterrell granted him leases, but that on February 7, 1631, he and Henry Somerset, 5th Earl of Worcester, set forth for London. The journey was apparently for a last visit by the Earl with his boyhood tutor, for the next entry in Powell's diary is "10 m'cij, [March] Wm Sterrell died."

Sterrell's Younger Brother(s)

As noted already, William Sterrell had a brother, Henry Sterrell, and a half-brother, Clare Frauncis, of his mother's second husband. Sterrell was very close to Henry, but we see little of the half-brother other than William apparently escorting him to Oxford in 1591 (Clare was named in the wills of Henry Sterrell and his Margaret). As suggested earlier, William Sterrell probably wrote the early sonnets of *Shake-speares Sonnets* to Henry in about 1593-95 while Henry was a young law student at the Middle Temple. It is probably because of Henry, who was fully aware of his brother's writing under a false name, that we find early traces of Shakespeare-the-author.

When their mother remarried, William was sent to Oxford while Henry went to live with maternal cousins, the Meres family whose seats were Kirton, near Boston, and at Auborne, not far south and west of Lincoln. Henry was apparently raised in the household of his great-uncle Anthony Meres. Here, he will have become well-acquainted with another of the close-knit Meres family, Francis Meres, who was about the same age as Henry. Both Henry and Francis were living in London in the 1590s and it will have been from Henry Sterrell that Francis learned of the writings of Shakespeare-the-author. In Meres's 1598 *Palladis tamia, Wits Treasury,* we have the earliest discussion of Shakespeare's work as an author; the book identifies twelve plays as well as "sug'red sonnets" that were said to circulate "among his private friends." These sonnets were surely the sonnets numbered 1-19 in the 1609 book of *Shakes-speares Sonnets*. These were addressed to Sterrell's younger brother, who would have shared them with Francis Meres; they were relatives.

One of Henry's fellow Middle Temple lawyers was John Manningham, who kept a diary during 1602-03. Several entries pertain to Shakespeare and one to John Florio's translation of Montaigne. Pertinent to us is Manningham's attending a performance of *Twelfth Night* in February 1602 at the Middle Temple, the only known performance of the play. William Sterrell probably wrote the play to commemorate Henry being called to the Utter Bar about a year earlier. Also in 1602, Manningham related a story told to him by "Mr. Sterrill" that was apparently taken from Florio's *Montaigne's Essays before* the book was published in 1603; William Sterrell would have had a draft of the book from his long-time friend John Florio.

Words and Writings of William Sterrell

The contention that Sterrell wrote the poetry and plays of Shakespeare would be extravagant, indeed unfounded, if there were no writings that would support the argument. Were there? We could turn the query around and ask the same of the Stratford Shakespeare who produced nothing whatsoever before *Venus and Adonis*. Was "Shakespeare," like Venus (and *Venus*), fully formed at birth? Only in myth. No artist begins a career with a masterpiece. No pianist or soprano has a first performance at Carnegie Hall. No runner's first race is for the Olympic games. Excellence has precedents.

Unlike Shakespeare-of-Stratford, we can be certain of Sterrell's exceptional command of the classics of Roman literature and history, or he would not have been appointed university-wide lecturer at Oxford. He lectured in Latin. He demonstrated written proficiency to attain his degrees and his position as university praelector. But there is other evidence we can consider.

Spoken Words of Sterrell

There are at least four instances in which William Sterrell's spoken words have been reported in writing. Two record him quoting Latin aphorisms in the course of personal exchanges. In both instances, Sterrell's words correspond to lines uttered by characters in Shakespeare plays reflecting the same point made by Sterrell to the persons reporting what he said. The third is the transcription of questions King James's Secretary of State propounded to Sterrell in 1605 as he interrogated Sterrell about correspondence with England's perceived enemies; these will not be examined. The fourth is from a legal proceeding at Oxford in 1587.

The first of the Latin statements was made in 1585 to a young man, one of six whom Sterrell was attempting to spirit out of England: *amo proditionem sed non amo proditorem* — I love the treason but not the traitor. It is discussed below, where you will read of Edward Dodwell's confession.

The second instance is from a letter written to Sterrell in which we learn of a Latin saying he often used. Hugh Owen, a leader of the Catholic exiles in the Low Countries and regular correspondent of Sterrell, wrote Sterrell in July 1602: "Me thinks I see you (in reading of this) make a grim scornful smile and say to yourself, *Ne sutor ultra* etc & that I find not those discourses in my breviary nor mass book." The adage is more fully given as *Ne sutor ultra crepidam - Let not the cobbler overstep his last.* The meaning is a person should not meddle in those matters he does not understand. We find the adage reflected in at least two Shakespeare plays. *Romeo & Juliet* (with humorous jumbling):

> **Servant**. Find them out whose names are written here? It is written that the shoemaker should meddle with his yard and the tailor with his last, the fisher with his pencil and the painter with his nets; but I am sent to find those persons whose names are here writ, and can never find what names the writing person hath here writ. I must to the learned. Act 1 sc. 2.

And in *Julius Caesar* is another clever play upon the aphorism:

> **Flavius**. Thou art a cobbler, art thou?
> **Second Commoner**. Truly, Sir, all that I live by is with the awl; I meddle with no tradesman's matters, nor women's matters, but with awl. I am indeed, sir, a surgeon to old shoes; when they are in great danger, I recover them. Act 1 sc. 1.

Latin aphorisms and quotations are found often in Sterrell's letters, and their direct counterparts are seen in Shakespeare works.

Sterrell's Letters

We have many letters that Sterrell wrote. They speak strongly of his command of language. Highly intelligent and learned, they are given force by apt Latin aphorisms and allusions. A compilation of 250 plus key words and phrases, often archaic or obscure, extracted from those letters all have the same usage as they are found in the works of "Shakespeare." To list a few common to Sterrell's letters and the Shakespeare works:

caluminate	designment	hollow heart	nighard	quietus
care not a pin	discourse of reason	intervalla	out of heart	reconforte/ recomfort
compassed	espial	inward man	outface	shent
condign	fain	malapert	overweening	starting hole
conjuration	folded (hid-den)	meed	palter	vendible
constant man	froward	methinks	pelt	waft/waift
cooling card	garboil	middest	prating	well willers

The letters offer other parallels to the Shakespeare works. A letter of Sterrell of 1602 uses a Latin aphorism: "Their lives and conversation in the mean is *toto* scandalous, *qualis arbor talis fructus.*" That is, what kind the tree, of such kind the fruit. This Latin adage illustrates the deductive method of logic. It is given a clever twist in *1 Henry IV,* Act 2, sc. 4: "If then the tree may be known by the fruit, as the fruit by the tree . . ."

Other proverbs or colloquialisms used by Sterrell have their parallel in Shakespeare's works:

Sterrell letter: "seeing himself deceived, and perceiving the queen's ships, he made virtue of necessity,"

Richard II **–** There is no virtue like necessity.

2 Gentlemen of Verona **–** To make a virtue of necessity,

Sterrell letter: "I care not a pin for any copy till it be printed by authority,"

Loves Labours Lost – By the world, I would not care a pin if the other three were in.

Sterrell letter: "the proverb is true, it is an ill wind that blows nobody good."

2 Henry IV **–** Not the ill wind which blows no man to good.

3 Henry VI – Ill blows the wind that profits nobody.

Occasionally the letters of Sterrell employ phrasing similar to sentences in the Shakespeare works. We would cite, for example, the repetition of ***many***:

Sterrell letter: "in returning they will do more mischief; Yet

many of them are dead, **many** sick by being so long at sea, **many** fled from them.

3 Henry VI - Thou hadst not liv'd to kill a son of mine. And thus I prophesy, that **many** a thousand Which now mistrust no parcel of my fear, And **many** an old man's sigh, and **many** a widow's, And **many** an orphan's water-standing eye. Act 5 sc. 6.

Henry V - As **many** arrows loosed several ways
Come to one mark, as **many** ways meet in one town,
As **many** fresh streams meet in one salt sea,
As **many** lines close in the dial's centre;
So **many** a thousand actions, once afoot, Act 1 sc. 2.

Another fascinating facet of Sterrell's letters are his many Latin quotes; their authors are also drawn upon in the Shakespeare plays and poetry. Seneca (4 BC – 65 AD) was a favorite Roman author of Sterrell, and the playwright refers to the Roman dramatist directly in *Hamlet*: "Seneca cannot be too heavy nor Plautus too light" (*Hamlet* 2.2.396-97). Sterrell quotes Seneca in multiple letters and these exact quotes are the direct sources of lines in the Shakespeare plays and poetry. We will recount below the full context when he quotes a line from *Phaedra (Hippolytus)*: *Quanti casus humana rotant* - "How on the wheel of fate we mortals whirl!" This Senecan line is the source of the statement of Coriolanus: "O world, thy slippery turns!" (4.4.12) followed by his discussion of how fate had revolved for him. When Sterrell used the quote, he found himself in the position depicted for Coriolanus in the play.

We see the Senecan line again in *2 Henry IV*: "O God! that one might read the book of fate, And see the revolution of the times." Again it appears in *King Lear* with Edmund's line, "The wheel is come full circle; I am here" (5.3). We find in *Antony and Cleopatra* that Cleopatra references the same idea, pleading, "let me rail so high/That the false huswife Fortune break her wheel." Pistol in *Henry V* speaks of "giddy Fortune's furious fickle wheel," and Fluellen responds, "Fortune is blind; and she is painted also with a wheel, to signify to you, which is the moral of it, that she is turning, and inconstant, and mutability, and variation."

Another, later, letter quotes from Seneca's *Medea*: *Qui nil sperare potest desperet nihil.* This translates as "He who cannot hope will not despair." It reflects Seneca's stoicism. Placing the quote at the top of his page, Sterrell was telling his correspondent how he would react to negative news about diplomatic developments. A few months later he echoed the same Seneca lines — now Englished — and added a quote from Lucan's *Pharsalia*: "The extract you inclosed, as now I understand was sent unto you after the last proroging of the match, *wherefore I can neither hope nor despair* of it, *semper nocuit differre paratis*." (Away with delay - it always injures those who are prepared; Lucan - *Pharsalia* (I, 281)).

From his first published writing, *Venus and Adonis,* we find the same Senecan expression: "Despair, and hope makes thee ridiculous: The one doth flatter thee in thoughts unlikely, In likely thoughts the other kills thee quickly." The message: avoid both despair and hope. The same sentiment is in *Sonnet 140*: "No news but health from their physicians know [i.e. hope], For if I should despair I should grow mad." Helena in *All's Well* suggests stoic reflection on his health worries: "Where hope is coldest, and despair most fits."

In multiple letters thirty years apart, Sterrell repeated the Lucan aphorism, *semper nocuit,* delay is loss. Its point in repeated in the Shakespeare plays. In *Richard III* Stanley tells the Queen: "Take all the swift advantage of the hours . . . . Be not ta'en tardy by unwise delay." King Edward in *3 Henry VI* says: "The sun shines hot; and, if we use delay, Cold biting winter mars our hop'd-for hay."

When Sterrell accompanied Worcester on Queen Elizabeth's progress about the country in 1602 he wrote his correspondent expressing his resignation and weariness in Latin: *Sic ut quimus quando ut volumus non licet* - When what we want is not possible, we do what we can. [25] It is from Terence's *Andria* (sic ut quimus, aiunt, quando ut volumu' non licet). The sentiment is paraphrased in *Julius Caesar* (Act 4, Scene 3) when Brutus says: 'And we must take the current when it serves, / Or lose our ventures.' Both *Twelfth Night* and *A Midsummer Night's Dream* had part of their plot from Terence's *Andria.*

These are a few of the Latin quotes of Sterrell that have their direct counterpart in Shakespeare plays and poetry. More will be explored in the context of Sterrell's crisis of 1592-93.

There is a high degree of congruity between the vocabulary and usage of the letters of William Sterrell and the works of William Shakespeare. Such close congruity cannot be found in the words and usages of other contemporary writers when they are compared to the vocabulary and usage in the works of William Shakespeare. As can readily be seen, many of the words Sterrell used are uncommon; many of these were uncommon for their time. Sterrell's letters mostly concern political, military and religious events and topics. This vocabulary would be more restricted than what we would find in the poetry and plays attributed to Shakespeare. The fact that Sterrell's Latin quotations are found repeatedly in the Shakespeare works has no counterpart in the period from any other writer.

♦♦♦ ♦♦♦

Bardophilus: I'm supposed to be impressed that someone has compiled a database. But this has only given us a list of words. Put them in the context of the poetry and the plays and then we'll talk about it. And you'll have to show that the same words and phrases weren't used by many of Shakespeare's contemporaries.

Skepticisima: Be patient, Signior Bardio. The author has compiled just such a comparison as you demand. He calls it an *idiolect;* that's a fancy name to describe an individual's unique use of language. Language consists of sentence constructs, word choices, and expressions of style; an *idiolect* comprises an individual's uses of these facets. You have one. I have one. Every person has a unique idiolect influenced by their language, socioeconomic status, and geographical location. Because you and I have similar backgrounds, educations and shared interests in Shakespeare, our language usage will have commonalities. Forensic linguistics analyzes idiolects. The author's full table would add many pages to this little book but not add a whole lot more than what he has demonstrated. You would just give us your dismissive *harumph.* And will you speak to the fact that Sterrell and Shakespeare often use the same Latin quotes?

Bardophilus: No. We all know that the "small Latin" of a provincial grammar-school boy in the age of the first Queen Elizabeth would have been large by the standards of many a university Classics graduate in the age of the second. We're not surprised or impressed that there would be a coincidental overlap. It must have been the same with writers of the period.

Poetry by Sterrell

Two poems were published in 1591 and 1593 that were surely Sterrell's work. These two examples anticipate his later poetry and suggest his interactions with other literary figures prior to hiding himself behind an invented identity borrowed from an unknown commoner from Stratford.

The Phaëton Sonnet

We have already met John Florio, the outstanding linguist, multi-talented man of Italian descent. He had arrived at Magdalen College, Oxford by about December 1577 when his pupil Emmanuel Barnes was enrolled at Magdalen College and himself was enrolled at Magdalen at age 36 in May 1581, noting that he was "serviens Mri Barnes."[26] While associated with Oxford, Florio published in 1578 a manual for teaching Italian, which he called *Firste Fruites*. Dedicated to Robert Dudley, Earl of Leicester (Chancellor of Oxford), its front matter included commendatory verses from actors in Leicester's company of players. Among them were Richard Tarlton, Robert Wilson, Thomas Clarke, and John Bentley; others contributing praise were Steven Gossen, John Cowland, R. Collines, I.P., R.H., and I.H.

Sterrell was a Fellow of Magdalen during this time of Florio's period at Magdalen. They were next together in the London embassy of France when Florio was tutor to the daughter of the French ambassador and Sterrell was coordinating with the ambassador the illicit voyages of Catholic youth to Douay/Rheims and elsewhere on the Continent.

When Florio published a second book of Italian/English dialogues, his *Second Frutes*, he dedicated it to "Master Nicholas Saunder of Ewel, Esquire," expressing his gratitude for the "rare courtesies you vouchsaft me at Oxford" and "great liberaltie" since continued in London. The two men had matriculated at Oxford a day apart in May 1581, Saunders at Balliol and Florio at Magdalen. Saunders had later studied law at the Inner Temple and was a Justice of Peace in Surrey at the time of the dedication. Where the *First Fruits* had commendatory verses or remarks by ten men, the *Second Fruits* had but one, and it was anonymous.

Just as the dedication to *Second Fruits* was to a man Florio knew from Oxford and London, so, too, was the commendatory verse probably from a man Florio knew from Oxford and London. It was likely William Sterrell who composed an Ovid-inspired poem that opened Florio's book, "Phaëton to his friend Florio." This sonnet was derived from the Phaëton legend of Book 2 of Ovid's *Metamorphoses,* about a young man who flew his chariot too close to the sun (Florio's emblem was Helios, the sun). The poem itself has nothing to do with the tale. A sole anonymous dedicatory verse was itself an oddity for the period and unlike any other publications by Florio. Here is the poem:

Phaëton to his Friend Florio

Sweet friend whose name agrees with thy increase
How fit a rival art thou of the spring?
For when each branche hath left his flourishing,
And green-lockt Sommer's shadie pleasures cease:
She makes the winters stormes repose in peace,
And spends her franchise on each living thing:
The dazies sprout, the little birds doo sing,
Herbes, gummes, and plants doo waunt of their release.
So when that all our English witts lay dead
(Except the Laurell that is ever greene,)
Thou with thy Frutes our barrennes o'er-spread,
And set thy flowrie pleasance to be seene.
Sutch frutes, sutch flowrets of moralitie
Were nere before brought out of Italy.

Phaëton is an excellent example of the Petrarchan sonnet. Though Florio did not name his poet-friend, scholars have often attributed it to Shakespeare.

What are we to make of a poet who identifies himself as *Phaëton*? Ovid's story is a cautionary tale about the dangers of a young man's excessive pride (hubris) and the folly of attempting feats beyond his capabilities. *Phaëton* is essentially the same admonitory fable of *All's Well* in which Parolles's hubris leads to his humiliation. If the two works have the same author who views himself in the same way, there is no surprise they reflect a common theme.

Florio knew well that Sterrell's name was potentially tainted by his Catholic activities in September 1585. He must have known of an informant's confessions to the Queen's officers about Sterrell's activities with the French ambassador and with his butler at the embassy. The informant's confessions are discussed in the next section of this chapter. The arrests of six young men as they sought to leave England on the ambassador's boat and the informant's confessions coincided with the departure of the ambassador and with Florio's appointment as the ambassador's agent to handle all of his affairs in his absence. The new French ambassador took Florio into his service and Florio handled the transition of the embassy to this new envoy.[27] Government agents will surely have questioned Florio about Sterrell's actions with the former ambassador and his butler based on the confessions. The sonnet seems to allude to Sterrell's having flown too near the sun, with Florio contributing to his rescue. Florio was in a perfect position to provide alibis for Sterrell's activities as he worked with Secretary of State Walsingham on behalf of the French embassy and to counter the informant's statements. A controversy over Sterrell and the French ambassador could have roiled the government plot against Mary Queen of Scots.

The poet preferred to remain anonymous for his own sake and for Florio's. But he cleverly placed a direct synonym of his name within the *Phaëton* sonnet: "Thou [Florio] with thy Fruits our *barrenness* o'erspread." The wordplay is doubled, as another synonym of "sterile" is *fruitless.* It is the same wordplay that Sterrell will make upon his name with *sterile* as a synonym of *barren* in *Venus and Adonis* and in *Shake-speares Sonnets.*

Phaëton's "thou" indicates a close friendship between the two rather than a superior speaking to an inferior. This use of "thou" to a close friend or relative is more frequent than "you" in *Shake-speares Sonnets.*[28] It was probably in reference to Sterrell that Florio in his next book of note, *A World of Words* (1598), talked about "a friend of mine that loved better to be a Poet than to be counted so . . ." Florio further identified his friend, probably the anonymous friend of the *Phaëton Sonnet.* After referring to the excellence of the Queen in her language (as well as the tongue of others), Florio wrote:

> That the best by her pattern desire to do as much, I doubt not; but I doubt how they can without such help, and that such help was to be had till now, I deny; yet do I understand that a gentleman of worshipful account, well travelled, well conceited, and well experienced in the Italian, has in this very kind taken great pains, and made as great proofs of his inestimable worth. Glad would I be to see that work abroad: some sight whereof, gave me **twenty years** since the first light to this. But since he suppresses his, for private respects, or further perfection, nor he, nor others (I hope) prize the less.

Twenty years before 1598: Florio would have first met Sterrell at Magdalen College about 1578 when Florio accompanied Emmanuel Barnes to Magdalen College.

A Notable Description of the World

In another poem, published this same year as *Venus and Adonis,* Sterrell subscribes his initials and status: "W.S. Gent." This poem is called *A Notable Description of the World.* The book is a miscellany named the *Phoenix Nest.* The poem's first stanza combines Ovid's description of Creation in Book 1 of the *Metamorphoses* with a summary of the principal features of Aristotle's science or "natural philosophy."[29] The second stanza contrasts the first with a free summary of the opening of the *Book of Genesis.* That is, the poem depicts creation from separate perspectives and sources.

Of thick and thin, light, heavie, dark and cleere,	**Mixtures.**
White, black, & blew, red green, & purple die:	**Coulors.**
Gold, Silver, Brass, Lead, Iron, Tin, and Copper,	**Mettals.**
Moist aire, hot fire, cold water, earth full drie:	**Elements.**
Blood, Choler, Flegme, and Melancholie by,	**Cõplexiõs.**
A mixed masse, a Chaos all confusde,	[complexion]
Such was the world, till God division usde.	**Chaos**
In framing heav'n and earth, God did divide,	**1**

The first daies light, and darkth, to night and day. 2
The second, he a firmament applide, 3
Third, fruitfull earth appeerd, Seas tooke their way, 4
Fourth, Sun and Moone, with Stars in skies he fixt, 5
Fifth, Fish and Foule, the Sea and land possest 6
And God made Man, like to himselfe, the fixt: 7
The seaventh day, when all thing he had blest:
He hallowed that, and therein tooke his rest.

Some have thought *Notable Description* might be Shakespeare's, but this has been rejected on the ground that "Shakespeare was not a 'gentleman' in 1593." William Sterrell, however, was a "gentleman" in 1593. As son of Henry Sterrell, Esq., Sterrell had the social status of gentleman; he is identified as "William Sterrell, gent." on Court grants to him in 1603 and in 1610-11.

There is special reason to believe that this is the work of Sterrell: it directly grows from his teaching of "natural philosophy" as an Oxford praelector. The entry on "natural philosophy" for the *Stanford Encyclopedia of Philosophy* observes of Dr. John Case, Sterrell's mentor who taught the same course as Sterrell, that: "Scholars like John Case (d. 1600), who considered Aristotelianism compatible with Christian dogmas such as creation and divine providence, were particularly fond of searching for ways to syncretize theology with natural philosophy."[30] The same entry observes that "authors like Virgil, Horace and Ovid were common presences in discussions about botany, and even a philological evaluation of the text of the *Bible* provided material to natural philosophers."[31] This is exactly the conceit of *A Notable Description*, a correlation of Aristotle, Ovid, and the Bible on Creation.

Reformation scholars held a bias against Aristotle, the philosopher whom they held responsible for sustaining the scholastic edifice of Catholic theology, especially for Thomas Aquinas's heavy reliance on Aristotle. Sterrell's poem posits the compatibility of Aristotelian scientific theory and Christianity.

The listing of the four humours, "Blood, Choler, Flegme, and Melancholie," is significant in Sterrell's thought. The theory of "humours" as the foundation of character pervades the Shakespeare plays. The "Introduction" to the Bevington 2003 edition of the

Complete Works of Shakespeare, p. xxvi, has an extended discussion of scientific thought during the Shakespeare period that closely follows the "Notable Description of the World":

> Traditional learning apportioned all physical matter into four elements: earth, air, fire, and water. Each of these was thought to be a different combination of the four "qualities" of the universe: hot, cold, moist, and dry. Earth combined cold and dry; air, hot and moist; fire, hot and dry; and water, cold and moist. . . . Humans, as a microcosm of the larger universe, contained in themselves the four elements. The individual's temperament, or 'humor' or 'complexion,' depended on which "humor" predominated in that person. The four humors in humans corresponded to the four elements of physical matter. The blood was hot and moist, like air; yellow bile or choler was hot and dry, like fire; phlegm was cold and moist, like water; and black bile was cold and dry, like earth.

On the theory of the Humours, it concludes: "practice of medicine in Renaissance times remained under the influence of the 'humors' theory until quite late, and its ideas are found throughout Shakespeare's writings."[32]

Most of the identifiable poets of the *Phoenix Nest* were associated with Oxford University as discussed below. They were contemporaries of William Sterrell and would have known him as a praelector of "natural philosophy"; *A Notable Description* is a poem that would be expected of someone teaching such a subject. More on *Phoenix Nest* will follow as it relates to *Venus and Adonis.*

Noted earlier were Shakespeare-the-author's direct references to Aristotle. Other of his poetic work shows a deep comprehension of Aristotle's scientific thought. The highly abstract *Phoenix and Turtle* draws on Aristotle in several ways. Take these two stanzas about the loving couple depicted as birds:

> So they loved, as love in twain
> Had the essence but in one;
> Two distincts, division none:
> Number there in love was slain.
>
> Hearts remote, yet not asunder;
> Distance, and no space was seen

'Twixt this turtle and his queen:
But in them it were a wonder.

The lines reflect Aristotle's criticism of the "Number Theory" of Pythagoreans who believed that things are numbers or that they are made out of numbers; they conceived of numbers as physical entities.[33] A parallel is in *Sonnet 136*. Aristotle also rejected the Platonists who thought of a line as composed of actual points such that there was always some space between the points that made up a line.[34] The poem depicts a couple who through holy love become a unity; they were a continuity with no space separating one from the other - metaphysically bound though in different locations.

♦♦♦ ♦♦♦

Bardophilus: Do you agree with our author that *Phaëton* and *Notable Description* are from the same writer who gave us *Venus and Adonis* and the *Sonnets*? They're nothing like the work of Shakespeare. Everyone knows that Shakespeare had a distinctive sonnet form. He used it over and over.

Skepticisima: Oh my, you fell into that one, didn't you? As Touchstone says to Corin in *As You Like It,* I say to you: "Shallow, shallow. A better instance I say. Most shallow man. ... learne of the wise and perpend."

It's true that the *Phaëton Sonnet* and the 1611 sequel uses a Petrarchan scheme of an octave - ABBA ABBA - and a sestet - CDCDEE, while *Shake-speares Sonnets* of 1609 use three quatrains - ABAB CDCD EFEF - and a concluding couplet - GG. You guys have noted this difference to reject the notion that Shakespeare penned *Phaëton,* and you've said that Shakespeare avoided Ovid in his sonnets. Not so!

Even you must admit that Shakespeare didn't always use the same rhyme scheme. No. The scheme of *Shake-speares Sonnets* follows one pattern because the little volume of poems published in 1609 is a sonnet sequence of 154 poems using a single pattern across recurring themes. Its design is to use that rhyme scheme for that entire collation, not because it was the only rhyme scheme used by the poet.

To support your contention that Shakespeare confined himself to his special rhyme scheme, you must excise from *Shake-speares*

Sonnets the more lengthy poem that appears immediately after Sonnet 154 under the heading "A Lovers complaint By William Shakespeare." It consists of forty-seven stanzas of seven-lines in the rhyme scheme ABABBCC, known as the rhyme royal. You must ignore both *Venus and Adonis* and *Lucrece. Venus* consists of some 199 six-line stanzas using a pattern of ABABCC, known as the Italian *sesta rima.* With *Lucrece,* our poet uses 265 seven-line stanzas with a pattern of ABABBCC, each in iambic pentameter which is the same pattern of *A Lovers Complaint.*

Nor does the 1601 *Phoenix and Turtle,* which is unquestionably Shakespeare's, use the Shakespearean pattern. Like *A Notable Description,* it employs its own distinctive rhyme pattern. The haunting *Phoenix and Turtle* consists of 18 stanzas: 13 quatrains and 5 tercets. The poet uses an ABBA rhyme scheme for the quatrains and AAA for the tercets. Like *Venus,* it draws on Ovid's *Metamorphoses*: Book XV (Teachings of Pythagoras), rather than Book X. *Phaëton, Venus and Adonis,* and *Phoenix and Turtle* all have their roots in Ovid, as does the *Phoenix Nest* in which *A Notable Description* appears.

Some sonnets internal to the Shakespeare plays follow a non-*Sonnets* pattern. Others do. You Stratford guys ignore Parolles's poem in *All's Well.* The playwright has the Second Lord ask Parolles, "will you give me a copy of the sonnet you writ to Diana?" The pattern is ABAB CCAA E. I'll grant you that *Romeo and Juliet* has two sonnets that are like the *Sonnets* of 1609. But *Loves Labours Lost,* written soon after *Venus and Adonis,* has multiple sonnets and fragments of sonnets. The sonnet read by Nathaniel in Act 4, sc. 2 (using hexameters rather than pentameters), and another by Longaville in Act 4, scene 3 use the Shakespeare pattern of ABAB CDCD EFEF GG. Dumain's poem from the same scene is a "sonnet" that uses 10 couplets of seven syllable lines rather than pentameters. You'll admit all this, won't you?

Bardophilus: What I think is, you're hijacking the narrative.

Skepticisima: I tend to do that. Okay, I'll slow down.

Bardophilus: You've convinced me that Shakespeare-of-Stratford may have written the *Phaëton Sonnet.* You can't show that our Stratfordian and Florio weren't friends at the time. But *A Notable Description*? It's just not poetic, is it? And few people think *A Lovers*

Complaint is really by Shakespeare, even if the *Sonnets* were authorized by the poet. And this business about the "humours." Everybody with a college education at the time knew about the "humours." Shakespeare's reading was wide and deep. He could have read Aristotle for the *Phoenix* poem; or someone could have appropriated his name.

Skepticisima: I've said enough.

Sterrell's Mission and Crisis

Now we must turn to the events immediately preceding the publication of *Venus and Adonis* and why the poem was so important to Sterrell's life as a writer. As recounted earlier, he was recruited by Thomas Phelippes and Francis Bacon for an overseas mission for the Earl of Essex in 1591-92. The fallout from the mission put him in great danger. The reality of his fears is amply seen in the murder of one man and the execution of another who faced the same charges as Sterrell: complicity in plots arising in the Spanish Low Countries in 1592-93. These two were Christopher Marlowe, murdered May 31, 1593, and Richard Hesketh, executed November 29, 1593. Sterrell and Hesketh had been operating in the Spanish lands among the members of the extended Stanley family; it was likely on behalf of the Stanleys that Marlowe was also in the places where Sterrell and Hesketh both worked.

It is mid-March 1593, the time of his great crisis. William Sterrell is a thirty-two year man in serious trouble. Six months before, the former Oxford University *praelector* of natural philosophy had returned to England unexpectedly from a spy mission in the Spanish Low Countries. Immediately, he came under suspicion by government officials that extended to the Queen of England herself. His future, even his life, is now at stake. We can almost see him in a rented room at the Saracen's Head Inn, Snow Hill, London. It had been his familiar lodging when he had come to visit the French ambassador at Salisbury Court in 1582-85. He had hoped to continue to stay at the Earl of Worcester's London residence. The great earl, however, now distances himself, despite Sterrell's intermittent but loyal service over near a decade.

Parliament is concluding its meetings. Worcester, his senior, first lord, is departing with his large entourage to Raglan, his great castle in Wales. Worcester leaves his disconsolate former servant without his protection in the country's capital. Government officials and shadowy agents are closing in on Sterrell. The earl had warned him of the dangers two years ago.

Looking out his window, from the Saracen's Head Sterrell can see the church of St Sepulchre-without-Newgate. It is no comfort. What had been for centuries a holy site of the Church of Rome was now subject to the rule of a secular woman solely by virtue of the bloodline of her usurping father, not a holy descendant of the authority given by Christ to St. Peter. Perhaps he prays. What other resources does he have? His father was a man of substance in Lincolnshire, but he is long dead, leaving meager inheritance to him. He has had little to do with his mother's new family. His younger brother is just beginning his legal training and can be of no help. Only his skill with words may he turn to. How best to deploy them?

Sterrell reflects on the events that have brought him to this moment of crisis. Thomas Phelippes and Francis Bacon had drawn him into an undertaking for the bold, ambitious young nobleman who had dispatched Sterrell overseas in 1591: Robert Devereux, Earl of Essex.

Essex is Queen Elizabeth's most favored courtier. At twenty-eight (1593), he is four years younger than Sterrell. He and Robert Cecil, Lord Burghley's equally ambitious son, are jealous rivals for Elizabeth's favor in the conduct of foreign affairs. Each has a lawyer lieutenant – Essex has Francis Bacon (the greater intellect) and Cecil has Edward Coke (the more tenacious). Each also has a spy network as each seeks to prove he can better protect the Queen and realm from foreign threat. The shrewd Queen plays them against one another.

Running Essex's spy network are Thomas Phelippes and Francis Bacon, in coordination with Francis's older brother Anthony, in France until recently. Phelippes and Bacon had come to know each other well in France when they lived in the same household. They initiated the network in early 1591 with a plan to use Sterrell as their operative. The two, ambitious to associate themselves with Essex's rise to greatness, had approached Essex with a proposal to employ an agent to "practise" among Catholic exiles in the Low Countries - Sterrell. Those exiles were considered a dire and continuing threat to England, fomenting rebellion and working with the Spanish for invasion of the country. Phelippes and Bacon used the spying proposal, with Sterrell as the tip of the spear, as a means to greater things in the service of Essex and the Queen. Neither man had found favor with the Cecils, father or son.

Sterrell was special for Phelippes and Bacon because they knew of his ties to the English Catholic exiles abroad. He had carried Catholic youth of their families over the English Channel to seminaries. He had facilitated correspondence for the exiles and was known and trusted among them. In the years since Elizabeth came to the throne there has been a continuing exodus of English Catholics to the Continent, where they can practice their religion while awaiting the return of the true church to England. They have left behind many relatives and friends. Contact with them is dangerous or forbidden.

Since 1587, Sir William Stanley's company in the Low Countries has been the nucleus for the support of the English emigré community. Sterrell's letters show that many of the Spanish king's pensioners were, and are, his correspondents.[35] He is a man with contacts who can facilitate correspondence and provide the pensioners with news of home and assistance. There is no established mail service at all; even harmless news of family births, marriages and deaths is dangerous and subject to seizure by the government - assuming one could find a courier to run risks of arrest. Nothing maintains morale and hope for those exiles better than letters from home. Sterrell has resources and channels for maintaining those crucial relations — or had, if he has been exposed as a double agent. Queen Elizabeth has built a wall between English Catholics and the exile community. Sterrell has spent and will spend years breaching that wall, maintaining community among the English Catholics and their loved ones in exile on the Continent.

Sterrell had been open to recruitment because Phelippes held out both carrot and stick. The stick was Phelippes's possession of incriminating letter(s). They show that Sterrell has engaged in illicit correspondence with those Catholic exiles: Sterrell has been well-known among them for more than seven years. One letter in particular is Mr. Skinner's, a man from Stratford-upon-Avon, a lawyer by training. Skinner had arrived at Exeter College, Oxford in 1577 at age 17 while Sterrell was a fellow student at Magdalen.[36] The letter(s) pertaining to Skinner were of special importance. Skinner and another of Sterrell's friends, from Magdalen College, Oxford, were apprehended at Gravesend coming up the Thames in a small boat from Calais just as Sterrell left on the mission late in 1591. The writings could condemn Skinner or Sterrell. Or both.

ꕤꕤꕤꕤ--ꕤꕤꕤꕤ

Phelippes maintained careful files for his intelligence work that stretched back to 1580 or so. When Sterrell was recruited in 1591, Phelippes doubtless had other files on Sterrell from Phelippes's service to Walsingham. He surely knew of Sterrell's work in the household of the French ambassador to England during 1582-1585. One document in particular sheds great light on Sterrell: the 1585 confession of Edward Dodwell.

As Secretary Walsingham's agent, Phelippes had monitored the Frenchman's activities on behalf of Mary Queen of Scots. Phelippes's claim to fame was decrypting the letters that the ambassador passed on to her. Phelippes was an able man but one who always served others. He was not a leader, apparently lacking character or convictions. Drawn to power and wealth, Phelippes achieved success only through scheming in which he could be serviceable to others. He had been highly useful to Walsingham.

Phelippes probably became aware of Sterrell in the mid-1580s when Sterrell was first discovered working secretly for Catholic interests overseas. Among his activities was helping to convey young lads to seminaries at Douay and elsewhere on the Continent. Reports had been forwarded to Walsingham which Phelippes will have shared. One youth turned informer to the government, telling the Queen's men that the French ambassador shared with Sterrell the correspondence of the captive Mary Queen of Scots. Anthony Skinner, Sterrell's friend whose correspondence Phelippes used to recruit Sterrell, was likely one of the men who had been transported overseas by Sterrell. In 1584 Skinner had gone abroad to Douay and then to Rome, where he served Cardinal William Allen, the Oxford scholar who founded the college/seminary at Douay.

In mid-August, 1585, the French ambassador to England, Mauvissière, welcomed into his chambers at Salisbury Court a group of three young men. The first of them was aged 24 and was going by the name of Kirby/Kerby. "Kirby" was the first of many aliases that we know for William Sterrell. The two youths "Kirby" brought with him no doubt had aliases too, but their real names were Edward Dodwell and William Norton. Through Mauvissière, "Kirby" arranged to get these two, and four more companions, out of England on a ship of the ambassador's, so that they could return to seminaries in Europe. Dodwell, however, had also been an Oxford student and recognized "Kirby" as Sterrell. For at least two years, Dodwell had been a government informant, and he was very familiar with the Catholic network in England and overseas. When the youths were taken from the ambassador's ship and held at Dover before being sent back to London, Dodwell began a tale of what had occurred at the French embassy. He said that Sterrell had "haunted" [frequented] the French embassy for three or four years and was a chief figure on all things Catholic in England. Secretary Walsingham, and surely Phelippes, was duly informed of Sterrell's activities.

In one of his confessions, the informant Dodwell said that Sterrell/Kirby smuggled Catholics overseas. Dodwell reported that Sterrell took him and other youths ("unbaked and dowy," we will describe them) to meet personally the French ambassador at the embassy. Dodwell's words – with his quotes of Sterrell – will introduce you to Sterrell's forceful personality as he tried to persuade Dodwell to remain stalwart: [37]

> And now to the matter: Sterrill (whom I called Kerby) is a master of arts now resident in Magdalen College at Oxford. He has been acquainted with the French Ambassador three [iij] or four [iiij] years, and has had conferences with him diverse and sundry times.
>
> He met with me at London 3 or 4 weeks past and talked with me in this manner:

> 'My friend, sayeth he, you know what credit you have left of late in detecting so many seminary priests to my Lord of Hunsdon. You know also that the fact is so heynous that you can hardly make satisfaction for the same. Wherefore I would wish you to be poenitent for that which cannot be recalled, and return to the seminary and take upon you that profession which will be profitable for your self and your [cause or country?]. If you will follow my counsel I will procure you safe passage and give you money to defray your charges to the place.'

I thanked him and consented to him, and being agreed together we went to Salisbury Court to talk with the Ambassador as concerning this matter. He welcomed both of us and promised me his furtherance in this journey, saying these words to Norton [another of the 6 taken from the ship] and me being then present: [in Latin]

> 'Sailors will hide you in my boat and if anyone opposed to your religion by chance looks at you and asks about your names, the sailors will respond that you are my servants and you are ill.'

With these words we held ourselves content and from that time we took our leave. The next day I told Mr. Sterrill that some were of the opinion that the Ambassador did but dissemble with us; their reason was because he had been too familiar with my Lord of Leicester to be good. He [Sterrell] answered that they were unwise men that thought so of the Ambassador, affirming that he had showed him letters which he received from the Queen of Scots, the teanure [tenor] whereof if he should utter would verify the contrarye; then he began to cut off those speeches and talked of my journey, persuading me to go forward with the same, swearing that I could not take in hand a better action: you are now sayeth he *fabula vulgi* [vulgar fame]: your uncle and other catholics heretofore your benefactors have utterly rejected you: my Lord of Hunsdon will use you as an instrument for the . . .

[page break and part missing, next sequence appears as

follows:]

> and at the last despise you still beating those speeches in my head: *amo proditionem sed non amo proditorem* [I love the treason but not the traitor].

Other matters I must let pass for they are in hast to have me to the Marshalsea [prison] where I must continue your honor's pleasure.

The admonition Sterrell gave to Dodwell in Latin, *non amo proditorem,* is attributed to Plutarch and to Julius Caesar. It is a theme repeated in a number of the Shakespeare plays. The lesson is that men may love the treason of another but that they will know then that he who has been false to another will be false to them. Here are several:

<> In *Othello,* Othello's suspicions of Desdemona begin when she is false to her own father, Brabantio. He warns Othello of his daughter: "Look to her, Moor, if thou hast eyes to see; she has deceived her father, and may thee."

<> In *Antony and Cleopatra,* after Cleopatra knows Antony lies to his wife Fulvia, she can no longer trust him, declaring: "Why should I think you can be mine, and true — though you in swearing shake the throned gods — who have been false to Fulvia?"

<> And in *All's Well,* Parolles demonstrates that no man can serve any honest use after proving himself false to his friends.

With his own deceptions as an undercover operative "practising" among Catholic exiles, Sterrell is acutely aware how quickly trust can be lost. Nor, perhaps, could he be trusted by those on whose behalf he "practised"; they had engaged him because of his ability to deceive.

Let us return to the Sterrell mission of 1591 and his crisis of 1593. The biographer of the Earl of Essex, Paul Hammer, has summarized the plan that Thomas Phelippes and Francis Bacon presented to Essex in 1591: Sterrell would pose as an agent for the exiles in order to feed them false information. He would try to learn their secrets, especially whether any were plotting against the Queen.[38]

The reward for Sterrell could be monetary and the possibility of greater service in the future with the Earl of Essex and the Queen. This was the same goal of Phelippes and Bacon: to work a way into Essex's household as trusted aides.

♦♦♦ ♦♦♦

Bardophilus: Pardon me for interrupting the flow. Why would the Phelippes-Bacon plan have appeal to Sterrell? After all, he had a secure position at Oxford as professor. He could have remained secure at Oxford.

Skepticisima: Your reasoning is distorted by your repeated projection of your own present circumstances as a celebrity scholar into the past. They did things differently there. You think "Oxford professorship" and are envious. You think of our academic celebrities who appear on BBC and NPR, who earn big royalties from their bestselling books, who maintain a social media presence with many thousands of followers. In Sterrell's day, his Oxford position had little promise. Its small prestige was offset by the necessity of dealing daily with rowdy young men.

Unlike many of his students, Sterrell had no inheritance to count on. His father had died while he was young. His mother had immediately remarried and bore another male child. Like Christopher Marlowe, Sterrell's status at his university depended on a scholarship for poorer youths. Sterrell's stipend as a "demy" arose from the will of Sir John Fastolfe. The seven senior "demies" of Magdalen were known as "Fastolfe's buckram men." Inflation had made the maximum allowance for college uniform insufficient for any but the cheapest cloth (buckram).[39]

With no paternal legacy, Sterrell would have to live by his wits – his skill with words that impressed others at Oxford from his earliest days. It got him his lectureship, but there was little more to be achieved. The only avenue to a more remunerative future was entering the service of a nobleman.

Let's compare Sterrell and Francis Bacon. Bacon, too, would have no inheritance. He would have to live by his sharp intelligence, especially his facility with words as a lawyer and as a writer. Bacon and Sterrell (only two months apart in age) could best advance by serving a nobleman with a political future. In Bacon's case, it led to his becoming, by a winding staircase, the Lord Chancellor of England. In Sterrell's case . . . .[40]

Bardophilus: Still, it . . .

Skepticisima: Not so fast, Sir Bardo. There was something more important for an ambitious man like Sterrell. Going into service for Essex had another sort of enticement. Call it an occupational hazard. As a serious student and as a professor, Sterrell lived with the great figures of history, Roman and English. Imaginatively, he could participate vicariously in their deeds and triumphs. He could explore the challenges they faced and the aspects of character that caused them to succeed or fail. But why, he will have asked, should he not himself participate in the making of history as they had. Why remain a passive observer when he could be an active participant? Essex was clearly a man of destiny. Placing himself in Essex's train could bring Sterrell's own powers to bear as a party to great events. He could be in France himself as one of a band of brothers under Essex, not remaining a gentleman in England in bed thinking himself accursed that he was not there; he would not hold his manhood so cheap.

Bardophilus: Do you really think you hear this Oxford professor in *Henry V*?

Skepticisima: I know it.

When Phelippes and Bacon approached William Sterrell in 1591, he was already in the service of a wealthy nobleman, Edward Somerset, the 4th Earl of Worcester. The Somersets traced their lineage back to the Plantagenets: Henry Beaufort's legitimized son Charles Somerset was knighted by King Henry VII. Sir Charles continued to gain honors under Henry VIII, who made him the first Earl of Worcester. Royal favor continued, with grants of land and privileges to him and his descendants. The wealthy Somerset family had occupied for generations the magnificent castles of Raglan and Chepstow in Wales.[41] The Somerset/Worcester family history is important for understanding the celebration of pageantry and grandeur in courtly entertainment by the 4th Earl and by his aide,

William Sterrell.

The forebears of Sterrell's patron figure significantly in the Shakespeare treatment of English history, including the Wars of the Roses. The bloody dynastic struggle between the Houses of Lancaster (red rose) and York (white rose), is portrayed through a historical tetralogy of four plays: *Henry VI*, Parts 1, 2, and 3, and *Richard III*, chronicling the conflict from Henry V's death to the rise of the Tudors. Sterrell's own maternal ancestor, Sir John Bussy/Bushy, has a prominent role in *Richard II* in which Richard II's deposition by Henry Bolingbroke (Henry IV) in 1399 laid the groundwork for the Wars of the Roses, creating a precedent for seizing the throne and challenging royal legitimacy. Sterrell's maternal ancestor, Henry Sotehill, fought in the snow with the Yorkists on Palm Sunday 1461 in the Battle of Towton, reenacted grimly in *3 Henry VI*.

William Somerset, 3rd Earl of Worcester, faithfully served Queen Mary and her royal consort, King Philip of Spain. His service to them included a military expedition to France in 1557. When Mary was succeeded by her Protestant sister Elizabeth Tudor, William Somerset gave her no opposition. Though regarded with suspicion as a Catholic, he added to his family wealth and prestige under Queen Elizabeth until his death in 1589. He became patron of his own acting company, Worcester's men, and left it under control of his son Edward, then known by his title of Lord Herbert.

The 3rd Earl of Worcester's sister Anne and his brother Thomas Somerset were not so fortunate as William. Anne was the wife of Thomas Percy, 7th Earl of Northumberland. It was she who, with Jane, Countess of Westmorland, was an instigator of the Rising of the North of 1569, pushing her reluctant husband into rebellion in a failed effort to have Mary Queen of Scots replace Elizabeth. Anne fled into exile after the failure of their coup attempt; her husband was beheaded. More than a decade later, Thomas Somerset was imprisoned for his support of Mary Queen of Scots and his Catholicism; he died in the Tower in 1586.

By the time Edward Somerset became the 4th Earl of Worcester in 1589, he had learned the lesson not to oppose the ruling monarch; he had observed what happened to both his aunt Anne and his uncle Thomas. His support for the Roman church would have to be covert, no matter what the dictates of his conscience might urge.

When Sterrell and Worcester first came together around 1583-84, Sterrell was close to the French ambassador who was seeking to help the Scots Catholic queen, as was Thomas. Worcester's father had been briefly arrested for the same cause – suspicion of disloyalty. In 1591 when Thomas Phelippes and Francis Bacon proposed to Sterrell that he undertake a mission of Essex, Sterrell was a tutor for Worcester's sons. The relationship between Worcester and Sterrell was not as close as it would become. Worcester approved the proposed undertaking for Essex. Though he was years older than Essex, Worcester had only ascended to his earlship twenty-four months earlier. Sterrell's mission was potentially beneficial to Worcester. It could serve as a cover for Worcester maintaining his relations abroad and explaining away his past contacts.

Sterrell was willing to leave one earl for service to another not only because Phelippes held Sterrell's letters of Skinner, but because Essex seemed the gleaming future of an ascendant England. Essex and Worcester were a study in contrast. Worcester was reticent when Essex was bold, modest in manner where Essex was charismatic. Worcester spent much of his time in Wales, while Essex remained in exciting London, the seat of government, the place of theatres, taverns and musical performances. Essex was surrounded by dozens of well-educated and ambitious followers. Under Worcester, Sterrell would always have to subsume his own aspirations to Worcester's. With Essex, Sterrell might achieve great things through action, not through words. In 1591, it could not be foreseen that Essex's reckless behavior would bring him to an early grave and ruin to those following him too closely.

Sterrell entered the plan to "practise" abroad for Essex with eyes wide open. He candidly laid it out to Phelippes in a letter written about August 1591. Because it provides us with a sense of Sterrell's writing "voice" and is not easily accessible, it will be quoted at length. His proposed mission would be risky, he asserted, one that could cost him his life. He craved protection:

> to have some things to show that I go over for her Majesty or the Earl of Essex's service that at my return I be not reputed a fugitive. You may die in the meantime, then what shall be

> thought of me? When I have practised among such markable persons and so inwardly as I must, it will not be sufficient to say that you employed me. They may ask, where is your warrant or what have you to show? And so I shall be well rewarded ***if I live.*** I am not ignorant how little service is esteemed when it is past, and what light occasions are taken to shift men off.

Sterrell wanted his assignment put in writing; he wanted it to show he would be well-rewarded for his service:

> Therefore let me entreat this much. Let the Earl of Essex write his letter to this effect, to require me that I go over to do her Majesty service as one appertaining to his Lordship and employed under him, and that he will see me rewarded and preferred according to *the due deserts of my service.*

He also requested a similar letter under Phelippes's own hand:

> Let me also have your worship's letter to require me to go over to do her Majesty service among papists or any of her majesty's enemies whosoever, according as her Majesty's pleasure if I should, *with promise of condign reward.*

Finally, Sterrell wanted to meet face-to-face with Essex so it would be harder for the earl to deny him:

> The third thing I desired, and now do, is that I may speak with the Earl and be known to him *de facie* [face-to-face] that I may press him with his words at my return.

He told Phelippes he didn't have to take the role he and Bacon sought of him. He was already "towards" [near; in attendance] a nobleman (Worcester):

> I have 40£ a year during my life and might have had more had not my unthrifty friends mispent it. I am towards a nobleman whose fortune I may follow, and have been ever brought up in the University, something acquainted with matters of state, and [in] every way as serviceable as others. I have therefore no need to endanger myself upon a slender ground. I am not far from preferment and I hope I shall not be so far from reason [for preferment].

Sterrell pushed Phelippes to inform Lord Burghley of Sterrell's mission. Burghley was the Queen's most trusted counselor; few matters of state escaped his attention. Sterrell inferred that Essex intended to succeed (or supplant) the authority of Burghley and his son Robert Cecil. But Sterrell agreed to go even without the written assurances.

To prepare for his work, Sterrell went among his circle of Catholics and sought their views on issues of religion and the challenges of Spain. Essex wanted such information for his political plans to seek some English Catholics for support, but he did not identify his contacts. He established his bona fides by getting some Catholic prisoners released from jail through Phelippes.

Reading Sterrell's letters, Phelippes would learn that his new agent had a sense of humor and enjoyed puns. Pressing Phelippes to fund his trips by seeking recovery of a debt owed Sterrell by a moneylender named Robert Cutt, Sterrell playfully urged: "Cut is an iron monger, whom I would wish you to turn to silver."[42] As a man adept in languages and learned himself, Phelippes must have enjoyed Sterrell's wordplay and frequent aphorisms in Latin.

Sterrell made a preliminary journey to Calais and Lille in August-September 1591 where he met with several of his Catholic correspondents. They exchanged ciphers for future correspondence with a view to his upcoming mission. In January 1592, as he was embarking again for his more extended "practising," Sterrell offered heroic gestures on behalf of the Queen: "If you can persuade her Majesty to address some plot to entrap Sir William Stanley, I hope to effectuate it, at leastwise I will venture . . ."

This was foolish bravado. Sir William Stanley was a battle-hardened English colonel of foot soldiers who had been given command of the town of Deventer only to then turn it over to the Spanish in January 1587, a most notorious turncoat. Sir William had a regiment of Spanish soldiers in the Spanish Low Countries; Sterrell had a sole courier to accompany him.

After arriving in the Low Countries in late February—early March, 1592, Sterrell began sending reports from overseas to Phelippes, using false names, among them *Thomas Francquelin, Henry Saintmain* and *Robert Robinson.* He used ciphers and code names.

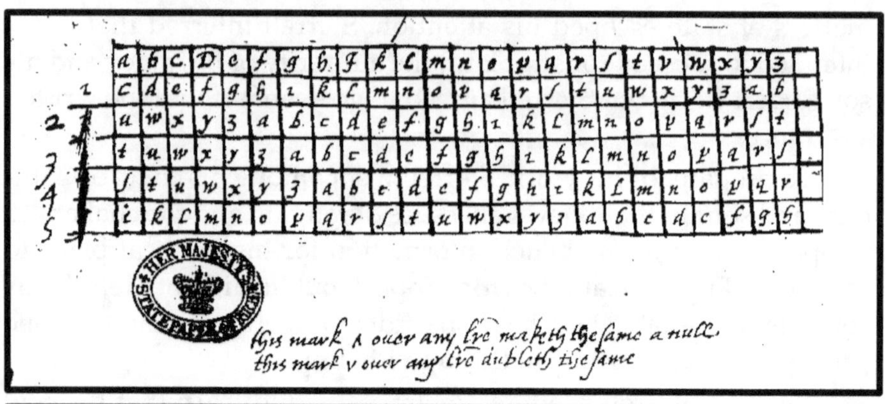

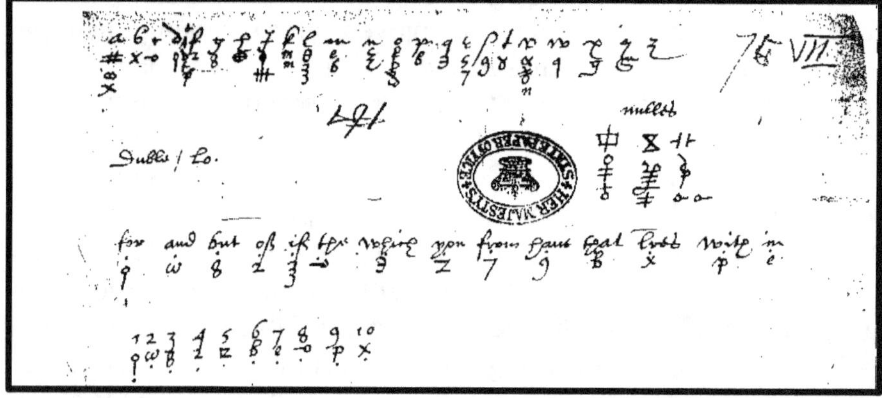

At times, Sterrell traveled with soldiers as they moved among encampments. In his mission, Sterrell risked exposure by both the agents of the Spanish and by the agents of the Cecils.

He failed, on both fronts.

In April 1592, Sterrell was arrested in Antwerp by the Spanish under his false name of Robinson. Thrown into the castle prison through the Spanish governor of the city, Count Mondragon, he was released by the influence of three English Catholic exiles. These included the man Sterrell had promised to spy on and entrap in the Low Countries, the notorious traitor, Sir William Stanley.

In a letter of April or early May, Sterrell as "Robinson" wrote to Ezekiel Staveley, his courier in Middleburg. This was an English-held town, about 40 miles from Spanish-held Antwerp. Sterrell had planned to meet with Staveley there. He informed the courier of what he faced:

> Kneel down upon your knees and thank God that you came not for if you had assure yourself you had died for it although you were the best Catholic in England not having anybody to give their word for you. I have had much ado and was like to have lain in the Castle. Sir Will Standley and Mr. Owen with my friend could scarce get me forth. I have been greatly accused by secret enemies.

Sterrell also prayed in this and several other letters that Staveley and Phelippes do all they could to have Anthony Skinner (whose letters with Sterrell were used by Phelippes to recruit Sterrell) sent over to him, away from danger in England. Skinner, however, was already in custody. Word of Skinner's fate from the Privy Council had not reached Sterrell yet. Subsequently, he wrote that "Sir William Stanley and Mr. Owen have friended me much."

In one letter to Phelippes Sterrell expressed his concern that he maintain good relations with both of his lords - Worcester and Essex:

> Forget not to do my duty to my own Lord [Worcester] I pray you as opportunity serves. I hope there is firm amity between him and the other [Essex] which I wish to continue.[43]

This letter reflects Sterrell's very odd setup: he continued to receive his regular payments as a servant to Worcester while now on assignment from Essex. How does one serve two masters and not feel conflicts looming?

After gaining his release in Antwerp, Sterrell had pressed on with his mission. He fell in with a group of about 800 soldiers, surely men from Sir William Stanley's command, marching to Namur, on the eastern side of the Low Countries. This was not far from the pleasant city of Liège, where Sterrell spent the next few months renewing contacts among exiles while pretending to spy on them. Instructing Staveley, his courier, on where to contact him in Liège, Sterrell wrote "inquire of me at Mr. Stanihurst's house near Saint Paul's Church." Soon, he took up lodging at the sign of the Lance Courone in Saint Hubert Street, near St. Martin's Basilica. Sterrell's quarters were situated on the Publémont hill looking down on the main part of the city. He had leisure time to write and could draw upon the libraries of his English Catholic friends. He spent time with Fr. William Birkbeck, a Cambridge graduate who had entered the English College at Rheims. Birkbeck, imprisoned in England and banished in 1585, was now chaplain at St. Martin's.

Some of Sterrell's missives to his courier and Phelippes were intercepted by Thomas Ferrers, deputy governor of the Merchant Adventurers company. Ferrers sent the letters on to Lord Burghley on June 30, 1592, along with a report of the suspicious treatment of "Robinson":[44]

> Robinson coming to Antwerp Mondragon did imprison him but forthwith the chief of the Jesuits there did cause him to be released, and as I hear he is now a pensioner to the King of Spain and hath 20 crowns per month. Stavely is by his occupation a tailor and doth keep an alehouse.

This report that Sterrell was a pensioner to the Spanish probably reflects the fact that he had traveled with a company of soldiers on the route to Liège. Robinson/Sterrell would have much to explain when he returned to England only ten weeks later. What might Lord Burghley do to this Englishman who was rescued by the great traitor to England, Sir William Stanley? After turning over the strategic town of Deventer to the Spanish, Stanley now was the English leader in whose orbit many English Catholic exiles circulated, perhaps organizing themselves for the return of England to the old religion.

Stanley and his fellow exiles were an ongoing threat to the kingdom, backed by Spanish soldiers. England feared a second Armada after the failure of the first only four years earlier. Burghley and the Privy Council constantly received reports from secret agents in the Low Countries, in France, in Italy, in Rome, fueling the fears. Whether true or not, those agents depended on finding – or manufacturing – conspiracies against the Queen. No threats, no need for spies.

Remember Sterrell's correspondent Anthony Skinner, whose letter Phelippes had used to recruit Sterrell? By the end of July, Sterrell learned of Skinner's conviction and sentencing from another of Sterrell's long-time correspondents, Richard Verstegan. He was an English fugitive publisher living in Antwerp. Verstegan wrote to Fr. Persons (yet another of Sterrell's correspondents) under date of August 3, 1592:

> Mr. Anthony Skinner is condemned, but not executed. Neither is it thought he shall be, for that some kind of offer of his pardon has been made to some of his friends for the sum of 500 pounds; and it is thought less will be taken. The Vicechamberlaine, as I hear, has undertaken to get it.

Sterrell must have been somewhat relieved. And who was this vice-chamberlain and from whom might he obtain such a sum? This was Sir Thomas Heneage, soon to become the second husband of the widowed Countess of Southampton. Another man highly important to the Countess, her business manager Edward Gage, in turn, will become father-in-law to Anthony Skinner (of Stratford).

Sterrell must have feared he would suffer the same fate as Skinner. He and his courier(s) had been caught and detained on several occasions, and he knew reports were sent to London that could seal his fate.

In early September 1592 Sterrell was back in England. His arrival was unexpected, and Phelippes, his handler and intermediary with Essex's secretariat, was away from London, unable to offer an explanation. Suspicion had fallen upon the returned spy from reports passed to the Queen's agents. That suspicion is laid out in a series of letters. First, Essex himself was perturbed. His own agent now was a risk to Essex and could impair his relation with the Queen. Those letters sent to Burghley had come to haunt Sterrell and Essex. Essex wrote Phelippes that:

> . . .we heard by my Lord Treasurer [Burghley] that the party [Sterrell] was come to London two days before we heard anything from him. Next that when I had received his first letters he gave us no satisfaction in anything of worth.

It is obvious from this that Burghley was tracking Sterrell's movements. It alarmed Essex that Burghley knew more about Essex's agent than Essex himself. Essex wrote to Sterrell and urged him to set down the reasons of his coming over and the means he had to do service. Sterrell gave answers but Essex's response, if any, is not known.

In a letter by Francis Bacon to Phelippes, dated September 15,

1592, Bacon told Phelippes that there was already suspicion of Sterrell, apparently extending up to the Queen herself:

> Your Mercury is returned; whose return alarmed as upon some great matter, which I fear he will not satisfy. News of his coming came before his own letter, and to other than his proper servant, which maketh me desirous to satisfy or to salve. My Lord [Essex] hath required him to repair to me; which upon his Lordship's and mine own letters received I doubt not but he will with all speed perform; where I pray you to meet him if you may, that laying our heads together we may maintain his credit, satisfy my Lord's expectation, and procure some good service. I pray the rather spare not your travail, because I think the Queen is already party to the advertisement [news] of his coming over, and in some suspect which you may not disclose to him.

Although Bacon met with Sterrell, suspicion of Sterrell only deepened.[45] These events depressed Sterrell. Writing still under the name Robert Robinson after visiting with Bacon, he told Phelippes the situation made him "in my dumps" and malcontent.[46] He had met with either Bacon or Essex but said "I could hardly make him [Essex?] understand me." [47] Somehow, Sterrell had to restore his credibility.

We sense Sterrell's distress as he wrote to Thomas Phelippes, to whom he had dispatched intelligence reports for eighteen months. Speaking of his relations with Worcester, who has turned on him despite his loyal service, he said:

> every hour with me here is worse than other, *coniectum oculorum ferre non posum.* And to assure me of their good will I am not allowed whittbred. Such a jest in an ale house were very pretty. It is a world to see how men's minds can vary. Not long since I was trusted with the very secrets of the inward man, now I am not worthy a half-penny whitt loaf. In lent last he would not leave for any a child he had, this lent he is with child with my absence. *Quanti casus humana rotant.*

Let us examine the second Latin line first. Sterrell tossed his Seneca with ease at a moment of a sense of abandonment or betrayal. His quote is from the chorus in *Phaedra (Hippolytus)*: "How on the wheel of fate we mortals whirl!" Let's look at the context in which the same line is uttered by Coriolanus in the eponymous play:

O world, thy slippery turns! Friends now fast sworn,
Whose double bosoms seems to wear one heart,
Whose hours, whose bed, whose meal and exercise
Are still together, who twin, as 'twere, in love,
Unseparable, shall within this hour,
On a dissension of a doit, break out
To bitterest enmity;

Coriolanus is describing his sense of betrayal by the people he has served, especially the tribunes who orchestrated his downfall, transforming him from a war hero into a political exile. Sterrell was "banished" by Worcester (both bed and meal – a 'half-penny whitt loaf'; white bread was a luxury), and the Privy Council, like the tribunes of *Coriolanus*, were working to charge him with treason.

Sterrell knows too well that Seneca suffered exile and death for suspicion of conspiracy against the state; just as Hamlet contemplates, Seneca took his own life with a "bare bodkin." Like Seneca and Coriolanus, Sterrell too is suspected of conspiracy against the state. He knows also he could be gruesomely executed. Such a fate awaits a man, Richard Hesketh, for bringing messages from Sir William Stanley in 1593. Sterrell probably had met with Hesketh in Sir William Stanley's camp. Or Sterrell could be murdered, as soon will occur to Christopher Marlowe, who, like Sterrell, had been working secretly in the Low Countries.

Now the second Latin line: *coniectum oculorum ferre non posum* - I cannot bear the gaze of [their] eyes. In Roman literature, the quote is a powerful rhetorical tool used to illustrate extreme shame, guilt, or the crushing weight of public scrutiny. In his history of Alexander the Great, Curtius Rufus records that the athlete Dioxippus committed suicide because he "could not bear the gaze" (*coniectum oculorum ferre non potuit*) of those who falsely accused him of theft. The direct quote from Curtius is "*coniectum oculorum, quibus ut fur destinabatur, Dioxippus ferre non potuit et . . .*"[48] Dioxippus, an Olympic wrestler, had defeated the Macedonian soldier Horratas in a duel using only a club while Horratas was fully armed. Jealous of his success, Alexander's courtiers framed Dioxippus by hiding a golden cup in his quarters and accusing him of theft. The shame of the accusation was more than he could endure, and he killed himself with a sword. Sterrell, too, thought he was being falsely accused by the agents of the Cecils, exactly as was occurring with Christopher Marlowe at exactly the same time in early Spring 1593. Marlowe was falsely accused by the Cecil agent Richard Baines.

The quote from Curtius was in Latin, not from the 1553 translation by John Brende. With Sterrell so familiar with the Latin biography of Alexander the Greek, that work was likely the source of the Alexander the Great allusions in the Shakespeare plays.

The quote and distressed sentiment of Sterrell's letter of early 1593 are Englished and expressed in Sonnet 29:

When in disgrace with Fortune and men's eyes,
I all alone beweep my outcast state,
And trouble deaf heaven with my bootless cries,
And look upon my self and curse my fate, . . .

We find similiar lines and distress in Lord Saye in *2 Henry VI*, act 4 sc. 4 for losing territories of the realm. In the midst of Cade's rebellion, this exchange takes place between Lord Saye and King Henry:

King Henry. Lord Saye, the traitors hate thee;
Therefore away with us to Killingworth.
Lord Saye. So might your Grace's person be in danger.
The sight of me is odious in their eyes;
And therefore in this city will I stay
And live alone as secret as I may.

Lord Saye (actually based on James Fiennes, 1st Baron Saye and Sele) seems drawn partly on Sterrell himself as an educated elite who has "most traitorously corrupted the youth of the realm" as charged by Cade [act 4 sc. 7]. Sterrell had been charged at Oxford by Simon Pett with corrupting the youth there, and Dodwell had similarly accused Sterrell of corrupting youth by taking them from the realm. Like Parolles in *All's Well*, Sterrell "would have made all the unbak'd and dowy youth of a nation in his colour."

Sterrell was painfully aware that he was under severe scrutiny from the Privy Council. He wrote a troubled letter to Phelippes on

January 2, 1593: "I would I could be with some of the Council for then would they desire to deal with me more roundly." He knew his relationship with Worcester had been impaired and that he would not be kept in his household. He told Phelippes:

> I was sorry that I put you not in mind to have imparted on to the Earl [Essex] in what terms I stand with my Lord [Worcester]. It might perhaps induce him to further my preferment but I would not have my Lord [Worcester] to have any notice of my discontentment for I would depart with his good will, as friends at least seeming for the very suspicion of untrusty dealing with him, notwithstanding my innocence would greatly prejudice my credit, were it but spoken of, and I would not for any good depart upon any such cause.

Because he was having to leave Worcester, he believed Essex should provide for him. He continued, "Methinks that the Earl [Essex] might be brought to make some allowance to be paid monthly considering that it is of necessity that I abide in London which of myself I cannot do. . . . If therefore I find no other place, he must needs to be good onto me and liberal, else I can not tell what to do." But Sterrell was unwilling to seek support directly from Essex. He expected that when Essex sent him aid he would be revived, but in the meantime he was "out of heart . . ." [49]

Realizing he was nearly alone, Sterrell made plans to provide for himself: "When my chamber is taken and furnished, I will endeavor to live of my self, because I may make some suit to the Earl hereafter *for some things of worth*."

What "things of worth" did Sterrell have in mind that would please Essex? We may suspect it is a poem that he has written that he considered dedicating to Essex. He has no money for a gift. He has no dramatic spying intelligence yet to reveal, for if so he has withheld it for six months, all the more reason to condemn him. Unless it is a literary work, he has nothing "of worth" to offer to a lord such as Essex.

When Sterrell learned that Essex himself was upset with him and that Sterrell's work would discredit Essex, he had to change his plans. He must seek another dedicatee. Sterrell looked now for work with some other nobleman — as a secretary. In early April

1593, he wrote Phelippes that he would be satisfied if Phelippes would do two things:

> The first is to let me have the remainder of such money as you promised me that I may furnish my chamber presently. The other is that as opportunity shall be offered, you would not be unmindful to *prefer me to the service of some nobleman* or other like to be employed. I doubt not but to discharge the *duty of a secretary which is convenient sufficiency, as many others do.* Loath I am to solicit the Earl in these two suits, hoping upon your courtesy and being desirous that all favours should be derived unto me by your means and mediations to the Earl.

Two things stand out: Sterrell believed Phelippes could try to mediate with Essex. And Sterrell wanted Phelippes to recommend him to "some nobleman" for employment as a secretary. What nobleman was closest to Essex? The Earl of Southampton. And Southampton's mother was a Catholic who was a blood relative of the Earl of Worcester.

♦♦♦ ♦♦♦

Bardophilus: I'll grant you that's a pretty dramatic tale of this fellow Sterrell. He's gotten himself into hot water. And it sounds like he was in pretty much the same dilemma as Christopher Marlowe. But he gets out of it, as his short biography has told us. Apparently, he was reunited with Worcester by late 1593. How did he survive?

Skepticisima: By his wits, his pen. That's the most reasonable explanation, all things considered. Something dramatic must have happened in early June 1593 to account for Sterrell's sudden return to grace with Essex, Bacon and the others of their circle.

Within a few weeks, Sterrell was reunited with Essex and Southampton at an important gathering taking place at Gains Park, Epping, fully restored to work. He was assigned to gather intelligence of the Spaniards whom Essex had brought over, Antonio Perez and his followers.

We hear no more of an investigation of William Sterrell by the Privy Council. It will be 1605 before his overseas correspondence again lands him in trouble, this time interrogated by Robert Cecil himself.

Bardophilus: But how does it support your thesis that Sterrell is really Shakespeare-the-author?

Skepticisima: Patience, my friend. We are not even half through our journey. Wait and see that Sterrell's mission and recovery is the source for *All's Well that Ends Well*. Or as Sterrell himself would say, *exitus acta probat*.

Bardophilus: You know something happened, but you don't know what. Is that what you are saying?

Skepticisima: All the available evidence points to one thing, the publication of *Venus and Adonis*.

Bardophilus: So, you think Sterrell is Shakespeare-the-author and that the Earl of Southampton was powerful enough to get the authorities to back off. Is that what you claim?

Skepticisima: You're right to look at the dedication of *Venus and Adonis* to young Southampton as instrumental. But he was a callow youth, a minor still, with no influence with the Privy Council or the Queen. The dedication was to Southampton, but its purpose was to influence others who were close to him.

Chapter 3
English Literary Life in 1593

Why *Venus and Adonis*? Books and their Origins

We take books for granted because we have used them from childhood. So, too, language, so much so that we forget how language works. We spend little time thinking about gerunds, indirect versus direct objects, or the nominative and genitive cases. Perhaps we can hear the voice of the rebel Jack Cade in 2 *Henry VI* who condemns Lord Saye for his literacy: "thou hast men about thee that usually talk of a noun and a verb and such abominable words as no Christian ear can endure to hear." In looking at a poem or a book, we may see the words without reflecting on how they work together nor how they came into being.

Because we are talking primarily about two books by Shakespeare-the-author and a number of related books of the era, we will begin with a broad perspective on books. Observations that apply today are equally applicable to 1593, with some differences.

No book springs into existence by itself. How did this one get into your hands? A book is the product of multiple hands and minds. From the first words on a page (or screen) to the bound volume on a shelf, a book reflects a series of choices, many choices. Every book or poem, like every individual, every religion, every nation, has an origin story.

Form. You want to be an author. You have an idea that you can turn into something you wish to share. You believe it's worth someone else's reading. Do you write a poem, or will you say something in a play or a novel or a history? Masque or play? You must choose. Fiction or nonfiction. Blank verse or rhyme. How many lines to a stanza? What is the order of rhyming – ABBA or ABAB? Each is a choice.

Behind the book. An author's name goes on a book. But is the book solely the creation of the author? A publisher of law books may approach prospective authors about a book on, say, Texas property law. The publisher and the editor(s) make most of the choices about the book's coverage and content and style. Books in a series such as *The Hardy Boys* (1927-2005) may be conceived by a syndicator but then written to specification by multiple writers under the pseudonym Franklin W. Dixon.

In the 1590s, we will ask often who is really responsible for the making of a book. Is it the poet/author, or is it the patron who pays for a poem/book for a special occasion? When a tailor makes a bespoke suit or dress, the tailor crafts the outfit, but it must conform to the needs and wishes of the customer and often the occasion, such as a wedding.

A poet today expects to publish in a magazine, such as the *New Yorker*, or a quarterly, such as *Sewanee Review* or *Southern Review*. There were no such publications in the 1590s. Back then, publication by a printer was possible only if you had a patron or expected to have one. How a book of poetry came into being was rather different in 1590 from 2025. Most often, the printer demanded money in the purse in advance; they did not count on compensation coming solely from sales.

Let us distinguish between a play and a masque. Both were popular for entertainment in the Shakespeare period (1593-1613) but were significantly different in form. No author would write a masque without someone else telling the author what they wanted. A play or a poem might be self-generated or it might be composed-to-order; a masque uniquely reflected a patron's wishes and a chosen occasion. A masque would have an author, but behind the writer was a patron, seen or unseen. So, too, would a play presented at Court have a writer. However, someone else was responsible for selecting the play for staging at Court and perhaps was the source for its concept and themes as well. That "someone else" was the true patron of the play and the acting company, even if it was the King's Treasury paying for the production.

Purpose. Why does a writer compose a poem or book or play or masque? Perhaps money is a motive. But even a monetary purpose may take different forms. One-time payment by a publisher? Or a sharing arrangement, such as a royalty, or a portion of the box-office receipts from sales of seats? Payment can be in the form of employment that is not tied to book sales. A writer may produce a book in anticipation of another sort of gain, such as securing tenure on a college faculty or establishing one's credentials to become a consultant or expert witness. A book or pamphlet or broadside may be called into existence to advance a political or religious cause with no regard to personal financial gain to the writer or sponsor. Many or most of the publications of the Shakespeare era were of this sort, paid for in advance and not in anticipation of sales revenue.

You may be surprised to learn of the political purposes that might be behind some of the books of the 1590s. Those living in the period were painfully aware of political realities, even from mere dedications. Consider the example of John Hayward. His dedication to the Earl of Essex of a work of history, published in early 1599, led to his imprisonment for the remainder of Elizabeth's life. Message to writers? Be very careful not only about what you say but with whom you associate.

The *To* and *For* of Dedications and the *Why*

Let us have a few words also about dedications and prefatory letters during the Shakespeare period. They are part of what publishers call "front matter" and scholars now refer to as "peritext."

The epistles dedicatory to a patron or potential patron were of two types - prospective or retrospective. One expresses hope for reward in the future; the other, gratitude for past support. These are two "whys" for dedications of patronage. We see the first type in *Venus and Adonis* and the second in *Lucrece*.

A dedication will be ***To*** a person. The named dedicatee may be a person who is alive or who is deceased. But why dedicate ***to*** a dead person? Because it is ***For*** the benefit of another. Like the song says, headstones are for the living, they're no good to the dead. Similarly, a dedication ***to*** someone living, say for example an infant, may actually be ***for*** another, the parent we'll say.

Here's familiar example. Who has not attended the visitation of a dead person prior to their funeral, or visited the website of the funeral home to view an obituary? We will sign a guest book; we will be asked to share a memory. Writing our name and words in memory are not for the benefit of the deceased but for the living person(s) who will read the words to which we have subscribed our name. That third person is likely unseen and unnamed. But it is to them we are directing our communication; they and we share this awareness. So, too, with literary dedications.

Ordinary language fails us as we try to sort these possibilities of dedication of a writing. Yes, the writer dedicates - a dedicator - to a named person - the dedicatee. Do not make the common error of assuming the dedicatee is the patron or potential patron. If the words are meant for another, what do we call that third person(s)? Those persons may be the ones we are actually seeking to honor or from whom we seek patronage.

Linguists distinguish between the *signified* (an object, for example) and the *signifier* (a sign for the object whether it is a word or a symbol or hand gesture). Now meaning of the sign (a word, say apple) and the signified (the object) will depend on the context of use by the persons communicating by the sign. If you tell me "I bought an apple," it will be understood as one thing if you have come from a grocery store and another if you have visited a computer store.

The relationship between a signifier and its signified is arbitrary. There's no inherent connection between the two. Metaphor comes into play when the signifier and signified are not related in a direct or literal way, but a connection is established through comparison or association within a given context.

Sometimes an *apple* will really be in reference to (signify) a piece of red or green or yellow fruit. But in a different context, the meaning shifts - the sign really means something else. It may be then a metaphor. In context, we understand one another, though an alien with a translation device will be at a loss. We might say, "She's the *apple* of my *eye*." Neither "*apple*" nor "*eye*" is meant by the sign we use. There is no congruence between sign and what is signified. Only in context do we understand that the idiom is a metaphor. And that idiom is a linguistic unit; substitute *peach* for *apple* or *ear* for *eye* and all meaning is lost, signifying nothing.

So, too, with dedications. We must see them in context. We must ask, who is the dedication intended to influence and how and why? What does an author or poet seek to achieve through the dedication?

We will return to the ***For*** of a dedication shortly after we take up other "peritext," our front matter, and its purposes.

Other Prefatory Epistles/Verse

Dedications are to be distinguished from endorsements. Such modern endorsements are *blurbs,* as our contemporary writers seek to ornament their own works with lofty panegyrics by celebrities. Often these are from a friend, an established fellow writer, a publisher or a highly esteemed person praising the author or the author's work – *aka* backslapping. Writers call upon friends to say a few laudatory words without regard necessarily to their sincerity. Like mercy, a book blurb is twice blest: "It blesseth him that gives and him that takes." The more magnificent the praise, the greater the blessing.

Prefatory letters were a customary part of most books published in the Shakespeare period. They served both a social and an economic function for the author and publisher (and gained recognition for the contributor). Until the *First Folio,* "Shakespeare" had no such support and made not a single contribution to the work of any contemporary. In this, he was virtually unique among Elizabethan writers. Our conclusion: the elusive playwright and poet had no friends and lent no support to others by use of his pen; nor did he feel he needed it. He was but a shadow of a writer. The businessman of Stratford may have had fellow investors, but the *writer* "Shakespeare" remained unseen. He must have been a loner among all fellow writers during the period 1593-1616. Like the title of a play by one of Sterrell's friends, Thomas Heywood: "If you Know not me, you Know Nobody." Shakespeare was Nobody; no one seems to have known him nor he any of his contemporaries.

Oh, but you say, he only wrote plays and these were never directly published by him or by the acting company; the quartos all appear to have been unauthorized or unendorsed. My point is made. His work was admired, his name appropriated by others, but neither he nor his company sought regular publication. And if he was known, why didn't other writers gain his endorsement, even if plays didn't need dedicatory epistles? Even as a company playwright, nothing prevented him from publishing poetry or issuing endorsements like nearly all other contemporary noteworthy playwrights and poets.

Finally, front matter/peritext often included a letter "To the Reader" explaining the book's purpose and managing the author's public image. Today, writers put their credentials somewhere up front (or on the book jacket) or tout their successful works. They may provide an abstract of the book that follows and/or a foreword. In the Elizabethan era, an "epistle to the reader" might be written by the author or it could be the publisher's letter. An especially amusing one is found in the *First Folio* of 1623 exhorting purchase. It is addressed to "the great Variety of Readers"[modernized]:

> From the most able, to him that can but spell: There you are numbered. We had rather you were weighed. Especially, when the fate of all Books depends upon your capacities: and not of your heads alone, but of your purses. Well! It is now publique, & you will stand for your privileges we know: to read, and censure. Do so, but *buy it first*. That doth best commend a Book, the Stationer says. Then, how odd soever your brains be, or your wisdoms, make your licence the same, and spare not. Judge your six-pence worth, your shillings worth, your five shillings worth at a time, or higher, so you rise to the just rates, and welcome. But, *whatever you do, Buy*.

The only other instance of a front letter in a Shakespeare book was by the publisher of *Shake-speares Sonnets* in 1609, Thomas Thorpe, who spoke of "The Onlie Begetter of these Insuing Sonnets, Mr. W.H." to whom he wished all happiness and eternity. Thorpe was playful -- a prankster. Once as a grand jest, Thorpe and his very good friend and collaborator Edward Blount reprinted as a lark all the 55 or so panegyrics to Thomas Coryate's *Crudities*. They were, each and all, parodies of traditional commendatory verses - such as the contributors themselves had often written. They were the Monty Pythons and Spinal Tap of their day, the wittiest of oddball British intellectual humor. Called *The Odcombian Banquet* (1611), Thorpe concluded by saying the text was omitted to save money for the purchasers of the book.

With his obscure dedication of *Shake-speares Sonnets*, Thorpe knew he was tantalizing us and his contemporaries to guess at the identity of Mr. W.H. And Thorpe said absolutely nothing of the Shake-speare fellow who contributed only a possessive surname to the title. Is that title the same as naming the poet of the sonnets or does it only signify that the sonnets are attributable to that name? Thorpe is careful to give the book a title but does not even include the name of the poet as "William Shakespeare." How odd is that? That may be why Thorpe is sometimes called "Odd" Thorpe.

♦♦♦ ♦♦♦

Bardophilus: I'll grant you that Shakespeare didn't endorse other writers that we know of. But that could just be a matter of lost publications. Besides, he had as many as six or eight or ten co-authors who were themselves well-known. Many scholars now accept that. He must have been a familiar among the contemporary playwrights or they wouldn't have collaborated with him. They recognized his mighty pen.

Skepticisima: And how do we know this? Stylometrics. To find a co-author based on style you must begin by identifying a distinctive Shakespeare style across a body of 36 (or more) plays and group of poems that you must presume to be authentic works of the author. You must then take a single play to focus upon and run it through your style model — a Shakespeare stylometer — and determine which, if any, portions of that play depart significantly from your style model to deem that portion to be inauthentic Shakespeare. Remember that the same play was part of the body of work you used to build your model! What you presumed to be authentic, you must now deem partially inauthentic. Then you go to a series of other models, say the Lodge Model or the Fletcher Model or the Marlowe Model or the Kyd Model, and compare the inauthentic portion of the single Shakespeare play to these other models and select one of them as closer in style to the inauthentic portion of the single Shakespeare play that lets you know that the other playwright must have co-written the play, despite the absence of a single record of the two men ever knowing or meeting with one another.

The major and minor premises of the approach are patently flawed. One is the assumption that the author didn't try writing in different ways at different times for his own amusement or to satisfy a particular occasion. Good writers vary their styles unless they're conforming their own writing so as to appeal to a known audience seeking assembly line literature, like an Ian Fleming's James Bond series or a Clive Cussler thriller. Second, you're buying into the "magic file" theory that all the plays in the *First Folio* were preserved by persons of the acting company in master manuscripts exactly as the playwright had written them such that there was essentially no editing by a team in the period 1619-1623. Variant styles in the plays of the *First Folio* could well have been the result of editorial reconstruction of a play. Don't modern editors splice together parts of a *First Folio* play with a better portion of a quarto version? More importantly, let's assume you and the co-author crowd are correct, how does that diminish the possibility that the co-authors were collaborating with William Sterrell?

Bardophilus: They would have known that Sterrell was the author. They would have revealed that Shakespeare wasn't Shakespeare.

Skepticisima: Why? If they didn't identify themselves as Shakespeare co-authors, why would they do otherwise if they were Sterrell co-authors? Maybe they did. Would anyone care?

There's another problem with stylometrics. What if *Shakespeare* was a co-author with, say, Kyd on one of the plays in the Kyd Model or Middleton in the Middleton Model? Wouldn't that throw considerable confusion into the model comparability? You would be arguing that Shakespeare co-authored with Shakespeare based on the similarities. And while I'm ranting, stylometry looks at text but ignores the audience. Good writers write for their audience. Many or most of the Shakespeare plays were written for special occasions and tailored to the audience. Take the two plays we know were written for a law audience: *Comedy of Errors* for Gray's Inn in 1594 and *Twelfth Night* for Middle Temple in 1602. Both have lots of inside humor and topical items for those two Inns of Court. Those jokes and subjects would have been lost on a common audience. So, too, with the plays that were written for an aristocratic audience such as *Merry Wives of Windsor, Midsommer Nights Dream,* and *Measure for Measure.* The language and characters in such plays would be different from plays for mass audiences.

Bardophilus: But nobody has suggested the possibility of Shakespeare co-authoring with any of his co-authors. Do you have any evidence that Sterrell was a co-author?

Skepticisima: So, you think collaboration could only work in one direction? Ridiculous on its face and such collaboration contaminates the whole set of assumptions of stylometrics. There is indeed the possibility that William Sterrell was himself a co-author. Or reviser. Of *Locrine*.

Bardophilus: I'm vague on *Locrine*. Refresh my memory.

Skepticisima: The play, depicting legendary Trojan founders of England and of Troynovant (London), was entered in the Stationers Register July 1594 with a title page declaring that it was "Newly set foorth, overseene and corrected, By W.S." According to Stanley Wells and Gary Taylor, *Wm. Shakespeare: A Textual Companion*, there are apparent links between *Locrine* and *I Henry VI*. *Locrine* has long been regarded as part of the Shakespeare apocrypha. Its author was apparently Charles Tilney, a young Catholic executed in 1586 for supposed involvement in the Babington Plot to overthrow Queen Elizabeth in favor of Mary Queen of Scots. He was cousin of Edmund Tilney, long-time Master of Revels and evidently also a cousin of George Buc, Master of Revels after Tilney. George Buc once owned a copy of the verse drama *Locrine;* a note in it in Buc's handwriting said that it was written by his cousin Charles Tilney. Sterrell was on the fringes of the Babington Plot when he was working with the French ambassador. Let's consider the possibility that William Sterrell had known Charles Tilney and that it was in his memory that "W.S." oversaw and corrected the verse drama of Charles Tilney. Recall, too, Sterrell became landlord to Tilney and Buc when he was granted proprietorship of the palace which housed Revels. Stylometrics is so imprecise a tool that scholars link it to possible authorship or revision by Christopher Marlowe, Thomas Kyd, Robert Greene, Thomas Lodge or George Peele . . . . despite the note of Buc himself about his own cousin.

Venus and Adonis – The Poem Itself

The Book Business of 1593. A person visiting a bookshop or stall near St. Paul's Church in 1593 would find for sale broadsides (single page), quartos (sheet folded twice to produce eight pages), and octavos (sheet folded three times to create 16 pages). Another, more substantial form, was the folio. A folio is created by folding a standard sheet of paper in half once, resulting in two leaves and four pages, thus substantially larger than quarto or octavo.

By law, a book's cover had to include a title, the date of imprint, and the name of the printer or stationer. Books authorized for sale were required to be entered into the Stationers' Register, the record book maintained by the Stationers' Company of London, and approved by the Master and Wardens of the company. Inside a book, the shopper would find the title again, often with a lengthy subtitle, and multiple pages of front matter. We would expect a dedication, by the author or by the publisher. Present usually were commendatory words or verses by fellow poets. The publisher or author might have included a letter "to the reader," offering an introduction to the work that followed. To understand *Venus and Adonis* in its time, we will need to discuss specific examples of front matter.

Books, pamphlets and broadsides were the mainstream media of the 16th and early 17th centuries. This was an era before newspapers. No radio. No television. No internet. No social media. There was no freedom of the press. Despite the strong political and religious censorship in England (or rather because of it), there were illegal printing presses within England, and disapproved books were smuggled from overseas.

We Visit John Harrison's Shop

To understand *Venus and Adonis* we must put ourselves in the moment. We must see things as others saw them at the first appearance of the book.

Imagine that you and I are gentlemen of London in early June 1593. Perhaps you are beginning your legal career at Gray's Inn or the Middle Temple. Perhaps you are secretary to an official in Whitehall; you keep the members of the Queen's Privy Council informed of their proceedings. You are educated, with a degree from Oxford or Cambridge. You might even be a literate freeman of the

Grocers Company engaged in the wholesale trade of medicines to shops throughout London.

Business is slow. The plague is still hot. So is the weather. The theaters are closed. The Parliament that met from February to the second week of April has adjourned. The 116 Members of the House of Lords and the 464 Members of Commons have all dispersed, returning to their palaces and manors in the countryside, taking their many hundreds of retainers and followers with them. Activity has diminished, but the streets are still busy - noisy and rank.

From the Temple or the government offices in Whitehall it is not a long walk to St. Paul's Cathedral and its broad spaces. I will accompany you. We have had time for a leisurely meal just after noon. Now we visit the yard of St. Paul's where we can take in "Paul's news" by visiting some of our acquaintances.* Rumor, gossip and reports of recent occurrences are exchanged among those milling around.[50] You share your knowledge of recent developments in your profession. Such news is a sort of currency, useful for those to whom you report, and for our own careers. How else would anyone know what's happening in the city, the country and the world? It pays to stay informed. Even if much of it begins "Some say . . . ." "It is said . . . ." "I have heard . . ."

The most striking rumor this day is that a playwright was killed at an inn in Deptford. Christopher Marlowe. No one can confirm the story. A coroner's report will provide details when it becomes available. I remind you, he was under investigation by the Privy Council for coining or treason or blasphemy or some such. Nodding, you respond, yes, a violent end to a man whose plays were known for their violence. *Paul's news.*

Several men speak of their sightings of the Spaniards roaming the streets of the city as though it were their own. They are easily identified by their fantastic apparel, all scarves and taffeta and ruffled breeches and out-of-fashion codpieces. They are among the followers of the flamboyant defector from Madrid, Antonio Perez,

* William Sterrell to Phelippes, April 6, 1593: "There is Paul's news sufficient always to furnish a letter with."

who (they say) is making the most of his new English host, the Earl of Essex, drawing heavily on his generous purse. Most recently, they decamped from Paris where, it is reported, they had been a major irritant to the French Court. The Earl of Essex brought Perez over with the Vidame de Chartres, son of the resident French Ambassador. Through them, it is said, Essex wants to learn all he can of Spanish plans in the Low Countries. Some say the French king may return to the Roman church, however unlikely it might seem. *Paul's news.*

Now we approach one of our regular haunts, beneath the sign of the White Greyhound in Paul's Churchyard. It is the shop of the bookseller John Harrison. A book begins with its cover. John Harrison has a board next to his door that displays the covers of his offerings inside. Here we see a new one, a quarto at eye height.

Our eyes fall upon the printer's distinctive top banner. This one is a smiling mask with facing peacocks on either side.

Beneath is the title:

VENUS

AND ADONIS

Latin verse is just below:

Vilia miretur vulgus; mihi flavus Apollo
Pocula Castalia plena ministret aqua

We both read Latin well enough to get a sense of the meaning. But you ask me to English the words on the cover of *Venus and Adonis*. Roughly, it runs:

Let common people admire cheap things;
let golden Apollo serve me cups full of Castilian water.

In the middle of the page is the decorative symbol used by the printer for many of his works.

The bottom of the cover informs us that the book is "Imprinted by Richard Field, and are to be sold at the signe of the White Greyhound in Paules Church-yard. 1593."

Intrigued by the ambitious cover, we enter the shop together to see if Apollo's cups may satisfy our literary thirst. Displayed on a table are copies we may examine. The book is not large; it is a quarto. Nor, at 52 pages, is it heavy. The first interior page proclaims in large letters the name of the dedicatee, the Right Honourable Henrie Wriothesley, Earle of Southampton, and Baron of Titchfield. Now we learn the name of the poet, subscribed beneath the 13 justified lines of the dedication. William Shakespeare. It is a name unknown to us. No other books in the shop nor other shops we have visited bear the name of this poet. Compared to other dedications of other books in the shop, this one is rather brief and less obsequious than many with which we are familiar.

We look at what the poet says to the very young Earl of Southampton and other readers:

> I know not how I shall offend in dedicating my unpolished lines to your lordship, nor how the world will censure me for choosing so strong a prop to support so weak a burden: only, if your honour seem but pleased, I account my self highly praised, and vow to take advantage of all idle hours, till I have honoured you with some graver labour. But if the first heir of my invention prove deformed, I shall be sorry it had so noble a godfather, and never after ear so barren a land, for fear it yield me still so bad a harvest. I leave it to your honourable survey, and your honour to your heart's content;

which I wish may always answer your own wish, and the world's hopeful expectations.

When we turn the page, we are surprised that the first stanzas of the poem appear. More often than not, books of any consequence carry commendatory epistles praising the author and the work. Often, too, the publisher will inscribe a letter to the reader concerning the work in hand. This one is different. Neither type of introductory material appears in this little book. Is this strange? Or is it distinctive? Why has it no words of approval attesting to the poet's merit by his fellow poets? Why didn't the publisher seek to boost sales by having such recommendations?

With the printer's decoration and the title repeated on the first page, there's room only for three stanzas of six lines each. The pages that follow all have four stanzas. With a quick calculation, we see that each page carries twenty-four lines of verse. That would add up to about 199 stanzas in fifty pages for a total of 1194 lines. The poem is both prodigious and sustained. But will it please the eye and the ear? Will is awaken our senses and sympathies? Or will it prove as barren as the author feared?

Harrison's clerk sees our interest and offers to sell us two copies for 12 pence. We open our purses and walk away with our purchase. Tomorrow or the next day we can share our impressions. Now we separate for our own pursuits.

The Poem Considered

Now, a one line summary of *Venus and Adonis*:

Young man, indifferent to romance, comically resists the amorous advances of an older goddess/queen (a frustrated seductress) then is gored by a boar.

As a comic masterpiece, *Venus* anticipates the mock-heroic epic, Pope's *Rape of the Lock*. When we read the name of the author, William Shakespeare, it tells us nothing except that the poet is male. His name has never appeared in print. We begin reading.

For its length and polish, we would assume it has been written over a period of some months. Its form and presentation are enticing, its rhetoric impressive, making it pleasing for us to read. We can compare it with the work which its author closely imitates while improving on the form.

Lodge in 1589 had published *Scillaes Metamorphosis or Historie of Glaucus and Silla.* Its cover, too, presented a quote from a Roman poet: *O vita/misero longa, faelici brevis.* This aphorism from Publilius Syrus may be translated as "For the wretched, life is long; for the happy, it is brief." The Ovid quote of *Venus and Adonis* is an elegant response – its poet is promising cups of Apollo from the Castalian spring.

Compare now the first page of Lodge's similar poem and that of *Venus and Adonis*:

The moſt pithie and pleaſant
Hiſtorie of Glaucus and Silla.

Walking alone (all onely full of griefe)
Within a thicket nere to Isis floud,
Weeping my wants, and wailing ſcant reliefe,
Wringing mine armes (as one with ſorrowe wood);
The piteous ſtreames relenting at my mone
Withdrew their tides, and ſtaid to heare me grone.
From forth the channell, with a ſorrowing crie
The Sea-god Glaucus (with his hallowed heares
Wet in the teares of his ſad mothers dye)
With piteous lookes before my face appeares;
For whome the Nimphes a moſſie coate did frame,
Embroadered with his Sillas heauenly name.
And as I ſat under a Willow trée,
The louelie honour of faire Thetis bower;
Repoſd his head upon my faintfull knée:
And when my teares had ceaſt their ſtormie ſhower
He dried my chéekes, and then beſpake him ſo,
As when he waild I ſtraight forgot my woe.
Infortunate, why wandreth thy content
From forth his ſcope as wearied of it ſelfe;
Thy bookes haue ſchoold thée from this fond repent,
And thou canſt talke by proofe of wauering pelfe:
Unto the world ſuch is inconſtancie,
As ſapp to trée, as apple to the eye.
Marke how the morne in roſeat colour ſhines,
And ſtraight with cloudes the Sunnie tract is clad;
Then ſee how pomp through waxe and waine declines,
From high to lowe, from better to the bad:
Take moiſt from Sea, take colour from his kinde,
Before the world deuoid of change thou finde.
A 2 With

VENVS AND ADONIS.

EVen as the ſunne with purple-colourd face,
Had tane his laſt leaue of the weeping morne,
Roſe-cheekt Adonis hied him to the chace,
Hunting he lou'd, but loue he laught to ſcorne:
Sick-thoughted Venus makes amaine vnto him,
And like a bold fac'd ſuter ginnes to woo him.

Thriſe fairer then my ſelfe, (thus ſhe began)
The fields chiefe flower, ſweet aboue compare,
Staine to all Nimphs, more louely then a man,
More white, and red, then doues, or roſes are:
Nature that made thee with her ſelfe at ſtrife,
Saith that the world hath ending with thy life.

Vouchſafe thou wonder to alight thy ſteed,
And raine his proud head to the ſaddle bow,
If thou wilt daine this fauor, for thy meed
A thouſand honie ſecrets ſhalt thou know:
Here come and ſit, where neuer ſerpent hiſſes,
And being ſet, Ile ſmother thee with kiſſes.
B

Which page invites us in? The Shakespeare poem is more attractive to the eye; it draws a reader into its text. And what a text it is.

♦♦♦ ♦♦♦

Bardophilus: Wait! The author can't allege *soto voce* that Shakespeare is a plagiarist and just move on.

Skepticisima: I don't think that's the point. The poet himself acknowledges in the *Sonnets* what his greatest talent was:

all my best is dressing old words new,
Spending again what is already spent.

Bardophilus: I don't think that's what he meant.

Skepticisima: You don't have to accept my interpretation. What you have to agree with is that *Venus and Adonis* is built from two templates. One is the story line. Shakespeare-the-poet takes up Ovid's brief tale and reworks it to his own theme and purposes. Lodge chose one Ovid tale and Shakespeare plucked another from the same book. The second template is the form. As the two first pages of poetry above demonstrate, *Venus* follows the exact rhyme scheme as *Scillae*. Same form, different words.

Bardophilus: You mean *Venus and Adonis* is an imitation, a knockoff, a faux-Gucci bag of a poem?

Skepticisima: Good lord, no. How many paintings and sculptures of the *pietà*, the dead Jesus cradled by his grieving mother, were created before Michaelangelo sculpted his *pietà* in 1499 or Giovanni Bellini painted his *pietà* in 1505? Each artist created a masterpiece that was based on the same form used by many predecessors. Shakespeare, like Michaelangelo and Bellini, showed what separates artistic genius from the product of a mere workman, however competent. We could continue, but the point is made. It's not the inspiration we admire but the execution. Where Lodge is dull and plodding and predictable, Shakespeare is lush, sensual, and erotic. It is Salieri and Mozart, Edison and Tesla, Roadrunner and Wile E. Coyote.

Bardophilus: Now you're making fun of me. You can't distinguish pathos and bathos. Soon, I'll have to respond in kind.

From beginning to end, the language and increasing intensity of *Venus and Adonis* is superior to *Scillae*. It is lascivious, its scenes erotic and impassioned. In the opening stanzas, Venus spots the beautiful young man; "trembling in her passion," she plucks him from his horse. She ties up her own steed. On the ground she begins to caress and kiss him. She's like an eagle devouring her prey. She kisses "his brow, his cheek, his chin, And where she ends she doth anew begin." He is unmoved.

If Venus is a bird of prey, Adonis is like "a bird lies tangled in a net, So fast'ned in her arms Adonis lies; Pure shame and awed resistance made him fret . . ." His coldness only enflames her more: "Her fire must burn. 'O, pity,' 'gan she cry. 'flint-hearted boy! 'Tis but a kiss I beg; why art thou coy?" All he wants to do is to hunt the boar.

After more stanzas of his resistance to her beauty and charms, Adonis springs to his horse to escape the "love-sick queen." His flight is foiled when his stallion sees a "breeding jennet." The horse breaks his reins and races to mount the mare. The reader is treated to several pages of vivid description of equine sex. Then, having satisfied their lust, the two horses run away, leaving poor Adonis to curse his horse for deserting him.

Venus resumes her efforts to woo him. She takes his hand; it is a "lily prisoned in a jail of snow." He tries to withdraw it from her grasp, but she refuses: "'Give me my heart,' saith she, 'and thou shalt have it'." She argues he should take a lesson from the coupling of the stallion and the mare and experience their joy. He demands that she "Remove your siege from my unyielding heart." She appeals to all his senses: the "deep-sweet music" of the ears; the "heart's deep-sore wounding"; the beauty seen by the eyes. If she had no eyes nor ears, then "love by touching thee" or smelling "breath perfumed, that breedeth love"; or taste of the "banquet wert thou to the taste."

After much more back and forth of pleading and resistance, Venus finally extracts a kiss from Adonis and rages for more: "Her face doth reek and smoke, her blood doth boil, And careless lust stirs up a desperate courage . . . ." Taking pity from his prayer that he be allowed to depart, she lets him go, saying they will resume tomorrow. But no, he replies that he'll be hunting the boar. She warns of the fierceness of the wild hog and urges him to unleash dogs and hunt timid animals like the hare or the fox or the deer, but he will not be dissuaded. She chides him for preserving his chastity, like a vestal virgin or a nun, burying within himself his posterity as though a suicide. Her entreaties, he tells her, only makes him like her worse and worse.

Eventually, the pursuer and the pursued both sleep. On waking, Venus seeks her love, listening for his hounds and horn. Finally, she spies the boar. The sight is not pretty: "frothy mouth, bepainted all with red, Like milk and blood being mingled both together." Frantic with fear, she searches until she discovers his wounded hounds but not their master. She addresses Death itself, berating, then pleading, that Adonis be not taken. Finding the corpse, she at first draws back but finally looks in grief at "the wide wound that the boar had trenched in his soft flank." As she gazes, she imagines how loved Adonis was by all creatures. The lion and tiger were tame in his presence. When fish or birds beheld him they took great pleasure, spreading their gills for him or bringing him berries. Even the boar loved him! The killing of Adonis was an accident: the "loving swine" was trying to kiss him and "nuzzling in his flank, . . . sheathed unaware the tusk in his soft groin."

Reconciling herself to Adonis's death and her unrequited love for the beautiful youth, Venus declares in five stanzas that love hereafter will only bring unhappiness – "fickle, false, and full of fraud." Love will breed jealousy, suspicion, war, and dissension within families. Because death came to her great love, "they that love best their loves shall not enjoy."

With the spleen out of her system, Venus looks on as the youth's body is melted like a vapor from her sight. He is transformed into a purple flower, checkered with white, resembling his pale cheeks flecked with his blood. She cuts the flower and clasps it to her breast. Now the silver doves who pull her chariot fly her to the empty skies.

ﭏﭏﭏﭏ--ﭏﭏﭏﭏ

If we knew nothing about the poet, we would surmise that he is a highly educated, well-read person. He takes a short tale from Ovid's *Metamorphoses* and gloriously expands it to ten times its length, enhanced by far more psychological depth and drama. But the critical reader spots a flaw. This poet Shakespeare has made a fundamental error in his reading of Ovid and his understanding of mythology. Or has he?

The mistake? In this, his first published work, he mocks "sick-thoughted Venus" as "the love-sick queen." Six times in *Venus and Adonis,* Venus is referred to as a queen. But nowhere in Ovid is Venus a "queen." Ovid's Venus is a goddess, but the title of queen is reserved to Juno, who is the "queen of the gods," or Proserpina, who is the "queen of the underworld."

Did the poet misread Ovid? Did he misunderstand the

mythical hierarchy in which Venus could be a goddess but not a queen? Venus appears in a half-dozen or more plays of Shakespeare as a goddess but never is she a "queen." "Great Juno" is depicted in the *Tempest* as "Highest Queen of State," but Ceres and Iris are mere goddesses; absent is the goddess Venus who is mentioned by name but excluded from the wedding of Miranda and Ferdinand so as to contrast pure, socially sanctioned love with the potentially destructive force of passion and desire.

No, Shakespeare-the-author did not mistake Ovid; he deliberately distorted Ovid and the Venus of myth. His purpose was that the critical reader would take the hint that "love-sick" Venus was patterned on Queen Elizabeth.[51] The mockery is just at the edge of explicit. But this is what Ovid himself had done with the tales of *Metamorphoses*: he inverted the accepted order; he elevated humans and their passions, especially ardor, but made the gods objects of farce and ridicule.

Would Southampton see Queen Elizabeth in the poem? Why would he find it suitable for *his* poem or even amusing? Or was the poet reaching past Southampton? And if Elizabeth is Venus, who is Adonis? And why? What was the poet up to?

Chapter 4

Dedications - Dedicatees

The poet of *Venus and Adonis* invested his time and his future in writing such a large poem. He would have chosen his dedicatee with the greatest care. At first, the Earl of Southampton does not appear to be an auspicious choice. He was only nineteen and still a ward of Lord Burghley, Lord Treasurer and the Queen's principal advisor. Nothing about Southampton suggested substance or gravity. One long poem in Latin had been dedicated to him, but it was an effort by Lord Burghley, through the pen of his secretary, to prod Southampton into marrying Burghley's own granddaughter. She was Elizabeth, daughter of Edward de Vere, the Earl of Oxford. Written by James Clapham and called *Narcissus*, it produced no reward for the poet from Southampton himself. Only when he turned twenty-one would Southampton have access to his substantial inheritance, but it was already encumbered by debt, not the least of which was £5,000 that Burghley was charging him for refusing to accept his choice of a bride for his ward. So, even though the named dedicatee of *Narcissus* was Southampton, the poet's patron was his employer Lord Burghley, and that was to whom the dedication was really directed. Southampton, a narcissistic and defiant youth, was the thinly disguised subject of the poem.

Let's take another example of a dedication to a nobleman's son in which the author was honoring the parent by the dedication. A buyer in 1609 at John Jaggard's book shop on Fleet Street who purchased Thomas Heywood's translation of two of Sallust's Roman dramas would find that the 120 plus page book was dedicated to Sir Thomas Somerset. The dedication identified Sir Thomas as Queen Ann's Master of the Horse. The translator acknowledged "many and extraordinary favours" of the dedicatee. No where was mentioned the person to whom Thomas Heywood was far more grateful: Sir Thomas's father, Edward Somerset, the 4th earl of Worcester. For a decade or so, Heywood had been writing plays for

Worcester's company (now the Queen's Men). The pride of a parent seeing one's child honored is as great, if not greater, than a gift to the parent.

Similarly, to understand the dedication of *Venus and Adonis* we must look to Southampton's family and friends. Only then will we have the context of the *Venus and Adonis* dedication. The man named in the dedication is the Earl of Southampton, but that dedication is really intended for the eyes of three others close to him—as with *Narcissus* and Lord Burghley. Those three others are Robert Devereux (Earl of Essex), his sister Penelope Devereux (Lady Rich), and Southampton's mother, Mary Browne (Countess of Southampton).

♦♦♦ ♦♦♦

Skepticisima: Before we go down that trail, let me ask you, Bardophilus, a question. Why do you and your fellow Stratfordians think your guy chose Southampton?

Bardophilus: Well, that's obvious. He was a wealthy young earl and a patron of the theater. He could be a big supporter in the future.

Skepticisima: Really? The very young earl was an unlikely candidate to choose for a patron unless it was for employment as a secretary. What do you think a patron would pay for the honor of being a dedicatee to a long poem?

Bardophilus: Off hand, I'd be guessing. Surely a lot.

Skepticisima: You'd be mistaken, at least by our standards. Let's take one example, a fine long poem also dated June 1593, exactly contemporaneous with *Venus and Adonis*. You're familiar with George Peele?

Bardophilus: Of course.

Skepticisima: By any measure, Peele was a successful playwright and poet whose talents were sought by patrons. But even a successful writer lived a hand-to-mouth existence unless he could find a permanent patron. In 1593 Peele published *The Honour of the Garter*. It was a poem similar to *Venus and Adonis* of similar length (851 lines to 1,194 lines) and also was preceded by an elegant Latin quote. The poem was written to celebrate the award of the Order of the Garter to five men on June 25, 1593. Sterrell's own senior lord,

Worcester, was one. The lord who commissioned Peele was Henry Percy, Earl of Northumberland. What was Peele's recompense? The sum of £3. No one could earn a bare living on such an amount.

Or consider Thomas Nashe's 92 pages of fevered religious prose, *Christ's Tears Over Jerusalem,* published a few months later in 1593. It was dedicated to Elizabeth Carey, wife of George Carey, the couple who were soon to become the patrons of the Lord Chamberlain's Men. The dedication earned a reward of £5, and the book's publication led to jail time for the author for railing against the sinfulness of London. Like the dedication to *Venus and Adonis,* the author promised (twice) a better book in the future ("more polished labours of mine ere long shall salute you"). The next year, Thomas Nashe dedicated *The Terrors of the Night* to the daughter of George and Elizabeth Carey, praising her "sharpe Wit" and "religious piety."[52]

Bardophilus: Shakespeare must have thought he could do better.

Skepticisima: Why would you think that? Southampton's had no association with the theater as patron or donor. Unlike Peele and Northumberland, Southampton had not even commissioned *Venus and Adonis* from "Shakespeare." For all the world knows, this little epic, *Venus,* was a speculative venture by an unknown writer who risked a barren harvest for all his efforts. Once published, it could not be shopped to another patron. If you offended the dedicatee, where would you be?

Bardophilus: Perhaps you have a point. But where are you going with this?

Skepticisima: Let's follow up by asking: How did things stand in early 1593 with 1) Shakespeare-of-Stratford, and 2) Southampton?

1) The Stratfordian you are so fond of is a twenty-nine-year-old man, presumed by scholars to be an actor, who is married to an older woman and father of three children. He is unpublished, and theatres have been mostly closed since June 1592. There is no reason to think he has had in 1593, or ever, access to a library in which he has read deeply Ovid in Latin. Excerpts in grammar school Latin texts? Nah. Neither he nor his presumed acting company has any

connection with the young earl, Southampton.

2) Southampton, a nineteen-year-old earl, has recently received his M.A. from Cambridge and has been admitted to the legal society of Gray's Inn but has no intention of studying law. He is not yet of age. While bearing the title of earl, he still will have no access to his inheritance until attaining twenty-one in another year and a half. He lives on a modest allowance, suitable to allow for a secretary (if approved by guardian or mother) but not likely to waste his pounds on a reward for a single dedication by someone he's never met and has nothing in common. His close friends are knights (the brothers Sir Charles and Sir Henry Danvers) and he is building his relationship, the strongest of his young years, with the powerful, swashbuckling Earl of Essex.

Bardophilus: Many people believe Southampton and Shakespeare were attracted to one another. A recent article suggested this in answering its own question with a question: "[W]hy this particular dedicatee for this particular poem? Is it a coincidence that Adonis is a beautiful young man with a disdain for the opposite sex?"[53] Shakespeare could have been seeking both money and sex in a highly refined manner.

Skepticisima: George Carey, patron of the Lord Chamberlain's Men wrote his wife in 1594 that Elizabeth Brydges had become mistress to Southampton. She gave up the Earl of Bedford for Southampton. Why would the poet think Southampton would be attracted to an unknown player/poet ten years his senior? Why would Shakespeare-of-Stratford risk everything by becoming a predator of a closely-watched nobleman ten years his junior? That's just creepy and sleazy. If there is a homosexual relationship between the two, why would the poet be so foolish as to display it publicly with *Venus* and *Lucrece*? It would embarrass the young earl with his friends and family. Why would Southampton jeopardize his relationship with his religious (Catholic) mother and sister Mary, his religious (Protestant) guardian, Lord Burghley, and his nobleman ideal, Essex, by a romantic entanglement with a common player? When the nobility sponsored acting companies, actors were identified with their social status: they were servants. They were not companions, not in 1593, not ever. Will Kemp was the exception.

The idea of a romantic relationship between the Stratfordian and the ambitious young earl is absurd on its face and lacking a smidgen of factual support.

Bardophilus: Love can't be explained.

Skepticisima: Leaving sex aside, let's look at the pecuniary side of things. If Shakespeare-of-Stratford is looking for reward and advancement, why wouldn't he dedicate his exquisite creation to someone far more promising for a playwright? There are companies in London and elsewhere that are constantly in need of plays, less so perhaps in plague times. Worcester's Men, Lord Strange's Men, the Lord Admiral's Men, Lord Hunsdon's Men and Sussex's Men to name the most prominent. Each of them had a patron and other family members who were interested in theater and poetry. Why not dedicate to one of them? In fact, the named patrons of two of those companies were married to sisters who were themselves important patrons of poets. They were two of the daughters of Sir John Spencer of Althorp. Elizabeth Spencer Carey, wife of George Carey whose company was Lord Hunsdon's Men. And Alice Spencer Stanley, wife of Ferdinando Stanley who was in charge of Lord Strange's Men. Their sister Anne was newly married to Robert Sackville. He was patron to the poets of the *Phoenix Nest* published near the time of *Venus and Adonis*. Sackville's father was himself a well-known poet/playwright and patron, Lord Buckhurst. Any of these three sisters or their husbands would have been a much better candidate to be a patron than the Earl of Southampton, whether Shakespeare-of-Stratford wished to succeed as a playwright or as a poet.

Bardophilus: We think he was already associated with a company. As an actor and as a playwright. It would have been impolitic to dedicate to another company's patron.

Skepticisima: That's lame even for you, Bard-Man. All the more reason to dedicate to his own patron or his patron's wife. If he was in a company, whether it was Lord Hunsdon's or Lord Strange's or the Lord Admiral's, that patron would surely be offended to be ignored. That's what would be impolitic. But, of course, you can cite no known company and no known patron and no known plays.

I'll forgive you. Your opponents with other candidates are

even weaker when it comes to the dedication of *Venus and Adonis* to Southampton.

Bardophilus: We're on the same side?

Skepticisima: Only because you decline to engage with those folks, not that I blame you. Start with the cult of Edward de Vere, the Earl of Oxford. The Oxfordians forget that Lord Burghley was his father-in-law. In 1592-93 Oxford knows that Burghley has failed to persuade young Southampton to marry Oxford's daughter with Burghley's own sponsored poetry, namely *Narcissus*. Why would the Earl of Oxford pretend to be a poet named Shakespeare who pleads for a reward? If and when Southampton tracked down the poet who dedicated *Venus and Adonis* to him, would he now find Elizabeth de Vere more appealing? Would Oxford think he was flattering Southampton to compare him with Adonis, who looks to all the world like a passionless celibate? What sort of father-in-law would that be? If Edward de Vere was willing to have his name/initials associated with other poetry published in 1593 (in the *Phoenix Nest*), why use a false name for *Venus and Adonis*?

Marlovians don't even try to explain why Christopher Marlowe would have written poetry simultaneously under the name of Shakespeare. In April 1593 he's under arrest waiting for criminal charges from the Privy Council. Why would he publish an appeal for reward from an earl who has no influence with the Queen or the Privy Council? Why wouldn't he dedicate under his own name to Lord Strange or to his sometime patron, Thomas Walsingham? Southampton could do nothing for Marlowe.

And Francis Bacon? He's tied to Essex himself. Why seek favor with Southampton? The minor has nothing to offer Bacon. Although lacking a title, Bacon has more influence at Court than Southampton. He's trying to become the Queen's Attorney General, and many others could help him far more than Southampton. Bacon himself may have been gay, but he wouldn't have preyed upon Essex's protege, Southampton.

If none of these three candidates composed *Venus and Adonis*, we can rule them out as authors of any of the plays. Unless their supporters want to claim that the Shakespeare of *Venus and Adonis* is a different Shakespeare from the playwright. Maybe it's like the

Kirk Douglas movie *Spartacus*. When the Roman soldiers demand that Spartacus surrender himself, one after another of his fellow captives stand to say "I'm Spartacus." .... "No, I'm Shakespeare!" The stylometrics folks would make Shakespeare the front for a whole staff of co-authors/collaborators, all together as one in the *First Folio*. They would make the Shakespeare plays like the Hardy Boys and Nancy Drew books. Both series were created by Edward Stratemeyer who had a crew of journalists.

Venus and the Weary Knight

The source of *Venus and Adonis* is, of course, Ovid's *Metamorphoses* but why did the author choose this story? What was its appeal in 1592-93? It's because Southampton's closest friend and his sister had already made use of Ovid's tale for their own political amusement and advancement as they courted the future king of England. To understand the appeal of Ovid's story for Sterrell, we must go back some months before he was recruited into Essex's service.

Thomas Fowler was an agent of Lord Burghley. In October 1589 Fowler passed to Burghley and his spymaster Sir Francis Walsingham copies of letters written by *Ryalta*, a pseudonym used by Penelope, Lady Rich. These were letters to King James of Scotland which Penelope and her brother, the Earl of Essex, used to encourage the Scots king to hope for the succession to the English crown to be his. It mattered little that Queen Elizabeth put to death James's mother, Mary Queen of Scots. Essex let James know his accession would be with the support of the powerful young earl and his network of followers.

Penelope's pseudonym in the secret letters was *Ryalta*, the name of the quarter of Venice in which the Exchange in *Merchant of Venice* was situated, the Rialto. The other pseudonyms in the Penelope/Essex secret letters were *Victor* for King James himself, Queen Elizabeth was *Venus*, and Essex was called the *Weary Knight*. Indeed, Essex had recently been made a Knight of the Garter, in April 1588. Though an earl, he was thus also a knight. James's naming as a member of the Order of the Garter had to await 1590 when Queen

Elizabeth sent the Earl of Worcester with the role of investing James.

Fowler told Burghley how the *Ryalta* letters emphasized Essex's weariness of the Queen: "I can tell few of their Names, but the Queen's Majesty is Venus, and the Earl [Essex] the weary knight, as I remember, but *always that he is exceeding weary, accompting it a Thrale*, that he lives now in . . ."[54] To be in *thrale* or *thrall* describes one who is in bondage to a lord or master, a slave or low servant. Essex planned for his political future by cultivating the young king to their north, Elizabeth's most likely successor, James VI of Scotland. He and his sister stressed Essex's unhappiness, his weariness, with Elizabeth *alias* Venus. The similes drawn from Ovid would have pleased James who loved theater and was himself a poet (*Lepanto*, 1585). Essex's rival, Robert Cecil, also undertook correspondence with James at the same time but lacked the imagination and wit of Essex and Penelope.

Sterrell refashioned the Penelope-Essex insider jest into an extraordinary little epic. His creation, *Venus and Adonis*, was an elegant, sensual elaboration of the inside jest that they and a few others of their circle shared as a private amusement about Essex and his Queen. The poem was entered with the Stationer's Register on April 18, 1593. When published by the end of May, it was dedicated to the Earl of Southampton but with an indirect appeal to the eyes of others. It was Sterrell's hope to find a new employer as well as to save himself and restore his credibility. The poet chose his dedicatee with the same care as his subject. And the goals of the poem itself were to impress Essex and to gain employment as Southampton's (or his mother's) secretary or similar patronage.

Sterrell could not subscribe his real name to *Venus and Adonis*. It would jeopardize his achievement, threaten his future, and cause great damage to the earl (Essex) who sent him overseas and the earl (Southampton) from whom he now sought a harvest of patronage.

Even without Sterrell's true name, the small audience for whom the poem was intended would immediately recognize the poet and the source of his poem. He was well-known among them (unlike the obscure burgher of Stratford whose name he borrowed).

While Essex courted King James in the guise of a weary knight, he had nurtured his relationship with Queen Elizabeth, and she with him, since the death of his stepfather (the Earl of Leicester). Essex was her favorite at her Court. He was a younger, gallant version of her former favorite, Leicester. Essex fought for his Queen overseas, at the side of the now dead Leicester. She made him her Master of the Horse and a Privy Councilor. But the Queen was much older than Essex, as is Venus to Adonis. Unlike Venus, she was mortal, which was why Essex sought to advance himself with James of Scotland.

When they received their copies of *Venus and Adonis*, Penelope, Essex, and Southampton immediately would have seen that the Queen and the Weary Knight were the inspirations for *Venus and Adonis*. Sterrell drew on Ovid to reimagine their playfulness about Essex and his weary relationship with his Queen. The Queen wouldn't get it, but they would.

In Ovid's telling, Adonis is depicted as enjoying his outdoor pursuits with Venus. In *Venus and Adonis*, Adonis is described (with an exercise in *synonymia*) as *weary* of the insatiable Venus, using the words of Essex so plainly noticed by Burghley's agent Fowler — *weary* and *Thrale/thrall*: [55]

Hot, faint and *weary*, with her hard embracing,
Like a wild bird being *tamed* with too much handling,
Or as the fleet-foot roe that's *tired* with chasing,
Or like the froward infant *stilled* with dandling,
He now obeys and now *no more resisteth*,
While she takes all she can, not all she listeth.

Venus herself says: "How love makes young men *thrall*, and old men dote . . . "

Weariness suffuses the *epyllion*:

<> Evening is weary: "*What hour is this? or morn or* ***weary*** *even?*"

<> The sun proceeds across the sky at a weary pace: "*Look, the world's comforter, with* ***weary*** *gait.*"

<> The legs of the Wat [a hare] are weary: "*Each envious brier his* ***weary*** *legs do scratch.*"

<> A bird of the air is tired of leisure: "*Lo, here the gentle lark,* ***weary*** *of rest.*"

<> Venus finds even a waiting hound weary: "*And asks the* ***weary*** *caitiff for his master.*"

<> At the end, Venus herself becomes weary: "*Thus* ***weary*** *of the world, away she hies.*"

There is no weariness to Ovid's Adonis, nor do the words "weary" and "thrall" appear in any translation of Book X of *Metamorphoses,* which was unquestionably the source of the story of *Venus and Adonis.*

The Essex circle would have delighted in the parallels of the poem with the Elizabeth-Essex relationship – the same *Venus* and *Weary Knight* of their correspondence with *Victor*, the Scots king. Like Adonis, Essex was the Queen's darling, despite a thirty-two-year difference in their ages. As the poem was written, he was twenty-seven and the Queen sixty. They were playful with one another, she the ingenue, he her gallant knight. Essex was her "fierce soldier" as John Sanford had described him at Magdalen College, Oxford with her in September 1592.[56] She showered him with gifts and offices; she sought his wit, charm, affection and company.[57]

Essex's sister, Penelope Devereux Rich (*Ryalta*), was very familiar to Sterrell. Not only was she Essex's sister but when their father (Walter Devereux) had died in 1576, both she and Essex had been placed under the guardianship of their father's cousin, Henry Hastings, 3rd Earl of Huntingdon, living at his house in Leicestershire. Hastings's sister was Elizabeth Hastings, the Countess of Worcester, the wife of Sterrell's master (to mid-1591). Sterrell owed his M.A. degree and his appointment as a *praelector* of Oxford to Essex's and Penelope's stepfather, the University chancellor, Leicester.

Sterrell was well-known to people in the Essex-Southampton social set. As Parliament began deliberations in late February 1593, Sterrell told his handler Phelippes of social activities in which he participated:

> We had many lords and lordings at dinner, who spent all the day in music, you might have done well to come among them. Here was Sir Harry Gray, Mr. Vavasour, and young Mr. Dudley, the great Lord's son, men I suppose well known unto you.

This brief mention would have impressed Phelippes, and it gives us insight into Sterrell's associations at this time and later in his life. A word about each should establish Sterrell's familiarity with the Essex-Penelope circle. They probably knew Sterrell only as a polite, quiet, unassuming professor from Oxford who recently had done some sort of work for Essex. He would have appeared a gentleman, but also as servant to an earl, one knew his place was in the background. For his part, he observed them closely, studying everything about their backgrounds - even as we do here. As a writer, he made use of all materials available to him.

Sir Henry Grey was first cousin to the Countess Southampton, mother of the Earl of Southampton. He was a former M.P. and was lieutenant of the Gentleman Pensioners (1588-1603) at the time of this dinner. His sons, John and Henry, had served under Leicester and Essex in the Low Countries.

"**Mr. Vavasour**" was Thomas Vavasour, from a prominent Catholic family with Lincolnshire connections. He had been in Parliament with Philip Sidney as well as serving as a captain in the Low Countries when Leicester, Sidney and Essex went over. Leicester entrusted Thomas Vavasour with the very delicate task of informing the Queen that he had accepted the title of Governor-General of the United Provinces, which was certain to enrage her. Essex's trust of Thomas Vavasour was such that he would later captain the *Antelope* on the Azores Islands expedition of 1597 when Essex would knight him. He would go on to hold office in King James's household, perhaps with the assistance of Sterrell and Worcester.

Essex's sister Penelope had a close connection with Anne Vavasour, Thomas Vavasour's sister. Anne was the notorious mistress of the Earl of Oxford, mother of his out-of-wedlock child. Anne Vavasour and Penelope Devereux became maids of honor for Queen Elizabeth within months of one another in 1580-1581. Thomas Vavasour famously had challenged Oxford to a duel because of the dishonor he had brought upon the Vavasour name. Another of his sisters, Frances, had secretly married Sir Thomas Shirley, the adventurer who was a cousin of Will Kemp, the comedian in the Shakespeare company. Because the marriage had not secured the blessing of the queen, Sir Thomas was locked in the

Marshalsea prison until early 1592.

The young **Mr. Dudley**, age nineteen in 1593, was Leicester's natural son who bore his name and inherited lands but not title. Dudley and Essex thus shared a father in Leicester: Dudley a "natural" son and Essex a stepson. Both were heirs to Leicester and knew one another well. Young Dudley was of course educated at Oxford, where his father was Chancellor. Although Dudley was at Christ Church College, not Magdalen, his tutor (in 1588) was Thomas Chaloner who was a fellow student at Magdalen College with Sterrell a decade earlier. Sterrell will have known Dudley both as his own likely student (as *praelector* in 1588) and through Chaloner. Sterrell would have paid special attention to Dudley, for Dudley's father had intervened at the University to save Sterrell's academic career, when it was in danger for his religion. Thomas Chaloner served Essex in France and was there knighted in 1591. Some of Sterrell's secret correspondence with Catholic exiles was shared with Chaloner. Years later, Sterrell will play a significant role in Dudley's life through Chaloner (then serving in the household of King James) by way of Sterrell's strong standing among Catholics in Rome. Sterrell and Chaloner have overlapping roles in the first decade of James's reign. Both Sterrell and Chaloner are given supervisory roles for masques written by Ben Jonson for the royal Court (*Oberon* for Chaloner and *Love Freed from Ignorance and Folly* for Sterrell).[58]

At the time of the February 1593 dinner and the dedication of *Venus and Adonis*, Sterrell was also a fast friend of Southampton's tutor and companion: John Florio. Florio was an Anglo-Italian linguist who knew Sterrell from two very close associations in the past dozen years. Florio, too, had matriculated from Magdalen College while Sterrell was a Fellow of Magdalen. He and Sterrell both had spent several years associated with the French ambassador in London, Monsieur Michel de Castelnau, Lord Mauvissière. If Southampton's mother had employed Florio as tutor and companion for her son, why not engage Florio's friend, William Sterrell?

♦♦♦ ♦♦♦

Bardophilus: Why didn't this Sterrell fellow just dedicate the poem to Essex himself? Or to Penelope?

Skepticisima: Essex had become suspicious of Sterrell. He doubted his loyalty. He was even withholding money he owed to Sterrell from his mission. As Sterrell expressed it to their middleman, Thomas Phelippes, Sterrell was "loath to solicit the Earl." He preferred that Phelippes play the mediator and that Phelippes help Sterrell find some other nobleman to serve as secretary. It would have been unseemly to solicit through dedication of a poem. Essex was already distancing himself from Sterrell. A dedication to Essex as Sterrell would have only drawn the Privy Council to come down on both men, even though Essex was one of the Council.

The England of Queen Mary and her Consort, King Philip

To understand why Sterrell would look for favor from Southampton's mother, we must go back to 1553. That was the year when Mary Tudor became queen of England for five years. Historians have not been kind to her, and they have neglected those whom she and her husband favored. After the death of her younger half-brother, Edward VI, a Protestant, Mary was proclaimed his successor in London in July 1553 and crowned in October. She immediately sought to return England to the Roman church.

Great scenes of celebration took place in the following summer. These were for the royal wedding (Wednesday, July 25, 1554) of Mary to Philip of Spain and King Philip's ceremonial entry into London (August 1554). The new king remained in England for the next fourteen months before leaving for diplomatic reasons. He returned again for three months in 1557.

King Philip, with his wife's full participation, was active in restoring England's relations with Rome. After all, Mary herself had been cut off from direct participation in the Roman Church since childhood. It was Philip who had connections in Europe. Three families who were close to the royal couple are of interest to us in our story of the origins of Shakespeare-the-author: Anthony Browne (Viscount Montagu), William Somerset (3rd Earl of Worcester) and Eleanor Kemp. Their children and grandchildren are directly connected to Shakespeare-the-author.

Anthony Browne had immediately established himself with Queen Mary Tudor when she succeeded her brother, King Edward VI, in 1553. In her brief reign he became one of the most important men of the realm. He was created Viscount Montagu and dispatched with several others to Rome to restore Catholicism in England with the Pope. King Philip made him his Master of the Horse. The viscount was inducted into the Order of the Garter and made a member of the Privy Council.

Similarly important was William Somerset, 3rd Earl of Worcester, who took part in Queen Mary Tudor's Coronation, October, 1553. Then he was sent to Spain April to May 1554 to meet and escort Prince Philip of Spain back to England. He remained close to the royal Court.

While the offspring of Anthony Browne and William Somerset of Queen Mary's Court and reign are most important to our story, of interest to us also is one of most important ladies of the privy chamber to Queen Mary Tudor, Eleanor Browne Kemp, widow of Sir William Kemp (d. 1539) of Wye, Kent. Descended of the same family as Anthony Browne and William Somerset, she was part of Mary Tudor's household by 1547 and was still there in 1558 when the queen died.

We can imagine these families with the Queen and the King at feasts in Lud's Town (London) as described (reimagined) in the Shakespeare play *Cymbeline:*

> **Cymbeline:** Laud we the gods;
> And let our crooked smokes climb to their nostrils
> From our bless'd altars. Publish we this peace
> To all our subjects. Set we forward; let
> A Roman and a British ensign wave
> Friendly together. So through Lud's Town march;
> And in the temple of great Jupiter
> Our peace we'll ratify; seal it with feasts.
> Set on there! Never was a war did cease,
> Ere bloody hands were wash'd, with such a peace.

The Countess of Southampton's father, and the third Earl of Worcester, along with a son of Queen Mary's lady-in-waiting, were all important in the reestablishment of Catholicism in England. It was the great goal of their descendants to see again a "Roman and a British ensign wave friendly together," just as they had witnessed in their childhood.

The lines just quoted are also the final words - and aspiration - of the *First Folio* of 1623, carried forward by the 4th Earl of Worcester and his faithful secretary, Sterrell. When the *First Folio* was published it appeared to them that the restoration of Catholicism was close to fruition with the Spanish Match. This was the long-planned marriage of England's future king Charles to the Catholic granddaughter of King Philip II, once King of England. And the first play of that *First Folio* is the *Tempest* which concludes with the marriage of Miranda, daughter of the exiled Duke Prospero, and Ferdinand, son of the King of Naples, a relationship that forms a political and personal resolution, uniting their kingdoms. Substitute *Spanish Infanta* for Miranda and *Charles,* son of the King of England, for Ferdinand and the message of the *Tempest* in the context of 1623 is immediately obvious.

Both the *Tempest* and *Cymbeline* celebrate the reunion of two opposing realms after long separation. We find the same theme in *As You Like It,* written in anticipation of peace between England and her rivals, Spain and the Low Countries under the Archdukes.

Readers of the *First Folio* will have noted the words of Cymbeline which preceded the vision of a reunited Rome and Britain. He blamed the rupture on "our wicked queen" who had dissuaded Britain from submitting to the "Roman empire." It was a clear allusion to Queen Elizabeth whose accession to the throne had disrupted the Roman church in England.

Viscount Montagu's Little Twins

Family history is a maker of destiny. Could there have been a more Catholic family in England than the Brownes? Anthony Browne (1528-1592) was sent to Rome by Queen Mary and King Philip to make wave together the ensigns of Rome and Britain. He was father of the little twins, Anthony and Mary, who were born July 22, 1552. Their mother (Lady Jane Radcliffe) had died in childbirth. Their only mother was the pious Magdalen Dacre, whom Anthony Browne soon married. He fathered eight more children by Magdalen. Lady Magdalen served as one of Mary's bridesmaids when the new queen married Philip II of Spain. So, she knew well Eleanor Kemp with whom she served in Queen Mary's household for five years. From the same period, the Brownes surely knew well also Eleanor Kemp's family (Will Kemp's uncles and aunts) who served the royal Court.

Surely, Queen Mary and King Philip often saw Viscount Montagu's two young children (whom they knew to be motherless). As fraternal twins, the small Brownes were a charming rarity. The royal couple probably entertained the little boy and girl as they prayed to have children of their own. The futures of two kingdoms depended on their having children to succeed them: If Mary died childless, the crown of England would pass not to her husband but to her younger Protestant half-sister Elizabeth. Philip's status as king did not extend beyond his wife's life.

All that Anthony Browne, Viscount Montagu, had achieved ended with Mary's death and Elizabeth's accession in 1558. The viscount made little trouble for the new queen, Elizabeth, and so retained his title, his lands and his head. The six-year-old twins would never be welcomed at Elizabeth's Court.

ꕥꕥꕥꕥ--ꕥꕥꕥꕥ

Viscount Montagu died only six months before the dedication of *Venus and Adonis* to his grandson, the Earl of Southampton. At the time of that dedication, May 1593, not only had the Countess of Southampton recently lost her father, her beloved twin brother had died only four months before their father had passed. She had suffered two grievous losses in less than a year. As she grieved early in 1593, she would have reflected on how her family had fallen in status and was excluded from the Court of Elizabeth, how her father and brother were denied Catholic burials. Her son could participate at Court but only if he embraced the religion of the queen and William Cecil, Lord Burghley, the fierce Protestant whom Elizabeth had appointed Secretary of State on the first day of her reign in 1558. Cecil was already guardian of the Countess's only son; he was trying to make the young earl his own grandson by pressuring him to marry his granddaughter. Would she lose her son to the house of the Cecils?

Mary Browne's marriage in 1566 to Henry Wriothesley, 2nd

Earl of Southampton, had begun well. She was strong in his support when he was imprisoned for his efforts on behalf of Mary Queen of Scots. But the relations turned sour when he suspected her of infidelity. When the 2nd Earl died young (36), his will provided for his son, the 3rd Earl to be attended by Thomas Dymock, a servant in the household, and his daughter to be raised by his sister or another aunt. Thus, it was that the eight-year-old earl became the ward of one of staunchest promoters of the Protestant regime, Lord Burghley, who profited greatly by assuming the wardship and who steered the boy away from his mother's and grandfather's ardent Catholicism. Lord Burghley was, as we have seen, attempting to make the young earl his own grandson-in-law. Mary Brown, dowager Countess of Southampton, must have felt forlorn in early 1592-93.

The Future Patron of William Sterrell

Returning to the royal Court of Mary and Philip, another child, perhaps three or four years old in 1553, could be seen with Eleanor Kemp and the Browne twins. He was little Lord Herbert, Edward Somerset. His father was William Somerset, 3rd Earl of Worcester. The 3rd Earl took part in Queen Mary Tudor's Coronation, October 1553. He was then sent to Spain April to May 1554 to meet and escort Prince Philip of Spain back to England where the prince became King Philip upon his marriage to Queen Mary in July. Moreover, William Somerset's sister Anne Somerset was a maid of honour (one of six) in the household of Queen Mary Tudor. In 1558 she married Thomas Percy, 7th Earl of Northumberland. The 3rd Earl of Worcester was surely a frequent presence while Philip was in England, and his small boy, Edward, was likely near at hand with his father and his aunt.

The Browne twins and little Edward Somerset would have been together frequently during Queen Mary's short reign because they were cousins. Their lives and fortunes intersected for at least the next four decades as will be seen. They shared a grandfather, Sir Anthony Browne (1443-1506). Viscount Montagu and the 3rd Earl of Worcester were first cousins: Montagu's father (Sir Anthony Browne) and Worcester's mother (Elizabeth Browne) were brother and sister. They were also closely related to Queen Mary's lady-in-waiting, Eleanor Browne Kemp. Their common ancestor was Sir

Thomas Browne (1402-1460), Eleanor's grandfather, who had served as a Member of Parliament and Chancellor of the Exchequer.

A Cavaliero, Will Kemp

It will come as a surprise to Shakespeare scholars that the famous comedian Will Kemp was probably among the children playing at Mary and Philip's Court. This would be due to his grandmother, Eleanor Browne Kemp, and his aunts and uncles who were all close to the royal couple. The biographer of Will Kemp in the *Oxford Dictionary of National Biography* notes "he was linked in some way to the Kempes of Ollantighe." The basis for believing this is the fact that Will Kemp had a famous meeting in Venice or Rome with Anthony Shirley who was part of this Kemp family. To account for Kemp's forceful personality and Catholic heritage, we will trace this background in depth because it explores unfamiliar territory. Kemp's family relations with the 4th Earl of Worcester, the Brownes (Viscount Montagu/Southamptons), and the Shirleys, will explain aspects of the comdeian's biography that have eluded historians.

What do Shakespeare scholars know of Will Kemp the actor?

<> Courier of letters and performer in the Low Countries, 1585-1592;

<> Actor and shareholder in acting companies 1593-1599 and Globe theater;

<> Traveler to Rome and elsewhere on the Continent where he met the adventurer (and Spanish agent) Anthony Shirley 1600-1601 and others, including the "Emperor of Germany."[59]

In each of these three, Will Kemp is most often referred to as "Mister" or its equivalent, indicating status as a gentleman (gentry). Although it is not possible to name Will's father, we can reasonably identify his aunts, uncles and grandparents. These identify him as the Will Kemp who, with his uncle George Kemp, was a pensioner of King Philip of Spain. Will Kemp is useful to us in further exploring the Catholic exiles in the Low Countries and connections with the Earl of Worcester (his relative) and William Sterrell.

Will Kemp's grandmother was one of the longest serving ladies of the privy chamber to Queen Mary Tudor, Eleanor Browne Kemp, widow of Sir William Kempe (d. 1539) of Wye, Kent. She was part of Mary Tudor's household from at least 1547 to 1558 when the queen died. Sir William's will of 1538 mentioned his eldest son Thomas and "my six younger sons" (i.e. seven total). The names of six Kemp sons are known from Sir William's widow's (Eleanor) will of 1560, and these six include Thomas. Thus, it appears that an unnamed son died between 1538 and 1560. Perhaps that son was Will Kemp's father. Or his father might be one of the other six sons for whom family data is incomplete. Eleanor Kemp also had five daughters of the marriage as well as two daughters from her first marriage to Thomas Fogge.

The Kemp family - Shirley/Sherley connection. Sir William Kemp's heir was Sir Thomas Kemp (1517-1591). This Sir Thomas Kemp's daughter Anne married Sir Thomas Shirley I (c.1542-1612), of Wiston, Sussex. Sir Thomas Shirley I and Anne Kemp were parents of Sir Thomas Shirley II (1564–1633/4), Anthony Shirley (1565-1636?) and Robert Shirley (*c.* 1581–1628), who were all adventurers. If Will Kemp the actor is Sir Thomas Kemp's nephew, this would make him first cousin of these Shirley brothers.

The Kemp family – Low Countries connections. Several of Eleanor Kemp's seven sons had important positions in the royal household of Queen Mary and King Philip. Even before Mary became queen, Anthony Kemp (bef. 1529-1597) followed his mother into the service of Mary Tudor. According to his biography in *The History of Parliament,* he had a role maintaining contact between the princess and the imperial court. Anthony Kemp evidently combined with attendance on the Queen dowager of Hungary, regent of the Netherlands, to whom on the eve of her coronation Mary sent a request for his return to England for that event and for two or three months' stay. After Mary Tudor became queen and married King Philip of Spain, the same source says that Early in 1554 Kemp was sent to Spain; for the rest of the reign he was regularly employed as a messenger between England and the Continent. Anthony Kemp frequently traveled between Greenwich and Brussels and was made aide of the chamber to King Philip. Two of his brothers also served Mary and Philip.[60]

After Elizabeth became queen, both Anthony Kemp and George Kemp were active in maintaining connections with the Catholic exiles in the Low Countries and in connection with them apparently continued to serve King Philip. These connections readily explain how their nephew Will Kemp became a courier of messages between England and the Low Countries, a role enhanced by his status as an actor. Performers were easily able to obtain passports to leave England based on their employment on the Continent. It was a perfect cover for a courier of messages and funds.

Will Kemp (often suggested to be the actor) first appeared in records in 1585 in two letters of November 12, 1585 from Thomas Doyley at Calais to the Earl of Leicester and to Secretary Walsingham speaking of "Mr. Kemp, called Don Gulihelmo/Gulielmo," [a Spanishing of William] as amongst those "English inhabitants" in Dunkirk. This immediately suggests "Mr. Kemp" had a Spanish identification. Don is "Mister" and that is itself a title, as is "Mr. Kemp."

Thomas Doyley was a physician and scholar of Spanish who was also a trusted intelligence agent for Walsingham and Leicester. What was so important about Kemp that he was informing Leicester and Walsingham, two of the highest men of England, about seeing him? Shakespeare scholars dangle the Kemp name but ignore this question of context. Doyley was reporting on the presence of Will Kemp among a group of English Catholic exiles.

The ship on which Doyley was sailing was captured off Dunkirk on October 14, 1585. He was questioned by the Spanish governor about English affairs in Flanders. In letters to Leicester and Walsingham of November 12, 1585, he told of three Englishmen living in Dunkirk. A printed transcription of the Leicester letter states that the three were "Mr. Stanyhurst, Tunsan's [Dunsany] brother, and Mr. Copley, surnamed Lord, whose sister Mr. Stanyhurst married: also Mr. Kemp, called Don Gulihelmo."[61]

The identification of the first two is easy: Richard Stanihurst, formerly of Dublin whose first wife was Genet/Janet Barnewall, sister of Mary Barnewall who married Patrick Plunkett, 7th Baron of Dunsany (Stanihurst dedicated a 1584 book to him); hence, they were brothers-in-law. Mr. Copley "surnamed Lord" would have to be William Copley, heir to Thomas Copley (d. 1584) and not his brother Anthony Copley who he did not succeed to his father's title/estate. The sister of these two Copley brothers was Helen

Copley, who was the second wife of Richard Stanihurst. The Stanihurst and Copley families were landed gentry. They were abroad for religion. Stanihurst had been very close to Edmund Campion; so were the Copleys and their relations among the Shelleys of Michelgrove, Sussex.[62]

Doyley supplied intelligence for years for Walsingham. In the letters of November 1585, as England entered military support of the Dutch rebels, Doyley was assessing conditions in the region for Leicester and Walsingham. The three men Doyley calls attention to are English inhabitants of Dunkirk, not men who were on the ship seized by the Spanish. They are notable as members of the gentry, not commoners, and are part of Dunkirk's English exile community.

If this "Mr. Kemp" were a Catholic priest, we can assume that Doyley would have told Leicester and Walsingham that the man was a priest. Now the full reference is to "Mr. Kemp, called Don Gulilhelmo." In English at the time ***Mr.*** is a title to address a man with the status of ***gentleman***. In Spain, **Don** is a title to address a man with the status of ***caballero***/gentleman.[63] In England, one would commonly use the title "Mr." with a man's surname, not his given name; one would say "Mr. Kemp" not "Mr. William" when speaking of or to William Kemp. Doyley reflects this universal usage by referring to "Mr. Stanyhurst" and "Mr. Copley" with no given name, though he knew their full names.

In Spanish, one would often use the title of "Don" with the man's given name not necessarily followed by the surname; it would not be impolite to use the given name with the title, Don. Thus, in *Much Ado about Nothing*, the characters of Spanish background are referred to as *Don Pedro* and *Don John*.

In English society, the prefix "Sir" is used with the holder's given name or full name, but never with the surname alone. It is still the English custom. For example, while Sir Mick and Sir Mick Jagger would be correct, Sir Jagger would not.

In linking these three men in Doyley's letters to William Sterrell and to Will Kemp the actor, we observe that a list of the English men and women receiving Spanish pensions during the 1580-90s includes:

<> Three Copleys: "Lord Copley" of the letter, William, as well as his father Thomas and brother Anthony;

<> Three Stanihursts: Richard Stanyhurst, as well as his two relatives, John and Walter;

<> Two Kemps: Will Kemp, as well as his uncle George (entry for Will states "Recommends Kemp to secure service. (E 588/137. Letter of King 23 June 1584)").

Richard Stanihurst (with Hugh Owen) helped secure the pensions for the two younger Copleys, his brothers-in-law. Stanihurst had lived in London from 1575 to 1581 and surely aided his old friend Edmund Campion and Campion's fellow Jesuit, Robert Persons, during their 1580-81 mission before he was briefly imprisoned in London.[64] Present and working among the Catholic exiles in Flanders and France 1585-86 was Fr. Robert Persons. Persons would certainly have known well the Stanihursts and the Copleys and likely became acquainted with Will Kemp during 1585-86 if not earlier. This is likely of importance to Kemp's trip to Rome during a time of Persons's crisis in 1600-1601, in which Anthony Copley played a role (as reported by Sterrell's letters to Fr. Persons).

Sterrell was familiar with quite a few of the English exiles on the pension lists, even staying at the Stanihurst house in Liège in 1592. The Copleys were related to at least one of the youths for whom Sterrell arranged transportation to seminary in 1585. It is very likely Sterrell knew "Will Kemp" through others of the Spanish pensioners, such as Anthony Skinner.

Will Kemp the actor was well known by the Spanish term for "gentleman" - caballero. In fact, he calls himself exactly this in his own book of 1600: "my selfe, thats I, otherwise called Caualiero Kemp, head-master of Morrice dauncers, . . . " We find Will Kemp carrying correspondence (March 24, 1586) from Leicester's camp back into England, identified by Philip Sidney as "Will, my lord of Lester's jesting plaier." Later in the same year he was in Denmark performing with other English players.

Will Kemp's appearances in the Low Countries in 1585-86 can be associated not only with his carrying Leicester's correspondence but due to the presence in Leicester's camp of one of his cousins and two of this cousin's sons. Will Kemp's uncle Sir Thomas Kemp was father of Anne Shirley (thus Will's cousin). Anne Shirley's husband (Sir Thomas Shirley I) and two of their sons (Sir Thomas II and Anthony) went to the Low Countries with Leicester in 1585 where Sir Thomas Shirley II commanded a company of cavalry and his brother Anthony Shirley served as a captain of infantry. Their father, Sir Thomas I, was appointed as treasurer-at-war in the Netherlands in 1587. This Shirley connection can explain how Will Kemp could easily move among the English Catholic exiles (who knew well his uncles Anthony Kemp and George Kemp) and among the English troops with his Shirley cousins.

We see again Mister Kemp, the actor, associated with Spain in a 1589 publication, *An Almond for a Parrat,* referring to him as "that most Comicall and Conceited Cavaliero, Monsieur du Kempe, Jestmonger and Viceregent-generall to the Ghost of Dicke Tarlton [a famous comedian actor]." As above, *Cavaliero* is the Englishing of the Spanish term *caballero,* a gallant or gentleman. And *Monsieur* is the French for Mister, a gentleman. The dedication to Kemp related an incident (likely fictitious) in which its author (probably Thomas Nashe) was in Bergamo on his way to England when a certain Harlequin inquired if he knew in London, "Signior Chiarlatano Kempino." Here in Italian we have again the title of a gentleman: *Signior.*

When a certain William Blackwall registered an entertainment known as a "Jig" in May 1595, it was entered as "a ballad, of *Mr* Kempes Newe Jigge of the Kitchen stuffe woman." In a trio of related plays (1598-1602), the third of which is *Return from Parnassus,* Will Kemp enters as himself, recently returned from Rome and Germany. Another character as himself is Richard Burbage, his fellow actor. Burbage and Kemp meet the two principal characters, Philomusus and Studioso; both welcome him as Mr. Kemp. Philomusus inquires: "What *Master* Kemp, how doth the Emperor of Germany?" and Studioso says "God save you, *Master* Kemp; welcome, *Master* Kemp, from dancing the morrice [Morris dance] over the Alps."

Why do these contemporary references to Will Kemp the actor emphasize his status as "mister" and "don" and "cavaliero" and "signior" and Spain? References to an actor as "mister" or "gentleman" at any time in the relevant period is very unusual (1560-1620).[65] A "gentleman" becoming an actor, especially a clown, was a rarity. Players were servants, not gentlemen. Kemp stood out as the exception, an oddity to be remarked upon each time he appeared.

Scholars know Will Kemp as a comedian/shareholder when the Lord Chamberlain's company was formed in 1594. In fact, his name appears first on a Treasury payment to "William Kempe, William Shakespeare, and Richarde Burbage, servants to the Lord Chamberlain" during the 1594-95 Christmas season. He was a shareholder in the building of the Globe Theater five years later.

Before he became associated with Worcester's Men around 1600 Kemp apparently had divested himself of his company shares, including the Globe.[66] This is a strange development in itself and may suggest an unpredictable personality or some instability within the company. And why this association with the Earl of Worcester? Probably because they were related by their common ancestor, Sir Thomas Browne (1402-1460). Worcester's father would have known well Kemp's grandmother and uncles during their common service to the royalty, 1553-1558. As Edward Somerset grew up, he may have associated with his Kemp kin. Will Kemp could well have been with Worcester's acting company when it toured Stratford and other towns in the 1580s.

The Worcester-Kemp kinship is seen with Kemp's famous Morris dance of 100 plus miles from London to Norwich in 1600. From his entertaining book (*Nine Daies Wonder*) his stops along the way are known. He stayed at homes associated with Worcester and with his grandmother: One was Ingatestone, the home of Worcester's daughter and son-on-law; that daughter and Will Kemp shared an ancestor, Sir Thomas Browne (1402-1460). Perhaps Kemp had already joined Worcester's company at this time. Another stay was at the home of the Colts, descendants of the same family as Jane Colt who was the first wife of Sir Thomas More and her sister Mary Colt, whose husband was William Kempe of another branch of the extended Kemp families. When Eleanor Kemp had her will prepared in 1559-60, she named as her executor the son-in-law of Sir Thomas More and Joan Colt, William Roper, along with several of her own sons, suggesting that these Kemps were associated with the Colt family.

In 1601, Kemp undertook an even odder journey to Rome and met with one or more of the adventurous Shirley brothers who were mysteriously involved with Persia. Anthony Shirley, now openly Catholic, was meeting with William Sterrell's correspondent Fr. Persons about April 1601. Fr. Persons supported Anthony Shirley as a claimant to the office of Persian envoy at the Vatican; Shirley also became an agent of the Spanish king. Kemp was already a pensioner of Spain.

Was Kemp's journey to Rome to meet Shirley or was it to meet with Fr. Persons or was it to meet with both? Coordinating a Kemp-Shirley meeting via secret correspondence while one was in Persia and the other in London seems extraordinarily difficult; rather, it seems likely the meetings of Fr. Persons with Kemp and with Shirley coincided. Persons knew from his letters from Sterrell that the Queen was nearing her death; a transition to a new government was rapidly approaching. Both Kemp and Shirley could help guide Persons as he saw the possibility of achieving the goal he had pursued unswervingly since his mission into England with Edmund Campion in 1580-81.

The meetings of Will Kemp with Shirley were so noted that they were included in popular entertainment and news, such as *Return from Parnassus* noted already, and in Day, Rowley, and Wilkins's *The Travailes of the Three English Brothers* (1607). And a diarist named Smith in September 1601 entered the following comment in Latin (here translated):[67] "Sept. 2, 1601. Kemp, a certain actor, who had undertaken a certain journey into Germany and Italy, after many wanderings and his own misfortunes, returned: he reports many things about Anthony Sherley, a knight, whom he had met at Rome (acting as the Persian Legate)."

After Kemp's return from Europe, scholars have assumed he died around 1602 based on the burial of a "Kemp" in the neighborhood where he was thought to have lived. In a later case mentioning Shakespeare in connection with the Globe and Blackfriars theaters and Kemp's former ownership of shares, the actor/comedian is described as a gentleman ('William Kempe, late of London, gentleman, deceased').[68]

What all Shakespeare scholars have avoided was that Will

Kemp was pensioner of the Spanish king *via* Sir William Stanley's company in the Low Countries where the player often performed. He had a pension of 20 escudos based on a 1584 recommendation to King Philip for Will Kemp to secure service. So, too, was George Kemp a pensioner, an uncle of Will; George had served since 1564. The biography of Anthony Kemp in *The History of Parliament* identifies George and Will Kemp as brother and nephew of Anthony Kemp, and thus they would be son and grandson of Eleanor Kemp.[69]

King Philip's solicitude and pensions for Will and George Kemp grew from his attachment to the family of Eleanor Kemp, especially her sons who served in his own household and as his and Mary's messenger. Eleanor Kemp's sons (Will Kemp's uncles) were strong Catholics who suffered reverses with Elizabeth's ascendance and reimposition of Protestantism.

Let us return to Anthony Kemp who was an uncle to the Shirley family and to Will Kemp. Not only did he have connections with the catholic exiles, he was well known as a Catholic recusant. He maintained the Roman ritual at the chapel of Slindon House which had a secret priest chamber. When Anthony was persecuted for his Catholicism in the 1588 and 1595, his cousin Sir Thomas Shirley testified to his loyalty and conformity with the law. This Shirley/Kemp connection should confirm that Will Kemp the actor is nephew to Anthony Kemp.

If we seek common associations between Will Kemp and William Sterrell, Anthony Kemp's second wife is important for her close connection to the Countess of Southampton and her son, the earl. That second wife was Margery Gage (married 1569). She was a cousin of Edward Gage of Bentley, the business manager for Countess of Southampton and her son the Earl of Southampton. Edward Gage of Bentley was an executor of Anthony Kemp's will (1597), and the same Edward Gage was the father-in-law of Sterrell's long-time recusant friend, Anthony Skinner. There were close associations between members of the Earl of Worcester's immediate family and Edward Gage's family. Several of the six youths for whom Sterrell was arranging passage across the English Channel in 1585 were closely related to Anthony Kemp and other Catholic gentry, including the Copleys. It would be surprising if Will Kemp were not acquainted with Sterrell at least by 1585. Kemp (*Don Gulihelmo*) was an ideal courier for Catholic correspondents to the Low Countries.

♦♦♦ ♦♦♦

Bardophilus: Dead horses shouldn't be beaten. Going back to the failed monarchy of Bloody Mary is misplaced nostalgia that even the imaginative Shakespeare would not have invoked. He was born in 1564, for Pete's sake. Mary was dead six years. Her husband had packed his Spanish trunks and trundled home. And their Court had long since dissolved. It's ridiculous to look at plays like *Cymbeline* and *The Tempest* through rose-colored opera glasses as though longing to return to a dead past, a wistfulness for the *ancien régime*. Players and audiences wouldn't be aware of events and people four decades earlier, nor would they have cared. They had moved on with Elizabeth. And she put an end to Bloody Mary's public immolations.

Skepticisima: Now, now, now, Bardy-boy. Calm thyself. The folks we're talking about weren't reminiscing on the porch steps. This was generational. The 3rd Earl of Worcester brought Philip from Spain in 1554. His son Edward, the 4th Earl, escorted James I into London in 1603. And Worcester's son-in-law Lord Thomas Windsor was rear-admiral in charge of the fleet sent in 1623 to bring Prince Charles home from Spain where a marriage to the Spanish princess was almost achieved. He is said to have spent 15,000 pounds in entertainments as part of his efforts, no doubt to advance the Match. The King personally chose Worcester's son Thomas Somerset to go to Spain with the same fleet to foster the marriage. Three generations of one family working to restore Catholicism. Sterrell was closely involved in the efforts of 1603 and 1621-23, in both periods working with officials in Brussels. The past was not only present, it was being reenacted.

Bardophilus: That's far afield from Shakespeare and the plays. And I can't speak to historical events that arose after Shakespeare retired back to Stratford. They're just not relevant to understanding his milieu.

Skepticisima: They're terribly relevant if Shakespeare-of-Stratford isn't your author. So, let's get back to a more comfortable spot for you, *Cymbeline* and *The Tempest*. You know full well that those plays, and I can say the same for most Shakespeare plays, weren't performed for mass audiences. You know these two weren't published in any form until 1623. Perhaps they were performed for small groups of Catholics just as they had secret services.

Bardophilus: You think the Elizabethans had an early form of Readers' Theater? We have such groups on my campus. Any evidence from back then?

Skepticisima: We have the example of the *Tragedy of Mariam*. It was by Elizabeth Cary, a Catholic. Her play was for reading or recitation, not for public performance. It's called closet drama and was written about the time of Shakespeare's *Othello*. We have the evidence from Francis Meres who identified twelve plays as well as "sug'red sonnets" that were said to circulate "among his private friends." The Catholic-themed plays by Shakespeare-the-author necessarily would have been performed in secret gatherings. We do have lots of arrests and executions for Catholic religious gatherings. Two events relate to Shakespeare. The *Phoenix and Turtle* was written in memory of Saint Anne Line soon after she was executed for participating in a Catholic service in 1601. And in Shakespeare's own backyard in London we have the doleful day at Blackfriars, known as the "Fatal Vespers."

Bardophilus: Backyard? I don't recall the event. Enlighten me.

Skepticisima: Tragic. In 1623 the Blackfriars property purchased in the name of Shakespeare in 1613 was used to access a great upper room where a Jesuit priest held services. The floor collapsed. Hundreds died or were gravely injured.

Bardophilus: But Shakespeare was dead. Why do I think you're going to connect this Sterrell fellow to both of these? You've got that sly look and eyes crinkling. Okay, I'll bite.

Skepticisima: But of course, my learned friend. Sterrell worked to bribe officials to get passports for Anne Line and her brother to join her husband Roger in the Low Countries. Roger's name was on the Spanish pensioners list, which included Will Kemp, Richard Hesketh, Anthony Skinner and relatives of the Countess of Southampton and the Earl of Worcester. Just after the 1623 building failure, Sterrell reported full details in a letter to the Secretary of State in Brussels. But you wouldn't know about that. It was after Shakespeare-of-Stratford died, even though it sheds lights on his property transactions.

Bardophilus: You keep bringing up the Blackfriars property. Why? It was just an investment.

Skepticisima: You can only claim that because the Stratford crowd have always averted their eyes from this property transaction. All of you focus on the silliness of a vague allusion to "Shakescene" by Greene in 1592 while ignoring the well-documented Blackfriars property. This real estate had title litigation while Stratford was still alive, and the owners were represented by lawyers. Who were Shakespeare's fellow owners in the friendly litigation? The records show that most of them or their families were strong Catholics who were willing to have their property used as a Catholic refuge, as the property had long been used and continued to be used up to the Fatal Vespers of 1623.

Bardophilus: Can you back that up?

Skepticisima: The history of the property as a Catholic refuge is long and complicated. Let's just mention one of Shakespeare's neighbors in the 1615 case: Robert Dormer, esquire and Marie Bannister, his wife. This Dormer is a close blood relative to the Countess of Southampton and to prominent Catholic exiles. His wife was a close relative to Fr. Robert Southwell, the poet/martyr. The lawyers were from the Middle Temple where they were associated with Sterrell's prominent brother. Sterrell himself had long known about the property's use as a hiding place for priests and other Catholics.

Bardophilus: You know you are taking me down a rabbit hole when you talk law cases and lawyers.

Skepticisima: Not a rabbit hole, a priest hole. Blackfriars functioned as a huge priest hole in the middle of London. One old document refers to its back doors and bye-ways, secret vaults and dark corners, its secret passages down towards the Thames. But we'll let that go and return to your places of comfort. And where were we?

Bardophilus: Closet drama?

Skepticisima: Oh, yes, private performances or readings of *Cymbeline* or *The Tempest* or *All's Well*. Maybe these plays were shared in manuscript as was forbidden poetry like the manuscripts of Fr. Robert Southwell before and after he was executed. You spoke of Bloody Mary. Tell me, is it easier to be burnt or to be castrated, eviscerated, beheaded and quartered? That's what happened to that gentle poet, Southwell. Ordered by Elizabeth's government. For Catholics, Elizabeth was brutal. Clare Asquith has written that "Elizabeth presided over a highly successful police state." Reading these plays together by Catholics could have been a shared experience that fortified their spirits and prepared the ground for a return to toleration of their religion.

Bardophilus: You make it sound like Shakespeare was making political statements rather than trying to entertain the audience.

Skepticisima: And why wouldn't you agree? Most of the plays reflect a life-long rumination on the foundations of political authority. Let's do this. From the *First Folio*, count the plays that are not primarily concerned with the legitimacy of a ruler or sovereign.

Bardophilus: That's a heavy and tedious task. I'd rather not.

Skepticisima: Sure. Fine. Anything else you want to get off your chest?

Bardophilus: Now that you mention it. Are we stuck to some script from our author? I think he's been editing my remarks to make me a Bumblefuss, a figure of straw to caricature.

Skepticisima: Maybe so. I know he's not unsympathetic to you, and he respects your immense learning. Human curiosity cries out for some explanation of why Shakespeare is such a mystery to human understanding. Speculation has had to fill the void. You have never had a viable alternative to Stratford. Speak up and we'll see what happens.

Bardophilus: All right. It's this Kemp thing. Where's he going with this? Nobody's ever paid much attention to Kemp. He's a clown. He's not connected to politics or religion.

Skepticisima: I can only speculate what our author is getting at. What should we call him? The "author" sounds too distant and may confuse our own readers. We're not on a first name basis with him, so Pat is out. I guess this is what Shakespeare-the-author went through when he wrote *All's Well*. What to call himself? He settled on Parolles – *Words* in French. Let's turn that on our guy. How about Palabras? Spanish. Or Verba, Latin.

Bardophilus: Palabras works for me. So speculate on Kemp to your heart's content. Maybe your buddy will respond.

Skepticisima: Okay, Verba has a conspiracy theory he's building. He's got his man Sterrell that few people know anything about. He's got to deal with the fact that a William Shakespeare shows up in the historical record in 1594-95 as a shareholder in the company called the Lord Chamberlain's Men, which is really Lord Hunsdon's company. This Shakespeare fellow appears out of nowhere. He's not shown as an actor or a playwright on any record before 1594. There's only the one poem, *Venus and Adonis*, a masterpiece appearing inexplicably. Does that get the poet a seat at the table with the producers of an acting company? Does this literary stranger have money to invest or costumes and props to contribute? So, someone must have brought him into association with the little group of actors/promoters and their patron. Only in this way could Shakespeare-of-Stratford front for Sterrell and presumably his master, the Earl of Worcester. Our Verba is setting up Will Kemp as the established actor who could be in on the plot to bring Shakespeare on to the stage, so to speak. Maybe Shakespeare-of-Stratford was a minor actor with Lord Strange.

Bardophilus: Okay, I'm with you. I don't accept it, but I see the logic. Will Kemp was well-known as an actor/comedian. He's clearly with Lord Strange's Men by 1592. If he really had the connections with the English Catholic exiles, as Palabras asserts, then he'd surely know Sterrell. Kemp would also know Lady Southampton and her family and Worcester and his family to whom he and his grandmother were related. When Sterrell needs to find a way to get Shakespeare-of-Stratford to serve his turn, Kemp vouches for Shakespeare as an actor and friend who wants to invest in the formation of new company out of the remnants of Lord Strange's Men and Lord Hunsdon's men. Is that about right? Not that I believe it.

Skepticisima: Amazing. We're together, but there's zero reliable evidence that Shakespeare-of-Stratford was ever an actor.

Bardophilus: Zero? Everyone knows that he was in *Every Man in His Humour* and *Sejanus*. And he's listed in the *First Folio* as a leading actor.

Skepticisima: I said reliable. There's only one source for Shakespeare actually acting, and that is Ben Jonson long after the fact. Jonson was closely associated with Worcester and Sterrell.

Bardophilus: You're ignoring other evidence of Shakespeare acting. It's universally recognized that William Shakespeare was one of twenty-eight "players" listed as receiving red cloth for King James's delayed coronation in March 1604. Players equals actors.

Skepticisima: Moi? Ignore the red cloth? Ha! Let me ask you, who made up the list?

Bardophilus: Who cares? It's an indisputable record.

Skepticisima: The Earl Marshal for the event was the Earl of Worcester working with his secretary, Sterrell. The entire plan for that procession must have been drawn up in the Office of Revels where Sterrell presided as landlord. Worcester and Sterrell made the list and naturally named their decade-long front man.

Bardophilus: But, but, we've always assumed . . . . There must be more. Maybe we'll leave Palabras or Verba the last words. Or at least, the next.

Verba: Not my words, my esteemed professor friend, not when we can look at the words of Worcester and Sterrell themselves. Worcester, as he finalized the plans, gave his friend the Earl of Shrewsbury a preview of the coronation in a letter of February 2, 1604. The royal procession was on the "15th to pass through London to Whitehall, without any feast at all; . . . this day it was decreed." He wrote that it was:[70]

> likewise resolved that every man shall wear what apparel himself listeth, and we here resolve to ride upon footclothes, some of one colour, some of another, as they like, but the most that I hear are of purple velvet embroidered, as far as their purse will afford means. The great Ladies are appointed to ride in chariots, the Baronesses on horseback, and they that have no saddles from the King must provide of their own; the number provided are twenty, which were provided against the coronation, of crimson velvet; and this is all I can advertise you of that matter.

Sterrell, under his alias of Rivers, wrote an account to a correspondent (perhaps Fr. Persons) of the coronation procession which indicates he was in it as it progressed. We can assume that he was close by Worcester:[71]

> The next day, being the 15th of March, His Majesty with the Queen and Prince, attended by all the nobility of both sexes and the principal officers of his household, passed in most triumphant manner through London, where arches or pageants were made in the way; all the streets railed and adorned on both sides, and the Companies of the City standing on one side all in order from the Tower to Temple Bar. The Earl of Worcester was Earl Marshal, the Lord Mayor carried the sceptre, all the aldermen attended at the cross, and presented the King, Queen, and Prince with three fair standing cups of gold. The Earl of Arundell had his place as *primus comes*. The Queen rode in an open chariot and gave good contentment by her pleasing countenance and affability to the people. The King kept greater state, saluting, by moving his cap, the Ambassadors of France and Spain, placed in several houses in Cheapside. The like he did to the aldermen. The Lady Arabella and the old Countess of Arundell followed the Queen in caroche, all the rest of the ladies on horseback; both lords and ladies were richly and gallantly attired; and so they passed to Whitehall.

Worcester chose Ben Jonson and the great actor Edward Alleyn, who had begun his career with Worcester's company, to give speeches to honor the new king. But not Shakespeare. If Shakespeare were a celebrated author and actor, why was he relegated to silence? Because the two men who planned the event were the truth about "Shakespeare."

The Countess of Southampton and the dedication

We should view Sterrell's goals for the dedication of *Venus and Adonis* to Southampton as multi-purposed – looking to the earl himself for employment as a secretary but also directed implicitly towards the persons who were closest to him, others who could favor the poet in a different sort. If Sterrell could sufficiently ingratiate himself with Southampton, how likely would Essex be to ruin Sterrell with the Queen and turn aside Southampton's entreaties on the poet's behalf? And there was another person close to Southampton who might be most pleased by the dedication: Southampton's mother, who sought to reclaim her son . . . and his soul. She also had great reason for animus against the queen (who is mocked in *Venus and Adonis*). Queen Elizabeth had displaced the Browne family (Viscount Montagu) from its lofty status at Court and deprived her father and brother of a Catholic burial.

Now William Sterrell was intensely aware of the dissension that had occurred between the Countess Southampton and her late husband. And he knew of the very recent deaths in her family. The man responsible (in some accounts) for the discord between the couple was Charles Paget, a Catholic exile who betrayed Sterrell to Ralph Winwood in 1602. The writer of "A Letter from a Catholic at Brussels to his friend, a Monk at Liège,"[72] probably William Sterrell himself, expressed the role Paget had played in alienating Henry Wriothesley from his wife in language that can only be described as Shakespearean. This passage is too impressive to reduce to a dull summary:

> It is a wonderful thing amongst the diversities of nature to see and consider the restless spirits and busy brains of some that can never be quiet nor repose in any estate, but be continually hammering new devices to the hurt many times of others and overthrow in the end of themselves: of this humour is Mr Charles Paget, who from the first hour that his years permitted him to converse with men hath evermore been tampering in broils and practices betwixt the bark and the tree, friend and friend, man and wife, and as his credit and craft increased betwixt Prince and Prince. And this being as natural unto him as to eat drink or sleep, it is as impossible to leave it as to forbear any one of the other.

The "man and wife" to whom he referred were Mary Browne and Henry Wriothesley. Charles Paget could be the model for Iago in *Othello,* tearing apart husband and wife with little motive except envy, even as he traduced the state. For his involvement in the Babington Plot (aimed at replacing Elizabeth with Mary Queen of Scots), Paget was attainted of treason by Parliament in 1587 and later accepted a Spanish pension. Paget and his co-conspirator, Thomas Morgan, continued in the Low Countries to roil relations among the English exiles. Sterrell mentions the Countess of Southampton in other correspondence with Catholic exiles later. We will return to Morgan in Chapter 7 when the playwright introduces him by name in *All's Well that Ends Well.*

William Sterrell was very closely connected to the tight circle of the Countess of Southampton and the business manager who oversaw her properties and her son's. Here we return to Sterrell's friend Anthony Skinner. When the Countess became a widow in 1581, the executor of her husband's will was Edward Gage. He now became the Countess's (and her infant son's) business manager. This Gage was closely related to Alice Gage, the grandmother of the Countess of Southampton, and to Will Kemp's family. Edward Gage of Bentley in the county of Sussex would become father-in-law to Anthony Skinner. Lady Southampton's second husband, Sir Thomas Heneage, was the man who saved Anthony Skinner from execution in 1592-93.

The person who would have been most pleased by a dedication of *Venus and Adonis* to the Earl of Southampton was the Earl's mother. As we have seen, Southampton's guardian, Lord Burghley, sponsored in 1592 *Narcissus* by his secretary, James Clapham. The Latin poem was dedicated to Southampton as a device to encourage Burghley's ward to marry his granddaughter or shame him for declining. Would the Countess not be highly pleased by the dedication to her son of a superior poem by a man whom she knew to be a Catholic assisting English exiles? Perhaps the poet could be her secretary or her son's secretary. Or she might otherwise reward such a lavish work for a noble son and for services to her friends overseas. The boy's father had tried to separate her from her son and daughter; now, too, did Lord Burghley. She could show her devotion to her son by rewarding the poet who honored him by the dedication of *Venus and Adonis*, which also mocked the woman who had deprived the Browne family of its intimate connection with the Crown and with Rome — the "wicked queen" of *Cymbeline*.

Only three years after the publication of *Venus and Adonis* we will see Sterrell undertake an extraordinary trip to Spain with Thomas Thorpe (publisher of *Shake-speares Sonnets*). The purpose apparently was to provide for the financial security of the Countess's beloved niece, the daughter of the Countess's recently-deceased twin brother. In a probate deposition/affidavit Thorpe gave no reason for his inexplicable trip to an enemy country as it prepared a new armada nor why he was the guest of the notorious exile Fr. Robert Persons.[73] So, we ask, who would benefit from Thorpe's extraordinary trip into Spain?

The estate of Wootton Bassett was held for life by Sir Francis Englefield, but it had been adjudicated to the crown for his treason. Upon his death, the property could still be inherited by the owner of the remainder interest under the entail. That was his nephew of the same name, Francis Englefield, who was married to the Countess of Southampton's niece, Jane. Thorpe's deposition as to the death of Sir Francis enabled the property to pass to the owner under the entail. Without Thorpe's eyewitness evidence, proof of death would have been impossible for years, if ever. Thorpe performed an invaluable service for the Countess of Southampton. Would that service not be a reason for her third husband to pass to Thorpe a collection of sonnets that were in her possession at her death in 1607? Her widower was her third husband, Sir William Hervey . . . the "Mr. W. H." whom Thorpe acknowledged as "The Onlie Begetter of these Insuing Sonnets" not long after her death. Perhaps it was pursuant to her wishes that "Mr. W. H." gave them to Thorpe, with the poet's personal blessing.

Another Example of Dedication, Content and Context: *The Phoenix Nest*:

We can better understand the poet's dedication to Southampton if we examine closely a book that was in preparation simultaneously with *Venus and Adonis* but by a different printer. It is the *Phoenix Nest* discussed briefly above for the poem contributed by "W.S. Gent."

Skip over this segment if you are bored by tedious details, however compelling they may be.

Here, too, scholars have been mistaken about an authorship/editor question for many years because they have failed to identify the persons in whose honor a dedication is intended. They have failed to see that the *Phoenix Nest* was directed in large part by its editor to Essex and his sister Penelope. They have tried to find a connection of "R.S. of the Inner Temple" to the contributors rather than the heirs/family of the Earl of Leicester and Philip Sidney, namely Essex and Penelope and to the father of "R.S. of the Inner Temple." This is the same error of scholars looking at the dedicatee of *Venus and Adonis,* Southampton, rather than at his close friends, Essex and Penelope, or his mother, the Countess. It was to Essex and Penelope that these two books were primarily directed (jointly with Southampton in *Venus and Adonis*) and they could not have mistaken the person(s) who edited and composed the contents of the books.

The *Phoenix Nest* collection is one of the most interesting and attractive of the Elizabethan poetical miscellanies, consisting of, as its frontispiece declared, "refined works . . . full of varietie, excellent invention, and singular delight" written by "Noble men, worthy knights, gallant Gentlemen, Masters of Arts, and brave Schollers." These compositions were "Never before this time published." The *Phoenix Nest* contains 79 poems, of which 28 have initials that partially identify seven of the poets.[74] Three more of the writers have been identified without initials, and conjectures have been made about the authors of the other poems. There may be as many as fifteen (or more) contributors, many very accomplished.

The *Stationer's Register* entry of October 8, 1593, for the *Phoenix Nest* said the book was "intituled *the Phœnix neste* & Compiled by RS." The publisher of *The Phoenix Nest* was John Jackson "and his partners." Jackson was a member of the Grocers Company rather than the Stationers Company. His partners were unnamed, but in other publications Jackson teamed with Arnold Hatfield (freed 1581) and Edmond Bollifant (freed 1583), both of whom are listed in the Stationers Company as freedmen (each had his first publication in 1586).[75] That Jackson was the named publisher suggests the publication was a business transaction differing from the partners' normal ventures. We later see John Jackson in a business transaction as a trustee for William Shakespeare in 1613, along with John Heminges and another person. Jackson and Heminges probably knew each other from the fact both were freedmen of the Grocers Company (not Stationers) and contemporaries who entered business in London.

Why is this book important to us? Most immediately, it is about the nature of dedications and the desire to associate with Essex and his circle through poetry. Second, if we are correct that "W.S. Gent." is William Sterrell, it suggests a second publication in which he wanted to favor Essex, and it places him in the company of the most active poets and writers of 1593 England. Sterrell thus should be counted as one of the "University Wits" who was solicited to contribute to the *Phoenix Nest* by its noteworthy compiler. It shows also an early association with John Jackson, a businessman of the Grocers Company who is later a trustee for Shakespeare in the purchase of property in London. Why Jackson was chosen to print the *Phoenix Nest* will de discussed in connection with the Shakespeare will below. Third, it takes us into the poetic environment of London into which the poet of *Venus and Adonis* thrust himself as a competitor in May 1593. This was the milieu of Shakespeare's "Invention."

Even if you are not open to the authorship controversy, you will profit by understanding the milieu of poetry and patronage of the period. An unpublished "Shakespeare" in 1593 was entering an arena of highly educated, well-connected writers and gentlemen who sought to establish their reputations and the support they needed to pursue their craft. The authors of the *Phoenix Nest* are a representative sample of these gentlemen competitors seeking to earn or burnish their literary reputations. When we examine their backgrounds and their patrons we see how improbable it is that an uneducated commoner from Stratford, with not even the title of gentleman and no connections to gentry or nobility could possibly have found access to a young nobleman, a printer, and a stationer to sell his "first heir," *Venus and Adonis.*

The *Phoenix Nest* collection begins with a dedicatory eulogy to Robert Dudley, the Earl of Leicester: a Preface that precedes "The dead man's Right." The author of the preface acknowledges the dedication is not for the dead dedicatee who cannot reward him for his work: "I write not (gentle Reader) to flatter, for the vain are not vainglorious: nor to gain, they reward not travels [travails, work]: for pride lesse [i.e. I write not for my own pride/reputation], they are other mens virtues not my own that I publish . . . I seek no other hire nor glory . . . ." He tells us directly he is wealthy enough to have no need for patronage, and his family name is already illustrious. If anything, he says, he wishes to clear Leicester's name. "The dead man's Right" seeks to do this.

The *Phoenix Nest's* preface is immediately followed by three anonymous elegies to Sir Philip Sidney, Leicester's nephew, who died in 1586 of wounds received at Zutphen, in the Spanish Low Countries. As we have seen, both of these men were closely associated with the Earl of Essex: Leicester was Essex's stepfather and Sidney was the closest friend of Essex, with him at Zutphen when Sidney received his fatal wound. Sidney left Essex his sword, and Essex married Sidney's widow. Sidney had written a series of love sonnets on "Astrophil" (Sidney) and "Stella" (Essex's sister, Penelope Devereux, Lady Rich), and their identities are alluded to in the first poem of the *Phoenix Nest*. That poem even speaks directly to "Stella." Penelope would know the book was for her eyes.

We can readily surmise the compiler and presumably all of the contributors were desirous of the good will of the people closest to the name and reputation of Leicester and Sidney: Essex and his sister Penelope/Stella. The poet-contributors all knew the identity of "R.S. of the Inner Temple," and they knew also his notable father. They would assume the work proceeded from both men. The contributors were friends of Essex, Penelope and "R.S." and had every reason to seek the good will of "R.S." and his very powerful father. Only a very influential sponsor could gather such an extraordinary group of living literary luminaries.

Let's look at the title page of the *Phoenix Nest*: It is exquisite, suitable for the "refined works" inside. From its announcement it was: "Set forth by R.S. of the Inner Temple, gentleman," The identification of R.S. of the Inner Temple seems simple enough. There was one well-known R. S. who was a member of the Inner Temple in 1593 and a gentleman: Robert Sackville, son of Thomas Sackville,

Baron Buckhurst (later Lord Treasurer and Earl of Dorset).

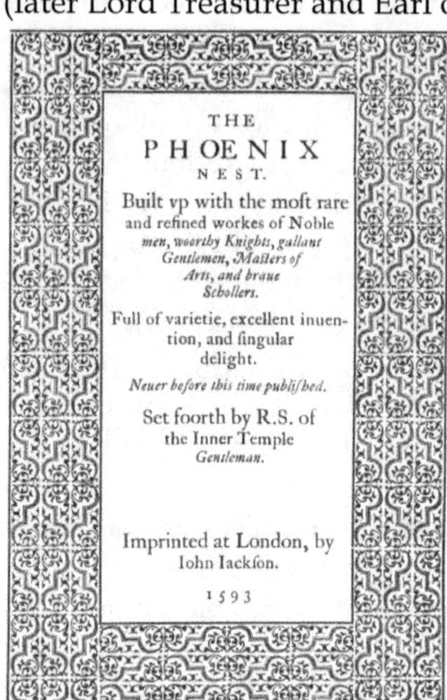
THE
PHOENIX
NEST.
Built vp with the most rare and refined workes of Noble men, woorthy Knights, gallant Gentlemen, Masters of Arts, and braue Schollers.
Full of varietie, excellent inuention, and singular delight.
Neuer before this time published.
Set foorth by R.S. of the Inner Temple *Gentleman.*
Imprinted at London, by Iohn Iackson.
1593

As a child Robert Sackville was tutored by Roger Ascham, most famous as tutor to Elizabeth I. Ascham dedicated his noted book *The Schoolmaster*, on the teaching of Latin, to little Robert, another instance of a dedication to a child to honor a parent/grandparent. The book was written at the encouragement of Robert's grandfather, Sir Richard Sackville, a cousin to Queen Anne Boleyn, a Treasurer of the Exchequer, and Privy Councilor under Queens Mary and Elizabeth. In a touching remembrance of Sir Richard, Ascham dedicated his thoughts to the young man who was the cause of the book's writing:

> I wish also, with all my heart, that young Mr. Robert Sackville may take that fruit of this labor, that his worthy Grandfather purposed he should have done: And if any other do take either profit or pleasure hereby, they have cause to thank Mr. Robert Sackville, for whom specially this my *Schoolmaster* was provided.

As an adult, Robert wanted to make a literary contribution of his own to England's literary heritage, like his grandfather, his father, and Roger Ascham.

Robert Sackville's father, Chancellor Buckhurst, was not only a member of the Inner Temple, he was an author of *The Tragedie of Gorboduc.* The play was first performed at the Christmas celebration given by the Inner Temple in 1561 and then at Whitehall before Queen Elizabeth on January 18, 1561. Lord Buckhurst had distinguished himself as a poet with the *Induction,* the most famous part of *The Mirror for Magistrates* (1563), and the poem *Complaint of Buckingham* in the same edition. He wrote other notable poetry in English and Latin.

Editors of the *Phoenix Nest* during the past century have been doubtful that Robert Sackville was the compiler and promoter because they could not find sufficient connections of Robert Sackville with the contributors. They failed to see those connections. They also did not perceive that Essex and his sister Penelope, Lady Rich, were the actual persons of interest for the contributors to dedicate their collected works to. The poems had not been published before 1593, so they were all written for the collection or taken off the shelf for inclusion. Moreover, they were among the best poets of the day. As they used only initials or honorifics they must have contributed to the book for their personal connections with the editor and/or the real honorees of the book. With only initials, they would expect neither fame or recompense - only friendship and honor which they could not receive from the named dedicatees, who were five and eight years deceased.

Robert Sackville of the Inner Temple had many reasons to put together one of the loveliest compilations of poetry of the period. One, it was a memorial to his late wife who was well known among some of the poets. Secondly, it was a tribute to his father's elevation to Chancellor of Oxford, where that father had earned an M.A. degree, and where Robert himself had earned the B.A. and M.A. degrees. Robert was a student at Oxford around the same time as a number of the poets in the *Phoenix Nest,* often referred to as the University Wits. The book demonstrated to his father Robert's own literary achievement, not only in bringing the book into being but probably by inclusion of some of the unnamed poems that Robert may have written. For many poets of the book, Robert was their Maecenas - as was also his father, their distinguished poet predecessor. Lord Buckhurst's own poetry had influenced strongly their poems and writings. As Chancellor of Oxford University, a knight of the Garter and a Privy Councilor, he could still influence their careers and their standing at Court. None would be surprised that he would later be created Earl of Dorset and appointed Lord Treasurer of England.

The dedications of *Phoenix Nest* to Leicester and Sidney would patch up relations of the Sackvilles with Essex and Penelope. Why? Leicester had incurred the great displeasure of Queen Elizabeth by accepting a title of governor-general of the Netherlands from the States-General of the Dutch, contrary to her express command. Lord Buckhurst was sent by Queen Elizabeth as a special envoy to the Dutch to convey her displeasure and concerns, and he became caught up in the feud between Elizabeth and Leicester. Buckhurst incurred the enmity of both, though he was later restored in relations to them, albeit with hurt feelings. In 1593, Lord Buckhurst had recently been appointed the Chancellor of Oxford University, after Queen Elizabeth forced the university to elect him over Essex, who had much popular support.[76] Robert Sackville and his father both had reasons to seek good relations with Essex and his circle. The dedications of *Phoenix Nest* coming from the household of the Sackvilles could soothe the multiple wounds of the recent past via Essex and Penelope. In addition, Robert Sackville and Philip Sidney served together as Members in the 1584 Parliament.[77] Likely, they had been friends and political allies, hence Robert Sackville wished to honor Sidney and Leicester by dedicating the *Phoenix Nest* to them.

Robert Sackville's late wife was Lady Margaret Howard, so that Sackville was connected with the Howard family, the Rich family (Penelope Devereux was Lady Rich) and the de Vere family Thus, Edward de Vere, Earl of Oxford contributed a poem to the *Phoenix Nest*.

Sackville was even more closely connected to the family of the Countess of Southampton and the young earl to whom *Venus and Adonis* was dedicated. A bit more than a year before the *Phoenix Nest,* Robert Sackville's sister Jane had married into the family of the Earl of Southampton. Jane Sackville, in February 1591, married Anthony Maria Browne, son of the Countess of Southampton's twin brother. On the death of his grandfather (Countess Southampton's father) in 1592, Anthony Maria Browne became Second Viscount Montagu, one of the wealthiest peers in England. Because his father was the twin of Mary Browne Wriothesley, he was nephew of the Countess of Southampton and first cousin of the young Earl of Southampton. Robert Sackville's sister then was part of the strongly Catholic network from which are drawn some of the poets of *Phoenix Nest* as was Sackville's late wife (Jane's sister-in-law).

Just how Catholic Anthony Maria Browne, Second Viscount Montagu and his wife Jane Sackville were we can learn from a letter of William Sterrell written just a few months after the *Phoenix Nest* was published. Sterrell as "Wicham" provided news of interest to overseas members of other families. To Fr. Richard Sherwood, an English Catholic priest in exile, he reported that "the young Lord Mountague [was] commited for Christening his own child, because no heretic should christen it as *he terms them*."[78] In June 1593, Montagu's first child had died on the day he was supposed to be baptized according to the rites of the Church of England. The grieving father blamed himself for consenting to a non-Catholic baptism. On the arrival of a second child within a year, he baptized the child himself at Lord Buckhurst's home where his wife Jane Sackville was recovering, saying he could find no seminary priest. Buckhurst was upset with his son-in-law, who remained under house arrest for about a year. Anthony Maria Browne grew more strongly Catholic after his experience with the hostility of the state to the privacy of a christening.

For Sterrell to have first-hand knowledge of such an intimate family problem indicates close associations with the family of the Countess Southampton and the Sackvilles. As Viscount Montagu was Countess Southampton's nephew, the child he had self-baptized was her very close relative. Sterrell may have received his information directly from the Countess, to whose son he had dedicated *Venus and Adonis*, or from Viscount Montagu's brother-in-law, Robert Sackville, to whose anthology the *Phoenix Nest* Sterrell had recently contributed a poem. Other intercepted letters under several of Sterrell's aliases as well as letters preserved in church archives discuss news regarding both the Earl of Southampton and his mother in the period 1599-1602. These demonstrate extraordinary familiarity with the highest members of the Court, including Robert Sackville and the Earl of Southampton.

One long letter of January 13, 1601, just before Essex's fall, was to Fr. Robert Persons in Rome. Among many topics of interest to Persons was discussion of Essex's visits from Robert Sackville carrying assurances from his father, Lord Buckhurst, "to tell him that he had dealt effectually with her Majestie in his behalf and was in hope to have brought it to good forwardness, had not his Lordship, in three respects hindered him. . . ." The three concerns of the Lord Treasurer were described, as were Essex's responses, which must have been related by Robert Sackville. The next paragraphs concerned Southampton: "The Earle of Southampton is now again in good grace with her Majestie and hath free access unto the court. The old quarrel continues between him and the lord Grey . . ." It goes on to describe at length a confrontation between the two men. William Sterrell clearly had direct access to the men or to members of their household.

Two other Sackville siblings were Catholic. Robert Sackville's sister Anne was Catholic and married to a strong Catholic, Henry Glenham. Glenham was put in prison for a time in 1600 for having visited Rome and there having conversation with Fr. Persons. Persons himself noted in 1600 that Buckhurst, Robert Sackville's father, was "at heart Catholic, though he does not appear so exteriorly." [79] Persons commented that Buckhurst married his son, Robert, to Lady Margaret as a good Catholic "and when she died, he married his son to another Catholic Lady. His two daughters also he has married to Catholics . . ."[80] Robert Sackville's younger brother, Thomas, himself traveled to Rome in 1602 and was received into the Catholic church by Fr. Persons.[81] On his return, his father told him to keep his trip secret but allowed him to return to Rome, where he met with the Spanish ambassador, the Duke of Sessa.

While there is no direct mention of Sackville's deceased wife in the *Phoenix Nest*, she is an important consideration to the collection. Her chaplain and close friend was the poet/priest Robert Southwell. He was in prison, sentenced to be executed, when the book was published. Several anonymous poems in the *Phoenix Nest* were probably by Southwell (his influential poetry circulated in manuscript). Also in prison for religion was the poet and Earl, Philip

Howard, Earl of Arundel, who was closely related to Robert Sackville. Margaret Howard, Sackville's late wife, was half-sister to Philip Howard. When Margaret Sackville died at the age of twenty-nine, Southwell composed a prose elegy, *Triumphs over Death,* that was addressed to Philip Howard, the Earl of Arundel, to console him for his sister's death. It was published in 1596 under Sackville patronage.[82] The book was dedicated to Robert Sackville and the children of his marriage with Lady Margaret.

We can see other ways in which *The Phoenix Nest* was connected with the circle of the Earl of Essex, as was *Venus and Adonis.* Leicester and Sidney were both closely identified with Oxford University, Leicester its Chancellor and Sidney a product of Christ Church College, Oxford. Most of the identifiable poets of *the Phoenix Nest* were associated with Oxford University at about the same time, as well as poets suspected of contributing, such as John Lyly (of Magdalen College). All the contributors probably knew one another. The *Phoenix Nest* editor Hyder E. Rollins observed that a "number of the contributors are known to have had associations with one another. Breton, Dyer, Eeds, Lodge, Peele, Raleigh, Roydon and perhaps Watson had been students at Oxford at about the same time and Greene was a Master of Arts there." [83] He added that "R.S. included poems only from those authors whom he knew personally . . . ."

Our compiler Robert Sackville matriculated from Hart Hall, Oxford in December 1576, aged fifteen, and graduated B.A. and M.A. on 3 June 1579 – just at the time many of the known contributors were at Oxford. And if in 1593 Robert, the son of the current Chancellor of Oxford, Thomas Sackville, Lord Buckhurst (himself a poet) called upon his old friends to share a poem or two in honor of their former Chancellor and one of their friends, Philip Sidney, from their time with Leicester and Sidney, who among them would have declined?

William Sterrell was well known among the Oxfordians as a prominent Fellow and *praelector.* So it requires little imagination to suppose him to be "W.S. Gent"; he was a man who owed a great debt to Leicester for his award of the M.A. and thus continuation at Oxford. Because both Leicester and Sidney were dead, the *Phoenix Nest* was designed to please the two people closest to them: Essex and his sister, as well as Leicester's natural son, Robert Dudley, whom we found dining in London with William Sterrell just as *Venus and Adonis* was about to be published and a few months before the *Phoenix Nest.*

Moreover, Sterrell had another very close connection to Robert Sackville in 1593. Sterrell had just spent the Christmas holidays at Raglan with Lord William Compton, (the Earl of Worcester's nephew). Compton was the stepson of Robert Sackville's new wife Anne, daughter of Sir John Spencer (married Dec. 1592). Anne was the widow of Baron Henry Compton (Lord William Compton's father), and her two sisters were married to the patrons of the two leading companies of actors, Alice to Ferdinando Stanley (Lord Strange's Men) and Elizabeth to George Carey (Lord Hunsdon's aka Lord Chamberlain's Men). As Worcester and Lord Compton and Lord Buckhurst (Sackville's father) were meeting in the House of Lords February 19 to April 10, 1593, they were all socializing with Sterrell and Robert Sackville likely present. There is evidence of other Sackville connections to William Sterrell and his brother Henry.[84]

"W. S. Gent." probably made his contribution to the *Phoenix Nest* miscellany in 1592, months before the published *Venus and Adonis* in May 1593. It would have taken Robert Sackville many months to collect and edit the 79 poems from 15 or more poets and get them into print about five months later. When *Phoenix Nest* appeared, the collection's poets and readers would have no reason to connect W.S. Gent. with Shakespeare and *Venus and Adonis.*

In short, William Sterrell surely knew many of the illustrious poets of the *Phoenix Nest.* He knew their works. He understood the poetry of the period and how *Venus and Adonis* would fit into this time of poetic flourishing. A number were at Oxford with him. They probably would have remembered him as a gifted professor at Oxford but lost track of him when he disappeared into the nether world of intelligence work overseas more two years before publication of the *Phoenix Nest.* We can imagine the exchange.

Q: "Whatever happened to Sterrell, that Magdalen Fellow?"

A: "Last I heard he was a follower of Worcester, but Worcester dismissed him last March."

Q: "Isn't the Privy Council charging him with something? Or was that Kit Marlowe?"

A: "Pity. So promising."

There is zero evidence that Shakespeare-of-Stratford ever had anything to do with any other poets of this era before his death in 1616. For traditional Shakespeare scholars, *Venus and Adonis* burst upon the literary world as if by spontaneous generation, perfectly in sync with the times and the poetry-consuming public.

With the *Phoenix Nest* and *A Notable Description* we gain insight into what life might have held for William Sterrell, Oxford scholar, had he not hidden his identity. Under his own name/initials he could have been one of the University Wits, a clever man-about-town in urbane London. Like his confrères, he could toady up to the nobility and solicit their patronage by effusive (but insincere) praise. His poetry would be constrained to the demands of the genre into which they fit: airy, pleasing, non-controversial, lightly amusing flights-of-fancy, even if they often claimed to be "wrapped in woe" in stylized "plaints" of grief and sorrow. Rather like his well-crafted and pleasant sonnet, *Phaëton to his Friend Florio,* the title of which hinted at some awful event as its source. Again we ask, why did Florio's friend see himself as Phaëton?

Writing behind the mask of unknown's name for publication had a liberating effect. As with the anonymity of the internet today, it allowed the writer to express himself in ways that he could not as an Oxford professor or as the secretary of a nobleman who could be embarrassed by the controversial writings of a mere servant. *Venus and Adonis* could be erotic in a way no Oxford professor would be allowed to express himself. Behind the name of an unknown actor the secretary to a great earl could mock Queen Elizabeth without consequence to himself or his master. Poets and actors, like Court jesters, had license to push the boundaries in ways not allowed to others in society.

Chapter 5

Shakespeare-of-Stratford to 1594

Shakespeare, Lost Years

Venus and Adonis must have an author. Its composer could not remain anonymous as he did for the *Phaëton* sonnet. He should not use his initials as he did for *A Notable Description,* published in an anthology with numerous poets. Initials would only invite inquiry if he were successful. Spies were despised, even then. Commonly, they were referred to with opprobrium as two-faced, deceitful, infamous, projectors, watchers. A single word pseudonym, such as *Ryalta* or *Publius* or *Roldan,* would excite a guessing game. And a purely made-up name? It would only heighten a search for the true author, as occurred with the apocryphal Martin Marprelate, the name used by the anonymous author or authors of seven notorious religious tracts that circulated during 1588-89. When discovered, his own name would likely expose Sterrell as a Catholic spy trying to shed an infamous background. Think here of the Hollywood writers of the 1950s, blacklisted as suspected communists, who adopted false names to continue their writing, even going to prison. Dalton Trumbo became Robert Rich and Hugh Butler; Ring Lardner Jr. continued to write in Britain as Oliver Skene (among others); Walter Bernstein used Paul Bauman and Leo Davis to disguise himself. Imagine how a man identified by multiple sources in 1585 at Oxford and at the French embassy as a corrupter of youth would have been treated. Sterrell could not publish under his own name.

There had to be a man behind a name, a name of someone obscure but credible as a source. A man associated with players might be both obscure and credible. We can't be certain how Sterrell settled on "Shakespeare," only that he did. Perhaps it was the young man whom scholars know as "William Shakshafte." This name appeared in a 1581 will and has been identified (not without dispute) as Shakespeare-of-Stratford. It is as good an explanation as any of how "Shakespeare" may have become a part of Lord Strange's men, which, in turn, was the core of the 1594 establishment of the Lord Chamberlain's company.

We will first locate young "William Shakshafte." We will then connect him with Will Kemp and the Stanleys who sponsored Lord Strange's Men. Into the mix we will add Christopher Marlowe.

ꟼꟼꟼꟼ--ꟻꟻꟻꟻ

Shakespeare scholars, eager to account for the playwright's "lost years" between childhood in Stratford and his appearance in records of 1593, have seized upon a young man named "William Shakshafte" who was found in the 1581 will of a wealthy Lancashire landowner. The testator was Alexander Hoghton, Esq. who made grants to his many servants, one of whom was Shakshafte. Hoghton's will recommended Foke Gyllome and William Shakshafte to Sir Thomas Hesketh of Rufford Hall together with Hoghton's play-clothes and musical instruments if his brother didn't want the latter. The will singled out two of his many servants for special consideration:

> And I most heartily require the said Sir Thomas to be friendly unto Foke Gyllome & William Shakshafte now dwelling with me & ether to take them unto his service or else to help them to some good master, as my trust is he will.

Hoghton also gave Shakeshafte (and Gyllome) a grant of forty shillings as a pension - a share of rents designated to a group of thirty servants in which Shakeshafte was named.

Shakespeare scholars debate whether the name Shakeshafte was an effort to disguise Shakespeare's identity. The scrivener of the will probably wrote down what *he* had heard - Shakeshafte, Shakshafte, Shakestaffe, Shakespeare, what's the difference? The mind in spelling works both phonetically and by retained images. A *speare* is a *shafte* and a *staff*. No scholar has ever claimed that Revels Accounts of plays performed at Court in the winter of 1604-05 by *Shaxberd* reflected anything but peculiarity of spelling by a clerk. The spellings of most names were inconsistent, as well as the spellings of many common words of English. There was no English dictionary before 1604. Throughout England there were regional accents and dialects that affected spellings based on phonetics. Much of the population did not consistently spell their own names and wrote infrequently, if at all.

Of the six supposedly authentic signatures of Shakespeare-of-Stratford, none is spelled as we all spell it now, Shakespeare. Instead they are:

1. 1612 (*Bellott v Mountjoy* deposition): "**Willm Shakp**"
2. March 1613 (Blackfriars conveyance): "**William Shakspēr**"
3. March 1613 (Blackfriars mortgage): "**Wm Shakspē**"
4. March 1616 (Will, page 1): "**William Shakspere**"
5. March 1616 (Will, page 2): "**Willm Shakspere**"
6. March 1616 (Will, page 3): "By me **William Shakspeare**"

Consider how the lengthy will of Alexander Hoghton must have come into being. With all the legal formalities, it is highly unlikely that Alexander wrote it himself. Nor is it likely he had a lawyer on staff, though his brother-in-law of Gray's Inn was a lawyer. So, a lawyer from a neighboring town comes in and takes down notes from what an ill man tells him (will of August 3, 1581, proved 5 weeks later, September 12, 1581). Upwards of fifty names are included in the body of the will. Based on the transcription by Ernst Honigmann, the spellings of names are internally inconsistent, Fulk Gillom is also given as Fulk Gyllom; John Hoghton is also given as John Houghton; Roger Crichlowe is also Roger Crichlawe (written Critchlowe or Croichlawe in other records of the period). Others who have made transcriptions of the same will have written Foke Gyllome, such as E. K. Chambers in *Shakespeare Gleanings* who also has it as "ffoke Gyllome." Another scholar, Douglas Hamer, has it "Fulke Gillom" and "ffowke Gyllom."

Someone in the household may have told a clerk or lawyer to write the bequest for William Shakespeare, and it was written down as Shakeshafte; the surname Shakeshafte was a not uncommon name in the local records. According to Hamer, there were 45 Shakeshaftes in the relevant period and few Shakespeares.[85] E. K. Chambers commented that he had "noted the numerous variations in the spelling of the name Shakespeare, the not infrequent appearance of Shakeshaft, an example of a Shakeschaft and a Shakestaff holding land together in Shropshire, and in particular the fact that the poet's grandfather, Richard, seems to be both Shakstaff and

Shakeschafte, as well as Shakspere, Shakespere, Shakkespere, and Shaxpere, in the Snitterfield manor records."[86]

It's impossible to say how many names of servants in the will were spelled wrong. The thirty or more named servants were surely not present at the writing of the will nor given an opportunity to correct a name. Even if an error was discovered, no one would rewrite a lengthy will to correct a seventeen-year-old servant's name when anyone reading the will would know exactly the person who was intended as beneficiary.

So, did William Shakespeare go from Alexander Hoghton's service to Sir Thomas Hesketh's service as a player and then into Lord Strange's Men?

Shakespeare scholars have struggled to have Shakeshafte end up in the company of players known as Derby's players or Lord Strange's Servants by first becoming part of the players for a company run by Sir Thomas Hesketh of Rufford . . . which has never been shown to exist. The Hesketh Players were called into existence by 1) the assumption that if Shakeshafte were to go to Sir Thomas, he must have a company of actors; and by 2) an obscure entry in a record of a visit by Sir Thomas to the Earl of Derby's house on December 30, 1587 which states: "On Saturday Sr Tho. Hesketh Players went awaie."[87] Scholars have incautiously read this as "Sir Tho. Hesketh's Players went away," rather than Sir Thomas and Derby's players went away on the same date, or as Douglas Hamer wrote: "The entry probably means, 'Sir Thomas Hesketh came and the players went away.'" There's no record of a Hesketh company.

But yes, surely Shakeshafte did have a route into the Derby/Lord Strange company of actors. That's because he was already well-known to the Stanleys by being a servant of Alexander Hoghton and his second wife Elizabeth Hesketh Hoghton.

Here is what all Shakespeare scholars have missed about Shakeshafte at Hoghton Tower: Alexander Hoghton's second wife Elizabeth was the daughter of Gabriel Hesketh of Aughton by Gabriel's *first* wife. Elizabeth Hesketh Hoghton had four Hesketh brothers (two are named in Alexander's will) by her father's second wife, the eldest of whom was Thomas Hesketh. This Thomas was a lawyer of Gray's Inn who was executor of the will, and

Bartholomew Hesketh was a witness and supervisor to the will. Cuthbert and Richard Hesketh were two other brothers.

These Hesketh brothers were from Gabriel Hesketh's *second* wife, Jane Halsall. Gabriel Hesketh seems to have died about 1570, and now his widow became the common law wife of a neighboring lord: Henry Stanley, the 4th Earl of Derby. She bore him four children, beginning shortly after 1570. This great man was estranged from his own wife but still close to his children by her; these children lived in or visited his household which he maintained with Jane Halsall Hesketh. He was So when Shakeshafte was in the Hoghton household, Alexander Hoghton's wife was close to her four half-brothers who were now in the household of their common law stepfather with their four half-siblings and Lord Derby's children by his lawful wife. These latter children included Ferdinando Stanley (Lord Strange), who will become the 5th Earl of Derby.

Ferdinando himself had recently married (in secret from Queen Elizabeth, but no secret to his family) to a well-educated young woman, Alice Spencer, who shared her new husband's interest in the theater; she's later a great patron of poets. If Jane Halsall and Henry Stanley were common law spouses, their many children may be called common law siblings. One of the children of the Henry Stanley–Jane Halsall Hesketh relationship, Ursula, may have a later Shakespeare connection.

Confusing? Yes. This is why it has always been overlooked. The chart below will make it clear(er) with ages at 1580 for a few of the family members.[88]

Gabriel Hesketh – Elizabeth Gerard (#1)	Gabriel Hesketh – Jane Halsall (#2)	Henry Stanley – Margaret Clifford (#1)	Henry Stanley (49)– Jane Halsall (#2 – common law) (54?)
Elizabeth Hesketh - Alex. Hoghton ---------- Their servant is William Shakeshafte (17?)	Bartholomew Hesketh (38) Thomas Hesketh (32) Cuthbert Hesketh (30) Rich. Hesketh (27)	Edward Stanley (23) Ferd. Stanley (21) William Stanley (19) Francis Stanley (deceased)	Henry Stanley (3) Thomas Stanley (10?) Ursula Stanley (10) Dorothy Stanley (?)

So, in 1580-81 William Shakeshafte/Shakespeare was a favored servant in a household of interacting Hoghtons, Hesketh (four by Jane Halsall Hesketh), and Stanleys (four legitimate by Margaret Clifford) and four illegitimates by Jane Halsall Hesketh (who are called Stanley or Halsall at different times). Quite the extended family. It's clear from Alexander Hoghton's will that he was close to at least two of his brothers-in-law, and they were sons of Jane Halsall. The Hoghton and Stanley families lived near one another in several manors. The acting company of Henry Stanley were present at the Stanley estate(s) from time to time. Ferdinando Stanley, Lord Strange, married Alice Spencer while Shakeshafte (a few years younger than the couple) was a servant to Alexander and Elizabeth Hoghton. Could Shakeshafte have been present at their wedding?

Shakeshafte never entered into the employ of Sir Thomas Hesketh of Rufford. After a period in Stratford for wife and family, he may have returned to the people he had come to know in the household dominated by the prestigious Stanley family, or at least, to their company.

To repeat, there is no need to conjure a Hesketh acting company. Shakespeare/Shakeshafte was well-known to all of the acting company Stanleys in 1580-81 and the Hesketh s, most of whom were Catholics, whose mother was the common law wife of the great patron of an acting company, the Earl of Derby.

The Gabriel Hesketh-Jane Halsall union produced not just Thomas Hesketh who later became a prominent persecutor of Catholics but also the two brothers, Batholomew and Richard Hesketh. Both were strong Catholics. Bartholomew was in trouble with the Privy Council for sheltering Fr. Campion (at the time his brother-in-law's will was being written and while Shakeshafte was a servant in the household). Richard was executed in 1593 for coming to Ferdinando Stanley with messages from Stanley's cousin, Sir William Stanley.

Through the Stanleys and the Hesketh s, Shakeshafte could have found his way into companionship with the charismatic, irrepressible William Kemp, the greatest comic actor of his day. The details are foggy. Shakespeare/Shakeshafte apparently joined Derby's/Lord Strange's Men by the time of merging with the Lord Chamberlain's company. It could be Will Kemp or Richard Hesketh or a Stanley who would bring Shakeshafte/Shakespeare and Sterrell together. Yet another person will be suggested.

Both Richard Hesketh and Will Kemp had occupations that

permitted them to travel freely between England and the Continent. Both were often asked to be letter carriers for their acquaintances. Both were pensioners of the Spanish via Sir William Stanley's administration and were surely known to Sterrell.

Richard Hesketh was a member of the Clothworkers' Company and became a cloth merchant importing/exporting with the Low Countries, residing in Antwerp when not at home. He was importuned to carry letters for the famous scientist and alchemist John Dee and to get books for him on his trips to Antwerp in the early-1580s. Others must have received similar service, especially those who became his fellow pensioners in the Low Countries. Among the pensioners were the same English inhabitants of Dunkirk whom Thomas Doyley encountered in October 1585: the Stanihursts, the Copleys, and "Mr. Kemp, called Don Gulilhelmo." Hesketh may have also worked with Anthony Kemp, whose biographer in the *History of Parliament* suggests that he may have been in the Low Countries among the English exiles at this time, who included his brother George and his nephew Will.[89]

Marlowe & Sterrell: Fellow Suspects

There's still another person who could have brought William Sterrell and William Shakespeare together in late 1592 or in 1593, another poet/playwright in great peril from the Privy Council. We must consider an exact contemporary of Sterrell who was covering the same dangerous ground as Sterrell himself in the Low Countries: Christopher Marlowe, poet and playwright.

Marlowe was arrested in Flushing in late January 1592 only a few weeks before Sterrell and his courier-companion Staveley passed through the same area. How long or where Marlowe was on the Continent before that is unknown. He was supposedly counterfeiting coins and was turned in by Richard Baines, his co-counterfeiter who was a notorious double agent of the English government. The governor, Robert Sidney, brother of the late Philip Sidney, sent Marlowe to the Privy Council, informing them that Marlowe: "says himself to be very well known both to the Earl of Northumberland and my Lord Strange." Because his plays were performed by Lord Strange's company during this immediate period, it's likely that he was in the Low Countries on behalf of Lord

Strange himself. It makes no sense that an English poet/playwright would leave England just to embark on a counterfeiting scheme overseas. Rather, Baines entrapped him as he stalked him for the Cecil spy apparatus.

All biographers of Marlowe suspect Marlowe was engaging in some sort of secret activity. It cannot have been for Sir Francis Walsingham, for he had been dead for more than a year and a half and his spy apparatus largely dissolved. It's unlikely to have been on behalf of Burghley and Robert Cecil, for he would have been released quickly after returning to England. Moreover, Marlowe would have invoked their names with Robert Sidney. And it could not have been work for Essex, for Sterrell and Phelippes would have been aware of Marlowe's actions.

Marlowe biographer Charles Nicholl has suggested that Marlowe must have been engaged in something for Lord Strange, Ferdinando Stanley but was doing so as "a Cecil projector."[90] This was in connection with the *project* of Sir William Stanley with Cardinal Allen and Fr. Persons to secure the English crown for a Stanley, whether the Earl of Derby or his son Ferdinando. It will be recalled that Sir William Stanley was Lord Strange's cousin; the two were living in the same household in mid-1560s.

It's doubtful that the playwright would be undermining for Cecil the patron who was putting on Marlowe's plays. Lord Strange's players were about to perform Marlowe's play *The Jew of Malta* at the Rose Theatre on February 26, 1592 (they performed it seventeen times between February 26, 1592 and February 1, 1593). The same players performed Marlowe's *Massacre at Paris* (*The Tragedy of the Guise*) in late January 1593. Lord Strange was surely familiar with his chief playwright, as Marlowe himself said.

Let's speculate instead that Ferdinando, Lord Strange (or his father), was communicating with his cousin and supporter through Marlowe. As detailed below, both Sir William Stanley and his brother Sir Edward were in the Low Countries serving the Spanish. Marlowe was (perhaps) a messenger between the Stanleys, as was Richard Hesketh in 1593, both losing their lives as a consequence. Baines, as a Cecil agent stalking Marlowe, used the supposed counterfeiting scheme to secure the arrest of Marlowe. If Marlowe had no incriminating letters of a Stanley to a Stanley on him, Baines could manufacture a criminal charge by producing a single forged coin to justify arresting him. Its modern equivalent is an agent's planting of a small amount of drug on someone, simple and highly effective, as convincing as say a stolen handkerchief with a distinctive emblem.

Although Marlowe's return to England had been early February 1592, he was still to meet with the Privy Council when he was later arrested on May 18, 1593. He was ordered to report daily until 'licensed to the contrary.' Both Sterrell and Marlowe were thus to appear before the Privy Council at about the same time for their suspicious activities in the Low Countries that related to Sir William Stanley and the projects for the succession to the crown.

Sterrell was surely aware of Marlowe's peril and that it was related to his own. Two well-known M.A.s, one an Oxford lecturer who had taught hundreds of well-connected students 1587-1591, and the other a rising poet and playwright, must have known of each other's plight. Both were in London in late winter and spring 1593. Likely, they would have gotten together about the problems they both faced and compared notes. It would have been foolish not to; both were brilliant and in the same predicament from overlapping travels in the Low Countries.

Numerous Shakespeare scholars have observed the influence of Marlowe in the works of Shakespeare, suggesting a nearly collusive relationship between the two dramatists. They may well have known each other for years. Marlowe is alluded to in *As You Like It,* in the *Dead shepherd* line spoken by Phoebe in Act 3, sc. 5, which is a reference to Marlowe's *Hero and Leander*. The reference to a "great reckoning in a little room" line in the same play is believed to be a reference to Marlowe's sudden death. *The Merry Wives of Windsor* quotes a line from *The Passionate Shepherd to His Love.* In *All's Well* (discussed at length below), the Clown draws from Marlowe's *Dr. Faustus* as he sings when referring to *All's Well's* character Helen, whose name is the same as Helen of Troy from Faustus: " 'Was this fair face the cause' quoth she 'Why the Grecians sacked Troy?" The lines of *Faustus* "Was this the face that launch'd a thousand ships," were not published til 1604.

Baines's accusations against Marlowe to the Privy Council are the sole sources for the notorious statements attributed to Marlowe ever since his murder. Those accusations included not only the original coining but numerous charges of blasphemy and homosexuality, including the most famous: "That all they that love not tobacco and boys are fools." Why should we believe a single word of them? Character assassination was followed by actual murder, state sanctioned by the release of the killer(s).

On May 30, 1593 Marlowe was stabbed to death at an inn at Deptford. He was in the company of three men: Robert Poley, Ingram Frizer, and Nicholas Skeres. Poley was an agent of Robert Cecil at this time and later. In 1585-86 Poley had betrayed Mary Queen of Scots. He was one of the chief *provocateurs* against Anthony Babington in 1586 (the Babington Plot). One writer has argued that Robert Cecil "guided a covert operation to demonize and then destroy Marlowe."[91] The continued efforts to prosecute Marlowe suggest strongly a desire of Cecil to undo Marlowe and at the same time his patron who was producing two of his plays.

Shortly after Marlowe's death, William Sterrell called Poley the "vilest spy that ever was" and, using a symbol in cipher, expressed danger to himself from Poley.[92] Ben Jonson, doubtless a close friend in later years of William Sterrell, composed a poem, *Inviting a Friend to Supper,* similarly vilifying Poley's [Pooly] name for posterity. Was Sterrell the unnamed friend at supper?

While in the Low Countries in 1592, Sterrell had directly or indirectly encountered two of Cecil's agents, Reinhold Bisley and Michael Moody; both were working under Poley. Sterrell cleverly reported them to Phelippes (and thus Essex) as supposedly Catholic spies. When confronted, they had to defend on the basis that they were working for the English government. This meant they were exposed to the Catholics, and Cecil's spying efforts were undercut. Another reason for the Cecils to spread suspicion of Sterrell. He was far too clever for them and their agenda.

Recently, Shakespeare scholar Stephen Greenblatt has argued that Cecil was behind the poisoning of the patron of the acting company performing Marlowe's plays, Lord Strange, 5th Earl of Derby. He finds it "more probable that someone in the queen's orbit—

Robert Cecil is the likeliest suspect—decided that it was better that the earl, with his Tudor claim to the throne and his ambiguous religious beliefs, be removed permanently from the picture."[93] If the Cecils were capable of securing the murder of Marlowe and the poisoning of his patron, Sterrell was right to be afraid for his life.

Even though Marlowe was not yet murdered when Sterrell chose to use another man's name, Sterrell knew that he was in great danger for his Low Countries activities. "If I live" he had told Phelippes before he accepted recruitment: "They may ask, where is your warrant or what have you to show? And so I shall be well rewarded ***if I live.*"** He desperately needed the protection of powerful figures at Court and could not go public with his name.

Marlowe's murder surely confirmed the wisdom of Sterrell's caution. So, too, the execution of Richard Hesketh. And so, too, the mysterious death of Ferdinando Stanley within a year must have concerned Sterrell. And who would have been actors in those two plays of Marlowe performed by Lord Strange's company in February 1592 (and sixteen more times within a year) and January 1593?[94] The roster of the players almost certainly included Will Kemp. Will not Marlowe have worked with the actors performing his plays? We must add Kit Marlowe to the persons who might have introduced William Sterrell to the company man, Shakespeare, if Shakespeare-of-Stratford was ever an actor.

When Sterrell needed someone to be his front for a poem, William Shakespeare could have been suggested by Kemp or Marlowe or another such as Richard Hesketh (who had known "Shakeshafte"). Shakespeare had nothing to lose, and he could gain substantially if Sterrell's gambit worked. In fact, it may have seemed like fun, a comic prank just as the poem *Venus and Adonis* itself is a wink that mocks the Queen of England while covered by the lush Latinate mask of Ovid.

We may surmise that a relationship developed between the two Wills, Shakespeare and Sterrell. As suggested earlier, some of the sonnets were addressed to Shakespeare by Sterrell, the real poet-playwright. Read the sonnets closely. You will see the relationship: one the public figure, the other the true poet. Each depended on the other; each was protected by their mutual secrecy.

Neither would benefit by exposure of their arrangement.

Worcester's close associates at the Court were aware that Sterrell was the man who planned and wrote the plays with the guidance of Worcester. The earl was co-creator of the entertainments that greatly enhanced his standing at the Courts of Queen Elizabeth and King James, just as Worcester and Sterrell were the men behind the masques. Shakespeare-of-Stratford earned substantial reward with no effort.

♦♦♦ ♦♦♦

Skepticisima: Well now, B-Man. Do you buy into this Shakeshafte thing?

Bardophilus: I'll acknowledge that the argument has been entertained by Stratfordians. I'm agnostic. Your friend whom we're calling Palabras has given the theory a new twist. Jane Halsall, Derby's alternate wife (what else can we call her), and her sons connected with Shakeshafte and Derby's son Ferdinando. That increases the likelihood that Shakeshafte is Shakespeare. But even Palabras seems to waffle.

Skepticisima: I'd waffle too. There's no evidence that Shakeshafte or Shakespeare was an actor in 1593.

Bardophilus: But, if Shakespeare wasn't a player, why bring Marlowe into the mix? If Shakespeare weren't acting in Marlowe's plays, Marlowe wouldn't introduce Shakespeare to Sterrell.

Skepticisima: True, true. Maybe Shakespeare was a minor player or an attending functionary. But Marlowe's presence here adds to the reasons why Sterrell would hide his name from the public. Our author had to bring in Marlowe somewhere. The Cecils went after Marlowe because of his visibility. Prosecuting a prominent playwright was a warning to other public personalities. Ask Ben Jonson! Linking Richard Hesketh with Kemp is another gambit by our author. Both are pertinent to Sterrell's insecurity and fear in 1592-93 irrespective of the Shakeshafte possibility.

Bardophilus: Too attenuated, if you ask me.

Skepticisima: Thanks. I did.

Bardophilus: Then let's press on. Our author here seems to be claiming not only that Shakespeare-of-Stratford was not the author of his plays, but that Shakespeare was a party to the conspiracy.

Skepticisima: Exactly so. The *Sonnets* say as much. But why are you so dismissive of a conspiracy?

Bardophilus: There's just no evidence of a conspiracy. Why should there be?

Skepticisima: Because the poet and playwright was a Catholic. Catholics in Elizabeth's England were persecuted. Catholic poets and playwrights were put in jail, their works shunned. And Sterrell was more than just a Catholic, he was a Catholic agent known as a corrupter of youth. If he had published under his own name, the government would have made an example of him. So long as his identity remained secret, he could continue to work for Worcester and draw on Worcester's resources. If Sterrell attracted attention to himself, it would have drawn into question Worcester's carefully cultivated reputation as a loyal subject who was reconciled to the Church of England.

Bardophilus: You exaggerate. Elizabeth didn't make windows into men's souls.

Skepticisima: Windows? She executed priests and had informants in every county to report on suspected Catholics. Do you deny that there were secret Catholic networks? Isn't that what you mean by a conspiracy?

Bardophilus: Shakespeare was never shown to be part of a network, even if some of his writings seem almost Catholic in outlook.

Skepticisima: My friend, that's the point of Sterrell hiding behind someone who wasn't publicly Catholic and not part of a Catholic network. Shakespeare-of-Stratford was well-compensated for supplying a name for the author.

Bardophilus: Others would have had to have been in on it.

Skepticisima: Of course. That's what a conspiracy is, a group of people working in secret for a common purpose. Look, there's even one of your own Stratfordians who's been tempted to accept the notion, even using the C word. That's Gary Taylor. In one essay he said we might "suspect that the Shakespeare First Folio was promoted . . . by a conspiracy of underground Catholics."[95]

Bardophilus: But Shakespeare was dead at the publication of the *First Folio.*

Skepticisima: Yes! I heard you say that earlier. The Stratford burgher had no connection with the poetry or plays. Nothing but the *First Folio* connects him to the plays. Let's look at the fact that the four men who wrote commendatory verses for the *First Folio* were "notorious hispanophiles" or openly Catholic. The leading figure of the four was Ben Jonson. He was well-known to Sterrell and Worcester and beholden to both of them for the masques that made Jonson famous at the Court of King James. Jonson was the only contemporary of Shakespeare who ever claimed that Shakespeare was an actor. He had every reason to dissemble for Sterrell and Worcester in the *First Folio* and in his own folio of 1616. Another of the four, James Mabbe, had been a student/colleague of Sterrell's many years earlier at Magdalen College. He, too, had been accused of being a secret Catholic agent and locked up for it. Hugh Holland, like Ben Jonson, also had been persecuted for his Catholicism on multiple occasions. Sounds like the making of a conspiracy to me.

Bardophilus: But a conspiracy for what?

Skepticisima: Sterrell and Worcester were both eager to promote a match between the heir to the English crown and a Spanish Catholic princess — as were their "pious fellows." Only with such a marriage was it likely that Catholicism could be returned to England. It was a holy conspiracy. Their life-long goal was an England tolerant of their religion.

Bardophilus: How would the *First Folio* help that?

Skepticisima: The dedicatees of the magnificent book were Worcester's friends and relations, the Herbert brothers. They were the Earls of Pembroke and Montgomery. Pembroke was a foe of the Spanish Match. The *First Folio* flattered them and lauded reconciliation. It was an overture to toleration.

Bardophilus: If Sterrell as Shakespeare was a Catholic conspirator, that would make him a traitor.

Skepticisima: So, you don't believe in religious freedom. Is that what you are saying?

Bardophilus: It's not that simple.

Chapter 6

The Printer and Publisher; Sterrell's Success

Let us now take up the circumstances of the publication of *Venus and Adonis*. Shakespeare-of-Stratford could have had some acquaintance with the man who printed the epic poem: Richard Field, a native of Stratford. But Sterrell knew him for his trade as a printer for other reasons. Because of his work with the Catholic community of exiles abroad, Sterrell was well-versed in surreptitious publication of religious and political tracts. He was familiar with the use of false imprints by his Catholic correspondents to make books and pamphlets appear as though printed in the Netherlands or France. Secret publication by the Catholics was their best hope to keep their religion alive in England, together with correspondence with friends and relatives. Let's examine Field's relation to such printing and printers.

Surreptitious printing

When *Venus and Adonis* was published, Sterrell had long been familiar with clandestine printing. He was at Oxford when Fr. Edmund Campion's bold challenge to Queen Elizabeth was distributed on the benches of St. Mary's Church before commencement ceremonies on June 27, 1581. The small book, called *Decem Rationes*, set forth ten arguments to the Queen against the validity of the Anglican Church and to advocate for the Catholic faith. It was printed at a secret press and made a powerful impression on the university. Years earlier, the Jesuit priest, as a learned young scholar, had debated before Elizabeth in her first visitation to Oxford in 1566.

Sterrell worked and corresponded with Catholic exiles who often published surreptitious, forbidden works, such as Thomas Fitzherbert and Richard Verstegan – both of whom were associated with editing and printing of the *Decem Rationes*. It is very likely Sterrell first made their acquaintance as they worked with Campion 1580-81. Later, Verstegan would use Sterrell as a channel of inquiry when Verstegan dedicated a book, *Restitution of a Decayed Intelligence* (1605), to King James. He also worked with Catholic priests, such as Fr. Henry Garnet and Fr. Robert Southwell, who published under false imprints from printers in London or from secret presses in England.

Another Jesuit priest using a secret press was Fr. Robert Southwell. Probably Sterrell's own cousin, the priest's excellent poetry was part of his ministry.[96] We encountered him earlier in connection with the Sackville family. We will return to him for his associations with Shakespeare's Blackfriars property in London.

Southwell and Henry Garnet arrived in England in 1586. Southwell's first book in England was *An Epistle of Comfort* written for imprisoned Catholics. Published in 1586/87, its cover declared it was "Imprinted at Paris," but it was in fact probably printed by John Charlewood in London, based on unique identifying characteristics. Charlewood is best known for his surreptitious printing of six books in Italian by Giordano Bruno (a peripatetic monk, philosopher, astronomer and seer). Those books claimed to have been printed in Paris or Venice. Bruno resided with the French ambassador in London during the years Sterrell was "haunting" the embassy and meeting with the ambassador. Sterrell would have been familiar with those books. Bruno was aboard the ambassador's boat when Sterrell's six youths who were supposed to use it for transport to seminary were taken into custody at Dover.

Two other printers using false imprints for political or religious publications were closely associated with one another, John Wolfe and Richard Field.[97] Wolfe, without a false imprint, printed Southwell's *Marie Magdalen's Funeral Teares* in 1591 for G. C. [Gabriel Cawood]. The author was identified as "S.W." A year later Southwell (S.W.) was imprisoned, tortured and then executed in 1595. Wolfe published in 1595 another book from a Southwell manuscript, *Saint Peter's Complaint,* which was dedicated by "The Author to his loving Cosen." A later edition read "To My Worthy Good Cosen Maister W.S. and was now signed "Your loving cosen, R. S."

Why Field and Harrison

Why would the poet use Richard Field for *Venus and Adonis,* a printer with only limited association with vernacular poetry?

"Shakespeare's" *Venus and Adonis* did not need to be published in secret as its poet was hidden behind a false name rather than a false imprint. He probably considered John Wolfe, a printer who frequently published tracts for the government as well as foreign language works. Often Wolfe's books had no imprint or a false imprint, in part because of his piracy of others' works. Instead, Sterrell had good reason for looking to Richard Field, who had begun his printing career with John Wolfe, and Field followed the practices of his former employer. Field was printing political tracts for Essex, when Sterrell was working with Essex on the same project.

Essex, Sterrell knew early in 1593, was bringing to England the most notorious defector from the Spanish government, Antonio Perez. He was once secretary to King Philip II of Spain. It was part of Essex's strategic planning against Spain, and Perez was useful for propaganda. Perez had already published in Paris his *Pedaços de Historia, ô Relaçiones* in 1591. By late September 1592, Perez had readied a new edition (in Spanish), dedicated to Essex.[98]

Perez's book would be printed by Richard Field and published by John Harrison by 1594. Only months before *Venus and Adonis,* the two had issued *The Spaniards Monarchie,* (1592) an anonymous publication ("Englished by H.O."), perhaps also with the backing of Essex. The introductory "To The Gentlemen Readers" by H.O. noted that his work "hath no title fetched from the Bull within bishops gate, as a figge for a Spaniard, . . ."[99] Shakespeare scholars have noted that the playwright apparently borrowed this expression for *2 Henry IV* where Pistol says "When Pistol lies, do this, and fig me like the bragging Spaniard, " and in *Henry V* where Pistol says, "The fig of Spain! " Sterrell acquired examples of such propaganda to send to his correspondents overseas.

Because Essex was behind the publication by Field and Harrison of Perez's work-in-progress (similar in purpose to *The Spaniards Monarchie),* the same pair would have been easily persuaded to issue a small pamphlet of only fifty pages at the encouragement of persons within the Essex circle. Why else would Field and Harrison work together to produce *Venus and Adonis* as the first publication of a completely unknown writer? Many or most publications of this period were contract work, paid for in advance, not speculative ventures by the printer and stationer dependent upon sales to cover production costs.

Richard Field entered *Venus and Adonis* at the Stationers Company Register on April 18, 1593, just as Antonio Perez arrived in England. The long poem could be purchased by early June at John Harrison's shop in Paul's Churchyard. No doubt early copies were distributed to Southampton and his mother, to Penelope Rich and to Essex. Did the poem yield "so bad a harvest?" Hardly.

Essex, Penelope, and the Countess of Southampton and her son the earl would have been highly entertained and pleased by *Venus*. How else to account for Sterrell's sudden return to grace with Essex, Bacon and the others of their circle? Within a short time Sterrell was reunited with Essex and Southampton at an important gathering at Gains Park, Epping, fully restored to work. He was apparently assigned to gain intelligence from the Spaniards whom Essex had brought over: Antonio Perez and his entourage. We hear no more of an investigation of William Sterrell by the Privy Council. It will be 1605 before his overseas correspondence again lands him in trouble.

Emerging from his crisis, Sterrell in 1594 wrote the *Comedy of Errors* for Francis Bacon's Inn of Court; Bacon had promised Phelippes that he would try to restore Sterrell's credit with the Earl of Essex. And Sterrell also wrote a play based on the events at Gains Park, with Essex, Southampton, Florio and Perez having recognizable parts: *Loves Labours Lost*.

Now Worth 800£

A year after *Venus and Adonis*, Sterrell wrote an overseas correspondent, Fr. Richard Sherwood, formerly a London merchant, that his fortune had greatly increased. Sterrell said:

> I have been used in vain baubles, not without danger of loss neither this long time and yet if *the world were turned tomorrow next, what account will be made of me: truly none*. I am worth 800£ yet if all were gold, I would not care to spend one half if I were employed so as I might be hereafter, *in aliquo numero* [to be of some importance], but when I so deal as I neither get *in hoc seculo, negue in futuro*, I must save my money to live upon myself.

The sentiment of the first line quoted is the same as we have seen in *Sonnet 81*: "I (once gone) to all the world must die." The latter Latin phrase is drawn from Latin Vulgate translation of Matthew 12:32, suggesting "I get nothing in this world, nor in the future."

Let us speculate on source of Sterrell's sudden wealth. Recall, he reported in 1591 that he was worth only 40£. The £800 he had recently come into was no reward for spying. No one in England was happy with his efforts in mid-1593 when *Venus* was published. Spies were seldom well compensated – if they lived. The benefactor was not likely the Earl of Southampton; he may have come into his inheritance but he was heavily burdened with debt, not the least of which was £5,000 owed to Lord Burghley.

We should instead suspect it was a gift from the Countess Southampton to her son's poet. The highly popular poem lifted the young earl in the esteem of his fellow Lords and established him as a patron of an impressive work. The Countess now had a poetic and Catholic counterweight to Clapham/Burghley's *Narcissus*. The Earl of Southampton will later marry Elizabeth Vernon, related to both Essex and Worcester. The Countess would not have wanted her son to wed the granddaughter of a stout Protestant who had worked so long to oust the Roman church.

As will be developed further in Sterrell's biography, Sterrell reciprocated a gift from the Countess by performing a great service for her on behalf of her beloved niece. And in more detailed analysis of specific plays we will see that she inspired further works of his. In seeing *Othello*, she would have recognized aspects of her marriage to Henry Wriothesley, 2nd Earl of Southampton, a couple torn apart by a malevolent lieutenant, probably based on Charles Paget. In *Twelfth Night* she would see herself and her deceased twin brother as the reunited twins Viola and Sebastian.

The Non-Poet

The success of *Venus* and to a lesser extent *Lucrece* ensured that its poet would abandon publication of poetry. This seeming contradiction must be explained. *Venus* went through seven editions before 1603 and *Lucrece* had four editions. *Phoenix and Turtle* and the *Sonnets* (1609) were put forth in "Shakespeare's" name without objection but likewise without his endorsement or apparent compensation. The publication of *The Passionate Pilgrim* in 1599 (and another edition in 1612) by William Jaggard is generally regarded as piracy. No money there. Shakespeare-the-author also wrote poetry that appeared as internal to the plays or as a feature of a character's lines. But there was no other significant published poetry to demonstrate his talents as a poet, very odd for a poet with such great success with *Venus and Adonis*.

A highly popular poet would not abandon publication of poetry without a good reason. Shakespeare scholars are at a loss to explain why Shakespeare-of-Stratford would sue on the balance of an account for malt and a debt of two shillings or a for a petty debt of £6, but would not compose poetry to receive the sort of income Jonson and Peele and other poet/playwrights were enjoying. The most reasonable explanation is that if the poet published more poetry, it would invite attention to the poet. Shakespeare-the-author had no need for the money if the wealthy Earl of Worcester was his exclusive patron. Shakespeare-the-burgher was avaricious, a hoarder of grain and money. They were two different men.

The Shareholder, a Proxy

The shareholder Shakespeare was useful for Sterrell and Worcester. Through him as their proxy, they could in effect become shareholders in the new company created out of Derby's/Lord Strange's Men after the death of Ferdinando Stanley in April 1594. The details need not detain us here. We can say that Shakespeare's becoming a shareholder of the acting company was just as Gary Taylor has noted of the playwright's investment in the Globe Theatre: "Shakespeare is not necessarily made a shareholder of the Globe [company] in recognition of his artistic talent; he may have bought his way in, like any other venture capitalist with sufficient liquidity."[100] Worcester or Sterrell (worth £800) had liquidity to acquire influence with the company through Shakespeare-the-sharer. Either man could afford to buy a way in through Shakespeare-of-Stratford. In short, Shakespeare-of-Stratford was a front man.

In business and in politics, we are familiar with Trojan horse investments. Hidden principals use a front to mask their identity and true intentions so as to gain access to a market they otherwise could not enter. Using "Shakespeare" as a false front, Worcester and Sterrell gained access and influence in London theatre.

The date of Shakespeare-the-sharer becoming a shareholder of the acting company is significant. It must have been after May 1593 because Shakespeare's name does not appear as part of the company in a license issued in their favor by the Privy Council on May 6, 1593.[101] The Privy Council allowed the Lord Admiral's company and Lord Strange's company to perform despite the plague "so it be not within seven miles of London or of the Court." The Privy Council named "William Kemp, Thomas Pope, John Heminges, Augustine Phillipes and George Brian, *being all one company*, servants to our very good Lord the Lord Strange." If "Shakespeare" were a shareholder in 1593, he would undoubtedly have been named. Three of these — Kemp, Pope, and Bryan — were all together as a group in Denmark as "instrumentist" [Kemp] or "instrumentists and mummers" [Pope, Brian and two others] for three months in 1586.[102] The earliest record indicative of Shakespeare as a shareholder is from March 1595.[103]

♦♦♦ ♦♦♦

Bardophilus: Isn't this making too much of a minor omission? Shakespeare might not have been available for the Council on the day the license was granted.

Skepticisima: Really? Of course you'll ignore something that doesn't fit your narrative. Here we have Conan Doyle's dog that didn't bark; he wasn't there to bark. The Council wasn't speaking to persons before them. It was responding to a petition signed by the company's principals. Look at the date of the Privy Council license - May 6, 1593. The poet was in London exactly at the time of the publication of *Venus and Adonis*. Wouldn't he have been zealous in trying to get his company in performance again?

Bardophilus: Are you saying that Sterrell or Worcester elbowed their way into an existing acting company through a minor player without anyone noticing? Why would the Lord Chamberlain's Men allow him in like that?

Skepticisima: Elbowing? That's where Kemp comes in. He's on record as working with Pope and Bryan in Denmark since 1586. Now Kemp would be able to vouch for Shakespeare and induce Pope and Bryan to allow Shakespeare into the company as an investor. Recall that Kemp was related by blood to both Worcester and the Countess of Southampton. He would have welcomed a part in seeing *Venus and Adonis* dedicated to her son, his kin.

Bardophilus: I'm not ready to buy it. We just don't know enough about the details on the formation of the Lord Chamberlain's Men in 1594.

Skepticisima: Look, you Stratfordians obfuscate what happened to the Strange/Derby company. You see it as a merger without seeing what really happened. In April 1594, the dying Ferdinando planned the company's future for his widow and his Carey in-laws, to whom he was very close.

Bardophilus: Just when I thought you might have a modicum of good sense. You don't have evidence to back that up.

Skepticisima: No, really. Here's the timeline. Ferdinando Stanley writes his will on April 12. He's reflected for eight days on his legacies. His widow will be Alice Spencer, age thirty-five. She was raised in a very literary family. When they married at age twenty, she and her husband together gradually assumed the dominant role for the family acting company. She continues to be a patron of literature and masques all her long life, even John Milton. Lord Strange's Men could have been called Lady Strange's Men. In fact, when her husband died, the company assumed her name: On May 16, 1594, the company performed at Winchester as "Servants of the Countess of Derby."

Bardophilus: Oh, Come on. We all know from the leading authority on the Shakespeare company that the decision to take over Derby's company was made in May 1594 by Lord Admiral Howard and by his father-in-law, Henry Carey who was Lord Chamberlain. The two men set up a duopoly to control the London theatre business.

Skepticisima: The Admiral had nothing to do with this. Nor did Henry Carey, Lord Hunsdon. The Lord Chamberlain was old. His company had been defunct for four years. The real story is far more dramatic.

Bardophilus: The real story? You'll serve up more Trojan Horse theories, I suppose.

Skepticisima: What you have are two very close sisters in the middle of great family turmoil. Here you have a pregnant Alice Spencer at the side of her dying husband. Ferdinando took ill April 6, 1594. Alice moved him to Lathom Manor and called for Dr. John Case of Oxford. An agonizing week later, Ferdinando made his last will, giving most of the estate to Alice and their children. Ferdinando's will left his brother William with only the shell of an earldom.

When Ferdinando died on April 14, the Countess was suddenly a widow. Her sister Elizabeth Carey was notified and hurried to her side. Immediately, the widow and her brother-in-law were in conflict. He was outraged that his brother had cut him off. If William could successfully challenge his brother's will, Alice and her three daughters would have little. William would even lose his title as Earl had not Alice miscarried.

Facing a legal onslaught, Alice turned to her sister and her brother-in-law, Elizabeth and George Carey. Elizabeth, too, was a patron of the arts. The three of them transformed what had been Lord Strange's Men into a new company, the Lord Chamberlain's Men.

Bardophilus: George Carey? Surely you must be thinking of Henry Carey, Baron Hunsdon. He already had an acting company. He was the Lord Chamberlain.

Skepticisima: Close. But he was already old. He had been patron of a company, Lord Hunsdon's men, now defunct. The new company was all the work of Elizabeth and George Carey, using the Baron's title. In these immediate weeks after Ferdinando's burial Alice, Elizabeth, and George Carey transitioned Alice's company to the new one under George and Elizabeth Carey. Alice would do this for herself and for the sake of the actors she had come to know well over the past fifteen years. She and her husband had built the company from its modest start as Lord Strange's Tumblers. Elizabeth and George Carey, working with their sister Alice, were responsible for bringing the "Servants of the Countess of Derby" under the patronage of a newly reconstituted company called the Lord Chamberlain's Men when they suddenly appeared on June 2, 1594. George Carey was perhaps prodded into it by his wife. Who can say? We know so little about the Carey family. Was he literary?

We do know his wife, their daughter, and his sister-in-law were well-lettered and long-time literary patrons.

Bardophilus: Is there any evidence for this ridiculous claim?

Skepticisima: Far more than any other account. When Ferdinando was dictating his will he would also have taken steps to shield the company he and Alice had built over a 15-year period from his brother. I'm sure he instructed her to arrange for Elizabeth and George Carey to bring the company under their patronage. Just five days after Ferdinando's death, we find George Carey very active in Alice's affairs. He initiated an inquest with a commission that included Alice's future husband, Thomas Egerton. Carey soon reported that the death was probably due to witches. George and Elizabeth Carey seem to have worked in the securing of the estate for their sister Alice and her daughters in her fight against William Stanley.

Bardophilus: You're speculating. Again.

Skepticisima: Where's the spculation? It's simple logic that fits the facts. The transfer of the company from Alice to George and Elizabeth was an obvious fit as George's father was Lord Chamberlain and had responsibilities for Court entertainments. Henry lent his title to the new company that was under the real patronage of Elizabeth and George Carey. And because George Carey's own sister was wife of the Lord Admiral, who also had an acting company, the two companies could make themselves a duopoly. By giving the company over to her sister, Alice could retain influence with the company. That role would have been lost if the company came under the control of her estranged brother-in-law. Ferdinando, Alice and the Careys were kindred spirits. Pastoral poems written by Ferdinando that he had shared with Elizabeth and George were found in their personal papers. I guarantee that Shakespeare's becoming a shareholder in the new company was with the backing of these Spencer sisters. The disruption of the existing company was an opportunity to create a new company, Phoenix-like.

Let's see how the Earl of Worcester and Sterrell would have

benefitted by using Shakespeare as their proxy with the acting company. Worcester had his own acting company, but it was excluded from public performances in London until the end of the decade. With a shareholder fronting for them, Sterrell and Worcester opened up London through a company sharer posing as a playwright. The plays of "Shakespeare" could reach London audiences without going through a middleman, such as theater impresario Philip Henslowe. So long as a "book" bearing the name Shakespeare as playwright was delivered, no further inquiries would be made.

There was no impediment for private performances of plays, so Worcester could stage plays for special occasions with his own actors or with some from the Lord Chamberlain's men: several of them had originally been with Worcester's/Lord Herbert's Men.

The only evidence of Shakespeare actually performing in plays comes from two highly unreliable sources: Ben Jonson who was beholden to both Worcester and Sterrell since 1603, and to the people who put together and financed the *First Folio* - Worcester, Sterrell and their associates. It was only with Jonson's own folio of his collected works in 1616 that "Shakespeare" was identified as an actor in Jonson's *Every Man in His Humour* (1598) and *Sejanus* (1603); he made no mention of Shakespeare as a poet or playwright prior to 1623 (his *Discoveries* was much later). No other record of Shakespeare as an actor has ever been produced, unlike other players of the same acting company. Ben Jonson and the *First Folio* creators had reason to perpetuate the Shakespeare myth.

To achieve their purposes, Sterrell and Worcester did not need the presence of their frontman. Shakespeare-of-Stratford could reside primarily in Stratford and be a comfortable (if unpleasant) burgher. The Stratfordians struggle to explain the contrast: the petty-minded hoarder and creditor of Stratford who was simultaneously writing and acting in the great dramas presented in London and at the Court of King James.

A record from 1598 suggests that Shakespeare-of-Stratford was hoarding malt in a time of shortage endured by the inhabitants of the town. Another has him receiving 10 pence from the borough for a load of stone for the repair of Clopton Bridge. Shakespeare sued a Stratford apothecary (Philip Rogers) for nonpayment for a purchase of malt c. 1604 and for a debt of two shillings. William Shakespeare of Rowington reported for militia muster in 1605.[104] The Cottage which Shakespeare purchased in 1602 was part of Rowington Manor (as confirmed by a 1604 record of Rowington showing "William Shakespere . . . holdeth one cottage and one garden"), and the militia were organized by manor. In 1608 he sued for a small debt owed by John Addenbrooke and also pursued the debt guarantor named Horneby. Was the author of great tragedy a tight-fisted litigant? Did the man who explored the depths of the human heart have the soul of a penny-wise shop-keeper? If the greedy burgher of Stratford wrote the plays that now bear his name, why did he not seek to monetize those plays and other poetry through publication during his lifetime?

The man of words was not divided. There were simply two men using the same name.

Recap

So, let's take stock and reflect on where we are on our journey. We have focused on *Venus and Adonis,* its literary setting, and the conventions of publishing in the 1590s. We have examined briefly relevant events in the lives of the three men of our greatest interest: William Sterrell, Edward Somerset, and William Shakespeare of Stratford. The origins of the Lord Chamberlain's Men have been traced. The political and religious dynamic of the Shakespeare period has been set forth.

Ahead are two topics to be explored in greater depth. One is the Shakespeare play *All's Well that Ends Well.* You will likely agree that the drama is a thinly veiled version of the crisis Sterrell faced in 1592-93 that led him to return to his old master, the Earl of Worcester. The second topic is the will of Shakespeare-of-Stratford. When we scrutinize its property provisions, perhaps you will be persuaded that the man is best understood as a surrogate for others who needed to work out of public view.

Chapter 7

Exitus acta probat

All's well that ends well. *Still the fine's the crown. Whate'er the course, the end is the renown.* Helena - *All's Well* [4.4.35-36]	*Exitus acta probat.* *Et item finis coronat et insuper a fine omnia denominari.* *de Scholarium Disciplina*[105]
All's well that ends well yet, *Though time seem so adverse and means unfit.* Helena - *All's Well* [5.1.25-26]	*Exitus acta probat.* *Careat successibus, opto, quisquis ab eventu facta notanda putat!* Ovid, *Heroides*[106]

The story of Sterrell's crisis in 1592-93 is told in the play *All's Well that Ends Well.* The story is perhaps the earliest example of a *roman à clef,* a work that treats real people and events under a façade of fiction. The key to understanding *All's Well* is to see that at its heart it depicts Sterrell's troubled relations with two masters, the Earls of Essex and Worcester. The playwright accomplishes his purposes by devising two plots that he weaves together.

The first plot centers on the love relation between two young people, Bertram and Helena. This story line is derived from Boccaccio's *Decameron.* Helena is a love-struck physician's daughter who cures the King of France. As her reward, the King requires Bertram, a nobleman, to marry her. Bertram rejects her due to class differences. After giving her impossible tasks, Bertram flees to a war. Helena uses a "bed trick" to fulfill Bertram's challenges, forcing Bertram to accept her.

The second plot depicts the relationship of Parolles, a foppish courtier who follows Bertram, and Lord Lafew. [107] It is not derived from Boccaccio or any other source. Throughout the play, Lafew mocks Parolles' pretentious behavior and labels him a rascally knave, while Parolles unsuccessfully protests. Parolles follows

Bertram into the war in Italy, where he is humiliated by Bertram and two other lords. After Parolles has been exposed as a coward and dismissed by Bertram, the disgraced Parolles is taken in by a mocking but merciful Lafew.

Most critics find both plots and principal characters unappealing. Some say it is the playwright's worst creation. Why quibble? Artistic merit is not our concern here.

From our perspective, the romantic plot from Boccaccio provides a storyline into which the more important story of Parolles and Lafew can be told. What seems a conventional romance of a young count and a physician's daughter becomes a character drama, for Parolles and Lafew are Sterrell and Worcester. That Parolles's story is central to the play is indicated by the fact that he is given 141 lines/speeches, compared to 109 for Helena and 102 for Bertram; Lafew has 97. It is only an illusion that the Parolles-Lafew story is a subplot.[108]

Parolles and Lafew are the two characters most fully realized in the play. Parolles is based on William Sterrell himself. His name in the play says directly what he is: "Paroles" which is "Words." His identity lies in his words, as a professor and as a writer. The plot is derived from Sterrell's mission abroad and crisis in 1591-93. Lafew is a favorable portrayal of the 4th Earl of Worcester, Edward Somerset. His name (as a French lord) is derived from *Le Feu*, French for "the heat." This is precisely the play on the name of Edward Somerset that Edmund Spenser made when he wrote *Prothalamion,* a long poem on the betrothal of two Somerset daughters in 1596: "were they bred of *Somers-heat* they say."

Bertram is drawn from the Earl of Essex, Robert Devereux, the young earl (count) whom Sterrell served in 1591-93. He comes across as shallow and deceptive up to the end, a liar even when confronted with undeniable evidence of his perfidy. Like Bertram, Essex was notorious for his unfaithfulness to his wife. The naming of Bertram comes from Essex's Christian name roBERT.

Both Lafew and Bertram are French lords. The setting of the play in France is suitable as both Essex and Worcester celebrated their French ancestry. Robert Devereux traced his lineage to Robert d'Évreux, who came to England with William the Conqueror during the Norman Conquest in 1066. Edward Somerset's family originated with John Beaufort, 1st Earl of Somerset, who was born around 1373 at Beaufort Castle in Champagne, France. This property was a possession of his father, John of Gaunt, Duke of Lancaster, who is a principal character in Shakespeare's *Richard II*.

The Clown is added to the play to heighten the characterization of Parolles and Lafew. He adds wit to a work that otherwise would lack levity.[109]

The take-away from this chapter is that *All's Well* is "Shakespeare's" treatment of the life crisis that transformed him into, as he puts it, "the thing I am." Parolles (Sterrell) undergoes an experience that existential philosophers call a boundary situation. The threat of imminent death can make a person aware of the urgency of living authentically, without self-deception. Stripped of self-illusions, a person can come to a more authentic existence. In a literary work, the moment of recognition is described by Aristotle's *Poetics* as *anagnorisis*. It is often paired with *peripeteia*, the sudden reversal of circumstances, changing the protagonist's fate from good to bad or vice versa. When the blindfold is removed, Parolles has a shock of recognition. As a result, he gives up ambitions for one sort of life to flourish through his true calling. This is what Sterrell experienced in 1592-93, at the end of which he returned to his old master, just as does Parolles.

ꕥꕥꕥꕥ--ꕥꕥꕥꕥ

All's Well is known only from its inclusion in the *First Folio* of 1623, never before mentioned in any records. The play's title is one translation of the Latin phrase *exitus acta probat*, an aphorism that recurs in Sterrell's correspondence over decades. For the title, the playwright once again drew upon Ovid, for the phrase is found in Ovid's *Heroides* as well as in another obscure source. It also translates to "the outcome justifies the deed" or "the result proves the act." Success or failure of a chosen action determines whether the decision is good. The phrase "all's well that ends well" is said twice by Helena. Its repetition suggests that we should focus on two outcomes - one is the plot of the relation of Helena and Bertram, the other is the second plot of the relation of Parolles and Lafew. Both end well, all things considered.

Parolles portrays Sterrell in 1592-93. Like Sterrell, he has the status of gentleman, not a mere servant. Seven different characters all refer to Parolles by the title of "monsieur," the French equivalent of Mister, for a total of eleven times. He is trying to rise above his station by associating with Counts (the same as English Earls). In this, Helena is his female counterpart. She, too, is trying to rise above her station. Here the playwright departs from his source, where Boccaccio's Giletta is a rich heiress with kin and suitors. Helena will rise by marrying Bertram; Parolles by serving Bertram. She knows Parolles for what he is, saying as he approaches: "I love him for his sake; And yet I know him a notorious liar, Think him a great way fool, solely a coward."

From their first words to one another, Helena and Parolles have an uncanny rapport.

Parolles. Save you, fair queen!
Helena. And you, monarch!
Parolles. No.
Helena. And no.

It's easy to miss the exchange. Each calls the other by a royal title, and each then denies the title. Parolles admits he's no monarch, and Helena that she's no queen. They are both social climbers and acknowledge each other as such.

Parolles is drawn into the service of a young lord, Bertram (Essex), just as Sterrell went into the service of the Earl of Essex in 1591. Essex and Bertram have features in common: both were made wards of the Crown at an early age. Essex was ten when his father died, and he was made a ward of Lord Burghley. Bertram is a ward of the King. Both are too young to go to war when they first set out on a foreign campaign. Bertram has to slip away, saying: "I am commanded here and kept a coil with 'Too young' and 'next year' and 'Tis too early'." Essex was only twenty when he accompanied Leicester overseas; his biographer observes he would have had to obtain the Queen's permission: "Essex was granted permission . . . to accompany his stepfather to war."

Bertram becomes "general of the horse" to the Florentine Duke just as Essex was named "general of the horse" to Leicester in the Low Countries campaign in January 1586 (age twenty) and then

Master of the Horse for Queen Elizabeth from June 1587 to his execution in 1601. Bertram as "general of the horse" has no cavalry nor other equine connections nor even a military role in the play; the title would appear superfluous if it is not intended to parallel the events upon which the story is drawn. In Boccaccio's tale, the Bertram character is said only to have been "made captaine of a certaine number of men." No "general of the horse" there. The playwright gave to Bertram the exact title that the Earl of Leicester conferred on Essex in 1586-87.

Another lord, Lafew (Worcester), is an older, insightful nobleman who knew Parolles before Bertram knew Parolles. When we first encounter Parolles, he makes clear to Helena that he serves Bertram. But when Parolles and Lafew first appear together in Act 2 sc. 3, they obviously know each other well, so well that they finish each other's sentences. Theirs seems to be friendly banter in this scene. The amiable exchange concerning the miraculous recovery of the King after receiving medication from shows the men's ease with each other:

> **Lafew**. They say miracles are past; and we have our philosophical persons to make modern and familiar things supernatural and causeless. Hence is it that we make trifles of terrors, ensconcing ourselves into seeming knowledge when we should submit ourselves to an unknown fear.
>
> **Parolles**. Why, 'tis the rarest argument of wonder that hath shot out in our latter times.
>
> **Bertram**. And so 'tis.
>
> **Lafew**. To be relinquish'd of the artists [scholars]-
>
> **Parolles**. So I say - both of *Galen* and *Paracelsus*.
>
> **Lafew**. Of all the learned and authentic fellows - [accredited members of the College of Physicians]
>
> **Parolles**. Right; so I say.

Parolles and Lafew speak familiarly of Galen (c. 129–c. 210) and Paracelsus (1493-1541) because both Sterrell and Worcester had close associations with the two most prominent philosopher/physician/professors of the Elizabethan period. They were Dr. John Caius of Cambridge and Dr. John Case of Oxford. Each of these appears in two other Shakespeare plays, Dr. Caius in *the Merry Wives of Windsor* by his own name and Dr. Case in *As You Like It* under the name Touchstone, derived from his final book, published shortly before the play in 1600, *Lapis Philosophicus — The Philosopher's Touchstone*. Both men wrote at length on Galen and Paracelsus.

Worcester had known Dr. Caius first-hand when he was a student at Cambridge 1567 to 1571. Educated in medicine in Padua, Dr. Caius was a devoted adherent of the medical science of Galen, the second century Greek physician whose works Caius translated and published with his own annotations. Dr. Caius was a member of the council of the College of Physicians - thus an "authentic fellow" as well known to Lafew/Worcester and Parolles/Sterrell.

Sterrell himself had lived with and studied under the other philosopher/physician/professor who was prominent at Oxford, Dr. John Case. Anthony à Wood in *Athenae Oxonienses* reported that Case lost his fellowship because he was "Popishly affected" and that his students were mostly of the Roman Catholic religion. To receive his B.A. in 1579 after only a year at Magdalen, Sterrell must have received credit for study at Oxford in a recognized private professor's home - John Case. In his writings, Dr. Case touched on Galen repeatedly. Case was particularly opposed to Paracelsus; his *Oxford Dictionary of National Biography* biographer asserts that "Case despised Paracelsus almost as much as Machiavelli, another recurring villain in his works."[110] In teaching "natural philosophy" at Oxford, Sterrell covered the science of both Aristotle and Galen. From Dr. Case, Sterrell received a harsh view of Paracelsus.

After the engaging exchange between Lafew and Parolles on Galen and Paracelsus, they are joined by others. The marriage of Bertram and Helena is set up by the King over Bertram's objection, whose shallow character is slowly revealed. When the others leave, Lafew and Parolles resume their badinage, only it now abruptly turns hostile. Parolles is reluctant to admit that Bertram is "My lord? My master?" Lafew says he used to think Parolles was wise. But now he knows better - he has found out Parolles, and Parolles is good for little. Lafew warns Parolles that if he is ever "bound with thy scarf and beaten," he'll be proud of his bondage. Parolles answers Lafew, "you do me most insupportable vexation." Lafew responds he'll maintain their acquaintance, though he says he will vex Parolles as long as he has life in him.

When Lafew leaves, Parolles speaks to the audience a parting shot aimed at Lafew: "Well, thou hast a son shall take this disgrace off me; scurvy, old, filthy, scurvy lord: Well, I must be patient; there is no fettering of authority."

Let us pause to focus on this passage as a critical moment for us in giving meaning to the play. There is no list of the play's characters in the *First Folio,* but most modern editors provide one. We look: there is no son of Lafew.[111] There is no further mention of a son. So, why does the playwright have Parolles say Lafew has a son? One explanation is that Parolles has said he would challenge Lafew to a duel to gain satisfaction for having been insulted, but Lafew is too old for Parolles to fight honorably. Yet he would gain satisfaction by beating the son, "if I could but meet him [the son] *again.*" From this, we surmise that the two men have a past together but not necessarily as master and servant. Until the next meeting with the son, Parolles says: "I must be patient; there is no fettering of authority." Plainly, Parolles and Lafew have a backstory with one another. Later, Lafew even alludes to Parolles having been a teacher of young men before the events of the play. It is also made clear that Parolles is multilingual.

There follows a curious exchange between Lafew and Parolles. Lafew alternates between using the insulting "thou," "thy," and "thee" and the more respectful "you" as Lafew berates Parolles for dressing in courtier's clothing. (Act 2 sc. 3).

> **Lafew**. The devil it is that's thy master. Why dost thou garter up thy arms o' this fashion? Dost make hose of thy sleeves? Do other servants so? Thou wert best set thy lower part where thy nose stands. By mine honour, if I were but two hours younger, I'd beat thee. Methink'st thou art a general offence, and every man should beat thee. I think thou wast created for men to breathe themselves upon thee.
>
> **Parolles**. This is hard and undeserved measure, my lord.

This passage suggests a master-servant relation had existed between the two. Is there a factual setting from which the author is drawing, one which some readers would recognize if real persons such as Sterrell and Worcester are the simulated characters,

Parolles and Lafew? To answer, you should know that Worcester was Sterrell's "old" lord in age (being eleven years the elder of Sterrell) and "old" in service, as having been Sterrell's employer prior to Essex. Essex was the younger lord, four years younger than Sterrell himself. Moreover, Worcester had more than three sons, the eldest presumptively his heir. Sterrell was very close to the Worcester sons, and Worcester's heir might "take this disgrace off me," as Parolles declares. With respect to the master-servant relationship, Sterrell's role was as a tutor, meaning he was a servant to Worcester. By becoming an operative for Essex in the overseas mission of 1591-92, Sterrell was more an agent than servant, just as Parolles had become an officer for Bertram after leaving his old lord, Lafew.

Lafew's insulting treatment that Parolles believes to be undeserved reflected the fact that Worcester disrespected (vexed) Sterrell in March 1593; Sterrell knew at the time he had to bear it. The exchange between Parolles and Lafew echoes Sterrell's letters of 1593 when he described Worcester's "unkind fickleness." He had informed his handler Phelippes that he had become as a voluntary follower of Worcester and referred to his continued though loosened bondage to Worcester: "these indignities I bear, perforce, *quia dominus opus habet* [like a slave who is made free owes service to his master]."[112] This appears to be the same sentiment of Parolles, that authority could not be "fettered."

Sterrell was ever conscious of his status in a stratified society. As an educated gentleman he was above the commoners - the tradesmen and merchants and servants of Elizabethan England. He was far more learned than the noblemen and sons of the nobility whom he taught for years at Oxford. But he was beneath the nobility. He was not presently a member of the landed gentry; he had little steady income and no expectancy of inheritance. He had no base from which to become a Member of Parliament. There was nothing in his background or anticipated future at age 32 (in 1593) that might lead to knighthood. Sterrell would have been stung by Lafew/Worcester's judgment that he aspired above his station.

In a scene that soon follows, the Clown and Parolles exchange witticisms that indicate that Parolles himself is a clown: "much fool may you find in you, even to the world's pleasure and the increase of laughter." This insight of the Clown foreshadows Parolles later accepting that he must become a clown, that is to say an entertainer. As a writer, he will give the world pleasure and an increase in laughter.

The action resumes when Lafew meets Bertram in Act 2 sc. 5, and warns Bertram that Parolles is no soldier. Bertram replies that he has it on good authority that Parolles is valiant, to which Lafew accepts that he might have misjudged Parolles. But when Parolles joins the two men, Lafew's hostility resumes. Parolles complains he doesn't know why he deserves Lafew's displeasure. You may have mistaken him, says Bertram. Lafew warns Bertam not to trust Parolles in any matter of consequence: "The soul of this man is his clothes."[113] Late in the play, the playwright tells us directly that Parolles's clothing is only a metaphor for his status. Hold the thought for when we see Sterrell identify himself with his clothing in a letter of 1592-93.

Two Brothers – Dumaine (Stanley)

Two "French" lords of *All's Well* who capture and interrogate Parolles are portrayals of two English knights who captured and interrogated Sterrell in Antwerp in 1592. As Act 3 opens, the Duke of Florence, two Frenchmen, and soldiers are apparently located near where battle is to take place. One is identified as "1. Lord"; there are also two persons identified by their speech as "French E." and "Fren. G." The Frenchmen have preceded Bertram, Lafew and Parolles to Florence and the fields of battle; no fighting ever occurs. Only in their seventh onstage scene, in Act 4 sc.3, are two of these two "French" lords given the Christian name Dumaine. It is only then that the naming of two officers serving with Bertram becomes consequential, when they are given specific English associations. We can best see how Sterrell is telling his own story by juxtaposing specific scenes and dialogue with Sterrell's letters and other sources recounting his experiences and character.

Parolles promises to enter the enemy camp: By Act 3 sc. 6 we find that Bertram is in Florence with the two Frenchmen. The two assert Parolles is a worthless man, "a most notable coward, an infinite and endless liar, an hourly promise-breaker . . .," just as Helena and Lafew had earlier labelled him. When Bertram objects, they propose a trap that will expose Parolles. They will induce him to recover a drum that has been taken by the enemy. Parolles enters the scene and takes the bait. With bravado, he promises that he will steal into the enemy camp and recover the drum. Bertram promises to reward him if he is successful.

Sterrell's promises to enter the enemy camp: In a January 1592 letter to Phelippes, as recounted earlier, Sterrell had offered heroic gestures on behalf of the Queen in the Spanish Low Countries or Spain: "If you can persuade her Majesty to address some plot to entrap Sir William Stanley, I hope to effectuate it, at leastwise I will venture . . . ." Such a proposal for a single-handed endeavor by a 31-year-old scholar in the midst of an enemy camp would seem sheer folly, just as Parolles's promise to go for the captured drum is folly.

Parolles and words: Bertram encourages Parolles to rescue the drum and departs, with Parolles saying, "I love not many words." This is the playwright's pun on Parolles name, to which Bertram's first lord jokes, "No more than a fish loves water." Words, after all, are what his name means. Moreover, he knows other languages ("he hath a smack of all neighbouring languages") and is a "manifold linguist."

Sterrell and words: William Sterrell apparently was competent not only in his native English but also Latin, Italian, French and probably Spanish. And words have been his identity - a *praelector* at Oxford, a reader of words/texts to students followed by elucidation of the readings.[114]

The play moves forward by indicating the Duke's camp and the enemy are very close together; Parolles can pretend to sneak to capture the nearby drum. The French officers are only a short distancc from the route which Parolles must follow. When Parolles in the night approaches what he thinks is the enemy camp, he speaks to himself (with "Lord E." speaking asides to the audience) about his own cowardice and empty promises. He knows himself. He says he will injure himself to make the others believe he has been wounded. Now his fellow Frenchmen led by the "Lord E." in the guise of enemies, beat a drum as they grab and blindfold Parolles. Because Parolles is multilingual, the principal Frenchmen disguise their nationality by speaking gibberish. One soldier acts as an "interpreter." Parolles, to save himself, immediately promises to tell these feigned enemies all that he knows about his own forces:

Oh, let me live,
And all the secrets of our camp I'll show,
Their force, their purposes; nay, I'll speak that
Which you will wonder at.

"Lord E." sends a report back to Bertram and his brother that they have caught the woodcock, a stupid bird that is easily tricked.[115] He tells the soldier with him that he will imprison Parolles: "I'll keep him dark and safely locked."

Several scenes later — the passage of time is uncertain — we learn that peace has been reached between the warring parties. Bertram will return home the next day. There's no reason to keep Parolles imprisoned. Bertram rejoins the two Frenchmen who have held Parolles captive. The two lords tell Bertram that Parolles is being brought in from the stocks. Bertram calls for "this dialogue between the Fool [Parolles] and the Soldier." When Bertram asks, "How does he carry himself?," the captain answers, "he hath confessed himself to *Morgan,* whom he supposes to be a friar." So Parolles has encountered while imprisoned a man named *Morgan* and confessed all his regiments actions. Was there a *Morgan* whom Sterrell would have visited in Antwerp in 1592?

Morgan is one of many instances of name-droppings and specific references in Shakespeare plays that baffle editors. Generally, they ignore them as random noise. For William Sterrell, such obscure references have pointed significance. There was a *Morgan* who was an English Catholic in the Antwerp prison in 1592 that briefly lodged Sterrell; other English prisoners were also kept there.[116]

This Morgan was Thomas Morgan. He was suspected of treachery towards the Spanish despite his being on the pension roll of Sir William Stanley. Morgan was a partner in scams and schemes with Charles Paget, who had the nemesis in the marriage of the 2nd Earl of Southampton and the Countess and who had betrayed Sterrell to ambassador Ralph Winwood in 1602. Morgan was no priest, but the playwright had to establish a reason for Parolles to confess - a confession by a prisoner such as Parolles would have to be to a member of the cloth. Sterrell knew of Morgan's misdeeds "from the time of his remembrance to this very instant disaster," *i.e.* dating back to 1583-85 when Sterrell was with the French ambassador while Thomas Morgan fed misinformation to Mary Queen of Scots from Paris.

In January 1590 Morgan had been arrested by order of the Duke of Parma and tried on suspicion of being an English spy. The report of Parma to the King of Spain said that Morgan "attempts to sew cockle and intrigues and to undo everything that Cardinal Allen and Father Persons and other good Catholics are doing . . . both within and without the kingdom."[117] Sterrell must have met with Thomas Morgan in prison and then persuaded the Spanish, through Sir William Stanley, to release and banish Morgan. In a letter of June 13, 1592, Sterrell reported to Thomas Phelippes from Liège: "Thomas Morgan is at liberty." This was shortly after Sterrell was in prison with Morgan and was rescued by Sir William Stanley. Because Morgan had long been an intelligence asset of Walsingham, Phelippes, and the English government, obtaining release for Morgan showed Sterrell's own worth to Essex, Bacon and Phelippes and to the Queen. He had done much the same to gain credit with the Catholics by securing release for several Catholic prisoners before going over to the Low Countries. Probably, the release of Morgan was one of the goals he and Phelippes set for his mission, and the letter informing Phelippes of the release showed he had achieved it. We sense this in the fact that Sterrell's letter had no need to explain to Phelippes who Morgan was. The Spanish were happy to banish Morgan.

The play drops in other names or identities of the real people with whom Sterrell was associated in his 1592 mission. One of the companies whose strength Parolles is swearing to is under "Jaques." His real life counterpart in Antwerp in 1592 was Jaques de Franceschi, one of Sir William Stanley's cannon masters. Despite the Italian name, he was one of the English exiles on Sir William's pension rolls. Sterrell met with Jaques on multiple occasions in Antwerp in the residence of Richard Verstegan, another of the exiles who achieved success as a printer, publisher, and polemicist. Jaques can be easily recognized again as the melancholy Jaques in *As You Like It*. His "Ages of Man" speech refers to the "Soldier, Full of strange oaths, and bearded like the Pard, Jealous in honor, sodaine [sudden], and quicke in quarrell, Seeking the bubble Reputation Even in the Canons mouth." This describes Captain Jaques who made his professional reputation as an officer under Sir William Stanley in the artillery, a cannon master. *As You Like It* has other allusions that make certain the character is the same Jaques as in Sir William Stanley's company.

Let's return to the next scenes of the plays. Soldiers bring in the blindfolded Parolles. As the "interpreter" interrogates Parolles before Bertram and the two French lords, Parolles confesses to the numbers of horses and men under Bertram and their condition. He is specific:

> **Int**. [as if reading] First demand of him how many horse the Duke is strong. What say you to that?
>
> **Parolles**: Five or six thousand, but very weak and unserviceable. The troops are all scattered and the commanders very poor rogues, upon my reputation and credit and as I hope to live.

Sterrell's similar account of "enemy" strength: This confession by Parolles has the same tenor as a report by Sterrell from the Low Countries in May 1592, in which he seemed to betray his own friends:[118]

> I am sorry for good sir William Stanley that he is in no more credit. His regiment is not above 400 in all and these nothing paid and ready to be cashiered but to say the truth there is no pay in the low countries and very few soldiers left. One regiment of Spaniards of some 2,000 do all the service.

When asked if he will swear to his account of the strength of his army, Parolles replies: "I'll take the sacrament on't, how and which way you will." Bertram, aside, tells the others: "All's one to him. What a past-saving slave is this?"[119] This passage is to demonstrate religious equivocation, another type of betrayal by Parolles. The author's intentions here would have been clear in 1593 or 1603. Parolles is saying, "I'll take an oath as a Catholic or as a Protestant," with Bertram commenting acidly that it's all the same to Parolles. Shortly before this, Bertram had asserted that Parolles "deceiv'd me like a double-meaning prophesier." Later the King makes the same slur upon Parolles, calling him "an equivocal companion."

In the period of the play, both comments were a reference to the Catholics who would take false oaths on religious issues: they equivocated, which is to swear to one thing while intending another. At the time, the word *equivocate* became synonymous with "Jesuitical." The *Oxford English Dictionary* defines a "Jesuit" as a "dissembling person, a prevaricator"; *Jesuitical*: "Having the character ascribed to the Jesuits; deceitful, dissembling; practising equivocation, prevarication, or mental reservation of truth." Recall that the June 30, 1592 report of Thomas Ferrers from Antwerp to Lord Burghley: Sterrell [Robinson] was freed from jail by the Jesuits: "the chief of the Jesuits there did cause him to be released." Sterrell was thought to be allied with the Jesuits, which, in fact he was.

Equivocation must have deeply troubled Sterrell; it is why Parolles is charged as an equivocator. To assist the Jesuits and the Catholic exiles he had to practice duplicity in dealings with most government officials over decades. He had to put on a false face and use a false name repeatedly, such as he did throughout his 1591-92 mission. We can sense it in a letter of April 1591 to Phelippes before going on his mission for Essex. Sterrell had, with cynicism, responded to a question Essex had raised about Sterrell's faith:

> I have now written something to try his [Essex's] conceit of me which will be to good purpose to prevent all future caluminators. I tell him that I am Catholic and desire a dispensation [from a Jesuit acquaintance] to come to sermons. That will please him I know, and it is true for the Queen is defender of the Catholic faith.

This was an equivocation. A good Catholic was supposed to refuse to attend Anglican sermons/services. If he received a dispensation from a Catholic priest or bishop, he could attend Anglican services and avoid recusant fines. Such a Catholic would only pretend to be an Anglican. In the Low Countries in 1591-92, was Sterrell a Protestant pretending to be a Catholic, or a Catholic pretending to be a Protestant? It must have seemed to those questioning him for the Spanish side or the English side that it was "all one to him."

We return to the plot. After Parolles is tricked into betraying his friends and divulging military secrets in exchange for his freedom, the captors search his pockets and find a letter he has written to Diana. She's a local woman whose favor Bertram has sought. Parolles's letter, in the form of a sonnet, warns that Bertram, whom Parolles serves, is deceitful and unfaithful. When the letter is read, Bertram is outraged.

The "captains" have specific questions about themselves, and the author discloses the Christian name of the brothers, Dumaine. Parolles, still blindfolded, throws invective upon both the brothers, not knowing they are his interrogators. The play becomes quite specific about these two "French" brothers in ways that have nothing else to do with the plot or the setting in France and Italy. As with *Morgan* and *Jaques,* the "son" of Lafew and the "general of the horse," the author is giving us clues to decipher the *roman à clef.* When asked by the interpreter about "Captain Dumaine's" expertness in war, Parolles responds:

> Faith, sir, *he's led the drum before the English tragedians.* To belie him I will not, and more of his soldiership I know not, except in *that country he had the honor to be the officer at a place there called Mile End, to instruct for the doubling of files.* I would do the man what honor I can, but of this I am not certain.

The playwright is thus very specific on details that do not move the story forward. Why? Because they parallel the real story depicted by the play; they are clues for seeing the story behind the story. If Bertram is Essex ("general of the horse"), can we identify the real life counterparts of the two brothers who are the captains/lords who have captured Parolles? When we identify two such brothers who served Essex as captains (near Antwerp in 1586) and who also were interrogators of William Sterrell (in Antwerp in 1592), then we are a long way towards confirming Parolles as Sterrell.

These two Dumaine brothers are the counterparts of Sir William Stanley and his brother, Sir Edward, both English knights or captains. It was Sir William Stanley whom Sterrell would have sought to "entrap" in the Low Countries, and it was Sir William Stanley who retrieved him from the Spanish prison in Antwerp and doubtless then interrogated him about his activities, if not already privy to what Sterrell was up to. Sir William's brother was Edward

Stanley, his chief lieutenant at Zutphen in 1586 where Edward's heroism led to his knighthood and a grant of a generous pension from the Earl of Leicester. The brothers, in that engagement, were fighting alongside Essex, Leicester's "general of the horse," just as the brothers Dumaine are fighting alongside Bertram, the "general of the horse."

Sir William Stanley once *"led the drum before the English tragedians."* The reference to "English tragedians" would apply to the acting company actively managed by Sir William's cousins and longtime close friends, Henry Stanley, 4th Earl of Derby, and his son Ferdinando Stanley, whose title was Lord Strange until he succeeded as 5th Earl of Derby in 1593. These English tragedians became the basis for the Lord Chamberlain's company formed shortly after the sudden death of Ferdinando in 1594.

Sir William Stanley's biography tells us that Sir William, born in 1548 to the head of the senior branch of the house of Stanley, became married at age 12. When the marriage was annulled five years later, records of the annulment establish that Stanley had served in the household of his aristocratic relative Edward Stanley (1509–1572), 3rd Earl of Derby. As a boy, Sir William came to know well Edward Stanley's son Henry (1531–1593, 4th Earl of Derby), and Ferdinando Stanley, (1559–1594, 5th Earl of Derby) when their acting company was quite active. [120] Young William would likely have *"led the drum before the English tragedians"* (the family enterprise) before becoming a soldier at age 19 for the Spanish under the Duke of Alba in the Low Countries. When enmity between Spain and England later arose, William Stanley joined the English regiment in Ireland, earning knighthood.

When might Sir William Stanley have been *the officer at a place there [England] called Mile End, to instruct for the doubling of files*? It was necessarily before January 18, 1587, the date when he turned the city of Deventer in the Low Countries over to the Spanish after winning it for the English under the Earl of Leicester. A little background is needed here.

In late summer of 1585, the Queen and her counselors decided to aid the Dutch in fighting the Spanish in the Netherlands. In early December 1585, Sir William Stanley was sent to Ireland to raise a thousand men for the Low Countries — new enlistees, not trained soldiers. [121] By early July 1586 he was back in London preparing his raw recruits for the Low Countries. This would have been at *Mile End,* where the London militia drilled. He would have given the new soldiers the most basic training: *instruction* for *doubling the files.*[122] By this time his younger brother, Edward Stanley, had joined him; both would have been drilling the troops. At the end of July 1586, they joined Leicester's men in the Low Countries.

Only six weeks after joining Leicester and Essex, the two Stanleys were key actors in England's operations to counter the Spanish. Soon, Sir William was placed in charge of the town of Deventer, only to turn traitor by handing the town over to the Spanish. His brother Sir Edward was evidently not working with him, for he was soon back in England.

In 1588 we find Sir Edward Stanley in London, now overseeing the drilling of new troops being raised in response to the approach of the Spanish Armada.[123] Thus, both Stanleys fit the description: *the officer at a place there [England] called Mile End, to instruct for the doubling of files.*

Nevertheless, Sir Edward returned to Sir William's Spanish regiment in 1591 in the Low Countries, probably because of informers' reports to the English government of his adherence to the Catholic faith and distrust because of his traitor brother. He was undoubtedly with his brother, Sir William, questioning Sterrell after Sir William sprang Sterrell from the Spanish prison in Antwerp.

ഩഩഩഩ--ഢഢഢഢ

After naming the Dumaine brothers and providing them with an English background, the playwright brings Parolles to his moment of truth. This device as seen in Greek and Roman tragedy is called *anagnorisis,* and can be found in the works of Sophocles (especially *Antigone* and *Oedipus Rex*), Aeschylus, Plautus, Virgil and Seneca, all of which were probably known by Shakespeare-the-author. It is the point at which the character changes their perception of themselves. This moment of profound insight is often termed an *epiphany.* It typically sparks a turning point. Playwrights from ancient times have used an internal monologue or soliloquy to show the process of this realization as the character reflects on their inner thoughts. The Shakespeare plays frequently employ *anagnorisis*, including *King Lear*, *Othello*, *Macbeth*, and *Twelfth Night*. It is especially seen in *All's Well* when Parolles declares his transformation in a dramatic soliloquy.

The playwright sets up the moment when he has the "interpreter" tell Parolles he must die. In response to his plea "let me live, or let me see my death," the blindfold is removed. He sees he's been made the fool. One lord (Lo.E) says he's returning to France and asks what message Parolles has for Lafew. This Lord, one of the Dumaines, is thus indicating that he knows of a special relationship of Lafew and Parolles, as William Stanley would have known of the relation of Sterrell to the Earl of Worcester. But he gets no answer.

Dismissed from the service, Parolles is alone on the stage. Now he expresses his moment of self-realization and transformation. He declares [Act 4 sc. 3]:

Captain I'll be no more,
But I will eat and drink, and sleep as soft
As captain shall. Simply the thing I am
Shall make me live. Who knows himself a braggart,
Let him fear this, for it will come to pass
That every braggart shall be found an ass.
Rust, sword! Cool, blushes! And, Parolles, live
Safest in shame! Being fooled, by fool'ry thrive.

This could have been the end of the play for Parolles, who plans to follow the French lords home. Critics have expressed surprise at his resilience when he is resurrected near the end of the play, but that misses the essence of the play, which is Parolles's reunion with his former master after attaining self-awareness, authentic selfhood.

Further parallels of Sterrell with Parolles are seen in subsequent exchanges between Parolles and Lafew after Parolles returns to the French court. Parolles is described as a snipt-taffeta fellow leading dowy youth when Lafew brings Parolles back in discussion. He tells Bertram's mother that her son had been misled into misdeed towards Helen. Lafew describes Parolles in the most unflattering of terms. He calls him "*a snipt-taffeta fellow there, whose villainous saffron would have made all the unbak'd and dowy youth of a nation in his colour . . . .*" [Act 4 sc. 5]. This is the author's continuing trope to characterize Parolles by his clothing while also revealing more of Parolles's past, saying he was once a leader of youth.

The identification of Sterrell as Parolles is furthered when we find Sterrell referring to himself as constrained in his double-faced relation with those upon whom he was practising. In a letter to Phelippes (probably in 1596) he wrote: "You must hasten the Earl [Essex] to resolve for our Lady day is at hand, and then I must leave to wear taffaty {taffeta} for so I promised and till I do so I shall not be able to discover any man among them here . . .." Sterrell thus identified himself as a "taffeta" man, doubtless with irony. In other intelligence letters Sterrell tells Phelippes he needs more money to dress himself up: "I am not yet appareled according to the fashion of the Spainards which doth hinder me." When he pretended to be a merchant, Sterrell also used the word "taffeta" in his letters to signify intelligence.

Sterrell's fancy clothing was noteworthy to a Cambridge historian who wrote a book on spying in the age of Elizabeth. Stephen Alford in *The Watchers* took up Sterrell's 1591-92 mission and pronounced it a complete failure. He came away with a perspective on Sterrell that nearly alludes to Parolles's comedown as a *snipt taffeta* fellow when he concludes: "So much for the life [Sterrell] had expected in Brussels, that of a *gentleman spy dressed in the latest Spanish fashions.*"

Dowy Youth and Oxford

In the same passage as *snipt-taffeta fellow,* Lafew says Parolles was one who "would have made all the unbak'd and dowy youth of a nation in his colour." This is on its surface rather odd, for there's nothing in the play to suggest Parolles in his service with Bertram has anything to do with the youth of France or England. Parolles is a captain in military service to a French count; he has no soldiers under him. This very brief mention of Parolles as a possible subverter of youth makes no contribution to character development or plot. It is as random as *Morgan* and *English tragedians* until we relate these to Sterrell. The snippet of information is yet another important fact in the *roman à clef* that is a clue to Parolles's identity: Sterrell was well-known among the zealous protestants of Oxford

University as a corrupter of youth leading them to papistry, his religious "colour."

The verb used *"would have made"* is a *conditional perfect verb form*, indicating a hypothetical, unrealized, or past intention in the past tense. Lafew is Parolles's old master, so he is speaking of Parolles as known for his former employment. This would suggest a teacher of young men, which would apply to Sterrell who was a *praelector* (University-wide lecturer) while also serving Worcester. The Oxford students to whom Sterrell lectured were "unbaked," as defined in the *Oxford English Dictionary*: "fig. Left in an unfinished or immature state."

Now, virtually all editors of *All's Well* revise the *First Folio* spelling of "*dowy youth*" to "doughy youth" to make a pun of "unbaked," as though referring to bread. Perhaps. But the pun works better in the opposite direction, adding "unbaked" to make the pun upon "dowy." It misdirects the audience from the real reference of "dowy." What is "doughy" about youth who might fall under Parolles's "villainous saffron" (fancy colored clothing or ruffles) spell? Consider a better reading that "dowy" is "Douai" or "Douay"(pronounced DOW-ee or DOW-y or DOW-ay, not Dōō-ay). *Douay* is the older, anglicized spelling historically used in English, particularly in reference to the Douay-Rheims Bible. Sterrell's letters that refer to the Catholic seminary spell it "Doway."

William Sterrell long had associations with Douay/Doway. The name identifies the town and the Catholic college/seminary in France founded by Cardinal William Allen, formerly principal of St. Mary's Hall, Oxford University. The college moved its location to Rheims in 1578 and returned to Douay in 1593. Sterrell was arranging transport of Catholic youth to Douay/Rheims in 1582-85, probably among them Worcester's first cousin, George Somerset.[124] The young men transported by Sterrell were "dowy/Doway" youth whom Sterrell was making "in his colour" i.e. the Catholic religion. Potentially, his many other students at Oxford had been at risk of being made Catholic, as was charged against him by other Fellows of the college. Worcester (Lafew) was very much aware of Sterrell's role as the seminary was supported by Worcester's uncle, Thomas Somerset. Lafew's use of the conditional past makes clear that the potential subversion of the nation's youth preceded

Parolles's mission abroad for Bertram (Essex).

We have already seen the confession of Edward Dodwell in 1585 reporting that Sterrell was responsible for transporting him and other Oxford students overseas to seminary. To that testimony we must add charges of a Fellow at Magdalen that Sterrell, like Parolles, was corrupting the young men of Oxford in religion. He essentially alleged that Sterrell "would have made all the unbak'd and dowy youth of a nation in his colour." This Fellow was Simon Pett who, with other puritan friends, complained in 1585 to higher authorities of the university that the president of Magdalen, Lawrence Humphrey, was too lenient with papist students and Fellows who were turning Oxford scholars to papistry. Bishop Thomas Cooper, who had long been associated with Magdalen, was appointed Visitor to the college to report on the complaints.[125]

Five depositions made by Magdalen Fellows survive. Referring specifically to Sterrell and several of his friends, Pett lamented that because President Humphrey was "a great friend and favorer" to them, "this house, which should be a house of prophets, and of the sons of the prophets, will become a receptacle of Papists, atheists, ruffians, idle bellies, unlearned and ungodly persons." Accusations specifically against Sterrell were also made by another Fellow, Edward Lord.[126]

Sterrell was named by Pett as one of the greatest offenders who was trying to turn into Catholics other students both at Magdalen and elsewhere in the university:[127]

> Mr. Sterrill and Sir [Paul] Browne [Fellow of Magdalen from 1583-1598] are greatly suspected for papistry, not only in our house [Magdalen], but in the University also; and so suspected that many of us dare take our oaths that we are persuaded that they are in heart papists, howsoever they dissemble the same. They communicate very seldom with us; come seldom to sermons. I have seen them and their scholars [younger students in their care] also walking in the cloisters in sermon time. They were companions with those that are gone to Rheims, and with those in the University that are grievously suspected for popery. . . . Mr. Sterrill did deal with one Presson, as that party told me, to corrupt him in religion,

> and since that party left Oxford, I hear that he is become a papist.

The "Presson" is almost certainly "Rowland Preston" of Shopshire, gent., who at age nine, in December 1576, matriculated at Magdalen Hall along with his brother William, age 18. Not long after Pett's allegations, Preston was at Douay/Rheims and thereafter Rome, where he apparently became a Benedictine priest. Sterrell, speaking through Lafew, relates the charges levelled against him by his fellow Oxfordians as a corrupter of youth in religion. Because Sterrell was known within Oxford and also to government officials like Lord Cobham and Secretary Walsingham as an agent of "popery" he needed a false identity if he were ever to succeed as a poet and playwright.

Thou and You - Parolles and Lafew

Another, more subtle, sign of the shifting relationship of Parolles and Lafew is directly drawn from another major event in William Sterrell's life. Throughout the play, the author reflects the contemporary language of social and personal status in using "thou" rather than "you" when a superior speaks to an inferior. This "thou" in usage to an inferior is traced in the *Oxford English Dictionary* which examines the changing usage of "Thou":

> *Thou* and its cases *thee, thine, thy,* were in Old English used in ordinary speech; in Middle English, they were gradually superseded by the plural *ye, you, your, yours,* in addressing a superior and (later) an equal, but were long retained in addressing an inferior.

Lafew, for example, consistently addresses the Clown as "thou" - an inferior - with rare exception. The Countess is close to Helena and addresses her with the intimate "thou," but not because Helena is of an inferior status as a poor physician's daughter. Bertram, himself a Count, speaks to Helena as "you" (e.g., Act 2 sc.5, 59-71), neither intimate, though his wife, nor inferior.

At the beginning of Act 2 sc. 3 Lafew and Parolles exchange friendly banter, with Lafew saying to Parolles, "A word with you." Twelve lines later, the usage abruptly changes. Lafew turns contemptuous, repeatedly addressing Parolles as "thou," "thee" and "thy." For example:

Lafew - Do not plunge *thyself* too far in anger, lest *thou* hasten *thy* trial; which if, Lord have mercy on *thee* for a hen, so my good window of lattice, fare *thee* well. *Thy* casement I need not open, for I look through *thee*. Give me *thy* hand. Act 2 sc. 3, 205-09.

Parolles is taken aback by the sudden change in attitude and can only sputter, "My lord, you give me most egregious indignity." The "thou-ing" is the indignity. When Lafew refers to Parolles as *you* rather than *thou* it signals change. Parolles in anger occasionally uses "thou" to Lafew but otherwise is respectful, with *you*.

Let's direct our attention to the changing relationship of Parolles and the Clown, and follow that by looking at the shifts for Lafew and Parolles. For their exchanges in most of the play, Parolles uses "thou" and "knave" in talking with the Clown. Here we will quote the study of Susan Snyder of *Naming Names in "All's Well That Ends Well."*[128] She notes that the usage changes with Parolles's precipitate fall in status:

> Formerly, as the companion of counts and lords, Parolles used "thou" and "knave" in talking with the Clown, aping his betters; now down and out, and indeed newly determined himself to live by fooling, he sees this same Clown as the back door into noble patronage. Parolles thus marks their new relationship by giving him not only the respectful "you" but a title and a name. The title, abbreviated in the Folio text as "Mr," could be expanded as either Master or Monsieur; "Monsieur" has been Parolles's own title in this play, exclusively his in eleven uses. He now applies the same honorific to the Clown, underlining his own loss of status as he reverses their former position.

So, Parolles and the Clown have a new relationship reflected in this passage as it appears in the *First Folio* (my emphasis):

> *Par.* Good **Mr** *Lavatch*, give my Lord Lafew this letter. I have ere now, sir, been better known to **you**, when I have held familiarity with fresher clothes; but I am now **sir** muddied in Fortune's mood, and smell somewhat strong of her strong displeasure.

Following the Clown's witty riposte seeking fresh air, Parolles replies, with respect:

Par. Nay, **you** need not to stop your nose, **sir**. I spoke but by a metaphor.

Then Parolles requests the Clown deliver a message to Lafew, again with "sir." The Clown calls Parolles "Fortune's close-stool" (toilet), but there is no need to deliver the letter because Lafew immediately enters. Lafew again berates Parolles, using *thou* and *thee*.

These differing usages of ***you*** and ***thou*** permeate the Shakespeare plays and the sonnets. The playwright follows a consistent approach that correlates to the social understandings of these terms reflected in the *Oxford English Dictionary*'s history of the usage.[129] To give an example, in *A Midsummer Night's Dream*, Oberon, as master, says *thou* to Puck, his servant, and Puck replies with *you*. The pronoun choices reflect social status rather than deliberate insult.

As an insult, we see the usage of "thou" and "you" with Lafew to Parolles and in other plays. The usage is especially clear in the play *Twelfth Night*. Sir Toby uses *thou* in speaking to his close friend Andrew Aguecheek but then tells him to taunt a youth, who was not a close friend, he is challenging by referring to him as "thou":

Sir Toby. Go, write it in a martial hand; be curst and brief; it is no matter how witty, so it be eloquent and full of invention. Taunt him with the license of ink; if **thou *thou'st*** him some thrice, it shall not be amiss; and as many lies as will lie in **thy** sheet of paper . . .

An equivalent usage violation today would be a lawyer addressing a judge in court by using their first name or an hourly employee of a Fortune 500 company calling the company CEO by their first name. Or an army private calling out to an officer, "Hey, you. Yes, I'm speaking to you." As a powerful social taboo, it simply isn't done.

The serious insult of "thou-ing" another who is equal in status but not an intimate friend is illustrated in a contemporaneous historical event. The same treatment of *thou* as a grave insult is found in the exchanges between Attorney General Edward Coke and Sir Walter Ralegh at Ralegh's trial in 1603. Coke goaded Ralegh by calling him *thou*: Coke said that all Cobham (Ralegh's co-conspirator) "did was by ***thy*** instigation, ***thou*** viper; for I ***thou thee, thou*** traitor."[130] To *thou* and *thee* Ralegh was to insult him, to treat him as an inferior. Ralegh responded: "It becometh not a man of quality and virtue to call me so . . ." Chief Justice Popham intervened to put Coke in his place for insulting Ralegh, addressing Ralegh more formally and explaining, "Sir Walter Ralegh, Mr. Attorney speaketh out of the zeal of his duty . . . ."

Thou-ing at Oxford, 1587

The "thou" usage in *All's Well* and in other Shakespeare plays reflects a significant event in Sterrell's life at Oxford. The "thou" event occurred in 1587.

In the middle of June 1587, a Convocation (gathering of all Masters) was called to consider new statutes for the University. Since November 1581, newly entering students had to subscribe their names to the Oath of Supremacy, the University's response to the distribution the previous June of Campion's *Rationes decem* at graduation ceremonies.[131] They were required to swear that they recognized the Queen dually as head of state and as head of the church. The Oath was necessarily a rejection of the Pope as spiritual head of the church and acknowledged a secular monarch as effectively the successor of Christ in all matters of faith and doctrine. Nothing but tradition and prudence bound the Queen's authority in religion. She was answerable only to God. Rejection of her primacy in religion was heresy. However, the statute did not apply to those already matriculated within the University.

Now, in the 1587 Convocation, the Masters took up a proposal for a statute requiring the Oath of Supremacy of all who had not been covered by the statute of 1581.[132] Sterrell himself would have been affected, but it was others of his friends for whom he spoke, named Thomas Warren and George Errington. Favoring the proposal was Richard Coxe, a minister who was new to Oxford: a Cambridge B.A. of 1582 and an Oxford M.A. of 1584. The youthful preacher expressed contempt for two Oxford Masters of Arts who had (re)turned to Catholicism. Warren and Errington were both M.A. of Trinity College, Oxford. The latter had been released from prison only a few months earlier. Coxe's words were more than William Sterrell could tolerate. Angered by the speech of this

Cambridge divine against Sterrell's friend Errington, who had suffered in prison for the very crimes of which Sterrell himself was guilty — transporting youth to Douay/Dowy — Sterrell spoke up. In a stage whisper, Sterrell said someone such as Coxe should not be speaking against Masters of Arts of nine or ten years standing. He drew closer to Coxe, and told him it was not well that Coxe should speak against them, they being absent and not there to speak for themselves.

Coxe now turned his invective upon Sterrell. If Sterrell were so impudent as to defend Warren and Errington, then he was as bad as they were, which in fact he was. Coxe openly declared that Sterrell was suspected and should not be suffered to speak in Convocation for any such men as Warren and Errington were or such like men suspected for religion. Growing more heated, Sterrell said that Coxe was not fit to be a witness: Coxe himself might be suspected of *felony!*

The matter was growing so serious that Dr. William James, the Dean of Christ Church College, intervened. As he was also the Vice-Chancellor of the University, Dr. James was the most important figure in the University in the absence of the Chancellor, the Earl of Leicester. Dr. James warned Sterrell: these were grievous words and would bear an action in slander. Sterrell said he could back them up with evidence of sheep-stealing and violation of Lenten prohibitions.

Such accusations would seem to make a *prima facie* case for slander against Sterrell, but this would be a misreading of the proceedings. Of greater interest is Coxe's next statement, which became the source of Sterrell's countersuit against Coxe. Two of Sterrell's witnesses gave testimony about what they had heard from Coxe, and they repeated precisely the same words in the countersuit. The scribe wrote that Coxe told Sterrell: "*Thou* carest not what *thou* swearest against any honest man." Sterrell's witness William Aubrey, an M.A. of Christ Church, testified that these "words were spoken openly in the hearing of many."[133] Another testified that he thought "the words to be greatly prejudicial to Mr. Sterrell's credit,"[134] and two more witnesses stated that these words greatly discredited him.

Sterrell's close friend Richard Easton, who was himself pulled off a boat bound for France while bearing Catholic religious items, testified that if this were his cause he was "esteame [value] his damages to an hundred pownds at the least." Aubrey agreed: "Mr. Sterrell may esteame his damage to as much as his credit is worth & this deponent thinketh his credit better worth than a hundreth powndes." On further questioning, Aubrey testified that Sterrell's name was discredited: "And this deponent never knew him but of good name and fame."

What in Coxe's statement is so offensive that it would support a Sterrell counter-suit against Coxe when Coxe sued Sterrell in Chancellor's Court for slander? The modern mind focuses upon Coxe's statement to the effect that Sterrell did not care what he would swear to. But this was merely a statement of opinion by Coxe. Hardly slanderous, even in Elizabethan times. The focus of an Elizabethan, and more particularly the focus of a Master of Arts at Oxford in 1587, would be upon the "*Thou*" used twice by Coxe in speaking directly to Sterrell, "spoken openly in the hearing of many" in Convocation. At every other mention of a name throughout the depositions in the suit of *Coxe v. Sterrell* and *Sterrell v. Coxe,* the formal title "***Mr.***" is carefully used.

The deposition of Coxe's witness, Arthur Laurence, is quite pointed, quoting Coxe as saying: "***you*** will not care what ***you*** say or sweare against any man with other words of heate which might seame to tend to Mr Sterills dyscredditt." Coxe's own deposition carefully avoids the "*thou*" statement while admitting that he said similar words: "he spake thus of all such as should show themselves so forward as Mr. Sterrill did in that cause and in that place. That is they that would speak in that place and that cause as Mr. Sterrill did would not shrink to say anything against any man & otherwise he speak not to his remembrance." The flawed remembrance has long been the refuge of the embarrassed litigant.

Despite the testimony that Coxe had said that Sterrell was as bad as Warren and Errington, the slander claim by Sterrell was not simply that Sterrell would swear to anything but that he was being addressed as an inferior in an insulting manner by Coxe. It was wholly inappropriate of fellows who were Fellows.

In the filings, Sterrell readily admitted that he said openly that it may not be suffered that such a one as Mr. Coxe should speak against Masters of Arts of nine or ten years standing who is suspected of felony. He only denied that he spoke openly the reports that the felles (sheepskins) were found in Coxe's chamber. He did confess that he spoke openly that he would prove suspicion of felony by persons not suspected of felony. His bold signature is followed by a penman's flourish. The case was settled without a judgment.

Oxford litigation between Fellows was very rare. Sterrell carried the experience in memory long after the event, and it is vividly reflected in *All's Well.* The accusation that Coxe made against Sterrell as he "thou-ed" him was: "Thou carest not what thou swearest against any honest man." This is essentially what Bertram says to the king against Parolles when he wrongly accuses Parolles of lying: "Am I or that or this for *what he'll utter that will speak anything*?"

Tearful Restoration

Let us now finish our play. Parolles has a new relationship with the Clown in which Parolles is humble and makes requests of the Clown rather than demands. But what of Parolles and Lafew? This relation is told in Act 5, sc. 2 and sc. 3.

Parolles tells Lafew that "I am a man whom Fortune hath cruelly scratched." Lafew asks what business is it to him and tosses him a coin. Parolles begs for a single word more. Okay, one word, responds Lafew. What is the word? Parolles says it: "My name, my good lord, is Parolles." Lafew jokes back that that is more than one word - meaning Parolles is the plural of word.

Delivery of the next lines is crucial here. How would the actors speak them? It makes all the difference in the meaning of the play. With your indulgence, I will propose my own stage directions.

Lafew [*with warmth and passion, extending his hand*]: Cox my passion [By God's passion], give me your hand. [*Now with irony*]: How does your drum?"

Par. [*falling to his knees and embracing Lafew's hand as he hopes for reconciliation*]: O my good Lord, you were the first that found me.

Lafew [*laughing indulgently*]. Was I, in sooth? [*Turning ironic* *again*] And I was the first that lost thee.

Par. [*pleading*]: It lies in you, my lord, to bring me in some grace, for you did bring me out.

Laf. [*with mock severity, playful*]: Out upon ***thee***, knave, dost ***thou*** put upon me at once both the office of God and the devil? One brings ***thee*** in grace, and the other brings ***thee*** out. [*Trumpets sound – as if announcing divine grace*]. The King's coming; I know by his trumpets. ***Sirrah***, inquire further after me; I had talk of ***you*** last night. Though ***you*** are a fool and a knave, ***you*** shall eat. Go to; follow. [*Lafew turns to leave, gesturing to Parolles to follow him, both home and into the future*].

Par. [*tearful in joy, overwhelmed by relief and grateful for the shift in usage from* thee *to* you]: I praise God for you.

In the final scene, Act 5 sc.3, the King declares to Parolles, "thou art a knave and no knave." It is as though the government has declared of Parolles that he had played the knave abroad but was not a traitor; charges dismissed, as seems to have occurred for Sterrell by the Privy Council's inaction in 1593. Lafew seems to agree, giving mixed judgment of Parolles, telling the King: "He's a good drum [entertainer], my Lord, but a naughty Orator [advocate]."

The penultimate lines of the play are by Lafew, just before the king's final pronouncements and the epilogue. We get the final indication of Lafew's relation with Parolles, speaking again to Parolles as a servant:

Mine eyes smell onions; I shall weep anon.
Good Tom Drum [Parolles], lend me a handkerchief.
So, I thank *thee*. Wait on me *home* [accompany me, attend], I'll make sport with *thee*. Let thy curtsies [bowing] alone; they are scurvy ones.

Parolles will again follow his old master home though treated as a servant: as Sterrell had written, "these indignities I bear, perforce, *quia dominus opus habet*" — like a slave who is made free owes service to his master. Sterrell could only flourish by remaining bound as a servant to his master so long as the master lived. Together they would make entertainment for years to come.

Why does the playwright have Lafew's eyes smell onions? It

is to make wordplay - eyes don't smell, but this is a common metaphor for weeping.[135] More pertinently, the onion is a stand-in for the leek, known as "the gourmet's onion." The leek is the national symbol of Wales where Worcester's castles (home) lie to which the two men are returning in their capacities as lord and follower, master and servant. Fluellen, a Welsh knight in *Henry V*, praises the leek memorably and reminds the king of his Welsh origins and that "there is good men [b]orn at Monmouth." Monmouth can refer to the town closest to Worcester's Raglan Castle (seven miles) or to the shire in which Worcester's great holdings were located, as well as those lands Worcester granted to Sterrell over time. The playwright always allows interpretation; he doesn't compel it.

ꕥꕥꕥꕥ--ꕥꕥꕥꕥ

When Sterrell returned to grace with Worcester after the 1592 Low Countries debacle, the two established an arrangement to their mutual benefit. Sterrell could write poetry and plays, some guided by Worcester, others not. Sterrell never had to worry about income or pleasing multiple patrons, unlike virtually all other poets and playwrights of the period. Worcester had at hand the greatest playwright of the age to provide magnificent entertainment and spectacle, thereby enhancing his own standing with the monarchy and among his own peers. Worcester also had a willing surrogate, an ever constant agent working to maintain the Catholic faith at home and abroad by his correspondence with Catholics in exile. Together, they cultivated friendly relations with the sovereigns in the Low Countries and with Spain. No one, including Robert Cecil, would charge Worcester with wrongdoing or disloyalty. And if Sterrell were caught, Worcester would protect him.

Poetic Work as Personal Reflection

All's Well was never publicly performed nor published, but it is obvious that it was closely edited by the time of its publication in the *First Folio*. Why would a writer compose such a personal work if not for fame or fortune? Why would he abase himself? Because many writers write for self-expression, as a way of organizing their experiences - much as many people keep a diary or notebooks. For many writers, the need to express oneself is embedded in their DNA; it is their identity.

A reflective playwright would write an introspective play to ruminate on a deeply personal experience of dread and abandonment. It is not unlike novelists who have lived with the pain and debilitation of tuberculosis inside their bodies and have transposed or reimagined their condition creatively. Consider, for examples, Albert Camus's *The Plague* or Thomas Mann's *Magic Mountain.* The protagonist of Dashiell Hammett's *The Glass Key,* Ned Beaumont, is a tall, thin, moustache-wearing, TB-ridden, drinking, gambling, hanger-on, like Hammett himself. Eugene O'Neill has two such introspective plays, *The Straw,* based on his experience in a sanatorium), and *Long Day's Journey into Night,* in which the character Edmund suffers from the illness.

Consider also the example of another, more recent Latin-quoting professor of Magdalen College, Oxford, who also was thoroughly religious in outlook and work. This was C. S. Lewis, a professor of English literature at Magdalen College, Oxford for three decades. He used the same library of the College where Sterrell studied, and where I examined very old books and records after climbing ancient spiral stairs. Like William Sterrell, Lewis based some work on Ovid and Boccaccio. His *Cupid and Psyche* is drawn from *The Metamorphoses* and *The Decameron.*

C.S. Lewis used two main pseudonyms to separate his academic work from his private life. He became Clive Hamilton for his early poetry publications. He wrote under the name N. W. Clerk, for the introspective book *A Grief Observed* to keep his bereavement following the death of his wife from the public. This book was compiled from four notebooks used by Lewis to explore his grief. Even his close friends did not realize he was the author when they recommended the book to him for consolation.

All's Well that Ends Well is a deep reflection by the playwright on a boundary experience in his life. The play must have served a purpose like C. S. Lewis's. And how does C. S. Lewis sum up his own account of his devastating experience? With these words that resonate with his Magdalen College predecessor's own:

> Two widely different convictions press more and more on my mind. One is that the Eternal Vet is even more inexorable and the possible operations even more painful than our severest

imaginings can forbode. But the other, that 'all shall be well, and all shall be well, and all manner of thing shall be well'.

It is almost as if C.S. Lewis/N.W. Clerk was channeling William Sterrell/Shakespeare as he worked within the same walls four centuries later.

Writers often project themselves in less than flattering terms. Timid T. S. Eliot sees himself in *J. Alfred Prufrock* who worries about eating a peach, who sees himself as the eternal footman. Ernest Hemingway presents elements of himself in the scarred-by-war Jake Barnes in *The Sun Also Rises.* We shouldn't be surprised to find the same in "Shakespeare," a man who had endured humiliation and threat of death, who had accepted his fate that he must hide himself behind a borrowed name if he were to find success as a poet and playwright.

♦♦♦ ♦♦♦

Skepticisima: Bardolby, you've been quiet throughout this discussion of *All's Well.* You didn't interject. That's not like you. Is all well with you?

Bardophilus: Don't be cute. I'm trying to show some respect and not interrupt the flow. That's quite a tall tale. I'm sure it has a simple explanation.

Skepticisima: Yes?

Bardophilus: I've heard your author Verba or whatever we call him has quite the imagination. He's written some historical fiction, and this book may just be another creative exercise. They tell me that if you read his novels, it's hard to distinguish his fictional characters from the real people they mix with. Did he make this book up whole cloth as a spoof, like Sokal's Hoax in *Social Text?* He may be laughing at us, starting with his title. It's all an *Invention,* his own fabrication. Nobody's heard of him. He's no more than a dilettante who's out of his element. Reflections on Shakespeare should be left to the professionals.

Skepticisima: I'll grant you that he's obscure. He writes outside your community. You could start with a non-fiction book of his that has lots more endnotes and covers some of the same ground. *Elizabethan Espionage*. There's bound to be inconsistencies and bad facts and lousy judgments. Nobody's read it. Dull. Pedantic. Too many facts, too little life. He's a plodder, not an entertainer, an amateur to the professionals we know among the Shakespeare elite who dazzle us with their wit, charm and erudition.

Bardophilus: Even so, he could be making up many of the letters and documents that he claims are in Vienna or in the Bodleian. He's not working from the published resources the rest of us all rely on. There have been some spectacular Shakespeare hoaxes, you'll have to admit. Maybe the author is channeling the spirits of John Payne Collier and William Henry Ireland in manufacturing documents, which they mixed in with the real records. Maybe he's concocted Sterrell as a new Piltdown Man.

Skepticisima: Maybe so, maybe so. How hard would it be for you to expose it and hold him up to ridicule?

Bardophilus: Meh. Is it worth the effort? Who will pay any attention to a self-published book anyway? But just for argument's sake, let's say we find that there really is this Sterrell guy, and Worcester was his employer. Sterrell could have told his story to the real Shakespeare who thought it could be developed into a play.

Skepticisima: I certainly expect you to spin this. But you may be missing out on the next big thing. Like one wag said, if Francis Bacon didn't write the Shakespeare plays, he passed up the opportunity of a lifetime. Maybe Sterrell-is-Shakespeare is what they will call a new paradigm. Lots of universities and colleges are dropping Shakespeare from the curriculum from disinterest. Think of the employment and scholarship opportunities that could open up just to put down this upstart who is so rash as to question the overwhelming weight of authority and impeccable credentials of the Stratford crowd. You can humiliate him like the captains do to Parolles. Ignore him and it will be one hand clapping – his alone. Engage, and you can make a big noise that will reverberate in the popular media as well as learned journals. The controversy will fuel hundreds of fires set off by the sparks in this *Invention*.

Bardophilus: Or not.

Skepticisima: Or not.

The Fatal Vespers

Before turning to Shakespeare's will, let us return to our discussion of the Fatal Vespers, a mass tragedy that occurred at Blackfriars in London on Sunday, October 26, 1623:

Upon Sunday last in the afternoon there was a famous Jesuit called as I hear Mr. Drewry [Drury] lately come from St. Omers, to preach in Blackfriars near to the French Ambassadors house who lieth in the Lord Hunsdon's house that was & is the Heirs still. Out of it were diverse ways into the Blackfriars. In brief as he was begining his sermon, the floor whereon they stood fell down & did beat down the next under it, and so the roof fell also upon them. How many are slain is uncertain, for the rubbish is so great a quantity that many laborers are still digging and have found 93 but there may be more. The Jesuit is found beaten all in pieces, many were sore hurt, many escaped, but few without some harm. There was a Benedictine (as I am told) that stood close to the preacher & cried aloud. Prepare yourselves, I absolve you from all your sins & escaped himselfe & went into the Ambassador's house. The report is, that there were assembled 400 persons. It is a doleful accident. The rooms in the friary have been many years decayed & some report, that father Fisher who provided them, was warned by the House Keeper not to trust to the large room for it would bear no weight. There was many there of account, but are not particularly known.

William Sterrell to Charles della Faille, Brussels, November 9, 1623

Sterrell succinctly and accurately describes the fatal occurrence, including the fact that Lord Hunsdon's House in Blackfriars is currently owned by "the heirs." He is writing to the Secretary of State of a foreign government and knows his letter might be intercepted by the English government, hence he uses the elliptical "as I hear," "(as I am told)" and "some report" to avoid his information being firsthand. The collapse of the floor was at a forbidden religious service, at which two Jesuit priests were celebrants as well as a Benedictine.

Here are three questions to consider as you read the next chapter on Shakespeare's will and its relevance to the Fatal Vespers.

1. How did 400 people manage to find their way to a secret service at a mansion in the heart of London? Each faced imprisonment and the three priests risked execution for a capital crime.
2. Where exactly was Lord Hunsdon's House in the old Dominican monastery known as Blackfriars?
3. How did William Sterrell know so much about the events and the building which collapsed? Or was this "Paul's news" as he had described the stuff of gossip and rumor as he had described such in April 1593?

Chapter 8

Shakespeare's Will

> *Then said he [Captain Jaques] there's no other way but two. When she [Queen Elizabeth] goes to walk or when she goes to a sermon. Take a dagger or a pistol and stab her or shoot her into the body for she takes no care of her goings. And if you can escape but two or three hours you are safe forever. But what means have you to go thither, you must go to Calais and abide with the spies and desire their help. But have you no friends about the court that you know? I said yes, Mr. Fortescue and Mr. Sterrell. Then said he, will Mr. Fortescue do anything for you? I said I think he will. . . . So if neither Mr. Fortescue nor Mr. Sterrell will do anything for you upon your letter [lre] and that you can not get a pardon go to Bullen [Boulogne] . . .*
>
> Confession of William Polwhele, Dec. 1593. *SPD, ccxlvi, 49.*

Polwhele is a would-be assassin of Queen Elizabeth. In late 1593 he confesses that he was put up to it by "father Sherwood" and Captain Jaques, both of whom as we have seen were close associates of William Sterrell in 1593. He confesses that he lived with Sir William Stanley for half a year as Sir William's page. Polwhele says he could escape after killing the Queen with the help of his friends at Court: Mr. Fortescue and Mr. Sterrell. You know who this Sterrell is. But who is Mr. Fortescue and how could he help Polwhele escape? When we learn his identity, clearly linked to Sterrell as part of an escape plan for a Catholic assassin, we will understand why Shakespeare acquired property in Blackfriars in 1613 as a front for others and why this property is so important in his will. Briefly, for now, Mr. Fortescue is the same man named in Shakespeare's deed of 1613 as a prior owner of the Blackfriars Gatehouse, and Sterrell had access to the property which Catholics used for refuge and escape.

I had not intended the extended treatment of the will in the early drafts of this book. But this chapter on the will's connections provides perspective on all that has come before.

What is a will? It is a writing that is always written in contemplation of death. When you write your will, you know these are your final words, a statement about who and what you are. In distributing the assets you acquired over a lifetime you are saying who is important to you and what you have valued in life. You make your declaration to the world about who you were in your time on this earth and how you wish to be remembered.

When King Lear relinquishes his kingdom, he distributes his assets. Though not strictly speaking a will, it is the virtual equivalent — a pre-will distribution. Tragically, he learns that the parceling out of his properties to favored daughters over another whom he thinks ungrateful only roils his heirs and destroys them.

Could the playwright of *King Lear* have been the man whom we see in Shakespeare's will? For Shakespeare's carefully designed will favors one well-to-do daughter over a younger daughter, incapable of providing for herself, and sets up a multi-generational conflict over the properties distributed by restricting future ownership to non-existent male heirs. The author of *King Lear*, or even an empathetic reader of the play, could not have done this to his daughters and his only grandchild in favor of a line of male heirs who might never come into existence.

Hidden within Shakespeare's will are clues that suggest Shakespeare himself was not really responsible for the principal features of his will. Not uncommon is it that someone other than the testator inserts themselves into a will. We are all familiar with testators who revise their wills at death's door as a caregiver or sibling or friend or child whispers into the ear of the dying. It is a concern in many families that such undue influence could occur.

What's Not in the Will

Let's begin with what is not in Shakespeare's will. Only two items suggest Shakespeare had any life outside Stratford. These were three names added as an afterthought that might suggest that the testator had a connection to three men associated with the acting company and a nominal bequest of a property in London, the Blackfriars Gatehouse. Of Ben Jonson there was no mention nor the Earl of Southampton, though both were alive. Nor, except for three interlineated names, any other person who had any connection whatsoever to plays or poetry or theatre or the Court. Two decades in the center of literary life in London and at the highest level of Court entertainment for Shakespeare-the-author and no connections of the testator except for the afterthought of those three interlineated names.

In no records of any literary or Court person of the period was the death of Shakespeare noted. He ignored them; they ignored him. Shakespeare-of-Stratford had never existed in London literary or Court life; only Shakespeare-the-author, a figure known only as a name on paper.[136] During his lifetime, not a single literary person or member of Court society ever recorded an encounter with Shakespeare-of-Stratford or acknowledged the man himself. Shakespeare-of-Stratford and Shakespeare-the-author were simply two different men. The very few contemporary references in London to Shakespeare-of-Stratford have nothing to do with poetry or plays.

Also not in the will were the shares in the acting company and the shares in the Globe Theatre and in Blackfriars Theatre. The Globe was rebuilt and operating again when the will was written. And the shares of other shareholders were being litigated; the documents are printed in Chambers. He traces the ownership of the shares to 1612 and then they disappear. [137] He suggests "the residuary bequest of 'leases' to the Halls [Susanna Shakespeare Hall] would cover them" but notes that they "do not appear in any of the recorded transactions of his heirs." This possible explanation by Chambers (and all who have followed him) is without foundation. Even if the sharers had "leaseholds" as lessees, it meant they had to pay rent (as seen in the company litigation records) rather than receive rents. A division of income from the Globe Theatre or the Blackfriars Theatre from their use would not pass under the residuary clause. This was a category error as the parties were not lessors. And if the sharers in the company and the theaters were active owners, they would be responsible for operating costs; there would be no passive income so far as we can tell from any documents. The company and theater shares were major assets that a catch-all clause would not be intended to convey.

As will be seen, Shakespeare's will disposed of certain assets in Stratford, but the will appears to be less concerned about the well-being of his immediate family than preoccupied with preserving the purposes served by the distant Blackfriars property in London. There is nothing that indicates Shakespeare ever had anything to do with Blackfriars. One stringent provision of the will insured that no heir could dispose of the property for a half-century; Shakespeare's granddaughter could do nothing with the property until the death of her Aunt Judith at age 77 in 1662.

What's in the Will

Now, to the will. Shakespeare's will went through at least one major revision over a period of several months in early 1616. The will was initially drafted in January 1616, but the date was crossed out and replaced with March 1616. The evidence establishes its three pages were drafted in stages rather than a single sitting. Interlineations indicate afterthoughts. Are they by the testator or by one whispering into his ear or guiding the hand of the scrivener? Analysis of the document indicates that page two was written at a different time than pages one and three; it is likely a surviving section of an earlier draft. Just before his death on April 23, 1616, the will added several personal bequests, including memorial rings for added friends (not covered earlier) and his "second best bed" for his wife, who was otherwise ignored completely.[138] The final document features the lawyer's signature and four other witnesses. The revisions reflect changing circumstances in his family and estate in the final months of his life. We may doubt whether Shakespeare was fully competent as the will went through these stages.

The primary assets specified in the will included monetary amounts as bequests (not physical cash), itemized goods, and interests in real property. The bulk of the assets were given to the following persons: the older daughter Susanna, age 33, and her husband Dr. John Hall, and the younger daughter Judith, age 31. Judith became married as the will was revised. Smaller bequests went to his granddaughter ("neece") Elizabeth Hall and to Shakespeare's only surviving sibling, Joan. The only bequest to his widow, Anne Hathaway, age 60, was Shakespeare's second-best bed.

The first £150 bequest (in two parts)

The first item of the will is £150 granted to the younger daughter Judith. The writer had crossed out "my son in L &. . . " before "daughter Judith." It is not what it first appears. As the first draft of the will was prepared in January, Judith was unmarried. She then married Thomas Quiney in February, accomplished only by ignoring required church procedures, before the final will was completed in March. At that time (February), another woman, Margaret Wheeler, was carrying Quiney's child; mother and child died in March, 1616. The will *by an interlineation* identifies that £100 of the £150 is "in discharge of her marriage portion," which means it is Judith's dowry. A dowry, or marriage portion, is parental property that is distributed to a daughter at her marriage, for the benefit or enticement of the husband, rather than at the holder's death. In England, failure to provide a customary, or agreed-upon, dowry could cause a marriage to be called off. That is to say, the bequest to Judith was effectively a bribe to her would-be husband. No marriage, no marriage portion to Judith. It looks as though Shakespeare was luring Thomas Quiney away from his lover Margaret Wheeler to provide his own daughter with a husband. Quiney took the bait, though it came with conditions. To be blunt, Shakespeare bought his spinsterish daughter a husband.

Moreover, the other £50 of the £150 was only to go to Judith if she surrendered to her sister Susanna any interest she might claim in his property of Rowington Manor, situated in Stratford. This is often referred to as the Cottage of Rowington Manor. It is a curious but extraordinary acquisition by Shakespeare in 1602. This conveyance was a copyhold, and it was not subject to entail imposed on all of the rest of the real property of the will. The real benefit of this £50 was to clear title to the copyhold in Susanna alone. It is as though Susanna were buying out the interest of her sister.

The second £150 bequest

The next item is another grant of £150 to Judith. Again, this bequest is far different than it first appears. It is not a present grant. It only vests at the end of three years if she or a child of her body is still living. In the meantime, she is to receive on the principal "two shillings in the pound" annually. If she's not alive at the end of the three years, the investment value goes to Susanna's child and Shakespeare's sister Joan in specified portions.

Even if Judith is alive at the end of three years, she doesn't get money; instead, Shakespeare's *executors and overseers* are to invest the value of £150 as follows:

> for the best benefit of her and her issue, and the stock not to be paid unto her so long as she shall be married and covert baron but my will is that she shall have the consideration yearly paid unto her during her life and after her decease the said stock and consideration to be paid to her children if she have any and if not to her executors or assigns, she living the said term after my decease, provided that if such husband as she shall at the end of the said three years be married unto or attain after, do sufficiently assure unto her and the issue of her body, lands answerable to the portion by this my will given unto her, and to be adjudged so by my executors and overseers then my will is that the said £150 shall be paid to such husband as shall make such assurance to his own use.

In effect, this £150 is to create what we would recognize as a "spendthrift trust." It is a device designed to protect a beneficiary's inheritance from their own financial mismanagement. It is a type of life interest in the money with only interest on the principal going to the beneficiary. What Judith will receive is a pension or annuity of "two shillings in the pound" which was "the rate aforesaied" in the first disposition. If I'm not mistaken, that would be £15 per year. Since the executors are Judith's sister Susanna and Dr. John Hall, the older sister is put in charge of money for the benefit of the incapable younger sister.

The £150 bequest is structured to incentivize a husband if Judith is married at the end of three years to provide the equivalent financial protection to Judith; only then could it go to "such husband" who has made provisions for her and her children's well-being as "adjudged so by my executors and overseers." Thus, the oversight of Shakespeare's executors and overseers extends to supervision of Judith's husband's financial transactions to provide for Judith, i.e. oversight of Judith's marriage relationship far into the future.

So, Judith gets something in the will, but it is only dribbled out as a living allowance for the rest of her life and under the strict scrutiny of her sister, her sister's husband, and the two overseers. The will provides comparatively little for a 31-year-old adult. From all indications, she was illiterate. Compared to the property interests given to her sister, how must she have felt about being treated like an incompetent child subject to the group of four? This is a formula for long-term grievance between the siblings and their spouses. Just like in *King Lear*.

Other bequests of money or goods go to granddaughter Elizabeth Hall and sister Joan and to the poor and a few friends. We'll hold off on a couple of those specifics to be discussed after the real property.

Real Property

The real property can be identified as five items or groups: 1) the Rowington Manor cottage; 2) New Place; 3) "two messuages or tenements . . . in Henley street"; 4) and "all my barns, stables, orchards, gardens, lands, tenements, and hereditaments, whatsoever, . . . within the towns, hamlets, villages, fields, and grounds, of Stratford upon Avon, Oldstratford, Bushopton, and Welcombe, . . . in the said county of Warwick"; 5) And also "all that messuage or tenement . . . wherein one John Robinson dwelleth, . . . in the Blackfriars in London."

Rowington Manor Cottage

The first item of real property is the Rowington Manor cottage. Treated separately in the will from other real estate, it had been acquired in 1602. Who was living there in 1616? Perhaps, contrary to the opinion of some scholars who assert Judith lived there, it was Susanna and her husband. Two things stand out: Shakespeare was insisting that all claims Judith might have had were turned over to Susanna, not Susanna and her husband. To see if this would give full ownership to Susanna, we must see what type of interest Shakespeare held. The will describes it as copyhold tenement. *Copyhold* was a form of English land tenure where land was held "by copy of the court roll" according to the custom of a manor. The interest would revert to the then current owner of Rowington Manor. E. K. Chambers tells us: "The copyhold followed the custom of the manor and the tenancy possibly ended . . . with Susanna's life." A "copyhold of inheritance" allowed land to pass to heirs, often requiring a fee called a "relief." Perhaps under the "custom of the manor" the copyhold tenure of the Cottage would have passed to both daughters, and Shakespeare was paying Judith so as to leave it solely to Susanna.

Chambers reproduces an October 24, 1604, record of Rowington Manor which states that Shakespeare held a cottage and garden on Chapel Lane in Stratford, part of the Manor of Rowington, and paid a yearly rent of 2 shillings and 6 pence. We see the nature of Shakespeare's interest more clearly in the 1606 record found in Chambers: 1606, Aug. 1. Extract from Survey of Rowington Manor.[139]

> Tenentes Custumarii. Willielmus Shakespere tenet copiam datam anno videlicet Domum mansionalem. Reddendo per annum Habendum. ijs heriettum annualis valor. dimittenda.

Translation and meaning: "Customary Tenants. William Shakespeare holds by a copy [of the manorial court's record] given in the year [blank], namely a dwelling house. Rendering annually [a rent] [blank], to have [and to hold]. Two shillings [is] the heriot; the annual value [is blank]. To be demised." A *heriot* of 2 shillings was a death duty or fine paid to the lord of the manor when a tenant died or transferred the land. *Dimittenda*: "to be demised" or "to be leased," indicating the property is available for transfer under these terms.

For Shakespeare to have acquired (about September 28, 1602) the Cottage of Rowington Manor, it had to be through the consent of the existing tenants and the proprietor. These were, respectively, the family of Sterrell's friend Anthony Skinner and Lady Anne Russell, Countess of Warwick. The Countess was the aunt of the Earl of Worcester's daughter-in-law, Anne Russell Somerset. Walter Getley represented the Countess of Warwick in conveying the property, acting through an attorney named Tibbottes. Getley was deputy seneschal or steward in the court baron, which was the feudal institution that dealt with property and land tenure disputes; he was not the tenant. The document indicates that this does not reflect *a sale* to Shakespeare but a *grant*; it was essentially a sort of sublease or substitution of one tenant for another. Shakespeare himself was not present. The property, the Manor of Rowington, was already under lease, and this Cottage and quarter-acre tract was a carve-out from the Manor.

Why would the Countess of Warwick concern herself and her steward with such a seemingly trivial transaction of only a small portion of a very large holding? Here's where Sterrell's friend Anthony Skinner again makes an appearance in the records. The *History of the County of Warwick* (1945) recites the following after recounting the Crown grant to the Earl of Warwick:

> Meanwhile, the site and lands of the manor with the rectory and tithes, had been the subject of a number of leases. The first of these was made in Feb. 1540, for a term of 21 years, to John Oldnall. He was Master of the Gild of St. Anne of Knowle and was baliff of Rowington in 1547 and until his death in 1558. His lease had been renewed in 1557, but in Dec. 1562 a fresh lease of the premises was made to William Skinner and Alice his wife (Oldnall's daughter) and their son Anthony for their lives. A further lease for 30 years, to date from the expiration of this, was acquired in 1597 by Thomas Audley, who at once sold his rights to Anthony Skinner. (vol 3, p. 150).

So, the immediate family of Worcester, which would include the Countess of Warwick, and Sterrell's friend Skinner made the transfer of the interest in the cottage to Shakespeare-of-Stratford. The wealthy Countess of Warwick hardly would have bothered herself with this one part of the Manor except at the instance of her niece's family and Skinner for his friend Sterrell. As a recusant in the 1590s and at the time of the acquisition by Shakespeare, Anthony Skinner's property interests were subject to fines and seizure, so his signature appears nowhere; it is unnecessary as the Countess herself had her steward Getley and attorney Tibbotts do it.

Shakespeare probably moved to the Cottage on leaving London. The survey of Rowington Manor in 1604 shows Shakespeare was holding the place and paying an annual rent. The Manor of Rowington overlapped several areas of Stratford so that the Cottage was very close to New Place. As noted earlier, William Shakespeare of Rowington reported for militia muster in 1605.[140] Probably he was living there, and New Place (below) was under lease to Thomas Greene, a Middle Temple attorney, at that time.[141]

Because of the copyhold title for the Cottage of Rowington Manor, Shakespeare couldn't subject the interest to the entailment that he imposed on all the other real property. If rentals weren't paid by Susanna, it reverted to the Manor and presumably the then current lessee. By the time of Shakespeare's will in 1616, Anthony Skinner was no longer involved: in 1609 he had sold his rights under the two leases to someone named Thomas Betham. If the copyhold reverted, it would presumably go to Bentham. Although the manor would have reverted to the Crown with the death of the Countess of Warwick in 1604, the underlying leases would continue according to the "custom of the manor."

New Place

New Place was a substantial house located on Chapel Street, the second largest house in Stratford. We must trace its twisted history to understand how it came into the ownership of Shakespeare. Again, we sense the influence of William Sterrell.

In 1567 New Place was purchased by an Inner Temple lawyer named William Underhill for £40. He was clerk of Assizes at Warwick and a property holder of other places in the county; he also acquired manors of Barton-on-the-Heath, Idlicote, and Loxley, and much other property in Warwickshire. The Manor of Idlicote had been granted by the Crown in 1562 to Lewis Greville who six years later sold it to William Underhill. This William Underhill died in 1570. The house passed to his fourteen-year-old son and heir, who was also named William. This son William was a strong recusant imprisoned for his faith in 1579. He married his first cousin Mary, daughter of Thomas Underhill of Ettington, and they lived both at New Place, Stratford, and at Idlicote. A report to the Privy Council of the Commissioners examining recusants in Warwickshire in about November 1592 listed William Underhill, lord of Idlicote [and New Place], as "Indicted" for his recusancy. The report noted that he had been presented as a recusant in their last certificate for Stratford upon Avon and continued as a recusant. The informants to the Commissioners said that Underhill had not been at Idlicote since the 22nd day of November 1590 when he buried his wife there. He would have been at another property, probably New Place.

Our connection to William Sterrell is through the brother of William Underhill's wife. Her brother was both brother-in-law and first cousin to William Underhill. His name was Edward Underhill, son of Thomas of Eatington (Ettington). This Underhill had entered Magdalen College in 1587 at the age of 14 as a demy, just as William Sterrell had been a demy. He remained with the College as a Fellow and then Proctor of the University until 1612; shortly before his death in 1613 he was knighted by King James.

We should point out that Edward Underhill was an exact contemporary of James Mabbe, one of the four "pious fellows" who contributed to the *First Folio.* Both Edward Underhill and Mabbe remained closely associated with Magdalen College for many years. They had been closely associated for a decade when the Underhill property was acquired by Shakespeare in 1597. Both Mabbe and Underhill were students under William Sterrell and would have known him well in the period 1587-1591. And they would have known well the sons of the Earl of Worcester when they matriculated from Magdalen in 1591. Both Underhill and Mabbe were probably involved when Worcester himself was awarded an MA during Queen Elizabeth's visit in September 1592.

Because Underhill and his sister shared a common ancestor with William Underhill, Edward Underhill probably had an interest in New Place or advised his close relative as he faced loss of property for his recusancy. And because William Underhill was an active part of the Catholic network of Warwickshire, it should be assumed that he would have been well acquainted with his neighbors Anthony Skinner and Anthony's father, William.

The deed of William Underhill for New Place to Shakespeare is dated May 2, 1597, and recites a payment of £60 sterling for the property. We must note how implausible this transaction was. Where did Shakespeare-of-Stratford get the money to make such a costly purchase? His name had first appeared for an entertainment in March 1595 to receive small payments as part of the company for plays the preceding winter. These were two plays by the Lord Chamberlain's Men and the plays were reimbursed at a flat rate of £10 each. That would be for the play script, the actors, the settings, the costumes and the company shareholders.

No credible record suggests that the poet received anything from the Earl of Southampton, who owed enormous debts when he came of age on October 6, 1594, for *Venus and Adonis* or *Lucrece.* Such poetry, as we have seen, did not generally receive more than a few pounds as patronage. Poets and playwrights did not earn royalties, and a play might fetch at most between £6 and £10 for a new play if purchased by Philip Henslowe. Shakespeare's father was still alive, so Shakespeare had no inheritance. It is unimaginable that the Lord Chamberlain's Men were so successful that a shareholder was taking home enough to live in London and then invest £60 in a property more than a hundred miles away — 3 to 5 days by horseback. He could not have been acting, writing three or more plays a year, and commuting this significant distance while supporting a wife and two daughters, aged 14 and 12; his son Hamnet had just died nine months earlier. So where did the nominal purchase price come from?

The events immediately after the New Place sale suggest that the transaction was a part of a plan to prevent the seizure of the property for the owner's recusancy; if so, no money was expected to change hands. Two months after conveying New Place, William Underhill was murdered; his son Fulke was executed for poisoning his father. We may suspect that the purchase of New Place was actually for the benefit of someone in addition to (or other than) William Shakespeare. Because William Underhill was a known and obstinate recusant, all of his lands were subject to seizure, with two-thirds going to the Crown. The same was even more true for Anthony Skinner: as a convicted felon for treason, he was not allowed to hold lands of the Crown. As seen above, in 1597 Anthony Skinner and his father had conveyed the leases to the Manor of Rowington to a third party, another trusted Catholic named Thomas Audley. Audley was a first cousin of Fr. Robert Southwell who accompanied Southwell on trips to Douay. Audley had then reconveyed the leases back to Anthony Skinner.

Thomas Audley had joined the Middle Temple shortly after Anthony Skinner. Both Audley and Skinner were very well known to the Sterrell brothers, William and Henry of the Middle Temple. The effect of such an interposition of a third party in the title, whether of the leases of Rowington Manor or the ownership of

New Place, was to make it more difficult for the government to seize the lands as they would have to divest the prime lessee to get at the sublessee (Rowington Manor) or undo the sale of New Place. This is so even if Shakespeare had simply acquired the property and leased it back to Underhill. Underhill's murder by his son intervened, forestalling any plan to lease it back to him. It is probable that Shakespeare's purchase of New Place was to protect William Underhill from losing it to the Crown because of his Catholicism. William Underhill himself was likely behind the purchase price nominally paid by Shakespeare.

Our supposition is supported by the fact that there was some problem with the title to New Place. In 1602 Hercules Underhill, the next son after Fulke Underhill (the murderer), confirmed the sale of New Place to William Shakespeare. Like his father William Underhill and his mother, Hercules Underhill must have been a Catholic. The woman he married not long after confirming Shakespeare's title was herself openly Catholic. She was Bridget Carleton (Underhill), sister of Dudley Carleton who was later Secretary of State for England. Dudley Carleton was a principal correspondent of John Chamberlain, the London letter-writer. In 1602 Chamberlain wrote his friend Dudley Carleton concerning Bridget: "Touching your Catholique sister I know not what to write or thinke, she is so irresolute and inconstant, and yet peevish and wilfull au bout. She doth exercise herself and her friends very much, and hath raised many tragedies since you went . . ." Did Hercules continue to have any interest in New Place while title was in Shakespeare? It would have been concealed because of the notorious recusancy of Hercules's wife and his own. Shakespeare was likely a front man for New Place just as he was for Blackfriars. His reward could have been the grant of the Cottage of Rowington Manor. The timing suggests that the two transactions of 1602 were probably linked.

The supposed evidence that William Shakespeare may have resided at New Place in 1597-98 is very weak and is equally consistent with the title to the property merely being in his name. For example, Samuel Schoenbaum asserts Shakespeare was a resident because a survey of malt and corn in February 1598 lists him as a resident of Chapel Street Ward, but this may be no more than listing Shakespeare as the record owner of the property for the survey.

What is clear is that within a few years, Thomas Greene - a Middle Temple lawyer and contemporary of Henry Sterrell - was living at New Place.

From the foregoing, it should be clear that the property transactions to William Shakespeare in 1597 and 1602 were closely related to people who were very well known to William Sterrell. We will return to New Place shortly.

Two messuages or tenements ... in Henley street;

These two seem to be the family home and a glove-making workshop of Shakespeare's father which Shakespeare inherited in 1601. Several documents exist that reference this property but uncertainly as to title. Presumably the properties were under lease and not unoccupied, yet there is no reference in the will to the current lessee. A properly executed lease would survive the death of the lessor Shakespeare (or his father) and burden the real property now given to Susanna and her husband. These could provide income to Susanna and her husband, but they could not sell them without approval of the overseers because of the entail.

all my barns, stables, orchards, gardens, lands, tenements, and hereditaments, whatsoever, . . . within the towns, hamlets, villages, fields, and grounds, of Stratford upon Avon, Oldstratford, Bushopton, and Welcombe, . . . in the said county of Warwick;

Because these are not included in an inventory, we cannot itemize what these may have been, though other records show interests acquired by Shakespeare that might fit the broad descriptive inclusion. These need not detain us as they, too, were included in the entailed properties. These interests could provide income to Susanna and her husband though they could not sell them without approval of the overseers. It is noteworthy that involved in several of the tithe and property transactions were at least three attorneys from the Middle Temple ,where they would have associated with Henry Sterrell): Thomas Greene, and the two Combes brothers, William and Thomas, as would have their uncle, William Combe of the Middle Temple. This same Thomas Combe was bequeathed Shakespeare's sword.

And also all that messuage or tenement . . . wherein one John Robinson dwelleth, . . . in the Blackfriars in London.

This brings us to what is most significant property to us. It will explain the design of the will. John Robinson is named as lessee of Shakespeare's interest; he is also witness to the will so that he can be certain his interest is being protected. Now we must go back to William Sterrell's very long association with "John Robinson," and we must examine the title to Blackfriars long before Shakespeare took his interest in 1613. Following the title, we also go back to the period just after Sterrell's crisis in 1592-93.

First, the location of Blackfriars Gatehouse. Originally part of a Dominican priory dissolved by Henry VIII, the Gatehouse was part of the Blackfriars district, near the Thames, across from the royal Wardrobe. There's no reliable map from the period for the immediate neighborhood, but descriptions allow us to conclude that the Shakespeare property was next to Lord Hunsdon's House and close to the Blackfriars Theatre, which was an indoor venue for plays dating back to 1596 or so. It was used by the King's Men from 1608. Also within a stone's throw was the home of the Brooke family (lords Cobham), where Queen Elizabeth stayed in 1600 when Henry Somerset married Anne Russell, as well as the home of Anne's mother, Lady Russell (Elizabeth Cooke Hoby Russell). The latter's home was smaller than the Cobham home, so the Queen only visited there at the time of the wedding. The Blackfriars Gatehouse had been detached in 1590 from the mansion of Henry Percy, the Earl of Northumberland, which continued in his tenure.

We would need to set forth a small treatise on English property law to go over exactly what Shakespeare purchased and what he might do with it in his will. Unlike real property transactions today, there was no courthouse system in which a property transaction was recorded with a complete description and a survey plat with a clerk of court to register all transactions in a book open to the public. There was a roll of certain conveyance transactions in the Chancery. Generally, it was necessary to have a document that you kept in your possession and with a copy in the hands of others such as lawyer or trustee or executor. A description of the property might be in the deed by metes and bounds which might be difficult to prove at a later time if one of the items of description shifted or changed. Another person might produce a document showing their own overlapping or competing claim. A court would have to sort out conflicts in descriptions or claims.

Here is the property description in Shakespeare's 1613 deed with the recitation of prior owners:

> All that dwelling house or Tenement with th'appurtenaunces situate and being within the Precinct, circuit and compasse of the late black Fryers London, sometymes in the tenure of James Gardyner Esquiour and since that in the tenure of John Fortescue gent, and now or late being in the tenure or occupacion of one William Ireland or of his assignee or assignes; abutting upon a street leading down to Pudle wharf on the east part, right against the Kinges Maiesties Wardrobe; part of which said Tenement is erected over a great gate leading to a capital Messuage which, sometime was in the tenure of William Blackwell Esquire deceased, and since that in the tenure or occupation of the right Honorable Henry now Earle of Northumberland; And also all that plot of ground on the west side of the same Tenement which was lately enclosed with boards on two sides thereof by Anne Bacon widow, so far and in such sort as the same was enclosed by the said Anne Bacon, and not otherwise, and being on the third side enclosed with an old Brick wall; Which said plot of ground was sometime parcel and taken out of a great piece of void ground lately used for a garden; And also the soil whereupon the said Tenement standeth; And also the said Brick wall and boards which do enclose the said plot of ground . . .

At the time of this conveyance, "Honorable Henry now Earle of Northumberland" in the recitation was imprisoned in the Tower of London as will be discussed.

There's no statement here of how much land is included or the nature or character of the structure and grounds. Were you a resident of London in 1613 or 1615 and you asked a constable or other official where Mr. Shakespeare of Stratford had his London property, you'd get a blank stare. Even with the deed in hand, if you walked down "a street down to Pudle wharf" and found a great gate, you might find a resident who could point out which tenement was "enclosed with boards on two sides thereof by Anne Bacon widow" some years before the transaction: Anne Bacon had transferred her interest 23 years earlier in 1590. Which boards, if the boards had been moved? If you asked a neighbor in 1614, "is Mr. Shakespeare living there?", they could not know if he was living there or a lessee or a sublessee of the lessee or a Catholic priest. You couldn't know from a telephone connection or a utility bill or a postal carrier or even a tax bill who was the occupant if the absent Mr. Shakespeare didn't make a court case against a trespasser. Moreover, it was no business of the neighbor to complain if they spotted a stranger there, unless they had reason to think he was a Catholic priest.

Does the deed identify Shakespeare as the sole purchaser or is the sale by Henry Walker to him as a co-owner with three others? On the face of the deed, there are four purchasers rather than Shakespeare and three trustees: "absolutlie bargayne and sell vnto the said William Shakespeare, William Johnson, John Jackson, and John Hemming, their heires, and assignes forever; . . ." From this habendum clause, there are four co-owners, not Shakespeare with three trustees as it later appears.

To trace the ownership of the Gatehouse, let's start with Anne Bacon. She was the daughter of William Blackwell, who had been a town official in the time of Queen Mary. When Anne Bacon inherited the Gatehouse about 1585, the Blackfriars property evidently had been used as a refuge for priests and other Catholics. In 1586 or thereabout Richard Frith, a neighbor who had a dancing school and tennis court within his quarters, reported his suspicions to the government, as quoted by E. K. Chambers:

> "One great house in or adjoining to the Blackfriars, wherein Mr. Blackwell, the town clerk, sometime dwelt." He said, "Now there dwelleth in it one that is a very inconformable man to her Majesty's proceedings. It hath sundry back-doors and bye-ways, and many secret vaults and corners. It hath been in time past suspected, and searched for papists but no good done for want of good knowledge of the backdoors and bye-ways and of the dark corners."[142]

A day-light search was needed, he urged.

Back doors and bye-ways, secret vaults and dark corners, secret passages down towards the Thames: perfect for hiding priests and giving them quick escapes. Chambers concludes that when Anne Bacon partitioned the property about 1590, Anne got the Gatehouse, and the "capital mansion" was soon acquired by Henry Percy, 9th Earl of Northumberland. Anne Bacon then passed title to the Gatehouse to her son Mathias Bacon.

Mathias Bacon was a lawyer, a member of Grays Inn, but he did not occupy the Gatehouse. As the Shakespeare deed recites, he let it first to a James Gardyner and then to John Fortescue, nephew and assistant to Sir John Fortescue, who was Master of the Wardrobe. Gardyner and John Fortescue, gent. are named in the Shakespeare deed. The Wardrobe offices were close by. Sir John Fortescue's steward was John Robinson, an active Catholic who sent sons to the Jesuit school at St. Omers, France. It was evidently Robinson's son of the same name who was to become the tenant of the Gatehouse when it came to Shakespeare in 1613. John Fortescue was himself a Catholic, though he protested he was not disloyal when his house was searched for priests alleged to be hiding there. A kinsman of the Earl of Essex, his wife Ellen was a Catholic who was related to the Countess of Southampton.

Tracing this history of the Blackfriars property, E. K. Chambers notes its use in 1591 as a refuge, quoting a contemporary record: "Fennell the priest doth use to come very muche to Mr. John Fortescue his house."[143] Chambers goes on to observe that so notorious was the Blackfriars Gatehouse as a refuge that John Fortescue and his uncle were warned by Richard Topcliffe, the priest-hunter, of the risk he ran.

On March 1, 1598, the house was searched for hidden priests on a report from William Udall, an informer who later was imprisoned himself. He described it as having "many places of secret conveyance in it," apparently communicating with "secret passages towards the water." Fortescue was away; his wife resisted the searchers, and, according to Udall, one of two priests who were there slipped away with Hugh the butler.[144] More priests showed up the day after the raid. Ellen Fortescue and her daughters Katherine and Elizabeth were examined. They admitted to recusancy, but denied the presence of priests, which crime would have been a basis for executing them – just as Anne Line was soon executed for that very offence. Later, John and Ellen Fortescue retired to the Catholic community at St. Omer(s). Their children proved to be strong Catholics as well.

Let us look briefly at the second property that resulted from the 1590 partition. Both the Gatehouse and adjoining property held by the Earl of Northumberland came to be used as Catholic refuges. A portion of this adjacent property, perhaps in the tenure of Earl of Northumberland, was owned by Fr. Robert Southwell's sister Mary and her husband Edward Bannister of Idsworth.[145] It can be assumed that Southwell himself spent time there. We'll turn our focus to this ownership in a moment.

Among the prominent Catholics living in Blackfriars was the Earl of Northumberland's aunt, Mary Percy. This Lady Mary was one of the daughters of Thomas Percy, Earl of Northumberland who was beheaded in 1572. She resided at Blackfriars before going on to the Low Countries around 1598. Fr. John Gerard, the Jesuit, sent her to Fr. Holt in the Low Countries where she became the principal founder of the English Benedictine convent at Brussels.[146] It is not surprising that Blackfriars was one of the hiding places of Fr. John Gerard. Lady Mary Percy and Fr. Gerard were both connected to William Sterrell. In a confession of May 11, 1594 John Frank, a servant of a Catholic family named Wiseman that entertained priests, testified about the activities of several priests he knew. He spoke of Gerard operating under the alias of Tanfield and said Gerard lay one night at the Lady Mary's in Blackfriars, and Ralph Willis, Gerard's servant, lay at John Frank's own house.[147]

We connect William Sterrell with Lady Mary and "Mr. Somerset" through a confession by a double agent of Robert Cecil named Renold Bisley. Bisley confessed to Thomas Phelippes that he had gone to the Low Countries on business for the daughter of the Countess of Northumberland, Lady Mary Percy.[148] This spy was being questioned because Sterrell, while in the Low Countries, reported to Phelippes that Bisley was an assassin who planned to kill the queen. Sterrell undoubtedly knew that Bisley was a double agent and reported Bisley as an assassin to expose the truth that he really was pretending to be a Catholic agent.

If Bisley was doing secret duties for the English government, he was betraying Lady Mary Percy and "Mr. Somerset," who were both Catholic. We will now more closely look at Mary Percy to see how she was connected with Sterrell. Her mother, Anne Somerset Percy, Countess of Northumberland (1536-1596), was the sister of William Somerset, 3rd Earl of Worcester, and aunt of Edward Somerset, William Sterrell's employer and patron. After her father was executed and her mother had fled abroad, the infant Lady Mary was apparently raised by her uncle Henry Percy, 8th Earl of Northumberland and thus was like a sister to Henry Percy, 9th Earl of Northumberland. She was a devout Catholic who sheltered priests in London, priests such as John Gerard with whom Sterrell had dealings. After living in the Blackfriars in the 1590s, Mary Percy returned into the Low Countries and established a Benedictine convent. She had business matters in the Low Countries in the 1590s arising from her mother's property there from her long years in exile and Mary's own plans to settle there. Sterrell, with his master Worcester, must have visited Lady Mary often at Blackfriars, and the priests whom she hid there.

The "Mr. Somerset" in the Low Countries who would have had some matters of concern that Bisley dealt with was George Somerset, son of Thomas Somerset (Worcester's uncle), who died in the Tower for his religion in 1587. George Somerset was nephew to the Countess of Northumberland and first cousin to both Mary Percy and Edward Somerset. Thomas Somerset was owed substantial sums by Cardinal Allen that still had not been paid when Allen died in 1594, and George Somerset was Thomas Somerset's heir to whom those debts were now due. In 1595 William Sterrell was helping this young man to return to England after years in the Low Countries when they were stopped by the lieutenant-governor of Flushing. Sterrell had earlier turned Bisley in as a potential assassin of Queen Elizabeth and thus prevented Bisley from doing harm to Mary Percy and George Somerset, the cousins of Worcester, Sterrell's longtime patron.

Perhaps all the controversy over the Gatehouse was a bit much for an attorney of Grays Inn, so Mathias Bacon decided to sell the Gatehouse. According to the deed granting the property to Shakespeare, Mathias Bacon sold the Gatehouse to one Henry Walker, "citizein and Minstrell of London," on October 15, 1604,[149] and on December 12, Walker had granted a lease to William Ireland, "citizen and haberdasher of London." Neither Walker nor Ireland has ever been satisfactorily identified. There was a Henry Walker who was a Catholic and who went to seminary on the Continent in the previous decade. It is possible that William Ireland was the William Ireland who was a nephew of William Byrd. Byrd was a Catholic composer whose patron was the Earl of Worcester and whose songs were in Shakespeare's plays. If correct, it would account for the Gatehouse continuing to be used for Catholic purposes.

Ownership may have changed, but it appears that the Fortescues were still living at the Gatehouse in 1605 when the Gunpowder Treason was revealed on November 5. The Blackfriars Gatehouse and Northumberland's mansion were immediately suspect. Lord Chief Justice Popham wrote to Secretary Cecil on the day of the discovery of the conspiracy, informing him that there were letters from abroad at "Fortescue's house by the Wardrobe."[150] E. K. Chambers reprints a document in Latin of Fr. John Gerard, the Jesuit priest well-known to Sterrell about seeking refuge from the Fortescues at the Gatehouse just after the Gunpowder Treason.[151] A translation conveys the drama and desperation: [152]

> Nevertheless after the discovery of the plot, and when Father Gerard had been publicly denounced all over the kingdom, he suddenly appeared without notice at Mr. Fortescue's house disguised by a false beard and hair, and asked him to take him in, as he knew not where to hide his head. Looking upon him, Mr. Fortescue said, full of heaviness, 'have you no one to ruin but me and my family?'

Suspicions about the Blackfriars property were a factor in the imprisonment of Henry Percy in 1605. Recall that when the Gatehouse was separated from the capital mansion, the latter was acquired by Henry Percy, 9th Earl of Northumberland, and was used by Lady Mary Percy as a shelter for priests. When the Earl of Northumberland's nephew and sometime tenant Thomas Percy was convicted and executed in the Gunpowder Treason, the Earl himself was arrested and imprisoned in the Tower of London for the next fifteen years. The Earl, mentioned in the Shakespeare deed of 1613, was in the Tower at the time of that deed.

Sterrell, Fortescue, John Robinson, Blackfriars

Now we will connect "John Robinson" of Blackfriars to William Sterrell in 1594 in Polwhele's confession quoted at the beginning of this chapter. We've already seen how he was connected to the companion mansion of the Earl of Northumberland through Lady Mary Percy who resided there in the 1590s.

What we know often cannot be separated from how we know it. A well-known intelligence device is the creation of documents that are placed carefully for "accidental discovery" by one's adversaries.[153] Most of the letters of William Sterrell that we have covered for the period 1591-93 came from the trunks and cabinets of Thomas Phelippes that were seized by Robert Cecil's government in 1605. However, one letter—to Sterrell from Hugh Owen in May 1594—fell into the government's hands, apparently by accident, but the accident was carefully contrived. The purpose of the letter was to counter a series of statements and confessions of various agents, including Richard Hesketh (executed in 1593, discussed above) and William Polwhele that had touched upon Hugh Owen, "Robinson," and the Earl of Essex. Recall that Robert Robinson was one alias of Sterrell, including the time when his papers were seized in 1592 and sent to Lord Burghley; and recall, too, that Hugh Owen was the man who with Sir William Stanley got Sterrell (Robinson) out of the prison in Antwerp.

The letter we are considering now reached the government on a "mistaken" delivery to the wrong person. The letter shows the Sterrell/Owen relationship and how the two men cooperated to send information to the English government. It also associates Sterrell closely with John Robinson of the Blackfriars.

The letter may seem too good to be true, and in one sense it is. It looks as though it was intended by the exile Hugh Owen to exculpate Owen to Essex via William Sterrell. But it was really intended to reach the eyes of Burghley, Cecil and the Queen. Contained in a packet addressed to 'Mr. Robinson in London,' it was delivered to the son of John Robinson of St. Helen's parish in Cheapside. From the Robinson father and son the letter was taken to the Lord Mayor of London. The Mayor was aware of the notorious exile Hugh Owen who was known as a practiser against the English state. Finding the letter addressed to 'Mr Sterrell, London' and signed by 'Hu: Owen', he took this packet to Lord Burghley.[154] We will return to the letter of the Mayor to Burghley in a moment. Owen and Sterrell doubtless planned for the letter to be reach Burghley, not Essex.

The letter ostensibly of Owen to Sterrell states, with mock naivety, that the writer (Owen) has but 'small acquaintance' with the recipient (Sterrell), they having met 'but twice' (once in Antwerp and the other time at the Spa). It then proceeds to a series of protestations of the writer's innocence of involvement in various recent plots against the state which had resulted in the execution of men who were officially said to have implicated Owen in their crimes. But though the letter was clearly intended to reach and influence the Queen's government, it was equally clearly written by Owen himself, whose acquaintance with Sterrell was by no means as small as he stated. Sterrell himself could safely be made a part of this ploy because he had been known for two years as an agent, often under the alias Robinson, of Essex in dealings with the Catholic exiles in the Low Countries. The ploy of a "discovered letter" was probably Sterrell's own. Secret letters that are discovered are favorite plot devices in *King Lear* (Edmund's forged letter); *Twelfth Night* (the Malvolio letter); *Hamlet* (the commission of King Claudius to England); *Romeo and Juliet* (the misdelivered message); *Love's Labour's Lost* (misdirected letters); *All's Well* (the Diana letter discovered in Parolles's pocket).

Sterrell arranged a message from Hugh Owen to go to the Council as if by accident. In denying the truth of the statements of certain named men interrogated, condemned and/or executed by the government, Hugh Owen sought to clear his own name and the names of Essex and "Robinson," i.e. Sterrell.[155] Owen alluded to the fact that accusations in the proceedings had touched Essex's name, and he was writing in part to clear Essex. He said that he knew Sterrell "wholly depend[s] on him [Essex]"; he authorized Sterrell to show his letter if it would give any contentment to Essex.

Owen's long letter took up Polwhele, among others, and

asserted that the Council was being abused by "perjured Jacks." He concluded by saying that the Duke of Parma (Alexander Farnese, Governor of the Spanish Netherlands from 1578 to 1592) had frequently received similar information of plots against him but made no account of them. If the Queen and Council likewise made no account of such fables and inventions, he said, they would never unquiet themselves as they did nor so easily permit false juries to cast away so many innocent men.

Let's examine further the persons associated with this extraordinary letter of Owen to Sterrell. The Lord Mayor's covering letter to Burghley says, "There came unto me . . . a young man named Robinson son to Mr. John Robinson stapler dwelling in St. Ellins [St. Helens - a parish within Bishopsgate Ward] " who about ten days before had received a letter to Mr. Robinson "without mention of any Christian name or place of dwelling." When young Robinson's father opened the letter, he saw it was to Sterrell from Hugh Owen. Let's recall the confession of William Polwhele set forth at the beginning of this chapter where he made the statement that the friends of the Catholics at Court to whom he was to turn for escape and refuge were Mr. Fortescue and Mr. Sterrell. This confession of Polwhele is among those discussed by Owen in this letter discovered by "John Robinson." We find that "Mr. Fortescue" and "John Robinson" are linked to one another.

As we have seen, Sir John Fortescue was Master of the Wardrobe (since 1559) but also Chancellor of the Exchequer and Privy Councilor. His nephew, also John Fortescue, hence "Mr. Fortescue," was a Catholic assistant of his, resident in the Blackfriars Gatehouse that served as a refuge for Catholic priests and laymen in London. [156] Sir John Fortescue's steward was John Robinson. The Catholic identity of this steward of Sir John Fortescue, his clandestine help to Catholics in hiding, and his use of the Blackfriars' house as a refuge are encapsulated in an intercepted letter of May 1599:[157]

> I am told that Dudley the priest (lately escaped out of the Marshalsea, as you have heard) doth yet remain in London. I hear he is in the Blackfriars in one Mr. Robinson's house who is steward to Sir John Foskewe [Fortescue]; his house is over against Sir John's door.

A steward of the Wardrobe may have had a background as a stapler, a merchant in woolens. Although dwelling in "St. Ellins" in 1594, we can surmise that by 1599 this Robinson and/or his son had come to Blackfriars. Here then was John Robinson living in Blackfriars property where a priest was hiding. He or his son was surely living there in 1613 when the property was purchased by William Shakespeare.[158] John Robinson's son who delivered the letter to the Lord Mayor was the same John Robinson who was Catholic and also associated with the Blackfriars Gatehouse refuge. It was easy for Sterrell to have the letter delivered to John Robinson and his son with the understanding it would be passed on to the Lord Mayor who would naturally send it on to Lord Burghley.

Yes, John Robinson is a common name. But the connections between Mr. Fortescue, John Robinson, Sterrell and the Blackfriars Gatehouse cannot be mistaken as a series of coincidences. It's right there in Shakespeare's deed: the property had been "in the tenure of John Fortescue gent." and in the confession of Polwhele.

Shakespeare's acquisition of the Blackfriars Property

On March 10, 1613, William Shakespeare purchased the Blackfriars Gatehouse from Henry Walker.[159] The price was £140, of which £80 was to be in cash. The remaining £60 was secured by a mortgage to Henry Walker. It was still under lease to William Ireland for 25 years. There is nothing to show that William Ireland actually lived there though an "Ireland's Yard" was nearby. On the deed with Shakespeare were John Heminges, William Johnson, and John Jackson. From subsequent transactions it can be inferred they were trustees for Shakespeare, not fellow investors. Heminges was the actor and promoter from the Kings Men company, but he didn't sign the deed. William Johnson, vintner, was apparently the proprietor of the Mermaid Tavern. John Jackson must be the publisher who had brought out *The Phoenix Nest* in 1593.[160]

Heminges and Jackson had long been associated. Before taking up acting, Heminges was for nine years, 1578-87, an apprentice of the Grocers Company. John Jackson was a member of the Grocers Company at the same time and took up printing about 1586. Jackson was in partnership with a couple of members of the Stationers Company for only a handful of books over a period of not more than a dozen years. Jackson's earliest association in printing was with John Charlewood who had freed Jackson as a member of the Grocer's Company. John Charlewood, a well-known publisher who had a monopoly on printing playbills, is generally identified as the printer who operated a secret press for Fr. Robert Southwell and the Countess of Arundel before Southwell was arrested in 1592. Until Philip Howard, the Earl of Arundel, was imprisoned in 1585, Charlewood styled himself: Printer to the Rt. Hon. The Earl of Arundel. When the Howards were ousted from their London house called Charterhouse, a secret press was evidently set up by Charlewood and his assistants in another of the houses to which the Countess of Arundel had access, probably a house at nearby Acton. John Jackson, we would surmise, was working with Charlewood at this time as he was making his first efforts as a printer.

Charlewood was dead in 1593 when *The Phoenix Nest* was published, and John Jackson as one formerly associated with Charlewood was a good choice to publish the work without drawing attention to the connections of "R. S. of the Inner Temple" and the contributors to the Howard family. Sackville's first wife, Margaret Howard, was sister of Philip Howard and sister-in-law of Anne, Countess of Arundel. Her chaplain was Fr. Robert Southwell whose work Charlewood (probably with his protege Jackson) had printed.

John Jackson in 1611 had been prosecuted in London for an alleged assault on Roger Semper, a barber-surgeon, on March 3, 1611. The jury found Jackson not guilty. Testimony against him was given by Anthony Munday, the anti-Catholic spy, pursuivant and dramatist, who probably was pursuing Jackson, among others, for Catholicism. A year later, Hugh Holland, a contributor to Shakespeare's *First Folio,* was found guilty of recusancy on the testimony of Munday.

Shakespeare granted a lease on the property to John Robinson, who may have already been occupying the property as far back as 1596. E. K. Chambers and Christopher Devlin acknowledge that this may be the same John Robinson who was a witness to Shakespeare's will.[161]

The 1613 Blackfriars conveyance was acknowledged before Gregory Donhault. Donhault, who served three times in

Parliament, had been made a special member of the Middle Temple in 1604. He had so offended Robert Cecil in the Parliament of 1601 that he was unable to secure a government job until near Cecil's death. After becoming secretary to Thomas Egerton, Lord Ellesmere, Lord Chancellor, Donhault was allowed to become a Master of Chancery in 1612. His cousin William Donhault was admitted to the Middle Temple in 1604 and was active in the Middle Temple through the next two decades. Gregory Donhault died one year after the 1613 Blackfriars transaction and made William Donhault the executor of his will.

The two Donhaults would have been well-acquainted with William Sterrell's brother, Henry. But there was a more important reason Gregory Donhault would have been involved with the Blackfriars transaction. As secretary to Thomas Egerton, he would have been closely associated with Egerton's wife: she was Alice, dowager Countess of Derby, Alice Spencer Stanley Egerton, and she was sister of Elizabeth Spencer Carey, the widow of Lord Chamberlain George Carey. Elizabeth was the patron of the Lord Chamberlain's Company when it was formed with Shakespeare as a member in 1594 (transferred in effect from her sister) and was now the life tenant of Lord Hunsdon's House of Blackfriars adjacent to the Blackfriars Gatehouse. Lord Hunsdon's House was the site of the Fatal Vespers of 1623 where Catholics had gathered in the hundreds for services. The Gatehouse was a primary access point to the site. Other neighbors were equally important for the Catholics gathering in Blackfriars.

The Blackfriars title confirmation, 1615

The Blackfriars Gatehouse and its adjacent properties were used as Catholic refuges from the mid-1580s to 1623. This was made possible by Catholic ownership of parties, a number of whom were named in 1615 title proceedings with Shakespeare. Catholic nobility and gentry and their sympathizers made the Gatehouse literally the gateway to a Catholic enclave in the heart of London. For London Catholics to have priests visit them in their homes for their Masses, the christenings of their children, the anointing of their sick, the funeral rites at death of their loved ones, the priests needed to be nearby, not forty miles away at a country manor. Blackfriars properties provided a safe base of operations for priests and

Catholics.

On April 25, 1615 a friendly lawsuit was initiated in the Court of Chancery to give Anne Bacon's son and executor, Mathias Bacon, authority to surrender letters patent and other deeds pertaining to the property. This suit was filed by "Sir Thomas Bendishe Baronet, Edward Newport, and William Thoresbie, Esquiours, Robert Dormer Esquiour and Marie his wife, Willyam Shakespeare, gent., and Richard Bacon Citezen of London."[162] The claim is addressed: "To the Right Honorable Sir Thomas Egerton, Lord Ellesmere and Lord Chancellour of England."

And who is Lord Ellesmere who was to preside? He was now the husband of Alice Spencer Stanley. She had been the patron of the acting company which became the Shakespeare acting company when Alice arranged for her sister Elizabeth Spencer Carey to become patron of the Lord Chamberlain's Men in 1594. She was still patron when it became the King's Men in 1603. The property, known as Lord Hunsdon's House, was immediately adjacent to the property in litigation. It was owned by Lord Egerton's sister-in-law, Elizabeth Spencer Carey, formerly patron of William Shakespeare. Possibly, Elizabeth continued to have an interest in that company as a patron after the company became the King's Men. Her great house was very close to the Blackfriars Theatre where the King's Men were performing from 1608 on.

From the litigation, we have a description of the property in which Shakespeare had purchased an interest only two years before. These parties claimed to be seised of the property, which consisted of one capital messuage or dwelling house with appurtenances, two court yards, one void plot of ground used for a garden, two stables and two hay lofts, a coal house, another messuage or tenement with the appurtenances now in occupation of Anthony Thompson and Thomas Perckes[163] or their assigns, and a void piece of ground whereon there was built a stable, and several other houses, together with all cellars, sollers [loft, attic], chambers, halls, parlours, yards, backsides, easements, profits and commodities.

It appears that the named parties were owners of the different portions of the property that had been divided up in 1590 when Anne Bacon's three-year interest terminated and she had to divide the interest with her brother. Thus, these were probably other owners of the Gatehouse and the remainder of the "capital messuage."

Mathias Bacon filed an answer and denied that he made any claim to the property or that he had any documents pertaining to the transaction. The plaintiffs obtained a decree in their favor that reveals that their attorney was Mr. Richard Moore.

Moore, the Attorney

Attorney Moore, who represented Shakespeare and the rest of the group, was an attorney from, you've already guessed it, the Middle Temple. Richard Moore would no doubt have been very well-acquainted with William Sterrell's brother, Henry Sterrell, as they were both very prominent and active in the Middle Temple in 1615. Richard Moore was also a Middle Temple contemporary of two Newports (brothers of Edward Newport) as further identified below. That he had some close Catholic connections is probably well indicated by the fact that in November 1590 when Robert and Thomas Winter entered the Middle Temple, they were both bound with Richard Moore. These were two Gunpowder Plotters, both well known to Frs. John Gerard and Henry Garnett, the Jesuit priest who was executed in 1606 for the Gunpowder Plot. Moore had come to Middle Temple from New Inn July 1586. The two Winters had arrived at Middle Temple from New Inn November 1590, and John Newport had arrived at Middle Temple from New Inn in February 1590. Robert and Thomas Winter and two Newport brothers, Charles, also of the Middle Temple, and Richard, were well-acquainted with the Blackfriars refuge in the decade of 1600-1612. These two Newports were priests hiding from the government that hunted them.

The Parties to the 1615 Suit with Shakespeare

The records that survive would suggest that most of the parties or their families were strong Catholics who would have been willing to continue to have their property used as a Catholic refuge. The property had long been so used and continued as a Catholic site to the tragic accident of 1623 when the crowds attending Catholic services in Blackfriars were so huge that the floors collapsed, the Fatal Vespers. In addition to Shakespeare, these owners in the 1615 litigation were:

<> *Robert Dormer Esquire and Marie his wife,*

<> *Edward Newport,*

<> *William Thoresbie, Esquire,*

<> *Sir Thomas Bendishe Baronet,*

From the pleadings, it is not possible to identify which of "seuerall lodginges or dwellinge howses" the named parties occupied, only that they traced their titles back to the common title from which Shakespeare's title was derived. Suffice it to say, they were close neighbors. Bear with me, the names, titles and relations are confusing, but the people seem to be close to one another in backgrounds.

Robert Dormer Esquire and Marie [Bannister] his wife

Robert Dormer and his wife Marie (often spelled Mary) Bannister had very close family relations to both the Countess of Southampton and Robert Southwell, the martyred priest/poet who was priest to the Countess's family. Robert Dormer's grandfather was Sir William Dormer of Wing, Bucks, who lived c. 1514 to 1575. Sir William had two wives, the first giving him two daughters: Jane Dormer, Duchess of Feria and Anne Dormer Hungerford. Jane Dormer was principal maid to Queen Mary Tudor when Viscount Montagu was a principal courtier. Her sister Anne was also a member of Queen Mary's household. By his second wife, Dorothy Catesby, Sir William Dormer had one son, Robert, and six daughters. Sir William was Catholic and evidently raised his children Catholic. The son, Robert Dormer born in 1551, was of Oxford 1569, and married Elizabeth Browne, daughter of Anthony Browne, 1st Viscount Montagu, by his second wife. Hence, Elizabeth Browne Dormer was half-sister of the Countess of Southampton; she and the Countess of Southampton had been raised together.

Robert Dormer was a Catholic whose house was from time to time a place of Catholic priests and masses, including Edmund Campion in 1580.[164] He evidently remained in contact with his half-sisters Jane and Anne. The Duchess of Feria, Jane Dormer, was for years the leader of the Catholic exiles in Spain. Her sister Anne was active among the exiles in the Low Countries until her death in 1603; she was a Spanish pensioner. By the title of Baron Dormer of Wyng, Robert Dormer, brother of Jane, was raised to the peerage on June 30, 1615. His eldest son William pre-deceased him in about October 1616, and he died November 18, 1616.

Baron Robert was succeeded by William's son, Robert, who was left a ward to King James; the king assigned the lucrative wardship to his favorite, Philip Herbert, Earl of Montgomery. The lad later became Earl of Carnarvon; his biography states: "He appears to have been brought up as a catholic, for a contemporary newsletter states that Dr. Prideaux, vice-chancellor of Oxford, devoted three days to catechising the young couple, and describes the mother of the bridegroom as 'an absolute recusant, and his brother like to prove so'." He married the daughter of Philip Herbert, Earl of Montgomery, in 1625. Hold this thought for when we come to Carnarvon's sister shortly.

Robert Dormer, who with his wife Marie was a party to the 1615 Blackfriars litigation, was a younger son of Baron Robert Dormer.[165] Because his father was a baron, he would sign his name Robert Dormer, *esquire*. His mother, the wife of Baron Robert who died 1616, was a prominent papist — Elizabeth Browne, daughter of Anthony, Viscount Montagu. Her half-sister was the Earl of Southampton's mother. Thus, Robert Dormer, esquire, was first cousin of the Earl of Southampton. His wife was Marie Bannister b. 1591 of Idsworth, Southamptonshire, daughter of Edward Bannister and Mary Southwell. Her parents were the sister and brother-in-law of Robert Southwell, S.J. who had visited the Blackfriars Gatehouse when Southwell was active.[166] So Robert Dormer, esquire, and his bride had at least part ownership of the Catholic refuge where her parents lived and where presumably she grew up. One can easily imagine that the infant Marie was baptized Catholic in the Blackfriars by her Jesuit uncle while he was in hiding there.

Marie Bannister Dormer's father was Edward Bannister/Banester. Born in 1540, he was a life-long Catholic, obstinate in his faith. His family had extensive lands: the manors of Idsworth and Wellsworth in Hampshire; Banester's Court in Millbrook near Southampton; houses in Portsmouth; a share in four manors in the Isle of Wright; and portions of two manors and other lands in Sussex. However, the Elizabethan fines on recusant Catholics sapped his wealth, and he was ousted from his manor at Idsworth by the Crown. By the late 1580s or 1590 he and his wife had moved into

Blackfriars. In a March 1588 report on Recusants and Priests in England, Banester's name was linked with Roger Line, husband of the martyr Anne Line, in Southampton; Line was a prisoner at this time in Newgate.[167] In 1606 Banester provided in his will that his son was to have the manor at Idsworth when he was 23 and his daughter was to have the Blackfriars property when she was 26, though his widow could remain at Blackfriars until the daughter occupied it. The daughter, Marie (b. 1591), was to receive £1000 as marriage money.

The closeness of the Dormer family to the family of the Earl of Worcester is seen in the fact that Sir William Dormer's daughter married Edward Somerset, the son of Henry Somerset and Anne Russell, in 1628. She was the sister of the Robert Dormer, Earl of Carnarvon, who married into the family of the Earl of Montgomery, one of brothers to whom the *First Folio* was dedicated. Thus too, she was the niece of the Robert Dormer whose wife Marie held the interest in the Blackfriars property.

Sir Thomas Bendishe, Baronet

Thomas Bendishe was of Steeple Bumstead, Essex. He was created Baronet in May 1611.[168] Perhaps the role of Thomas Bendishe in the 1615 transaction is explained by the fact that Edward Banester had spent some time at Middle Temple, at the same time when the father of Thomas Bendishe, also named Thomas Bendishe, was there.[169] The grandmother of the latter was Margaret Newport, so he may have been related to the Newport of the same Gatehouse proceeding.

Edward Newport

Edward Newport is likely the younger brother of two Catholic priests, Charles and Richard, and of two lawyers of the Middle Temple, the same Charles, and John Newport.[170] Their parents were John and Julyan (Ann) Newport of Welton, Nothamptonshire. John Newport was the eldest of the brothers. He was a student of Dr. John Case at Oxford in 1588, with whom William Sterrell had studied. Sterrell was lecturing at Oxford at the time and would likely have known the students who resided with Case just as he had. Also with Dr. Case in the next year was William Morgan who became a son-in-law of the Earl of Worcester in 1598 and who was a strong supporter of Catholic priests; John Newport and Morgan probably were well-acquainted through Dr. Case and Sterrell. John Newport entered the Middle Temple in 1589. Worcester's family and Sterrell would have known John Newport well and his brother Charles.

John's brother Charles Newport enrolled at Oxford while William Sterrell was praelector there: New Inn Hall, matric Oct. 25, 1589, aged 17; BA from St. Edmund Hall 6 Feb. 1593-4. Charles entered the Middle Temple in 1594 a year after Sterrell's brother Henry Sterrell and was bound with his brother John. Thus, both John and Charles Newport were associated with Henry Sterrell at the Middle Temple for several years. Charles gave up his chamber by May 4, 1597, and soon traveled to Douay, arriving there January 17, 1598, using the alias of Thomas Harris. Ordained in 1601, he was later that year sent into England and was banished in 1606.

Richard Newport, another Newport brother, entered the English College in Rome on September 30, 1595, and was ordained in April 1599. He left for England in April 1602 and was banished in 1606 with his brother Charles. He returned to England and was banished again but returned again. In 1611 he was imprisoned and then executed at Tyburn the following year. One of his brothers, a "heretic," accompanied him to the hurdle. Perhaps this was Edward Newport. Even if Edward pretended to adhere to the state church, Edward would have assisted his brothers.

When Richard Newport was brutally executed, the crowd of onlookers included prominent Catholics who wished to be present at his martyrdom. John Chamberlain in a letter of June 11, 1612 to Sir Dudley Carleton reported that the "earl of Arundel, with his young son were present at the execution and the viscount Montague with divers ladies and gentlemen in coaches."[171] The Earl of Arundel was Thomas Howard whose father Philip died in the Tower for religion, whose mother was Anne Dacre, Dowager Countess of Arundel, and whose aunt had been Margaret Sackville (d. 1591). Viscount Montagu was the son of Countess of Southampton's twin brother and grandson of Anthony Browne, 1st Viscount Montagu, and Mary Dormer. The Viscount was thus related to Robert Dormer who was the owner of the Blackfriars property with his wife Marie Bannister. Marie Bannister's uncle had been the priest/poet Robert Southwell who had been chaplain to Anne Dacre Howard, Margaret Howard Sackville, and the Countess of Southampton before he was imprisoned in 1591. The "divers ladies and gentlemen in coaches" at Richard Newport's execution likely included Robert Dormer and Marie Bannister. It is also likely that Edward Newport was the brother of the martyr and his brother Charles Newport. The two Newport priests had surely used Blackfriars as a refuge for their ministries to Catholics like the members of the Howard and Browne families.

William Thoresbie

I have been unable to establish the identity of William Thoresbie, esquire, who was in the 1615 litigation. The name is also spelled Thoresby or Thursby. Possibly he is the "William Thursbye of Durwardshall in Bockinge in com. Essex, Esquier," found in the *Visitations of Essex* of 1612. Two brothers of the wife of this William Thursbye had been students at Oxford (Brasenose College) and were members of the Middle Temple; William Peart, admitted 1607 and George Peart, admitted 1609. There are several priests in the late Elizabethan/early Jacobean period named Thursbeus (Douay spelling), Thoresby or Thursby: Thomas and Charles. Thomas Thorseby, priest, was among the list of priests banished from England in 1606 along with Charles and Richard Newport. We should suspect that Edward Newport and William Thoresbie were straw owners to mask the actual users or occupants of the property — as was William Shakespeare.

In sum, the lawyer and the property owners in the 1615 Blackfriars suit all were members of the Middle Temple or had close family connections with the Middle Temple and they were closely associated with Catholic priests. Being an owner in title deriving from the Bacon title did not mean that the owner was occupying the property. The persons using the property might be lessees or guests. If the intention was to preserve the Gatehouse area as a Catholic refuge, it would be imperative to have ownership in someone who would not object to the continued use of the property for Catholic gatherings, someone who would not report suspicious activities to the ever-vigilant authorities. Shakespeare was chosen to purchase an interest to front for others who needed to keep the ownership among Catholics privy to its secret use as a refuge.

All those Catholics in the 1615 litigation and the others who relied upon them had to be certain that Shakespeare's demise at the relatively young age of 52 would not disturb their continued use of the refuge. Hence, we should surmise that they stepped into the drafting and execution of the will to preserve the integrity of Blackfriars in friendly hands. They had no interest in any other parts of Shakespeare's assets, but they had to ensure that the Blackfriars interest would not be sold to a third party. This was accomplished by entailing the real property interests and by naming an overseer of the will who could prevent Shakespeare's heirs from making a settlement among themselves to cut off the entail.

Another property immediately adjacent to the Blackfriars Gatehouse was Lord Hunsdon's House.

When George Carey died in 1603, his will left a life tenancy in his house in Blackfriars to his widow, Elizabeth Spencer Carey, with the remainder interest to their daughter Elizabeth Berkeley. The will provided:

> I give and bequeath to my faithful, loving, virtuous and good wife, Dame Elizabeth, the use, occupation and profits of my dwelling-house in the Blackfriars, London, and of all other my houses, lands, tenements and hereditaments within the precinct of the Blackfrars or elsewhere within the city of London during her life; And after her decease, I give and bequeath the fee simple and inheritance thereof to my daughter, Elizabeth Berkeley, and to the heirs of her body lawfully begotten forever;

Lord Hunsdon's House in Blackfriars was located within the precinct of the former Dominican monastery; it was adjacent to the Gatehouse of the old monastic grounds. Let us note the name of one of his overseers: William Spencer. This was his brother-in-law, brother of George Carey's widow, Dame Elizabeth Spencer Carey. George Carey was also then the uncle of William Spencer's daughter, Elizabeth Spencer who had married Thomas Russell, esquire (later Sir Thomas), at Strensham on June 24, 1597. So, William Spencer was overseer of the property adjacent to Shakespeare's Blackfriars property, and his son-in-law, or his uncle of the same name, became the overseer of Shakespeare's Blackfriars property. An utterly incredible coincidence? Sir William Spencer died in 1609, so the two were not simultaneously overseers, though someone else close to the Spencer family may have assumed the role, such as his son-in-law, Sir Thomas Russell; I've not found who may have replaced Sir William Spencer as overseer. We will examine Thomas Russell shortly.

Sir William Spencer and William Sterrell had ample opportunity to have become acquainted at Oxford. Sir William is likely the William Spencer shown in Joseph Foster, *Alumni Oxonienses* (1891) p. 1398, as "scholar, Trinity Coll., 1573 B.A. 17 May 1576, fellow 1579, MA 21 April 1580." These dates almost exactly coincide with William Sterrell's own likely arrival at Oxford about 1574 and the dates of his degrees from Magdalen College. The biography in *The History of Parliament* of Sir William's father, Sir John Spencer of Althorp, notes that "Only the family of his third son William was to remain intermittently Catholic."

When Shakespeare acquired the Gatehouse, Dame Elizabeth Carey was the owner of Lord Hunsdon's House. On January 9, 1613, the letter writer Chamberlain noted that Lady Hunsdon was 'newly maried' to Ralph Eure, third Baron Eure (d. 1617). It was only two months later that Shakespeare, who had been associated with her and her acting company since 1594, acquired the property immediately next to her own. Her change in status may have potentially affected the use of Lord Hunsdon's House.

Let's look a bit further at the ownership of the property before considering its use. Chamberlain also recorded the death of Dame Elizabeth, Lady Hunsdon, "of a palsie as is supposed" on February 24 or 25, 1618; Sterrell himself had observed her fit of palsy at dinner in 1602. By operation of Lord Hunsdon's will, the Blackfriars property would pass to her daughter, Elizabeth Carey Berkeley, herself a widow since 1611.

Strikingly, it is as Lady Eure (Lady Hunsdon) is dying of "palsie" that we again see a transaction with Shakespeare's Gatehouse. The trustees of Shakespeare's Blackfriars property entered into a Declaration of Trust of February 10, 1618, that confirmed and noted the extension of the lease to John Robinson and transfers the trustee role to two men living in Stratford. The Declaration has a memorandum: "Memorand. that the xj." day of February in the years within written [1618], John Robinson, tenant of the premises within mentioned did give and deliver unto John Greene within named to the use of Susanna Hall within named five pence of lawful money of England in name of Attornment." This "Attornment" of five pence is the legal act of the tenant formally agreeing to recognize a new owner as their new landlord. It ensures the lease remains in effect, allowing the tenant to stay while creating a direct landlord-tenant relationship with the new owner. Susanna Hall's apparent worth derived from the property seems to have been only five pence. Nothing is said about a periodic rent. So much for the Blackfriars Gatehouse purchase being an investment for the good of Shakespeare's family. The February 1618 Declaration of Trust appears to have been a transaction to confirm John Robinson's control of the Gatehouse just as the ownership of Lord Hunsdon's House was changing.

Elizabeth Carey Berkeley continued to own the Blackfriars house even though she remarried in 1622 and was living in Cranford, Middlesex at an estate she had purchased for £7,000 in 1618. She **had not divested** herself of the title to the Blackfriars house. It had come into the possession of the French ambassador by the date of the Fatal Vespers — October 26, 1623. The house was now the residence of the French ambassador, Comte de Tillieres.[172] The spacious property was used for secret Catholic worship and probably had been for years. We know that title had not changed from William Sterrell's letter (above) confirming the ownership: "French Ambassadors house who lieth in the Lord Hunsdon's house that was & is the Heirs still." Similarly, Shakespeare's Gatehouse was in the hands of Shakespeare's heirs because the Gatehouse was entailed so that neither Susanna nor her daughter could alienate it during their lifetimes. The entailment, probably devised by Sterrell, allowed Catholics to continue using the Blackfriars Gatehouse. Let's see how the device of entailment worked.

The Entail

In Shakespeare's will, the real property interests in New Place ("wherein I now dwell"), the Henley street properties, the other interests in Warwickshire, and in Blackfriars ("wherein one John

Robinson dwelleth") were devised to his daughter Susanna Hall but all were entailed so that neither she nor her daughter nor Judith could never gain full ownership:

> To have and to hold all & singular the said premises with their appurtenances unto the said Susanna Hall for and during the term of her natural life and after her decease to the first son of her body lawfully issuing, and to the heirs males of the body of the said first son lawfully issuing and for default of such issue to the second son of her body lawfully issuing and to the heirs males of the body of the said second son lawfully issuing and for default of such heirs to the third son of the body of the said Susanna lawfully issuing and of the heirs males of the body of the said third son lawfully issuing. And for default of such issue the same so to be and remain to the forth, fifth, sixth, and seventh sons of her body lawfully issuing, one after another, and to the heirs males of the bodies of the said forth, fifth, sixth, and seventh sons lawfully issuing in such manner as it is before limited to be and remain to the first, second and third sons of her body and to their heirs males. And for default of such issue the said premises to be and remain to my said Niece Hall and the heirs males of her body lawfully issuing for def[ault of] such iss[u]e to my daughter Judith & the heirs males of her body lawfully issuing. And for default of such issue to the right heirs of me the said William Shakespeare forever.

Because of this entailment, the will of Shakespeare as to real property conveyed almost nothing of value except use or income during life of the property in Stratford. For the Blackfriars property in distant London, it provided neither use nor income of record. Nothing seems to have flowed to Susanna from Blackfriars.

English common law property recognized the creation of a "fee tail male" which was a legal restriction on real property ensuring it descended exclusively to a landowner's direct male heirs, typically the eldest son, to prevent breaking up estates. This mechanism prohibited selling or mortgaging the land outside the male lineage. It was designed to maintain family wealth, landed power, and status within the male line for generations. While intended to last for generations, a strict settlement could sometimes be broken (docked) if the current owner and the immediate next heir (once of age) agreed to it. Appointment of an overseer prevented the "fee tail male" from being broken by the heirs and executors without the overseers' consent. Because Shakespeare had no male heirs and it appeared unlikely that his daughters would, preventing his daughters or granddaughter from breaking the entailment seems intended to prevent them from alienating the Blackfriars property for their entire lives at little cost to the real parties in interest for Blackfriars.

It was not uncommon for great landowners to keep substantial tracts intact for their heirs, but this device makes no sense when applied to a property like Shakespeare's interest in Blackfriars some distance away in London. Nor were the other real property interests in Stratford part of some consolidated area. Although the Cottage of Rowington Manor was near New Place, it was not subject to the entail because it was only a copyhold interest.

So, what was Shakespeare's intent for the entailment? The legal effect of this entail for generations was to make the grants essentially worthless to the heirs except for lease income, if any. They could not sell the property nor even occupy it if it was under lease. E. K. Chambers suggested that the "hopes of the will" were that Shakespeare be followed by a long line of male heirs. But Susanna in 1616 was thirty-three and the mother of only one daughter. In that time, a woman of that age with only one child was unlikely to bear more. His other daughter had just married and had no children, but she was disfavored in the will, and Shakespeare could not bring himself to write her recent husband's name in; he had crossed out what was to be his name. Even if Judith had male children, they were in the line of succession under the entailment only if Shakespeare's granddaughter had no male children when the granddaughter died, however many decades later that might be. If Shakespeare hoped for male great-grandchildren from his granddaughter Elizabeth, it was unnecessary to entail the property.

No heirs under Shakespeare's will would ever bear his name. If a man did nothing to preserve his own priceless writings and pass those creations on as his heritage, why would he preserve the fragments of disparate bits of real property to the 7th son of 7th son?

Okay, maybe I'm stretching the effect of the entail. Shakespeare's bequest little benefitted a future heir in his bloodline and did not preserve his name. It seems designed to protect the lessee in the Blackfriars from being disturbed by members of his family and their descendants. The intent of the will appears to have been to prevent most of the properties from passing at all. It seems most likely that it was the intent of the lawyer and the overseer to keep the properties out of commerce, to tie them up and keep them from the hands of the executors and named beneficiaries. A certain recipe for family conflict. The Blackfriars property was already under the control of trustees prior to the will, and there seems to be nothing the executors could do to affect it; only the overseers could with the cooperation of the trustees.

Even when the London trustees of Blackfriars transferred their control to new trustees in Stratford by means of a Declaration of Trust of February 10, 1618, the use of Blackfriars was unchanged. The trustees stated that Shakespeare, along with them, had made a lease for a term of years unto John Robinson, "now tennant of the said premises."[173] The trustees conveyed the trust property to new trustees John Greene of Clements Inn and Mathew Morys of Stratford. These two were to control the property to the use of Susanna for her life and then for the life of her first son and so forth. The conveyance refers to the transaction being subject to the lease with John Robinson. A memorandum of the same date states that "John Robinson, tenant of the premisses within mencioned, did give and deliver unto John Greene within named to the use of Susanna Hall within named five pence of lawful money of England." Anything the new trustees would do with the property was subject to the oversight of the overseers. John Greene was brother of Thomas Greene, the lawyer who had lived at New Place.[174] Thomas Greene was an investor with William Shakepeare on certain tithes in 1605 and was involved with him in enclosing certain lands.

The overseers' could prevent the executors from violating the entailment by entering into transactions that would defeat it, thereby giving Susanna full ownership.[175] An effort was made to cut off the entail and thus bar Judith from inheriting in May 1639, as traced by E. K. Chambers.[176] Susanna Hall had no issue, other than Elizabeth. Elizabeth had no issue. Judith Quiney's last child died in February 1639. Steps were taken to bar the entail. A settlement of "the inheritance of William Shakespeere gent, deceased" was made by Susanna and Elizabeth with Elizabeth's husband, Thomas Nash, followed by fines and a fictitious legal action. Under the settlement the estate was vested successively in Susanna, Thomas and Elizabeth Nash and the survivor, their joint issue, the issue of Elizabeth, and the heirs and assigns of Thomas. Under Shakespeare's will, if Elizabeth died with no male heirs, all the real property would go to Judith and then to her male heirs. So, in 1639, even if Judith's sons were dead, Judith would inherit the property on the death of Elizabeth if she had no male children/heirs. That would mean nothing would go to Elizabeth's husband Thomas Nash. Judith, who lived another 23 years (age 77), could well have inherited the property on the death of Elizabeth, leaving nothing for Elizabeth's husband. The 1639 "new settlement" was a device to cut off the possibility of Judith inheriting the property; it instead attempted to vest it in Elizabeth and her husband, to the exclusion of the interest of Judith. It was not successful. After Judith's death in 1662 with no male heirs, Elizabeth, now married to Sir John Bernard, was free to claim the property under the will as her grandfather's only heir. According to a recent discovery, Elizabeth and her husband sold the Blackfriars property to Edward Bagley on March 27, 1665, who then sold the property to Sir Heneage Fetherston on August 28, 1667.[177] After the Great Fire of 1666, it was now only empty ground.

In short, the will of Shakespeare as to real property in Stratford conveyed value only for use or rent during life of Susanna and Elizabeth. Perhaps they leased some of the property to others. The overseer could have broken the entail for Susanna and Elizabeth. But what if the overseer were someone more interested in the Blackfriars property remaining in Catholic control?

The Overseer, Thomas Russell, esquire

Let's now inquire as to the role of the overseers. Whom did they represent? How did their duties differ from those of an executor? Executors of a will are responsible for managing a deceased person's estate, which includes initiating probate, inventorying assets, paying debts and taxes, and distributing property to beneficiaries. They hold a fiduciary duty to act in the estate's best interest, legally representing the deceased and fulfilling all instructions in the will. An overseer acts as a monitor to ensure the executors comply with the will's intent.

Thomas Russell, esquire, (abt. 1570 - 1634), was named as an overseer of Shakespeare's will along with the attorney Francis Collins. Beyond being named in the will, there is almost nothing to connect this overseer to Shakespeare-of-Stratford. Early biographers of Shakespeare thought he was a metallurgist of London. Leslie Hotson's 1937 book proposed that the overseer was Thomas Russell of Alderminster, the uncle of Sir Thomas Russell of Strensham.[178] Hotson apparently sought a Thomas Russell in the vicinity of Stratford rather than London, one who could be called *esquire,* and seized upon this Thomas Russell.

Apparently, Hotson ruled out Sir Thomas Russell of Strensham as the overseer because he was a *knight* while the will refers to Thomas Russell as *esquire*. Hotson also seemed to rely on Thomas Russell of Alderminster having had a connection (stepfather) to Leonard Digges whose name appears as a contributor of verse to the *First Folio*. There is nothing to indicate Leonard Digges ever knew Shakespeare in London or Stratford, though Leonard at the time of Shakespeare's death was a close friend of Sterrell's student James Mabbe, who also contributed verse to the *First Folio*.

The scrivener who drafted the Shakespeare will could have simply misidentified "Thomas Russell" as *esquire* rather than as *Sir* Thomas Russell. The two Thomas Russells were very closely related and both lived not far from Stratford. They were only a few years apart in age and both had attended Oxford within a couple of years of each other. Sir Thomas Russell had been an *esquire* as son of a knight before he was knighted as *Sir* Thomas Russell in 1603.

Thomas Russell, esquire, was the stepfather of both Sir Dudley Digges and Leonard Digges. He had married the wealthy widow of the mathematician Thomas Digges when she was 45 and he about 30.[179] Some background facts seem to connect Thomas Russell, esquire, with Sterrell and Worcester. Matriculating from Queens College, Oxford November 15, 1588, he could well have been a student of William Sterrell anytime between then and Sterrell's resignation as professor in March 1591. Thomas Russell, esquire, would not have encountered his future stepson Leonard Digges, but he would surely have encountered at Oxford Leonard Digges's very close friend James Mabbe. It was likely Mabbe who got Leonard Digges to join him in contributing verse to the *First Folio,* rather than Thomas Russell, esquire. Mabbe had enrolled at Sterrell's Magdalen College not long before Thomas Russell, esquire, at Queen's College. Is it coincidental that Thomas Russell, esquire, was of the same Russell family as Anne Russell who married Worcester's son Henry in 1600? But so, too, was Sir Thomas Russell of Strensham. Any connections between Thomas Russell, esquire, of Alderminster and Shakespeare-of-Stratford seem to have been the product of Hotson's vivid imagination.

When we turn to Sir Thomas Russell of Strensham (1577-1632), nephew of Thomas Russell of Alderminster, we encounter a cascade of correlations showing that he had strong connections to people discussed throughout this book. Sir Thomas Russell was a close companion to the family of the Earl of Worcester.[180] He had matriculated from St. John's College, Oxford, in 1591, just months after Sterrell had escorted two of Worcester's sons and Sterrell's own half-brother to Oxford. If Sir Thomas got his slightly older uncle of the same name to be overseer, it might have been because it was problematic for himself to be overseer of Shakespeare's will as he was openly Catholic by 1610.

When we look into Sir Thomas Russell's family of we find still stronger connections to both the Earl of Worcester and to the acting companies associated with Shakespeare-the-author. His father was Sir John Russell (a half-brother to Thomas Russell, Esquire) who was brought up in the household of his relative Francis Russell, the 2nd Earl of Bedford (c. 1527 - 28 July 1585). Thus, Sir Thomas Russell's father was like a sibling to Bedford's son John Russell, Baron Russell (c. 1553–1584), who married Elizabeth Hoby, widow of Sir Thomas Hoby. The daughter of Baron Russell and Elizabeth was Anne Russell who became the wife of Henry Somerset, Worcester's heir — Sir Thomas Russell's contemporary at Oxford. Sir Thomas Russell then is a close cousin of the Earl of Worcester's daughter-in-law, and this accounts for Sir Thomas being part of the social set of the Somersets and Russells. Sir Thomas Russell was certainly among the family members attending the great wedding of Henry

Somerset and Anne Russell in 1600.

The Russell family had close connections to Shakespeare's Cottage that was part of Rowington Manor. One of the daughters of Francis Russell, 2nd Earl of Bedford, was Lady Anne Russell (1548–1603), wife of Ambrose Dudley, 3rd Earl of Warwick. She was raised in the household in which Sir Thomas Russell's father was raised. As we have seen, Lady Anne Russell, Countess of Warwick, was directly responsible for one Shakespeare property transaction: the Cottage that was part of Rowington Manor, which Shakespeare purchased in 1602 and where he most likely lived. Now another Russell of the same family is overseeing the will that distributes the same property. But it doesn't stop there.

For Shakespeare to have purchased the 1602 Cottage of Rowington, it had to be through the consent of the existing tenants (the family of Sterrell's friend Anthony Skinner) and the proprietor, Lady Anne Russell, Countess of Warwick, who was the aunt of the Earl of Worcester's daughter-in-law. In connection with Rowington Manor we must now introduce Sir Thomas Russell's mother, Elizabeth Sheldon, daughter of Ralph Sheldon, from another strongly Catholic family of Warwickshire that had close connections with Sterrell and Sterrell's friend Anthony Skinner. This was through Ralph Sheldon's sister Katherine Sheldon Plowden. And it was Elizabeth Sheldon Russell's uncle William Sheldon who was a witness on the conveyance by William and John Combe to Shakespeare of the Old Stratford Freehold, May 1, 1602, which was nearly contemporaneous with the Cottage transaction.[181] From this same Sheldon family of Beoley was another William Sheldon (nephew of Elizabeth Russell and first cousin of Sir Thomas Russell) who married Elizabeth Petre, granddaughter of Edward Somerset, 4th Earl of Worcester. The only extant copy of the Shakespeare *First Folio* that can be traced back to its original owners was acquired by this couple in about 1628 (known as the Sheldon Folio or Burdett-Coutts Folio). The point of this recitation is to demonstrate the familiarity of these Russell, Sheldon, Somerset and Skinner families with one another and their property connections with William Sheldon of Stratford.

Even more significant for Shakespeare's will is Sir Thomas Russell's wife, whose family is directly associated with the playwright and the acting companies. She is Elizabeth Spencer, daughter of William Spencer, one of the sons of Sir John Spencer of Althorp. Her aunts thus included the three Spencer daughters discussed at length above, two of whom were patrons of the two acting companies: Alice Spencer Stanley, wife of Ferdinando Stanley whose company was Lord Strange's Men; and Elizabeth Spencer Carey, wife of George Carey whose company was Lord Hunsdon's Men. Those three Spencer sisters were likely present when Elizabeth Spencer at age 18 married Thomas Russell at Strensham on June 24, 1597. She was at an age and status in society when she (and her husband) could not have been unaware of the plays by William Shakespeare that were performed by the acting companies associated with her two aunts.

As we look next to bequests in Shakespeare's will to three members of the Shakespeare acting company, we should note both Alice Spencer Stanley and Elizabeth Spencer Carey were long acquainted with the three men and could have seen to their inclusion in the Shakespeare will and were closely related to the will's overseer. They had participated in the inclusion of William Shakespeare's name when they established, with the involvement of Elizabeth's husband, George Carey, the new company bearing the title Lord Chamberlain's Men.

Sir Thomas Russell's wife was niece of the owner of Lord Hunsdon's House immediately adjacent to the Shakespeare property conveyed in the 1616 will. That same aunt had long had a business relationship with John Heminges, the co-owner or trustee (with two others) controlling Shakespeare's Blackfriars property. Because John Heminges was a participant, whether as co-owner or trustee, in the purchase of Blackfriars and presumably was privy to the Catholic purposes behind the purchase, he would have been directly interested in the disposition of the Blackfriars Gatehouse in Shakespeare's will. Heminges himself may well have seen to the inclusion of his name in the will. It provided a link between his Blackfriars role and the will itself. That link was the purchase price of a ring, and the gift was interlineated in the only logical place in the will to make such a provision.

The Rings

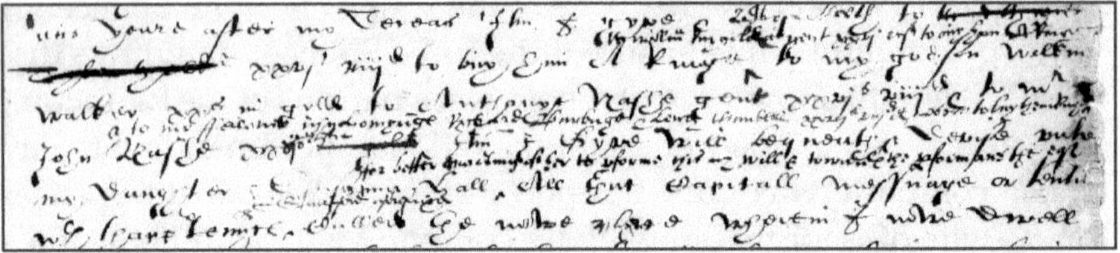

Item, I gyve and bequeath to [~~Mr. Richard Tyler thelder~~] *Hamlett Sadler* xxvj.s viij.d. to buy him a ringe; to *William Raynoldes gent., xxvj.s. viij.d. to buy him a ringe;* to my godson William Walker xxs. in gold; to Anthonye Nashe gent. xxvj.s. viij.d. [~~in gold~~]; *and to my fellowes John Hemynge, Richard Brubage, and Henry Cundell, xxvj.s. viij.d. a peece to buy them ringes.* [italics is interlineation].[182]

Shakespeare scholars point to the fact that Heminges, Condell, and Burbage were among seven men given small sums for mourning rings in *Stratford's* will but even that is dubious. The three names of company personnel were added by an interlineation to an earlier draft of the Shakespeare will. The addition of the three names preserved the illusion that Shakespeare-of-Stratford was a playwright companion to the three men.

The persons interested in the Blackfriars property, and a lawyer or overseer acting on their behalf, had reason to be concerned about the provisions of Shakespeare's will. These three names were well known to the woman who owned the property next to Shakespeare's Blackfriars Gatehouse, Elizabeth Spencer Carey, who had started up the Lord Chamberlain's Company in 1594 with Shakespeare, John Heminges, and Richard Burbage. She may have seen to their addition. Heminges himself may have been responsible for the interlineation. Adding the names made it seem that there was a basis for cutting Blackfriars off from what Susanna inherited by entailing it. There's no other mention in the will of John Heminges (with two others) having a controlling interest in the deed to that property, only that it was under lease to someone named John Robinson. If there had been no mention of John Heminges in the will, it would have been more difficult to establish why he (and two others) was connected to the Blackfriars property. To preserve effective control over use of the Blackfriars Gatehouse, Heminges had a personal incentive to see that his name was associated with it, just as the lessee of that property was himself a witness to the will.

♦♦♦ ♦♦♦

Skepticisima: Any thoughts, Mr. B?

Bardophilus: Frankly, I'm stunned.

Skepticisima: How so? I can't recall any such depth in treatment of the Shakespeare will.

Bardophilus: That's just it. It strikes me as sacrilegious. The author is maligning a sick old man on his deathbed. We owe too great a debt to the father of our national literature to pick apart his will. It's always seemed to me that he was generous to his daughters. He was a loving and doting parent. We know how much he loved his only son Hamnet. He felt grief deeply for having been an absentee father. That explains why he hoped so much that Susanna would bear a son.

Skepticisima: You know that from a movie, not from any evidence. He left his daughters what he had, but what else would he have done? It sure looks like he was keeping it from his wife. And the property going to the daughter was crippled in usefulness by the entail. You scholars see that Susanna and her husband were the executors of the will, and you conclude that they "would enact the design" of the will's execution. The presence of the overseers frustrated that. Chambers shows that Susanna and her husband tried to get around the entail and could not. More importantly, you Bardolators generally ignore the most significant piece of property in the will. The valuable real estate in the heart of London. The entail, with overseers, ensured that Susanna would get nothing from it.

Bardophilus: Perhaps there was rent from Blackfriars that we don't see from any records.

Skepticisima: Of course. Shakespeare was the inventor of the early modern Bed and Breakfast. He would rent out rooms to the gentry coming to London to see his plays. If we just keep looking, we'll eventually find a register of his guests. It'll make a great movie.

Bardophilus: Don't mock me.

Skepticisima: Teasing, not mocking. Your devotion to an idealized Shakespeare prevents you from dealing realistically with the facts.

Bardophilus: Maybe. But you suffer from your own silo vision. You and Verba have got this Catholic thing. We don't see a real Catholic influence on Shakespeare. Don't Catholics put Catholic religious language in their wills?

Skepticisima: Well, you're spot on there. I'm not saying that Shakespeare was a strong Catholic. But Sterrell was. Isn't that the point though for hiding things behind the name of Shakespeare?

Let's look at Sterrell's will. It opens invoking the Trinity in Latin: "In nomine Patris et Filii et Spiritus Sancti." It says that the testator is in perfect health and memory to proceed "according as it shall please God considering the frailty of mankind." Then Sterrell continues: "In the name of God, Amen. I do bequeath my soul to the holy, blessed and glorious Trinity, three persons and one God, from whence I had it. And my body to the earth from which it came, to be interred where it shall please our most blessed Saviour Jesus Christ, perfect God, and perfect man." Thus, the paradoxes of unity, in both the Trinity and the Incarnation, are reiterated with emphasis. And when he gives his directions for the annuities to two beneficiaries, Sterrell introduces a note of Catholic piety. He specifies the two days of the year on which payments are to be made. One of them is named more vividly than conventional: "at the feast of the Annunciation of the most blessed lady the virgin Mary, and at the feast of St Michael the Archangel."

Bardophilus: The Catholic conspiracy thing still.

Skepticisima: It fully explains Blackfriars. And most of the playwright's anonymity and career. And especially *Phoenix and Turtle*. Your real problem is that you can't accept the power of religious faith. It troubles you in your treatment of Eliot and Lewis and Percy even if you acknowledge that it haunts Joyce and Burgess.

Chapter 9

Reckonings

A reckoning is an accounting, a settling of accounts. It may be a bill that has come due or an inventory of an estate by an auditor. For the sailor, it is a calculation of the ship's position in its voyage, taking into account the log, the course steered, observations of wind, current, sun and stars. We have reached a point of reckoning for this book. As Touchstone would have it, "When a man's verses cannot be understood, it strikes a man more dead than a great reckoning in a little room." We must examine what it has accomplished and what it has not. Let's take account. Where are we on the voyage we began 300 pages ago?

The goal of this book has been to persuade you that William Sterrell was Shakespeare-the-author and that Shakespeare-of-Stratford was his false face, a serviceable front. To go against centuries of scholarship, in so brief a space within these covers, is a heavy burden. Instead of an all-encompassing examination of the Shakespeare poetry and plays, its method has been to focus on one poem and one play, *Venus and Adonis* and *Alls Well that Ends Well*. You have been given some treatment of major events in the life of William Sterrell and his patron-collaborator, the 4th Earl of Worcester. Of Shakespeare-of-Stratford, there is little more that can be said of his life, for there is so little of record; on his will, there is no more exhaustive coverage than what you have seen.

Perhaps this has been enough to achieve our primary ends. Much more could be written. And so it shall be. For a proper reckoning, there should be more complete explorations of many or most of the Shakespeare plays, the *First Folio* itself, and the full biography of William Sterrell together with an edition of his extant letters.

The Tasks Ahead

The *First Folio*

Before considering the plays, we must first sweep aside the encrusted story of the *First Folio,* the only authentic/authoritative work attributable to Shakespeare. Don't get me wrong. There is great scholarship concerning many of the details surrounding the 1623 publication of *Mr. William Shakespeare's Comedies, Histories & Tragedies*. What is wanting is a more realistic explanation of how it came to be. Once we accept that William Sterrell was the author of its plays, the absurd account of its preparation and publication can be replaced by an explanation that does not require we set aside common sense and human experience.

In 1623, Sterrell oversaw the publication of his magnificent *First Folio,* an achievement that far surpassed the folio that Ben Jonson had published in 1616. The hefty book remains the most important single publication in literary history. Though conducted with great care and scholarship, all explanations of its nativity have been unsatisfactory and essentially incoherent. Here is a sketch of the new approach to the *First Folio.*

With Sterrell as author, we can discard the "magic file cabinet" fiction that is the foundation of *First Folio* scholarship. Virtually all Shakespeare scholars start with an assumption that the different iterations of a Shakespeare company stored authentic copies of finalized plays throughout the period c. 1592 to 1613 and continued to protect them after Shakespeare-of-Stratford's death in 1616.[183] Accounts of the *First Folio* are premised on this magic file cabinet. The theory goes like this: Over a period of three decades, a cabinet containing the plays moved among multiple locations and even survived the fire that destroyed the Globe Theater in 1613. In about 1619, the contents were gradually taken out and faithfully put into type without material alteration.[184] In this fable, no editor had ever revised or corrected the authentic final draft of the genius who had penned them in so neat a hand than relatively few palpable errors made it into print. Stylistic changes from play to play must have been due to growth in technique by the author, not the product of differing editors; or the internal shifts reflected the hands of anonymous co-authors, which were preserved in a single final draft of each play, with no attribution to a co-author.

Let's ask, what was the incentive to engineer the very expensive undertaking of the *First Folio* on behalf of a man who had ceased writing a decade earlier and had been dead more than five years? To make a profit for the acting company? To make money for the printer and stationer? To honor the two Herbert brothers who were its dedicatees? Considering the cost, time and effort necessary to bring such a finely polished and well-organized collection into print, there can be no economic explanation. Nor can any of the suggested intentions explain why the dedicatory verses were written by the "pious fellowes," who wrote them or who edited the works. Shakespeare-of-Stratford provides us with no motive for the magnificent project.

On the other hand, Worcester and Sterrell had every reason to see the plays into print. In the version of the editing and printing of the *First Folio* in 1623 set forth briefly here and later in much greater depth, the playwright William Sterrell played an active role. and was aided by several trusted friends whom he had known for many years. This work of multiple hands accounts fully for the excellence of the product of 1623. The language of the plays reflects Sterrell's many letters written during the editing of the plays. Sterrell himself must have maintained the manuscripts of the plays and wished to preserve them. They needed competent editing for such an ambitious undertaking, as has been true of every other set of "collected works" for the last four centuries. In 1621 Sterrell was sixty and still very active at Court; he maintained a frequent correspondence overseas reporting on complex English political, economic and religious developments. He needed assistance with a massive literary project. Several eager helpers shared his political and religious outlook, his "pious fellowes."

The dedicatory verses of the *First Folio* were all by fellow Catholics, including Jonson and James Mabbe. Mabbe was a star student of Sterrell from their days together at Magdalen College, a genuine "pious Fellow" in the Magdalen College sense.[185] When the *First Folio* was published, both Sterrell and Mabbe were working together to secure the Spanish Match, to have Prince Charles marry the Infanta of Spain, setting the stage for tolerance of Catholicism in England. Thomas Thorpe, publisher of *Shake-speares Sonnets,* and works of Jonson, Hugh Holland, Mabbe and Digges, was not far in the background as the project was completed.

The *First Folio* of 1623 did secure immortal life for the named playwright, as the poet of the *Sonnets* had projected, but not the poet himself, as he also said. Those words of *Sonnet 81, "I (once gone) to all the world must die, The earth can yield me but a common grave,"* are echoed in Sterrell's will of 1631. In it, he directs:

> And upon my funeral my will is that my executors bestow no more than in humanity they need must. *Caelo tegitur qui non habet urnam.* [One who has no grave is covered by heaven].

Sterrell sought to remain hidden, down to the last words he wrote; he wanted only a common grave. With the *First Folio,* he saw to it that his words would not be buried with his body.

The Shakespeare Plays

With the *First Folio,* we have a comprehensive body of plays that we can treat individually and thematically. This will be done more fully in a forthcoming study of many of the plays and a more complete treatment of the relationship between Sterrell and Worcester and their careers at Court. Here is a preview of that deeper treatment of the Shakespeare plays. The work will treat masques as well as plays. These were two very different types of entertainment, but Sterrell and Worcester were deeply invested in both.

Of the 36 plays published in 1623, half were theretofore unpublished or completely unknown. What is poorly understood is that most of the known plays (i.e. of which there is some contemporaneous record) were "occasional plays." Written for special occasions, most of these started as commissioned one-offs for a single performance for special events in the lives of Sterrell and Worcester. They celebrated the occasion and its host, not the author. The audience at, say, *Measure for Measure* or *Othello* were there to attend King James, not to see a play because it was written by "Shaxberd." Most of the Court audience probably had no idea who wrote it. A few plays made it to a wider audience. A majority of the plays in the *First Folio* were unpublished or known to the English public only as a title. The common understanding from movies and books is that most of Shakespeare's plays were written for performance at public theatres. Not so, based on close examination of the likely circumstances of individual plays.

We can treat the plays as falling into two periods, two distinct decades: Queen Elizabeth's last decade, 1593-1603, and King James's first decade, 1604-1613.

Tudor: 1593-1603

Some early "occasional plays" were for Sterrell's own interests, such as *Loves Labours Lost,* his comic treatment of his experiences with Antonio Perez and the Essex crowd in June-July 1593. The *Comedy of Errors* was his gift to Francis Bacon at Gray's Inn for helping Sterrell overcome Essex's suspicions in those months of fear and despair in 1592-93. The marvelous *Twelfth Night, Or What You Will* was written to celebrate Sterrell's brother's elevation to Utter Barrister of the Middle Temple, where the play was performed in January 1602.

Plays written for and with the guidance of the Earl of Worcester during Elizabeth's reign for major Worcester occasions include *Merry Wives of Windsor* for the Order of the Garter four years after Worcester was inducted, *Midsommer Nights Dream* for the dual weddings of two of his daughters in 1596, and *As You Like It* for the marriage of Worcester's heir in 1600. These plays, which were likely performed before small audiences of courtiers in conjunction with the events, enhanced Worcester's reputation as a master of theatrical entertainments.

Stuart: 1604-1613.

It is no surprise that Worcester and Sterrell were appointed by King James to special entertainment positions as he became King in 1603. To fulfill their roles, Sterrell was made proprietor of the Priory of St John of Jerusalem, the home of the newly designated King's Men acting company. Here we will take up a topic we will call *Grandeur,* a quality of magnificence. This was an ideal of the Crown and nobility in the reign of King James in his first decade. He sought to establish and solidify his authority in a country in which he was a foreigner. With his Coronation, two crowns were united but not two distinct countries, each with its own polity.

No figure of this period was more associated with *Grandeur* in all its Courtly forms than Edward Somerset, 4th Earl of Worcester. Projecting *Grandeur* was the basis of his long influence with the King and his Court. Worcester's confidante Sterrell was an essential part of Worcester's success. Exploring the long collaboration of the two, we will see how Worcester used Sterrell's talents, often through entertainments, to further his personal authority.

Sterrell's plays now focused on royal entertainment, which amplified Worcester's role in the government. We have *Measure for Measure* written for diplomatic efforts to bring a reconciliation with the Spanish Low Countries in 1604. Other Court plays such as *Othello, Macbeth, King Lear, the Winter's Tale,* and *the Tempest,* were devised to flatter and amuse the King. The Court plays were similar in purpose to the Court masques that Worcester commissioned from Sterrell's friends Samuel Daniel and Ben Jonson, a fellow Catholic. Worcester and Sterrell were responsible for hiring Jonson's prolific pen for other occasions, including speeches for King James's ceremonial coronation March 15, 1604, and the orations on January 6, 1610, for *Prince Henry's Barriers;* Worcester was Earl Marshal organizing activities for both occasions. The entertainments were major events used to show favor to courtiers and to sway diplomats by giving them proximity to royalty and officials.

The Masques

Of particular importance for influence at Court were the Jacobean masques. Sterrell and Worcester were responsible for the evolution of the masque from the Tudor Court to the Stuart Court. We can sense this development in the precedents found in pre-1603 Shakespeare plays, often written for special occasions, that featured brief masques or masque-like scenes. These include *Loves Labours Lost, Romeo and Juliet, Merry Wives of Windsor, Midsommer Nights Dream* and *As You Like It.*

Let's take a Court masque and the masque in *As You Like It* for examples. The 1600 wedding celebration of Worcester's son Henry Somerset to Anne Russell included a masque attended by the Queen. Roland Whyte, the letter writer of Court gossip, described the plan of the Somerset-Russell masque as composed of eight ladies: "each hath a skirt of cloth of silver, a rich waistcoat wrought with silks and gold and silver, a mantle of carnation taffeta cast under the arm, and their hair loose about their shoulders curiously knotted and interlaced."[186] They came into the performance dancing to the music of Apollo. This wedding masque which featured Queen Elizabeth's participation was probably very like the wedding masque featured at the end of *As You Like It*, which dates from 1600; it was entered with the *Stationers Register* August 4, 1600 but "stayed" from publication. Hymen presides over the play's wedding masque, which features eight persons marrying in a group. The mid-June 1600 Somerset-Russell wedding masque and the 1600 *As You Like It* wedding masque probably were mirror images of one another.

The Somerset - Russell wedding masque and the *As You Like It* masque were previews of the Court masques overseen by Worcester and the Earl of Suffolk for King James and Queen Anne. The 1603-1613 masques featured lengthy productions that were more sophisticated than earlier masques. Sterrell was surely involved in most. They now included allegorical literary scripts, architect-designed sets, and elaborate costumes, such as were described by Whyte in the 1600 masque for Worcester's heir's wedding. Scripted performances with speeches were a central part of the gatherings of the courtiers, after which they danced into the night in resplendent costumes and masks, as had occurred at the 1600 wedding when Queen Elizabeth was led out to dance by Mary Fitton. Foreign diplomats vied with one another for invitations and favored seating.

Sterrell was put in charge of at least one Ben Jonson masque that served a critical diplomatic function in Anglo-French relations in 1611, *Love Freed from Ignorance and Folly*. For this, and perhaps other services, the King then awarded Sterrell £50. Sterrell had paid Jonson £40 from the Treasury for the masque, a substantial sum.

A Sterrell Biography

The present book is an incomplete portrait of William Sterrell. Its focus is on his early education and teaching, coupled with the formative experience of his mission undertaken under the aegis of the Earl of Essex in 1591-92. The larger work on the Shakespeare plays and Sterrell's workings with his patron, Worcester, will prioritize the plays and the men's associations in producing them.

Two more books will fill out our presentation of Sterrell's life. The first is a biography tracing his Lincolnshire roots and family up to his death in 1631 at age 69. This book will provide a more complete understanding of the man who gave the world the plays and poetry we know as Shakespeare. The second will be an annotated collection of Sterrell's letters (250+). Sterrell was active as a letter writer of English intelligence or news from his days at Oxford in the 1580s through the outbreak of war in Europe in 1626. As a stand-alone volume, it should be useful to historians of the period 1590 through the end of the reign of King James. These letters provide the perspective of a highly intelligent and well-placed observer and participant for many political events of those years. The letters from 1591 through 1605 are mostly under pseudonyms for secrecy from the English government. Those from 1616 to 1626 are all under Sterrell's own name. Many were translated into Spanish and forwarded to Spain. There are probably many more letters of William Sterrell in private collections and in archives that will emerge once historians know of his potential importance.

Conclusion

We finish with a final reflection on Sterrell's unwillingness to ascribe his own name to his creations. The name Sterrell, whatever the spelling, was very rare in England in the 16th century. In my research, I have only come across it in relation to William Sterrell's immediate family. The appearance of the name William Sterrell in any context during his lifetime would call attention only to the man who from his earliest days at Oxford was known for his Catholic identity. Even then, this association had imperiled his degrees despite his academic brilliance. His known correspondence with Catholic exiles marked him as a threat to Elizabeth's government, and he was suspected of being an enemy agent. Any publication under his name would be toxic, turning away potential readers and drawing government inquisitors. Anonymity under a single wealthy, powerful and Catholic patron was the only safe course he could follow as a writer.

The wisdom of the choice is seen when we compare the careers of William Sterrell and Ben Jonson. Jonson had many commissions and patrons but never the protection of a powerful, full-time employer such as enjoyed by Sterrell from the Earl of Worcester (*aka* Lafew). Ben Jonson retired to Westminster in the 1620s, complaining of penury and disappointed that he had never become Master of the Revels. Almost self-loathing, he lamented his hypocrisy by base flattery with his epigram 65, "To my Muse." Referring to himself as a parasite upon patrons, he complained that his muse:

betray'd me to a worthless lord;

Made me commit most fierce idolatry.

William Sterrell, with his young wife, lived in the same precinct as Jonson; he held multiple properties in the same neighborhood; and he received substantial rents from sizeable tracts in Wales gifted to him by Worcester. Sterrell lacked Jonson's public recognition, but he never wanted it. Jonson wanted to play at politics but never did. Sterrell had a deep, if hidden, role in the political developments of nearly five decades. He enjoyed a rich, full life at the highest level of Court through his employment by Worcester. No other writer of the period enjoyed such success and few since. All he lost was the immortal name his works had earned, as he had anticipated: "in me each part will be forgotten." *Sonnet 81.*

♦♦♦ ♦♦♦

Skepticisima: Any final thoughts, old friend?

Bardophilus: I just don't get the secrecy. Why would this fellow Sterrell not take credit for being the Ovid of English literature when and if he was behind the *First Folio*?

Skepticisima: Well, if your question applies to Sterrell, doesn't it apply equally to your man, Shakespeare-of-Stratford as of 1616? The playwright's non-participation in literary life in London was obviously deliberate. He never issued anything directly with his subscription or apparent approval after *Venus and Adonis* and *Lucrece*. Why would the "soul of his age," as he has been called, leave unpublished and unperformed half of his life's output? Nothing of the printed plays bore signs of his endorsement for publication. Why did the great Shakespeare display so little interest in his own work? Could he have had such little regard for his masterpieces? The sonnets shout that he knows his words are immortal.

Bardophilus: But why remain an obedient servant? Your Sterrell could have broken free of Worcester. He was the greatest playwright of his age.

Skepticisima: You dear man, you've missed so much of what has been said. Why should Sterrell want to leave Worcester? At James's Court, the playwright had the greatest companies in England at his command. There was no other such market for his plays. With Worcester he had everything, like Parolles with Lafew. He had the immense satisfaction that his writing was successful. He only forewent the accolades of an admiring throng. Probably, like Coriolanus, Sterrell refused to seek the approval of the plebian crowd: "You common cry of curs, whose breath I hate." Like Hamlet, he probably looked down on the commoners: "the age is grown so picked that the toe of the peasant comes so near the heel of the courtier he galls his kibe." Which of his plays were not meant for an audience of aristocrats or lawyers? Sterrell knew them intimately and lived among them most of his life. The burgher of Stratford, never. No writer of his time had a more fulfilling life.

Bardophilus: Surely, with the passage of time, secrecy was no longer a concern.

Skepticisima: Again, you err. Secrecy was still necessary. What would you expect him to do? Announce, "Hey, England, I'm the secret author you have known as Shakespeare! I've fooled you all these years." What would be the point? It would only be an embarrassment and spoil a long-time illusion. *Sterrellus ex machina*. Expose the puppet-master, the man behind the curtain, and you spoil the dumb show. More importantly, Catholics were still persecuted for years after the Gunpowder Plot of 1605. Look at Sterrell's contemporary, Hugh Holland, who was locked up in 1612 when he was found guilty of recusancy on the testimony of the anti-Catholic playwright Anthony Munday. Or the writer/translator James Mabbe, whom the Archbishop of Canterbury had imprisoned for most of a year on suspicion of being a Catholic spy around 1618.

Bardophilus: You're bringing us up to the *First Folio* again, or you wouldn't have mentioned Holland and Mabbe.

Skepticisima: Clever lad, you. Sterrell did not leave his brilliant body of work to suffer the ruin of neglect and loss through non-publication. Sterrell's own name would have poisoned his greatest achievement. We'll have to see what occurs now, now that the secret is out. If people prefer the fable, it will prove why he chose an inscrutable face and continued to use a dead man's name in 1623.

FINIS.

Notes

1 Among the works exploring the problems of attributing the authorship to Shakespeare-of-Stratford are John Michell's *Who Wrote Shakespeare?* (1996), Ian Wilson's, *Shakespeare: The Evidence* (1993), and Diana Price, *Shakespeare's Unorthodox Biography* (2001, 2012). None settles on an alternative. Bertram Fields, a prominent entertainment lawyer, fastens multiple authors to the plays, as suggested by his title: *Players, the Mysterious Identity of William Shakespeare* (2005). James Shapiro examines the question in depth in *Contested Will* (2010) and concludes that the Stratford man was highly imaginative. An engaging account is Elizabeth Winkler, *Shakespeare Was a Woman and Other Heresies* (2023).

2 Chambers, *Shakespeare* (1930), i, p. 23. Schoenbaum *William Shakespeare: A Documentary Life,* (1975) p. 88 is equally dismissive of the Rowington discovery of William J. Thoms, "Was Shakespeare ever a Soldier?" *Three Notelets on Shakespeare* (1865): "But Thoms has of course confused the poet with some namesake."

3 Lucy Gent, "Venus and Adonis: The Triumph of Rhetoric," *Modern Language Review*, 69 (1974), pp. 721-729.

4 Editors and scholars since Malone in 1790 and Steevens in 1793 down to the present have debated heatedly whether the Sonnets are self-revelatory or in Boswell's phrase mere "effusions of fancy." *See* Margreta de Grazia, *Shakespeare Without a Life*, 103-12 (2023).

5 Andrew Gurr, for example, concludes that *3 Henry VI* must have been performed often by 1592: "He was certainly known to Greene as a player when Greene complained about him in August 1592, with his allusion to the "tyger's heart" from *3 Henry VI* (1.4.137). That play, not in Henslowe's lists for 1592, must have taken Greene's attention at one of the Shoreditch playhouses (there would be little point in Greene making the allusion if the play was not being performed often enough for the reference to be recognizable). I am almost convinced that Shakespeare was with those plays in Pembroke's company at the Theatre in 1592 and 1593." Andrew Gurr, "Three Reluctant Patrons and Early Shakespeare," *Shakespeare Quarterly*, Vol. 44, No. 2 (Summer, 1993), pp. 159-174.

Others say that *1 Henry VI* was already in performance in 1592. *See* Lawrence Manley and Sally-Beth MacLean, *Lord Strange's Men and Their Plays*, (2014) p. 281: "Nashe's description of a play about John Talbot in 1592 (the date of Henslowe's/Strange's 'harey the vj') is an excellent match to *The First Part of King Henry the Sixt* in Mr. William Shakespeares Comedies, Histories, & Tragedies (1623). In the absence of any other play answering to Nashe's description, it would seem that Shakespeare's *1 Henry VI* is the "harey the vj" performed by Strange's Men at the Rose in 1592." They also give this the authority of another noted scholar: "Gary Taylor, in one of the most thorough accounts of multiple authorship of the play, concludes that Shakespeare's collaboration 'with three other playwrights in writing Henry the Sixth, Part One' is proof that he 'unmistakably had some connection at some time in the early 1590s with Strange's Men'."

6 The poet of *Shake-speares* Sonnets speculates in *Sonnet 81* that "I shall live your epitaph to make" and states more conclusively that "I (once gone) to all the world must die, The earth can yield me but a common grave." Someone, learned yet unidentified, did make an epitaph for William Shakespeare within a short period after his death in 1616. In Latin and English verse, that someone wrote an inscription for the Shakespeare monument on the north wall of the chancel of Stratford Church:

Iudicio Pylium, genio Socratem, arte Maronem.
Terra tegit, populus maeret, Olympus habet
Stay passenger, why goest by so fast?
Read if thou canst, whom envious death hath plast,
Within this monument Shakspeare: with whom
Quick nature died: whose name doth deck this tomb,
Far more then cost: since all, that he hath writ,
Leaves living art, but page, to serve his wit.

The Latin translates as "Earth covers, the people mourn, Olympus has him, a Nestor in judgment, a Socrates in genius, a Virgil in art." Pylium and Maronem are uncommon names to identify Nestor and Virgil, suggesting that the author of the lines was someone quite knowledgeable of Latin literature. The inscription's use of "Within this monument Shakspeare: with whom Quick nature died: whose name doth deck this tomb" echoes *Sonnet 81's* lines "When you entombed in men's eyes shall lie, Your monument shall be my gentle verse . . ." Was the inscription's author merely a reader of *Shake-speares Sonnets*, or was he the poet of *Sonnet 81* who in fact had lived to make Shakespeare's epitaph? Consider the further echoes of the sonnet and the Stratford Monument in William Sterrell's only epitaph, inscribed in his own will as he directed his executors to spend as little as possible on his funeral: *Caelo tegitur qui non habet urnam* – Heaven covers one who has no tomb [urn]. Sterrell, who taught Moral and Natural Philosophy at Oxford's Magdalen College in Latin, would have been well familiar with Socrates, Pylium and Maronem.

7 The dating of *Sonnet 107* is almost certainly 1603 ("The mortal moon hath her eclipse endured") and heralds the arrival of King James. It is auspicious for Sterrell and for the player Shakespeare: Sterrell has just been made landlord of the Palace of St. Johns of Jerusalem and the Shakespeare company has been taken under the support of the King as the Kings Men. Peace with Spain and the Low Countries was now anticipated: "Incertainties now crown themselves assured, And peace proclaims olives of endless age." The poet is not promising to rehabilitate the name of a man found guilty of treason and recently released from prison – the Earl of Southampton.

8 The 1609 print has the word "tell" as "fel" or "sel "but it's clear in context that "tell" is intended.

9 Crystal, *Dictionary of Linguistics and Phonetics*, 470 (2008).

10 Robert Cawdrey, *A Table Alphabeticall* (1604): "sterilitie, barrenness." John Bullokar, *An English expositor teaching the interpretation of the hardest words used in our language* (1616): "Sterill. Barren."

11 Del Soldato, Eva, "Natural Philosophy in the Renaissance", *The Stanford Encyclopedia of Philosophy* (Fall 2023 Edition), Edward N. Zalta & Uri Nodelman (eds.), URL = <https://plato.stanford.edu/archives/fall2023/entries/natphil-ren/>.

12 The *First Folio* dedication in part:

> it hath bin the height of our care . . ., to make the present worthy of your H.H. . . . Country hands reach forth milk, cream, fruits, or what they have: and many Nations (we have heard) that had not gums & incense, obtained their requests with a leavened Cake. It was no fault to approach their Gods, by what means they could: And the most, though meanest, of things are made more precious, when they are dedicated to Temples.

Pliny's *Natural History* dedication letter to the future emperor as translated:

> care is taken that what is dedicated to you may be worthy of you. However, country folk, and many natives, not having incense, make offerings of milk and salted meal, and no man was ever charged with irregularity for worshipping the gods in whatever manner was within his power.

13 Charles Schmitt, *John Case and Aristotelianism in Renaissance England* (1983), p. 83. As many as twenty-two students might be enrolled as Case students at a time.

14 Nine plays staged at Oxford in the first two months of 1582 make a cluster noteworthy not least for the fact that Shakespeare would subsequently make substantial use of central themes of at least four of them (*Menechmi* in *The Comedy of Errors*, *Supposes* in *The Taming of the Shrew*, *Caesar Interfectus* in *Julius Caesar*, and *Antony and Cleopatra*), not to mention the lines in *Meleager* which scholars have said anticipate some lines in *A Midsummer Night's Dream*. Grants to Sterrell by the College for "vestments" could well have been for costumes for plays.

15 *Oxford Dictionary of National Biography* entry for John Florio.

16 The subject Sterrell taught was aimed at understanding the nature of the world, not at using science as an instrument. Peter Dear, a historian of science, has explained: "Natural philosophy was not, then, generally seen as having a practical part at all; . . . . The content of natural philosophy was essentially and solely speculative because it was about understanding things, not doing things. . . . Natural philosophy stood out as different simply because it was not conceived as knowledge to be used for practical purposes." Peter Dear, "What Is the History of Science the History Of?: Early Modern Roots of the Ideology of Modern Science," *Isis*, 96, pp. 390-406 (September 2005), p. 394.

Art, science and metaphysics were not hostile to one another, as captured in Hamlet's statement: "There are more things in heaven and earth, Horatio, Than are dreamt of in your philosophy." Act 1 sc. 5. li. 176. The Bevington edition of the *Complete Works*, p. 1109 properly notes this line: "176 'your philosophy' this subject that is called 'natural philosophy' or 'science.' (Your is not personal.)"

17 John Case's biographer noted the "striking similarity" between Case's use of plant grafting as an example of the fruitful intervention of art into a prepared and receptive nature; *see* Charles Schmitt, *John Case and Aristotelianism in Renaissance England* (1983), p. 199.

18 Schmitt, *John Case and Aristotelianism in Renaissance England* (1983), p. 104.

19 Sterrell was the first of a number of capable, well-educated intelligence agents dispatched by Essex to Europe. Two others were Sir Anthony Standen and Robert Naunton who was later to become Secretary of State and Lord Privy Seal. Paul Hammer has written articles on them. Paul E. J. Hammer, "The Use of Scholarship: The Secretariat of Robert Devereux,

Second Earl of Essex, c. 1585-1601," *The English Historical Review*, 109, (Feb., 1994), pp. 26-51.

20 Rivers (Sterrell) to Ridolfo Perino (Fr. Persons), March 3, 1602 (Westminster VII n. 29).

21 SPD 12/283/75, Ralph Winwood to Cecil, 10 April 1602.

22 From Mary Sullivan, *Court Masques of James I* (1913), p 221:

"James by the grace of god king of England France and Ireland defender of the faith &c. To the Trer [Treasurer] and Undertrer of or Excheqr greeting. Whereas the Queene our dearest wife hath resolued for our greater honour and contentement to make us a maske shortly attended by most of the greatest Ladyes of the kingdome forasmuch as shee is pleased that the Earle of Suffolk chamberlayne of our houses and the Earle of Worcester Master of our horse shall take some paines to look into the emptions and provisions of all things necessary for the same Wee doe hereby require and authorize you to issue so much of our treasure at such tymes and by such porcons as they shall require under their hands and to such persons as they shall assigne to receaue the same for doing whereof this shalbe your sufficient warrant and discharge... Exchequer of Receipt, Warrants for Issue, Bundle, 141.

23 Some genealogical records suggest a later birth for Anne.

24 We must acknowledge that several other playwrights drew on the same epigram though not in their wills. John Lyly in *Endimion - The Man in the Moone*, 1591, and Thomas Kyd in *Spanish Tragedy* (bef. 1592) made use of the quote.

25 Sterrell/Rivers to Ridolfo Perino in Vinegia, September 1, 1602. He repeated the phrase in two other letters that year.

26 Clark, *Register of the University of Oxford*, (1887) ii, part i, p. 392. A 'serviens' (servant) was a student of a lower rank who received free or reduced-cost education in exchange for performing menial duties for a 'Master.' Barnes received his Master's in May 1581. As Florio's *First Fruits* was published in 1578 identifying as living in London, Florio was probably dividing his time as "serviens"; *see* Yates, *Florio*, p. 28.

27 Yates, *Florio*, pp. 65-70.

28 The sonneteer of *Phaëton* contributed a "dearly esteemed" 1611 poem in Florio's *New World of Words;* it drew upon Phoebe who appears in the same stories in Ovid's *Metamorphoses*. Here Phoebe, the moon, a feminine side of Phoebus, is the Queen, who has given warmth and light to Florio

as his current patron, thus extending the conceit of the 1591 sonnet. Both the 1591 and 1611 sonnets use an identical Petrarchan scheme.

29 Ovid, *Metamorphoses*, Book 1: "chaos: a rough, unordered mass of things . . . . No form of things remained the same; all objects were at odds, for within one body cold things strove with hot, and moist with dry, soft things with hard, things having weight with weightless things. God—or kindlier Nature—composed this strife." Frank Justus Miller, trans. (1951) The stanza draws on Aristotle's writings on *De Caelo* (On the Heavens); *De Partibus Animalium* (Parts of Animals), *De Sensu et Sensibilibus* (Sense and Sensibilia) and Galen's expansion of Aristotle on the four humours. The side bar of "mixtures" and "Cõplexiõs" etc. reflects Aristotle's "hylomorphism," the theory that every physical object is a combination or compound of matter and form. Based on the Oxford lecture timetable for natural philosophy from fifty years after Sterrell taught the materials, the books of Aristotle for the course would have included *Physici* (Physics), *de caelo & mundo* (On the Heavens and the World), *De meteoris* (Meteorology), *Parvis nat. anima* (Short Works on Nature), *De generatione & corruptione* (On Generation and Corruption). https://www.cabinet.ox.ac.uk / quadratura-circuli-1643.

30 Del Soldato, Eva, "Natural Philosophy in the Renaissance", The Stanford Encyclopedia of Philosophy (Fall 2023 Edition), Edward N. Zalta & Uri Nodelman (eds.), URL = <https:// plato.stanford.edu / archives/fall2023/entries/natphil-ren/>.

31 The entry notes of Dr. John Case, Sterrell's mentor who taught the same course as Sterrell taught: "Scholars like John Case (d. 1600), who considered Aristotelianism compatible with Christian dogmas such as creation and divine providence, were particularly fond of searching for ways to syncretize theology with natural philosophy." Del Soldato, Eva, "Natural Philosophy in the Renaissance", *The Stanford Encyclopedia of Philosophy* (Fall 2023 Edition), Edward N. Zalta & Uri Nodelman (eds.), URL = <https:// plato.stanford.edu / archives/fall2023/entries/natphil-ren/>.

32 *See also* the British website for the National Library of Medicine:

> Shakespeare understood human personality in the terms available to his age—that of the now—discarded theory of the four bodily humors—blood, bile [choler], melancholy, and phlegm. . . .
>
> The language of the four humors pervades Shakespeare's plays, and their influence is felt above all in a belief that emotional states are physically determined. Carried by the bloodstream, the four humors bred the core passions of anger, grief, hope, and fear—the

emotions conveyed so powerfully in Shakespeare's comedies and tragedies.
https://www.nlm.nih.gov/exhibition/shakespeare-and-the-four-humors/index.html, accessed December 10, 2025.

33 *See* Aristotle, *Metaphysics*, Bk I, ch. 5.

34 *See* Aristotle, *Physics* iv.1-5 and v.1 and vi; Mendell, Henry, "Aristotle and Mathematics," *The Stanford Encyclopedia of Philosophy* (Fall 2019 Edition).

35 The Jesuit historian Fr. A. J. Loomie gathered contemporary lists of English exiles enjoying the support of the king of Spain. *Spanish Elizabethans* (1963), pp. 242-265.

36 Anthony Skinner left the country for seven years in 1584, finding his way to Rome, where for some years he acted as a servant to Cardinal Allen. On December 28, 1591, the English Privy Council authorized a warrant to the keeper of the Marshalsea prison to receive into his custody Anthony Skinner and "Richard Acliffe" (Ailiffe/Ayliffe).

37 This document is calendared as "Confession of Edward Dodwell," September 15, 1585, CSP Domestic 1581-90, p 266. SPD 12/182/18. There is no date on the document, and these appear to be two documents placed together. The date of the Calendar is undoubtedly wrong. The young men seem to have been first examined on September 14 and were probably examined twice. Edward Stephens then questioned Dodwell while still at Dover and got a more elaborate story from him about Sterrell/Kerby than before, and Stephens sent this word on to Lord Cobham, who was warden of the Cinque Ports. The day following, the 23rd of September, Cobham sent the youths on to Walsingham, with a note about "Kerby." The written confession(s) must have been given in London. The two documents seem to be addressed to William Wade/Waad. The first, which is quoted at length here, closes with Dodwell saying he must hasten to the Marshalsea, a London prison. The second document or confession follows up to the first and adds additional information about the youths who were traveling with Dodwell.

38 The story of the recruitment of Sterrell by Phelippes and Bacon is told in Paul Hammer, *The Polarisation of Elizabethan Politics,* pp. 153-57. Hammer mistakenly thought Sterrell had been a Walsingham agent because Phelippes was a Walsingham man. Rather, Phelippes had learned of Sterrell's role as a Catholic agent during the time of Phelippes's entrapment of Mary Queen of Scots and as he had intercepted later letters of Sterrell.

39 In *1 Henry IV*, Poins and Prince Henry play a joke on Falstaff by disguising themselves in buckram and stealing from Falstaff the very goods he had recently stolen from others: *see* Bloxam, *A Register of the Presidents, Fellows, Demies* . . . (1873), p. xx: "the seven Senior Demies, who received the Fastolf liveries, were called *Falstalf's Buckram-men*."

40 Hammer notes that Essex sought out scholars for intelligence work and for his secretariat. "By late 1595, Essex's secretariat thus consisted of four men: Reynoldes, Wotton, Temple and Cuffe." Paul E. J. Hammer, "The Use of Scholarship: The Secretariat of Robert Devereux, Second Earl of Essex, c. 1585-1601,"*The English Historical Review*, 109, (Feb., 1994), pp. 26-51. Edward Reynoldes was Sterrell's contemporary at Oxford and obtained his Master degree in 1584. After service as a secretary to Sir Amias Paulet, he became a secretary to Essex by mid-1588. Reynoldes was arrested after Essex's insurrection in 1601 but was eventually let free. William Temple, an M.A. of both universities, had previously been a Fellow at King's College, Cambridge, where he had won an international reputation as a champion of Ramist logic before becoming secretary to Sir Philip Sidney. Henry Cuffe gave up his Oxford position as Regius Professor of Greek to be a secretary to Essex. In 1601 he was executed with his patron. Henry Wotton was another Oxford scholar who provided Essex with intelligence from abroad during the same period as Sterrell. When Essex was apprehended in 1601, Wotton fled to France and thereby avoided Cuffe's fate. Eventually he earned knighthood and prestigious diplomatic posts.

41 Tintern Abbey was given to the lord of Chepstow Castle, Henry Somerset, 2nd Earl of Worcester; lead from the roof was sold for building of Raglan Castle. Tintern Abbey is probably the source for *Sonnet 73's* line: "Bare ruined choirs, where late the sweet birds sang . . . ."

42 The name Cut in Shakespeare becomes a synonym for a rascal. Some scholars have thought that "cut" referred to a sort of horse and so it is in several places in the plays, but it is more likely that it referred to this antagonist of William Sterrell in one play: Shakes. *Twel. N.* ii. iii. 203 If thou hast her not i' the end, call me Cut. *Oxford English Dictionary*: #30 "A term of abuse, applied to a man or woman," citing *Twelfth Night*.

43 SPD 12/242/30.

44 The letters were seized from John Townshend, who had been at Magdalen with Sterrell and who was closely related to the Bacon brothers; he married a daughter of Nathaniel Bacon, half-brother of Francis and Anthony.

45 Three years later Phelippes himself reminded Essex how it had seemed; he explained what had happened on Sterrell's return from his mission in late 1592 to mid 1593. The mission had failed. Phelippes had to recount events later because he had spent some time in prison for debts and alleged mishandlings as a customs official. From a cell, Phelippes gave Essex an explanation for the failure, and for Queen Elizabeth's very personal hostility to William Sterrell and to Phelippes himself: ". . . it was in effect lost and quite overthrown: no good coming of his travails, and the party *himself [Sterrell] suspected without cause*, which should never have troubled me, but that it was told me the *Queen, being distasted with the man and the matter* seemed to impute it to weakness of judgment in me, that anything should be expected of the party's endeavours." *Hatfield Papers*, 9(6) p. 511.

46 State Papers, Domestic, 12/246/62.

47 Sterrell was describing a meeting with Essex or Bacon. Jardine and Stewart believe that the reference here was to Francis Bacon and that Sterrell was indignant at being sent to Bacon instead of going to Phelippes. *Hostage to Fortune*, p. 130. There is reason to believe this is correct. However, it also is possible that Bacon was a peacemaker between Essex and Sterrell and that Sterrell had seen Essex himself. Sterrell was reluctant to put Essex's name in a letter but not Bacon's name; Essex was reluctant to put Sterrell's name in a letter but not Bacon's or Cloudsley's (another courier).

48 https://penelope.uchicago.edu/Thayer/l/roman/texts/Curtius/9*.html.

49 *Henry IV Part 1,* Falstaff: "I shall be out of heart shortly, and then I shall have no strength to repent."

50 Paul's news is news to be gathered by gossip at St. Paul's where the book sellers were. St. Paul's Churchyard was the primary hub for news and bookselling in London, attracting crowds known as "Paul's walkers" who gathered to share information and browse stalls. Joad Wren, *The Great Exchange* (2025) xxii explains: "My title is appropriated from a description of Paul's Walk in London in 1628, a place where people gathered to talk news in many languages, making a great buzz, 'the whole world's Map . . . the great Exchange of all discourse'."

51 There are several rather clear allusions to Queen Elizabeth in a play and in at least one sonnet, the play anticipating her death and the sonnet after her demise. Neither is favorable to her. The play is *Hamlet*.

Apparently written in 1601, Hamlet's mother is Queen Gertrude who is now wed to the murderer of Hamlet's father. In the graveyard scene Hamlet reflects on death and tells the Clown to go to his "lady's chamber" (the queen's) and remind her she is mortal, "tell her, let her paint an inch thick, to this favour [death] she must come. Make her laugh at that." This bitter speech by Hamlet echoes a letter of Sterrell of January 1601 in which he described the Queen's appearance: "It was commonly observed this Christmas, that her Majesty when she came to be seen was continually painted not only all over her face but her very neck and breast also, and that the same was in some places well near half an inch thick." Sterrell/Rivers to Ridolfo Perino (Persons), January 13, 1601 (Westminster VII n. 1). Other letters of Sterrell to his exiled correspondents track the Queen's decline; they, of course, were eager to see her reign end. *Sonnet 107* notes the queen's passing with optimism and hope for a better future, despite predictions of a bad result. Uncertainty is ended:

The mortal moon hath her eclipse endured,
And the sad augurs mock their own presage,
Incertainties now crown themselves assured,
And peace proclaims olives of endless age.

52 "to the new kindled cleare lampe of virginitie, and the excellent adored high wonder of sharpe wit and sweete beautie, mistres elizabeth carey; sole daughter and heire to the thrice noble and renowmed sir george carey, knight marshall, &c."

53 "A woman's face ...," *TLS,* Sept 16, 2025. https://www.the-tls.com/arts/visual-arts/nicholas-hilliard-miniature-shakespeare-essay-elizabeth-goldring-emma-rutherford-jonathan-bate.

54 Murdin (ed), *A Collection of State Papers relating to ... the reign of Elizabeth* (London, 1759), p. 639.

55 Murdin (ed), *A Collection of State Papers relating to ... the reign of Elizabeth* (London, 1759), p. 639. Thrale or thrall is "One who is in bondage to a lord or master; a villein, serf, bondman, slave; also, in vaguer use, a servant, subject;" *Oxford English Dictionary.*

56 John Sanford's *Apollinis et Musarum Eukita Eidyllia (1592).* Translation by Dana Sutton, *https://philological.cal.bham.ac.uk/ sanford /trans.html.*

57 Lytton Strachey vividly describes the relationship in *Elizabeth and Essex,* 37-38 (1928):

He was lavish in the protestations of his worship—his adoration—his love. That convenient monosyllable, so intense and so ambiguous, was for ever on his lips and found its way into every letter—those elegant, impassioned, noble letters, which still exist, with their stiff, quick characters and those silken ties that were once loosened by the long fingers of Elizabeth. She read and she listened with a satisfaction so extraordinary, so unprecedented, that when one day she learned that he was married she was only enraged for a fortnight. Essex had made an impeccable choice—the widow of Sir Philip Sidney and the daughter of Sir Francis Walsingham; he was twenty-three, handsome, vigorous, with an earldom to hand on to posterity; even Elizabeth could not seriously object. She stormed and ramped; then remembered that the relations between herself and her servant were unique and had nothing to do with a futile domesticity. The fascinating bridegroom pursued and cajoled her with ardours as romantic as ever; and she felt that a queen could ignore a wife.

58 Their contemporary at Magdalen, Samuel Daniel, was author of a royal masque.

59 This would have been Rudolf II, Holy Roman Emperor, who also met with Sir Anthony Shirley in Prague at about the same time.

60 Francis Kemp was Clerk of the Hanaper [chief financial officer for the Lord Chancellor] and Attorney of Court of Chancery, and George Kemp was made a Sewer [server] of the Chamber.

61 Thomas Wright, *Queen Elizabeth and Her Times*, II, pp. 266-69 (London, 1838).

62 Sir Thomas Copley's mother was Elizabeth Shelley of Michelgrove; his sister was Bridget Copley, mother of the Jesuit martyr and poet, Robert Southwell. Michelgrove had been a shelter for Fr. Persons during the Campion-Persons mission of 1580-81.

63 "B" in Spanish is pronounced "v" and so spelled in English in various ways such as in *Merry Wives of Windsor*: "Host. How now, Bully-Rooke: Thou'rt a gentleman. Caualeiro Iustice, I say!

64 Colm Lennon, *Richard Stanihurst*, pp. 38-41.

65 Someone sought the status of gentleman for Shakespeare-of-Stratford by applying to the College of Arms for a grant of a coat of arms for his father in 1596. There was pushback in 1602 from another herald of the College over the grant to John Shakespeare and others.

66 Kemp "borrowed 20s from Henslowe 'for his necessarye usses' on March 10, 1602; authorized payment for the troupe on August 22, 1602; and had a suit purchased for him by the company early in September of

the same year. He and Thomas Heywood served as payees for a Court performance by Worcester's men on January 3, 1601." Nungezer, *A Dictionary of Actors*, pp. 219-20.

67 Chambers, *Elizabethan Stage*, II p. 326.

68 *Coram rege* roll in the Court of King's Bench (TNA KB27/1454, rot. 692), [9 October] 1615: plea of *Thomasine Ostler v. her father John Heminges*.

69 *The History of Parliament: the House of Commons 1509-1558* (ed. S.T. Bindoff, 1982), II, pp. 460-61.

70 Worcester to Shrewsbury, February 2, 1604, Edmund Lodge, *Illustrations of British History*, (1791) iii, pp. 88-89.

71 Rivers to Augustino Cornelio, April 4, 1604; copy from Jesuit Archives, London.

72 SPD 12/271/74, 4/14 July 1599.

73 Thorpe facilitated the printing of Catholic works and Catholic writers. Most had to be in secret. One of these printers was Valentine Simmes, a well-known printer who secretly published Catholic works and was jailed for such activity in 1607, where he was joined with another printer, Henry Owen, brother of Nicholas Owen whose freedom from prison Sterrell had secured. Thorpe and Valentine Simmes were openly associated with the publication in 1604 of Fr. Thomas Wright's *The Passions of the Mind*, which had introductory verse by the Catholic writers Ben Jonson and Hugh Holland, both contributing verse to Shakespeare's *First Folio*. Wright was a former Jesuit and associate of Fr. Persons in Spain. He had returned to England in 1595, seeking the protection of the Earl of Essex.

74 On the difficulties of working from initials in Elizabethan publications, *see* Franklin B. Williams, "An Initiation into Initials", *Studies in Bibliography*, ix (1957), 163-78.

75 The Stationers Company Register, vol. 5, says: "Arnold Hatfield, Ninian Newton, John Jackson, and Edmund Bollifant alias Carpenter were joint Master Printers in a Printing House [ii. 132, 140; iii. 702] in Eliot's Court in the Little Old Bailey."

76 Hammer, *Polarisation*, p. 301.

77 Hasler, *The House of Commons, 1558-1603*, vol. 3, p. 315, 384.

78 SP 12/283/75 I, Harry Wicham [Sterrell] to Francis Derick [Sherwood], June 1, 1594. The circumstances of this christening and Montague's commitment to his father-in-law's house (Lord Buckhurst) are discussed in M. Questier, *Catholicism and Community in Early Modern England*, 235-36.

79 Leo Hicks, "Sir Robert Cecil, Father Parsons and the Sucession," *Archivum Historicum Sociatatus Iesu* 24 (1955) 95-139, p. 115 n. 74.

80 Hicks, id. Ethelred L. Taunton, *The History of the Jesuits in England, 1580-1773* p. 25 (1901) quotes Persons's *Autobiographical Notes* as showing that Sackville and Persons were close friends when they were young: "I departed from England in May or June 1574, leaving all that ever I had in England in confidence unto the said Lord [Buckhurst], who dealt honourably with me afterwards when in Italy I entered religion; for he delivered all left to his custody with the persons I assigned." Lord Buckhurst, says Taunton, persuaded Parsons to go to Padua to study physic.

81 A. J. Loomie, "Toleration and Diplomacy," *Transactions of the American Philosophical Society* (1963), p. 12.

82 Devlin, *Robert Southwell,* p. 198. The dedication was to Margaret's four surviving children and was written by John Trussell. This same Trussell translated and published Thomas Watson's *Amintae Gaudia* in 1594 under the title *An Old Fashioned Love. See* F. W. Brownlow, *Robert Southwell,* (1996), pp. 52-3.

83 Rollins, xxxiii. *The Phoenix Nest* is also edited and analyzed by F. Etchells and H. Macdonald, *Haslewood Reprints* (1926). They likewise observed that most of the identifiable poets were associated with Oxford University at about the same time: "Breton, Dyer, Edes, Lodge, Peele, Raleigh, Roydon and probably Watson were all students at Oxford at about the same time . . . ." p. 7.

84 Robert Sackville's eldest son and heir by Margaret Howard was Richard Sackville, 3rd Earl of Dorset (1589–1624). His wife, Lady Anne Clifford, was tutored by Sterrell's friend Samuel Daniel and was first cousin to the wife of Worcester's son Henry Somerset, with whom she was close. Henry Sterrell apparently lent money to Richard Sackville, for in his will of 1618 he asserts, "Item the Earle of Dorset oweth me two hundred poundes."

85 Douglas Hamer, "Was William Shakespeare William Shakeshafte?," *Review of English Studies*, n.s. 21.81 (1970), p. 46.

86 Chambers, *Shakespearean Gleanings*, p. 53 (1944).

87 Chambers, *Shakespearean Gleanings,* p. 55-6 (1944). Chambers wrote this in WWII and lacked access to documents. A comma after Hesketh had been added by a much later editor. There is much silliness about Shakeshafte being too old to be Shakespeare because of the relative amount paid to Shakeshafte vis-a-vis the other servants. But this ignores the fact that Hoghton singled out Shakeshafte for special treatment in two other places in the will. Robert Bearman, "'Was William Shakespeare

William Shakeshafte' Revisited," *Shakespeare Quarterly* 53 (2002): 83-94; Ernst Honigmann, "The Shakespeare/Shakeshafte Question, Continued," *Shakespeare Quarterly* 54 (2003) pp. 83-86; Douglas Hamer, "Was William Shakespeare William Shakeshafte?," *Review of English Studies*, n.s. 21.81 (1970): 41-48.

88 I am relying on multiple online resources and the *Oxford Dictionary of National Biography* entry for Richard Hesketh. The entry in Hasler, *House of Commons* under Robert Hesketh of Rufford (son of Sir Thomas Hesketh of Rufford) identifies Richard who was executed in 1593 as a brother of Robert of Rufford, not as his cousin.

89 Kempe may "have spent some time abroad himself, perhaps in the Duchess of Feria's entourage [Jane Dormer, who had been a lady-in-waiting to Mary Tudor together with Kempe's mother, Eleanor Kemp], which included a man of his surname who is mentioned in letters between the duchess herself, George Kempe [Anthony's brother], Damascin Stradling and (Sir) Thomas Chaloner. It was this 'Mr. Kempe', too, whom King Philip planned to send to England with letters of encouragement from the Duke of Feria to the northern earls, a mission for which Anthony Kempe's connexions with the north would have well fitted him. . . . this could have been the final phase of his career as international go-between." *The History of Parliament: the House of Commons 1509-1558*, ed. S.T. Bindoff.

90 *The Reckoning*, p. 246. The implausibility of this argument is seen in the fact that Marlowe's arrest was through the machinations of Cecil operatives in the Low Countries; and Robert Poley was one of the three at Marlowe's murder.

91 Curtis C. Breight, *Surveillance, Militarism and Drama in the Elizabethan Era*, (New York, 1996) p. 129. Nicholl's view is that Marlowe's death was an Essex conspiracy.

92 SPD 12/283/75 ii. "I am afeard you are to open with '38 (Paget): he deals with one [symbol] (Poley) the vilest [symbol] (spy) that ever was and so you may undo '44 (Sterrell)."

93 Greenblatt, *Dark Renaissance: The Dangerous Times and Fatal Genius of Shakespeare's Greatest Rival*, p. 192.

94 Despite the plague, plays were being performed. For the chronology and venues of the performances by Lord Strange's servants, *see* Lawrence Manley and Sally-Beth MacLean, *Lord Strange's Men and Their Plays* (2014), p. 342.

95 Gary Taylor, "The Cultural Politics of Maybe," in *Theatre and Religion: Lancastrian Shakespeare*, edited by R. Dutton, A. Findlay and R. Wilson (Manchester, 2003), pp. 242-58, 250.

96 Southwell's manuscripts of poetry, prepared before his imprisonment in 1592, were dedicated to "To My Worthy Good Cosen Maister W.S.." On his mother's side of his family, Sterrell was a Sothill or Sotehill, a variant spelling of Southwell, all pronounced as "suttill," just as the martyr's name was pronounced. In fact, Sterrell's grandfather preferred to sign himself Gerard Southwell. And Maister/Mister is used to refer to a gentleman, which Sterrell was.

97 The relationship of Wolfe and Field in working together and use of false imprints is explored in Denis B. Woodfield, (1973) *Surreptitious Printing in England, 1550-1640,* chs. 4-5.

98 For a later translation to English Perez would be given editorial assistance by Anthony Bacon, brother of Francis Bacon. Both brothers were in Essex's intelligence service where they guided Sterrell's intelligence "practising." Anthony will have known Perez in Paris and probably coordinated his visit to England for Essex.

99 A year earlier, John Wolfe, who often worked with Richard Field, had published another Spanish propaganda book called "A fig for the Spaniard, or Spanish spirits wherein are liuelie [lively] portraihed [portrayed] the damnable deeds, miserable murders, and monstrous massacres of the cursed Spaniard." This work must have been after November 1591 as it talks of Antonio Perez being safe with the French king.

100 Taylor, *Reinventing Shakespeare*, p. 330. E. K. Chambers notes the investment of capital: "Shakespeare would have had to contribute to the original stock of the Chamberlain's in 1594, and possibly also, as a housekeeper, to the building of the Globe in 1599." Chambers, *William Shakespeare* ii, p. 71.

101 The Privy Council document is reprinted in Chambers, *William Shakespeare* ii, p. 313, and Chambers, *Elizabethan Stage*, ii, p. 123. Others have read the warrant as applying just to the Lord Strange's company and that Edward Alleyn was part of this company though the warrant identifies him as "servaunt to the right honorable the Lord Highe Admiral." *See* Lawrence Manley and Sally-Beth MacLean, *Lord Strange's Men and Their Plays*, (2014) p. 1. I think it more likely the syntax indicates that the license pertains to two companies and the phrase *"being all one company,"*

identifies the five named in a row as servants to Lord Strange, while Alleyn was servant to the Admiral's company.

102 Jacob A. Riis, "Hamlet's Castle," *Century Magazine*, lxi. 391.

103 Chambers, *Elizabethan Stage,* ii, p. 126: "Derby's men did not appear at Court during the winter of 1593-4. On 16 April 1594 Lord Derby died. On 16 May the company used the Countess's name at Winchester. It seems clear that during the summer there was some re-shuffling of the companies, that Alleyn took the leadership of a new body of Admiral's men, that several other members of the old combination, including Pope, Heminges, Kempe, and Phillips, joined with Burbadge, Shakespeare, and Sly, under the patronage of the Lord Chamberlain, Henry Lord Hunsdon, and that, after a short period of co-operation with each other and Henslowe, the two companies definitely parted." Chambers' only reason for associating Shakespeare with the company before 1594 was on the basis of Greene's "Shake-scene" reference of 1592; there was no other record of Shakespeare as actor or playwright or poet before *Venus and Adonis*. The first record as a basis for identifying Shakespeare as a shareholder is a payment of March 1595 that was to "William Kempe, William Shakespeare, and Richard Burbage, servants to the Lord Chamberlain," for two Comedies or Interludes before her Majesty at Christmas time.

104 William J. Thoms, "Was Shakespeare ever a Soldier?" *Three Notelets on Shakespeare* (1865).

105 I am in the debt of Professor John Finnis, the eminent authority on Aquinas at Oxford and Notre Dame, for recognizing that the pseudo-Aquinas is the source for Helena's speech. Finnis, "'The Thing I Am': Personal Identity in Aquinas and Shakespeare," *Social Philosophy and Policy*, 22 (July 2005), pp. 250 – 282.

The quote from the play tracks the full Latin quote of the pseudo-Aquinas and not simply the partial quotation that is the same phrase in Ovid's *Heroides.* It is exquisitely done by rendering the two lines of Latin of 15 beats to two lines of English of 10 beats. Scholars seeking Shakespeare's Latin were unfamiliar with the pseudo-Aquinas. They have thought, along with Boswell, that the quote is simply a translation of the Latin proverb "Finis coronat opus." *See* T. W. Baldwin, *William Shakespeare's Small Latine & Lesse Greeke* (Urbana, 1944) ii, p. 350.

106 The Loeb Library translation: "The event proves well the wisdom of her course. Let him come to naught, I pray, who thinks the deed should be condemned from its result." *See also,* John Langston's collection of Latin quotes and translations, *Lusus poeticus Latino-Anglicanus in usum scholarum*

(1675): "The End does crown the work, 'tis true: But good success to such I grudge, As by th'events of matters doe The actions goodness wholly judge."

107 In the *First Folio*, the spellings of the principal characters in *All's Well* differ in their spellings from scene to scene. For simplicity I have settled on "Helena" rather than Hellen or Hellena, and "Parolles," rather than Parrolles or Paroles unless context requires otherwise. I have used Lafew to be consistent with the *First Folio;* though many editors prefer Lafeu which suggests "heat."

108 We see in *Julius Caesar* a similar phenomenon. Most playgoers and readers focus on Antony or Caesar without seeing that Brutus's struggle over regicide is the most important aspect of the play. Brutus has 194 lines compared to Antony's 51 and Caesar's 42. Brutus comes to self-awareness and authenticity (acceptance of fate) while the other two resist development, as does Octavius.

109 A number of things in the play suggest the Clown is a gentleman as identified above of the real Will Kemp of Ollantighe. In Act 2 sc. 2 when the Countess challenges his breeding, he responds "I will show myself highly fed and lowly taught," which suggests he was well-born but did not complete a college degree. He also indicates he is a courtier, again suggesting gentle birth. Like Will Kemp, this Clown is a letter carrier. The Countess gives him a letter to carry to Helena in Act 2 sc. 2. In Act 3 sc. 2 he gives the Countess a letter from Bertram. In Act 5 sc. 2 Parolles directs Monsieur Lavatch to deliver a letter to Lafew, giving him the title of "monsieur" indicating gentle birth. The Clown tells Lafew "I am a woodland fellow, sir, ..." suggesting property or that he is of the landed gentry. Finally, the playwright associates Kemp with the morris dance for which the actor was famous when the Clown speaks of: "a morris for Mayday . . . ."

110 *See* Schmitt, *John Case and Aristotelianism in Renaissance England* (1983), pp. 210-14.

111 Lafew also has a daughter who is briefly mentioned at the end. Although the Earl of Worcester had a number of daughters, this one is not a counterpart to an actual daughter. Instead, the playwright gives her the name of Sterrell's College at Oxford: "fair Maudlin," which is the pronunciation of "Magdalen." It was the college Worcester's sons attended. Again, the playwright loves to leave little clues in playful use of names.

[112] In Roman law and custom a freedman was obliged to pay homage (*obsequium*) to his patron. *See* Susan Treggiari, "The Freedmen of Cicero," *Greece & Rome*, 2nd Ser., Vol. 16 pp. 195-204 (Oct., 1969) at 197: "Freedmen normally swore an oath on manumission to do a certain amount of work . . . for their patrons."

[113] Note how the man and clothes are identified together. As in *Sonnet 76*: "keep invention in a noted weed." A parallel to Parolles is found in *Sonnet 110* where the poet says he has "made my self a motley [to wear the clothes of the fool] to the view."

[114] The *Oxford English Dictionary* explains what the term meant anciently at Oxford: "prelector, præ- . . . [a. L. *prælector* one who reads an author to others, and adds explanations, agent-n. f. prælegĕre: see prelect.] A public reader or lecturer, esp. in a college or university. In Oxford formerly interchangeable with professor (as applied to all except the Regius Professors), as the Prelector or Professor of Poetry; . . ." Sterrell was "praelector" of natural philosophy: Sterrell "resigned his fellowship in 1586, but from that year, or probably from the year preceding, was Praelector of Natural Philosophy until 1591, when he resigned that lectureship on March 24." William Dunn Macray, *The Register of the Members of St. Mary Magdalen College, Oxford* vol. III (*Register of Fellows 1576-1648*) (London, 1901), pp. 80-81.

[115] In a later letter Sterrell speaks of a man who "was taken like a woodcock in a cock shoot."

[116] Another English prisoner in this same place at the time was a naval officer held for ransom by the Spanish. He was Sir Edward Winter who would marry a daughter of the Earl of Worcester soon after his release. There should be little doubt that Sterrell arranged to meet him while he was detained there.

[117] Loomie, *Spanish Elizabethans* (1963), p. 115.

[118] SPD 12/242/37 ccxlii #37.

[119] This characterization has its counterpart in *Macbeth*. The Gatekeeper says: "Faith, here's an equivocator that could swear in both the scales against either scale, who committed treason enough for God's sake, yet could not equivocate to heaven."

[120] Chambers, *Elizabethan Stage*, ii, p. 118.

[121] Loomie, *Spanish Elizabethans*, pp. 133-137.

[122] "simple drill maneuver in which the soldiers stand in a row two deep" Bevington 2004; "the simplest of drill exercises, in which every

alternate man positions himself behind the next." *The New Oxford Shakespeare: Modern Critical Edition.*

123 Motley, *History of the United Netherlands: From the Death of William the Silent to the Twelve Years' Truce,* (1888), ch. XVIII, p 452.

124 Worcester's uncle had helped Cardinal William Allen raise funds to establish the college at Douay. Thomas Somerset's deathbed wish was for his nephew, Edward, to order his affairs. George was among the pensioners on Sir William Stanley's rolls when Sterrell was rescued from imprisonment by Sir William in Antwerp 1592. In 1595 Sterrell was again in the Low Countries when he escorted George back to England. When George was detained in Flushing (the Dutch town held by England) in January 1595 while with Sterrell, George confessed he had been meeting recently in Brussels with Giacomo (Jaques) de Franceschi and Sir William Stanley, who had known George Somerset's father. Sterrell had satisfied the English official and was released before the two men he was conveying obtained their freedom.

125 C. M. Dent, *Protestant Reformers in Elizabethan Oxford.* Oxford: Oxford University Press, 1983, p. 47.

126 Dent, *Protestant Reformers,* p. 64. Magdalen College Archives MS/684/1 (photocopy kindly provided by Dr. Emily Jennings, Magdalen College, Jan. 5, 2026).

127 William Dunn Macray, *The Register of the Members of St. Mary Magdalen College, Oxford,* vol. II (Register of Fellows; 1522-1576) (London, 1897), p. 114. Bloxam, (1873), *Register* I, p. 201, reprints a record [in Latin] that Sterrell and Eston "are deprived of their commons [shared meals] for a day, because they attempted to uncover Mr. Pett's bald and shaved head." The "uncovering" was payback, perhaps by forcibly giving Pett a tonsure to mock his puritanism.

128 *Shakespeare Quarterly* , vol. 43 (1992), pp. 265-279.

129 In *Shakespeare's Words,* David and Ben Crystal have an excellent two page spread/chart treating on the complex interaction of THOU AND YOU (pp. 450-51) in a number of plays, though it omits *All's Well* from its treatment.

130 *Cobbetts State Trials,* II (1809), p. 10.

131 McConica, "The Catholic Experience in Tudor Oxford," in *The Reckoned Expense,* McCoog, ed., 1996, p. 57. On *Decem rationes* and *Venus and Adonis,* see above.

132 If you need to confirm the accuracy of my account, it may take time. The only record of what I recount here is on handwritten parchment in the Bodleian library archives. I may be the only person who has closely read the account in 400 years (and it was at noon during an eclipse of the sun).

133 Deposition of William Aubrey, M.A. of Christ Church College, and then associated with Oriel Cathedral in Oxford.

134 Robert Brook, M.A. of Brasenose College, testimony of July 17, 1587.

135 It is the same conceit (built on St. Paul in 1 *Corinthians* 2.9) in *Midsommer Nights Dream* where Bottom is transformed from an ass: "The eye of man hath not heard, the ear of man hath not seen, man's hand is not able to taste, his tongue to conceive, nor his heart to report, what my dream was."

136 Compare Francis Beaumont (1585–1616) whose career as a playwright spanned only six years, mostly in co-authorship with John Fletcher. Beaumont died only weeks before Shakespeare-of-Stratford but was buried in Westminster Abbey, near to Chaucer and Spenser: "this placement in what has come to be known as the 'Poets' Corner' was a tribute to his high standing as a writer." (*ODNB* entry).

137 E. K. Chambers, *William Shakespeare*, ii, p. 67.

138 E. K. Chambers is unconvincing that the widow was protected by common law for an interest. Many wills of the period expressed love to a spouse and provided for life tenancy in most property.

139 Citing R.O. Land Revenue Rentals and Surveys, ccxxviii, ff. 149-208.

140 William J. Thoms, "Was Shakespeare ever a Soldier?" *Three Notelets on Shakespeare* (1865).

141 Shakespeare-of-Stratford gave a deposition in a suit, *Belott v. Mountjoy*, in 1612 in which a maidservant testified about an event touching upon "one Mr Shakespeare that laye in the house." This was at some point in 1604 apparently, and the deposition indicates Mr. Shakespeare knew Mountjoy since about 1602. Charles Nicholl's book *The Lodger* (2008) turns "laye" into an indication that Shakespeare was a "lodger" and therefore he must have been a tenant of some sort. This one word in the deposition (with inferences about his acquaintance with the family) grows into an unfounded extrapolation of fact in the *ODNB:* "Shakespeare was living from 1602 to 1604 as a lodger with Christopher Mountjoy and his family in Silver Street in the respectable neighbourhood of Cripplegate." The possibility that Shakespeare briefly "laye" in a house in London is in no way

inconsistent with his primary residence having been the Cottage of Rowington Manor.

In August 1603 Greene was appointed Steward of Stratford-upon-Avon; and as Town Clerk in 1614-15 he withstood the Combes in the matter of the Welcombe enclosures in which Shakespeare also was involved. Prior to 1611 he seems to have lived for a while at New Place.

142 Quoted in E. K. Chambers *William Shakespeare,* ii p. 166. Spelling modernized.

143 Chambers, ii. 166-67.

144 Chambers, ii. 166-67.

145 Devlin, *Southwell,* p. 217.

146 Gerard, *Autobiography,* p. 40.

147 Foley's, ii p 576: "*Item,* he saith that the said Gerard lay one night at the Lady Mary Percy's in Blackfriars . . ."; SPD 12/248/103, May 11, 1594.

148 SPD 12/242/88, Notes of the examination of Renold Bisley, 25 July 1592; SPD 12/241/118, "Reinold Boseley [to Cecil ?]," 7 April 1592 (confirms that Bisley was in fact acting for the Queen's government, as a Cecil double agent on a trial basis).

149 The sale of this Blackfriars property by M. Bacon coincides suspiciously with a grant by the government of a "lease to Matth. Bacon, of lands of the Duchy of Lancaster, value 20*l* per ann." July 23, 1604 CSP 1603-1610 p. 136 (dacquet). On the same day, 16 recusants, including Sir Thomas Tresham, were released from their debts of 20*l* per month for their recusancy. *Id.*

150 CSP 1603-1610, p. 240. In G. Plot Bk., No. 10.

151 Chambers, *William Shakespeare,* ii, p. 168. It appears that Gerard attempted to lodge some of the conspirators at the Gatehouse before the plot was revealed. This does not mean Gerard knew of the plot itself.

152 Hotson, *I, Shakespeare,* p. 181

153 Allen Dulles, *The Craft of Intelligence* (1963), ch. 10; Ewen Montagu, *The Man Who Never Was* (1954).

154 SPD 12/249/7, Sir Cuthbert Buckle, Mayor of London to Lord Burghley, 7 June 1594. The letter of Owen to Sterrell is found in the State Papers in two widely separated parts. The first four pages are in SP 12/248/53 (CSP Dom. 1591-1594, pp. 475-7). The editor of the Calendar, published in 1867, thought the letter was from Owen to Phelippes. The last sheet is in

SP 15/33/13 (CSP Domestic Addenda 1580-1625, p. 363, published in 1872). The editor of this later volume did not connect the fragment with the other fragment calendared five years earlier. The link between the two is facilitated by Owen's epistolary practice of writing at the foot of each page the first word of the next page. Placing the fragments side-by-side leaves no doubt about the fact that they are one letter.

155 Among the men were John Daniel, Hugh Cahill, Richard Hesketh, John Annias and William Polwhele.These conspirators and related agents are discussed in more detail in Martin, *Elizabethan Espionage* (2016), pp. 120-27.

156 *See* Chambers, *Shakespeare* ii, 166. This nephew was evidently the son of Sir John's brother Sir Anthony Fortescue who was condemned for conspiracy against Queen Elizabeth. The *Oxford Dictionary of National Biography* says that he was still alive in 1611. Chambers, *Shakespeare* ii, 167: "In after life [an unspecified date after 1598], John Fortescue and his wife retired to St Omer."

157 Hatfield papers 9, p 186-7 [70.67], 31 May 1599, Fra. Duckett to Richard Brother.

158 The most recent effort to identify "John Robinson" of the Gatehouse and the will is Chris Laoutaris, "Who was Shakespeare's mysterious London lodger?" *TLS*, March 31, 2023. He says that "the steward was dead by 1613," and he was unable to find a son of the steward who was also named John Robinson. He offers a very young printer who was just finishing his apprenticeship, and Shakespeare was offering the young man a base close to the "precious hoard of texts" now stored at the nearby Blackfriars Theater where Shakespeare planned to prepare his works for publication. The thesis is expanded in Laoutaris, Shakespeare's Book (2023). See the discussion herein of the "magic file cabinet" and how implausible this is.

159 The deed is reprinted in Chambers, *Shakespeare* ii, 154-7 and https://shakespearedocumented.folger.edu/node/127. It states: "Henry Walker, citizein and Minstrell of London." For payment under a mortgage accompanying the deed, the location is where Walker was "nowe dwelling house of the said Henry Walker, situate and being in the parish of Saint Martyn neere Ludgate of London." Chambers thinks a different "Henry Walker, mercer, alderman, and bailiff of Stratford," was father of William Walker who was named as Shakespeare's godson in his 1616 will.

160 Leslie Hotson, *Shakespeare's Sonnets Dated*, pp. 133-140, 208-211, identified John Jackson as a merchant of Kingston-upon-Hull. Hotson's

linkage of this Jackson to Shakespeare is through a possible connection to Donhault. It appears from internal evidence relied on by Hotson that he ran multiple persons with the same common name together in his enthusiasm.

161 Devlin, *Southwell*, p. 217; Chambers, *William Shakespeare*, ii. P. 169. Supposedly a "John Robbinson" was a signatory to the Blackfriars Petition of November 1596 against the operation of a theater, supposedly spearheaded by Anne Russell's mother. The document is undoubtedly another of the many fabrications by John Payne Collier (aided by his protege James O. Halliwell-Phillipps) who pulled up the name from a series of documents that might make his forgery plausible. I will explain further in a later book. If the document is genuine and dated correctly, it indicates that "John Robinson" was dwelling in the Blackfriars Gatehouse as John Fortescue's steward well before 1599 when he was reported as hiding a priest.

162 Chambers, *Shakespeare* ii, 159. Richard Bacon was Mathias's brother. Shakespeare's three co-owners of 1613 are not now shown as owners.

163 Thomas Perkes was likely related to the George Perkes to whom the Jesuits were paying £20 per year in 1605. Fr Garnett while awaiting execution in 1606 wrote in orange juice to Anne Vaux (for whom Fr Fisher had been chaplain) that she should "tell Mr. Blunt we owe £20 per an. to Mary Green and George Perkes." Foley, iv, 109. A short time earlier he had written a similar letter telling Anne Vaux he left the "Society [of Jesus] charged with an annuity of twenty pounds yearly to Mrs. Mary Grene, and the like to a gentleman, a bachelor, whom you call uncle." Foley, iv, 103, SPD 14/20/11, Garnett to Mrs. Vaux, 3 April 1606. A Perkes was a tenant of the Littletons of the Gunpowder Treason. The Perkes who helped Humphrey Littleton and Robert Winter in their effort to escape was put to death for his efforts. Haynes, *The Gunpowder Plot*, pp. 95, 116; Hugh Ross Williamson, *The Gunpowder Plot* p. 200 ff. The Gunpowder conspirator Robert Winter was a member of the Middle Temple and had been bonded with Richard Moore, the attorney on the 1615 litigation.

164 Anstruther 1: "Harris, William. . . . He was at the house of a Mr East at Iffley, Oxfords. about 1577 and with Campion at Mr Dormer's at Wing, Bucks, in 1580 (SP, 12/168/25ii)."

165 Sir Bernard Burke, *A Genealogical and Heraldic Dictionary of the Peerage and Baronetage of the British Empire* (35th Ed 1873) p. 360: Sir William Dormer's son Sir Robert Dormer who was created a Baronet 10 June 1615 and elevated to the peerage by the title of Baron Dormer of Wenge 30 June 1615

had three sons: William (Sir, d. 1616), Anthony of Grove Park, Warwickshire, and Robert, of Peterley, co. Bucks, m. Mary, daughter of Edward Banester, Esq. of Illsworth, Co. Southampton.

166 Devlin, *Southwell* p. 217: "In the Gatehouse, . . ., was the lodging of his [Robert Southwell] sister Mary and her husband, Edward Bannister of Iddsworth."

167 CRS, XXII, 122.

168 John Burke, *A Genealogical and Heraldic History of the Extinct and Dormant Baronetcies of England, Ireland, and Scotland* (London 1844).

169 *Middle Temple Records*, II, 117, 120, 125.

170 Walter C. Metcalfe, *The Visitations of Northamptonshire made in 1564 and 1618-19* (London 1887), 115.

171 J. Nichols, *Progress of K. James 1*, II, 449; McClure, Norman Egbert (ed.), *The Letters of John Chamberlain* (1939), I, p 355.

172 Tanneguy Le Veneur, Comte de Tillières (Aug., 1619), ambassador in ordinary. Arrived in August, 1619; first audience at Windsor Sept. 15. Absent on leave Aug. to Oct., 1623. Firth & Lomas, (1906) *Notes on the Diplomatic Relations of England and France*, 1603—1688, P. 31.

173 The Declaration of Trust and the memorandum that accompanies it are reprinted in James O. Halliwell-Phillipps, *The Life of William Shakespeare* (London 1848) pp. 254-57.

174 E. K. Chambers, *William Shakespeare*, ii, pp. 152, 164.

175 A settlement was made respecting income from tithes in 1625 with John Greene signing on; this was of no interest to the holders of the Blackfriars property. E. K. Chambers, *William Shakespeare*, ii, pp. 126, 179.

176 E. K. Chambers, *William Shakespeare*, ii, pp 179. *See also*, Lucy Munro, "A Man of Property," *TLS*, April 17, 2026.

177 Lucy Munro, "A Man of Property," *TLS*, April 17, 2026. As best as I can determine, the essay incorrectly identifies the site of the Gatehouse owned in Shakespeare's name. It points to a place on a plat occupied by William Iles rather than the adjacent empty ground identified as "The Inheritance of Dr. Bacon." The 1613 deed recites: "part of which said Tenement is erected over a great gate . . . ."

178 Hotson, *I, William Shakespeare* (1937).

179 It is perhaps a very strange coincidence, but Dudley Digges was husband to Mary Kemp, daughter and co-heir of Sir Thomas Kemp of

Olantigh, Kent; she was a cousin of Will Kemp and perhaps knew the actor as a child.

180 An entertainment and celebration at Hereford in 1609 included Morris dancing and horse racing and other festivities. Among the 18 men named as the foremost participants were Lord Herbert of Ragland (Henry Somerset), Sir Thomas Somerset, Charles Somerset, Count Arundels & sonnes (one of these sons married Blanche Somerset), and Sir Thomas Russell (of Strensham). *See* David Klausner, *Herefordshire, Worcestershire* (Toronto, 1990) p. 127. The pamphlet was published in 1609 (STC (2nd ed.) / 12032).

181 E. K. Chambers, *William Shakespeare,* ii, pp 107-09.

182 Source: https://shakespearedocumented.folger.edu/file/prob-14-2.

183 Shakespeare-of-Stratford had not passed any manuscripts to heirs nor named a literary executor.

184 Greenblatt, *Will in the World,* p. 380, posits that the playbooks were all in the Globe Theatre when it burned in a fire in 1613 but were spirited away by unknown persons: "A more rapidly moving fire could have meant that half of Shakespeare's plays — those that had not already appeared in quartos — would never have found their way into print." He cites nothing to support this supposition.

185 The association of Sterrell, Florio and Mabbe (all of Magdalen College) is seen in Florio's 1611 *New World of Words* for which both Sterrell (anonymously) and Mabbe contributed verse; Florio (not John Fletcher) reciprocated with two commendatory poems that prefaced Mabbe's translation of Aleman's *Rogue* (1622), joined by Ben Jonson.

186 John Nichols, *Elizabeth Progresses,* iii pp. 498-99.

Blackfriars

Bibliography

I have examined original documents or microfilms of originals in Archives of Magdalen College, Oxford; Archives of Bodleian Library, Oxford, National Archives, Kew Gardens, London, (later with correspondent researcher R. W. O'Hara); Folger Shakespeare Library, Washington, D. C.; Jesuit Archives, London; and Vienna Austria Archives, (through Ruth Jaeneke-Elyas, a researcher in Vienna).

OED refers to noted entries in *Oxford English Dictionary* Second Edition on CD-ROM (v. 4.0)(2009).

ODNB refers to noted entries *Oxford Dictionary of National Biography*, ed. H. C. G. Matthew and Brian Harrison, 60 vols. (Oxford: Oxford University Press, 2004) and online access in 2025.

A

Akrigg, G. P. V. (1962), *Jacobean Pageant: Or, the Court of King James I* (Harvard).

Alford, Stephen (2012). *The Watchers: A Secret History of the Reign of Elizabeth I* (Bloomsbury).

------- (2024), *All His Spies: The Secret World of Robert Cecil* (Allen Lane)

Anstruther, Godfrey (1968), *The Seminary Priests: A Dictionary of the Secular Clergy of England and Wales 1558-1850, I Elizabethan 1558-1603* (Ware & Durham, England, 1968).

-------- (1953), *Vaux of Harrowden: A Recusant Family* (Newport, Monmouthshire: Johns).

Asquith, Clare (2005), *Shadowplay: The Hidden Beliefs and Coded Politics of William Shakespeare.*

-------- (2018), *Shakespeare and the Resistance.*

B

Baldwin, T.W. (1924), "Shakespeare's Jester: the Dates of *Much Ado* and *As You Like It*," *Modern Language Notes* 39: 447-55.

------- (1944), *Small Latine and Lesse Greeke* (Urbana, University of Illinois Press).

------- (1950), *On the Literary Genetics of Shakspere's Poems and Sonnets* (Urbana, U. Illinois Press).

------- (1931), *William Shakespeare Adapts a Hanging* (Princeton University Press).

Bakeless, John (1942), *The Tragicall History of Christopher Marlowe* (Cambridge, Mass.).

Bate, Jonathan (2010), *Soul of the Age.*

------- (2020), *How the Classics Made Shakespeare.*

Barroll, Leeds, "Shakespeare, Noble Patrons and Pleasures of 'Common' Playing," in *Shakespeare and Theatrical Patronage in Early Modern England*, ed. Paul Whitfield White and Suzanne R. Westfall (Cambridge, 2002).

Bearman, Robert, 'Was William Shakespeare William Shakeshafte' Revisited,' *Shakespeare Quarterly* 53 (2002): 83-94.

Bevington, David and Peter Holbrook, eds. (1991), *The Politics of the Stuart Court Masque* (Cambridge, Eng.).

Bevington, David (2004, 2016), *The Complete Works of Shakespeare*, (Chicago).

Bindoff, S.T. (ed.) (1982), *The House of Commons, 1509-1558*, 3 vols (London).

Birch, Thomas (1754), *Memoirs of the Reign of Queen Elizabeth* (London).

Black, Joseph (1997). "The Rhetoric of Reaction: The Martin Marprelate Tracts (1588-89), AntiMartinism, and the Uses of Print in Early Modern England," *Sixteenth Century Journal*, 28: 707-725.

Bloxam, John Rouse (1853-1881), *A Register of the President, Fellows, Demies… of… Magdalen College*, 7 vols. (Oxford).

Bossy, John (1965), "Henri IV, the Appellants and the Jesuits," *Recusant History*, 8: 80-122.

------- (1975), *The English Catholic Community, 1570-1850* (London, 1975).

------- (1973),"The English Catholic Community, 1603-1625," in *The Reign of James VI and I*, ed. A. G. R. Smith (London, 1973),

------- (1991). *Giordano Bruno and the Embassy Affair* (New Haven and London: Yale University Press).

------- (2001). *Under the Molehill: An Elizabethan Spy Story* (New Haven and London: Yale University Press.)

Bradney, Joseph (1914), *A History of Monmouthshire*, vol. 2 part 1, *The Hundred of Raglan* (London).

--------- (1923), *A History of Monmouthshire*, vol. 2 part 2, *The Hundred of Trelech* (London).

Breight, Curtis C. (1996), *Surveillance, Militarism and Drama in the Elizabethan Era*, (New York, 1996).

Brownlow, F.W. (1993), *Shakespeare, Harsnett, and the Devils of Denham* (Newark : University of Delaware Press).

------- (1996), *Robert Southwell* (New York, 1996).

Bruce, John (1844), "Who was 'Will, my lord of Leycester's jesting player'," *Shakespeare Society Papers*, 1:89-90.

Budiansky, Stephen (2005), *Her Majesty's Spymaster: Elizabeth I, Sir Francis Walsingham, and the Birth of Modern Espionage,* (New York).

Bullough, Geoffrey (1957-1966), *Narrative and Dramatic Sources of Shakespeare* (New York & London).

Burke, John (1844), *A Genealogical and Heraldic History of the Extinct and Dormant Baronetcies of England, Ireland, and Scotland* (London 1844).

Butler, Guy (1983), "Shakespeare and Two Jesters", *Hebrew University Studies in Literature and the Arts* 11: 161.

C

Caraman, Philip (ed.) (1951), *John Gerard: The Autobiography of an Elizabethan* (London: Longmans).

------- (1964), *Henry Garnet, 1555–1606, and the Gunpowder Plot* (London: Longmans).

------- (1995), *A Study in Friendship: Saint Robert Southwell and Henry Garnet* (St. Louis).

Carlson, Leland H. (1981). *Martin Marprelate, Gentleman* (Huntington Library).

Carter, Charles H. (1964), *The Secret Diplomacy of the Hapsburgs, 1598-1625* (New York: Columbia University Press).

Cecil, Algernon (1915). *A Life of Robert Cecil,* (London).

Chambers, E.K. (1923), *The Elizabethan Stage,* 4 vols. (Oxford: Clarendon Press),

-------- (1930), *William Shakespeare,* 2 vols. (Oxford: Oxford UP).

-------- (1944), *Shakespearean Gleanings* (Oxford: Oxford UP).

Chiasson-Taylor, Rachelle A.M., (2006), *Musicians and Intelligence Operations, 1570-1612: Politics, Surveillance, and Patronage in the Late Tudor and Early Stuart Years* (Ph.D. dissertation, McGill University).

Childs, Jessie (2014), *God's Traitors: Terror and Faith in Elizabethan England* (Oxford, 2014).

Clark, Andrew (ed.) (1887), *Register of the University of Oxford* II/i (Oxford: Oxford Historical Society).

Clark, Arthur (1951), *Chepstow, its castle and lordship* (Newport & Monmouthshire Branch of the Historical Association).

-------- (1931), *Thomas Heywood,* (Oxford, 1931).

Cooper, John (2012), *The Queen's Agent: Sir Francis Walsingham and the Rise of Espionage in Elizabethan England* (New York).

Crystal, David & Ben, (2002), *Shakespeare's Words: A Glossary & Language Companion* (Penguin).

Crystal, David (2008, 6th ed.), *A Dictionary of Linguistics and Phonetics* (Blackwell).

D

Daugherty, Leo (2013), *The Assassination of Shakespeare's Patron: Investigating the Death of the Fifth Earl of Derby* (2nd Edition).

Davies, David William (1967), *Elizabethans Errant* (Cornell).

de Grazia, Margreta (2023), *Shakespeare Without a Life* (Oxford).

de Schepper, Hugo and Geoffrey Parker (1976), "The Formation of Government Policy in the Catholic Netherlands under 'The Archdukes',1596-1621," *English Historical Review*, 91: 241-254.

Dear, Peter, "What Is the History of Science the History Of?: Early Modern Roots of the Ideology of Modern Science," *Isis*, 96, pp. 390-406 (September 2005).

Del Soldato, Eva, "Natural Philosophy in the Renaissance", *The Stanford Encyclopedia of Philosophy* (Fall 2023 Edition).

Dent, C. M. (1983) *Protestant Reformers in Elizabethan Oxford,* (Oxford: Oxford University Press).

Devereux, W. (ed.) (1853), *Lives and Letters of the Devereux, Earls of Essex ... 1540-1646,* 2 vols. (London).

Devlin, Christopher (1956), *The Life of Robert Southwell, Poet and Martyr* (London: Longmans, Green).

Dodd, A. H. (1938a), "A Spy's Report, 1604," *Bulletin of Celtic Studies* (1938), 9:154-67.

------- (1938b), "The Spanish Treason, the Gunpowder Plot, and the Catholic Refugees," *English Historical Review* 53: 627-50.

--------- (1937), "Two Welsh Catholic Emigres," *Bulletin of Celtic Studies* 8: 346-48.

Donaldson, Ian (2011), *Ben Jonson: A Life* (Oxford).

Duffy, Eamon (1992), *The Stripping of the Altars* (New Haven).

du Maurier, Daphne (1975), *Golden Lads* (N.Y.).

Katherine Duncan-Jones, "Was the 1609 Shake-Speares Sonnets Really Unauthorized?," *The Review of English Studies* 34.134 (May 1983): 151–71.

--------- (2010), *Ungentle Shakespeare* (London: Methuen Drama).

E

Eccles, Mark (1934), *Christopher Marlowe in London* (Cambridge, Mass: Harvard University Press).

-------- (1982), *Brief Lives: Tudor and Stuart Authors,* in *Studies in Philology*, vol. 79 (Fall 1982).

Edmondson, Paul; Stanley Wells (2015), *The Shakespeare Circle: An Alternative Biography* (Cambridge).

Edwards, Francis (2002). "The First Earl of Salisbury's Pursuit of Hugh Owen," *Recusant History* 26: 2-38 (2002).

--------- (1964), *The Dangerous Queen* (London: Geoffrey Chapman).

--------- (1985), "The Attempt in 1608 on Hugh Owen, Intelligencer for the Archdukes in Flanders," *Recusant History* 17: 140-57.

--------- (1995), *Robert Persons: The Biography of an Elizabethan Jesuit 1546-1610* (St. Louis, Missouri: Institute of Jesuit Sources).

------- (2006), *The Succession, Bye and Main Plots of 1601-1603* (Dublin: Four Courts Press).

------- (1973), *The Gunpowder Plot: the narrative of Oswald Tesimond alias Greenway*, (Folio Society).

Etchells, Frederick and Hugh Macdonald (1926), Phoenix *Nest* (Haslewood Reprints).

F

Ferguson, Craig, (1968), *Valentine Simmes* (Charlottesville).

Finnis, John (2005), "'The Thing I am': Personal Identity in Aquinas and Shakespeare", Social Philosophy & Policy 22: 250-282; also in Ellen Frankel Paul, Fred. D. Miller & Jeffrey Paul (eds.), *Personal Identity* (Cambridge & New York, Cambridge U.P.), 250-282.

------- & Martin, Patrick (2003a), "Shakespeare's Intercession for *Love's Martyr," Times Literary Supplement*, no. 5220, April 18th, 12-14.

------- & Martin, Patrick (2003b), "An Oxford Play Festival of February 1582, *Notes & Queries* 248:391-4.

Fitzalan-Howard, H. G. (ed.) (1857), *The Lives of Philip Howard, Earl of Arundel and of Anne Dacres, his Wife*, (London).

Foley, Henry (ed.) (1877-1883), Records *of the English Province of the Society of Jesus*, 7 vols. (London).

Foster, Joseph, (1891), *Alumni Oxonienses: The Members of the University of Oxford, 1500-1714*, 4 vols. (Oxford).

Fraser, Antonia (1996) *Faith and Treason: The Story of the Gunpowder Plot* (New York).

------- (1969), *Mary Queen of Scots* (London).

Freedman, Sylvia (1983), *Poor Penelope: Lady Penelope Rich, An Elizabethan Woman*, (The Kensal Press).

G

Gardiner, Samuel R. (1887), *History of England from the accession of James I to the outbreak of the Civil War 1603-1642*, 10 vols. (London: Longmans).

Gent, Lucy, "Venus and Adonis: The Triumph of Rhetoric," *Modern Language Review*, 69 (1974), pp. 721-729.

Goodman, Nathan Gerson (1925). *Diplomatic Relations between England and Spain, 1597-1603* (Philadelphia).

Greenblatt, Stephen (1988), *Shakespearean Negotiations: The Circulation of Social Energy in Renaissance England* (Berkeley: University of California Press.

------- (2004), *Will in the World: How Shakespeare Became Shakespeare* (New York).

------- (2025), *Dark Renaissance: The Dangerous Times and Fatal Genius of Shakespeare's Greatest Rival,* (Norton).

Greg, Walter W. (ed.) (1904), *Henslowe's Diary* (London).

Guiney, Imogen (1939), *Recusant Poets* (New York).

Gurr, Andrew (1996), *The Shakespearian Playing Companies* (Oxford: Oxford UP)

Gurr, Andrew "Three Reluctant Patrons and Early Shakespeare," Shakespeare *Quarterly*, Vol. 44, No. 2 (Summer, 1993), pp. 159-174.

H

Halliwell, J. O. (ed.), (1845)*Poetical Miscellanies from a MS. coll. of the time of James I* (London).

Hamer, Douglas, "Was William Shakespeare William Shakeshafte?,' Review of English Studies, n.s. 21.81 (1970).

Hammer, Paul E.J. (1999), *The Polarisation of Elizabethan Politics: The Political Career of Robert Devereux, 2nd Earl of Essex, 1585-1597* (Cambridge: Cambridge UP).

------- (1992), "An Elizabethan Spy Who Came in from the Cold: the Return of Anthony Standen to England in 1593," *Historical Research* 65: 277-95.

---------"The Use of Scholarship: The Secretariat of Robert Devereux, Second Earl of Essex, c. 1585-1601," *The English Historical Review*, 109, (1994), pp. 26-51.

Handover, P. M. (1959), *The Second Cecil 1563-1604* (London).

------ (1957), *Arbella Stuart* (London, 1957).

Hasler, P. W. (1981), *The House of Commons, 1558-1603,* 3 vols. (London).

Heath, Charles (1806), *Historical and Descriptive Accounts of the Ancient and Present State of Ragland Castle* (Monmouth).

Herford, C. H., P. Simpson, and E. M. Simpson, *Ben Jonson*, eds. (1925) 11 vols. (Oxford, 1925–52), cited as Herford and Simpson.

Heywood, Thomas (1612), *An Apology for Actors* (London).

Hicks, Leo, SJ. (1964), *An Elizabethan Problem: Some Aspects of the Careers of Two Exiled Adventurers* (New York: Fordham University Press).

------- (1957-8), 'Father Robert Persons, S.J. and the Book of Succession', *Recusant History*, 4: 104-37.

------- (1963), "The exile of Dr William Gifford from Lille in 1606," *Recusant History*, 7 214-38.

------- (1960), "The Embassy of Sir Anthony Standen," *Recusant History*, 5: 91-127; 184-222.

------- (1955), "Sir Robert Cecil, Father Parsons and the Sucession," *Archivum Historicum Sociatatus Iesu* 24:95-139.

------- (1942), *Letters and Memorials of Father Robert Persons SJ*, (London, Catholic Record Society no. 39).

Higgins, Ben (2022), *Shakespeare's Syndicate: The First Folio, its Publishers, and the Early Modern Book Trade* (Oxford).

Hogge, Alice (2002), "Closing the Circle: Nicholas Owen and Walter Owen of Oxford," *Recusant History*, 26:291-300.

------- (2005), *God's Secret Agents* (Harper).

Holmes, Peter J. (ed.) (1981), *Elizabethan Casuistry* (London, Catholic Record Society no. 67)

------- (1980), "The Authorship and Early Reception of a Conference about the Next Succession to the Crown of England," *The Historical Journal*, 23:415-429.

------- (1982), *Resistance and Compromise: The Political Thought of the Elizabethan Catholics* (Cambridge).

Honan, Park (2005), *Christopher Marlowe: Poet and Spy* (Oxford).

Honigmann, Ernst, "The Shakespeare/Shakeshafte Question, Continued," *Shakespeare Quarterly* 54 (2003) pp. 83-86.

------- (1998), *Shakespeare: the Lost Years*, (Manchester)

Hood, Christobel M. (1926), *The Book of Robert Southwell: Priest, Poet, Prisoner* (Oxford).

Hopwood, H. (1903), *A Calendar of the Middle Temple Records* (London).

Hotson, Leslie (1952), *Shakespeare's Motley* (New York & Oxford, Oxford University Press).

------- (1954), *The First Night of Twelfth Night* (London).

------- (1937), *I, William Shakespeare*, (London).

------- (1949) *Shakespeare's Sonnets Dated and Other Essays* (London, Rupert Hart-Davis).

Howell, Thomas Bayley (ed.) (1809), *Cobbett's Complete Collection of State Trials and Proceedings for High Treason and Other Crimes and Misdemeanors*, 2 vols. (London: T C. Hansard).

Hubault, Gustave (1856), *Michel de Castelnau: Ambassadeur en Angleterre* (Paris).

Hume, Martin A. S. (ed.) (1899), *Calendar of State Papers relating to English Affairs (Spain)* (London, HMSO).

------- (1901), *Treason and Plot; Struggles for Catholic Supremacy in the Last Years of Queen Elizabeth* (London).

Hutchinson, Robert (2007), *Elizabeth's Spy Master: Francis Walsingham and the Secret War that Saved England* (Phoenix).

I

Israel, Jonathan (1997), *Conflicts of Empires: Spain, the Low Countries and the Struggle for World Supremacy* (London).

J

Janelle, Pierre (1935), *Robert Southwell the Writer: A Study in Religious Inspiration* (New York).

Jardine, David (1846), *Criminal Trials*, 2 vols. (London, M. A. Nattali).

------- (1851) (ed.), [Garnet's] *Treatise on Equivocation* (London).

Jardine, Lisa and Alan Stewart (1999), *Hostage to Fortune: The Troubled Life of Francis Bacon, 1561-1626* (New York).

Jenkins, Gladys (1947). "The Archpriest Controversy and the Printers, 1601-1603," *The Library*, V [5th series], 2:180-86.

Jones, Emrys (1977), *The Origins of Shakespeare* (Oxford: Oxford UP).

Jones, Deborah (1933), "Lodowick Bryskett and His Family," pp. 243-362, in Charles J. Sisson (ed.) *Thomas Lodge and Other Elizabethans* (Cambridge, Mass.).

K

Kamen, Henry (1997), *Philip of Spain* (New Haven, Yale UP).

Kaula, David (1975), *Shakespeare and the Archpriest Controversy* (The Hague, Mouton).

Kelsey, Harry (1998), *Sir Francis Drake* (New Haven).

Kenny, Anthony, (1982), "Reform and Reaction in Elizabethan Balliol, 1559-1588," in John Prest (ed.), *Balliol Studies*, 17-52. (London).

Kilroy, Gerard (2005), *Edmund Campion: Memory and Transcription* (Aldershot: Ashgate)

Kinney, Arthur F., (1973), *Titled Elizabethans* (Hamden, Conn.).

Klause, John (2000), "Politics, Heresy, and Martyrdom in Shakespeare's Sonnet 124 and *Titus Andronicus*," in Schiffer, James (ed.) (2000), *Shakespeare's Sonnets: Critical Essays* (NY: Garland), 219-40.

--------- (2008), Shakespeare, the Earl and the Jesuit (Rosemont).

--------- (2002), "*The Phoenix and Turtle* in Its Time," in Moisan, Thomas and Bruster, Douglas (eds.) (2002), *In the Company of Shakespeare: Essays in Honor of G. Blakemore Evans* (Farleigh Dickinson U.P.), 206-229.

Klausner, David (1990), *Herefordshire, Worcestershire* (Toronto), p. 127.

Knox, Thomas Francis (ed.), (1878), *The First and Second Diaries of the English College, Douay* (London, D. Nutt).

L

Labanoff, Alexandre (ed.), (1844), *Lettres, instructions* et *mémoires de Marie* Stuart, *reine d'Écosse*, 7 vols (London).

Lacey, Robert (1971), *Robert, Earl of Essex* (Atheneum, New York).

Laoutaris, Chris (2014), *Shakespeare and the Countess: The Battle that Gave Birth to the Globe* (London).

--------- (2023), "Who was Shakespeare's mysterious London lodger?" *Times Literary Supplement*, March 31, 2023.

--------- (2023). *Shakespeare's Book* (William Collins).

Lee, A. G. (1964), *The Son of Leicester* (London).

Lee, Maurice ed. (1972), *Dudley Carleton to John Chamberlain, 1603-24* (Rutgers).

Lefèvre, Joseph (1925), "Juan de Mancicidor, sécretaire d'état et de guerre de l'archiduc Albert, 1596-1618," *Revue belge de philologie et d'histoire*, 4: 697-714.

Lennon, Colm (1981), *Richard Stanihurst* (Irish Academic Press).

Lindley, David (1998), *Court Masques: Jacobean and Caroline Entertainments, 1605-1640* (Oxford).

Lodge, Edmund (1838), *Illustrations of British History*, 3 vols. (2d ed. London).

Loomie, Albert J. (1971a), "Guy Fawkes in Spain," *Bulletin of the Institute of Historical Research* Special Supplement No. 9.

-------- (1973a), "Francis Fowler II, English secretary of the Spanish embassy, 1609" *Recusant History*, 12/2 pp. 70-78.

-------- (1973b), *Spain and the Jacobean Catholics*, vol. I: *1603-1612* (Catholic Record Society no. 64)

------- (1972), "Thomas James: The English Consul of Andalucia," *Recusant History* 11:165-178.

------- (1963a), *The Spanish Elizabethans* (London: Burns & Oates).

-------- (1971b), 'King James I's Catholic consort', *Huntington Lib. Q.*, 34:303–16.

-------- (1963b), "Toleration and Diplomacy," *Transactions of the American Philosophical Society*, n. s., 53/6 (1963).

-------- (1965a). "Richard Stanyhurst in Spain: Two Unknown Letters of August 1593," *Huntington Lib.Q.* 28: 145-55 (1965).

------- (1969), "Sir Robert Cecil and the Spanish Embassy," *Bulletin of the Institute of Historical Research* 42: 30-57.

------- (1965b), "Philip III and the Stuart Succession in England, 1600-1603," *Revue Belge de Philologie et d'Histoire*, 43: 492-514 .

Lunn, Maurus "Chaplains to the English regiment in Spanish Flanders 1605-6," *Recusant History*, vol 11, 133-55 (1971), p 137.

M

Maclean, John (ed.) (1864), *Letters from Sir Robert Cecil to Sir George Carew*, Camden Soc. o. s. no. 88 (London).

Macray, William Dunn (1897), *The Register of the Members of St. Mary Magdalen College, Oxford*, vol. II *(Fellows 1522-1575)* (London).

------- (1901) (III, *Fellows 1576-1648*), *A register of the members of St Mary Magdalen College, Oxford* (London).

Madan, Falconer (1895), *The Early Oxford Press* (Oxford).

Manley, Lawrence and Sally-Beth MacLean, *Lord Strange's Men and Their Plays* (2014).

Marañon, Gregorio (1953), *Antonio Perez,* Charles D. Ley, trans., (New York).

Martin, Patrick H. and Finnis, John M. (2002a), "The Identity of 'Anthony Rivers'," *Recusant History* 26: 39-74.

-------- (2002b) "Tyrwhitt of Kettleby, Part I: Goddard Tyrwhitt, Martyr, 1580", *Recusant History* 26: 301-313.

--------- (2003a), "Thomas Thorpe, 'W.S', and the Catholic Intelligencers," *English Literary Renaissance* 33: 1-43.

-------- (2003b), "*Caesar*, Succession, and the Chastisement of Rulers," *Notre Dame Law Review* 78: 1045-1074

-------- (2003c), "Tyrwhitt of Kettleby, Part II: Robert Tyrwhitt, a Main Benefactor of John Gerard SJ, 1599-1605", *Recusant History* 27: 556-569

------- (2005), "Benedicam Dominum: Ben Jonson's Strange 1605 Inscription", *Times Literary Supplement*, November 4th, 12-13,

------- (2006), "The Secret Sharers: 'Anthony Rivers' and the Appellant Controversy, 1601-2", Huntingdon Library Quarterly 69/2: 195-237.

Martin, Patrick H. (2015), *Elizabethan Espionage* (McFarland).

Mattingly, Garrett, (1957), "William Allen and Catholic Propaganda," in *Aspects de la propagande religieuse* (Geneva: Droz), 325-339.

------- (1959), *The Armada* (Boston).

McConica, James, "The Catholic Experience in Tudor Oxford," in *The Reckoned Expense*, McCoog, ed., 1996.

McCoog, Thomas M. (1988), 'The Slightest Suspicion of Avarice': The Finances of the English Jesuit Mission," *Recusant History* 19: 103-23.

--------- (1996a), *The Society of Jesus in Ireland, Scotland, and England 1541-1588* (Brill).

--------- (1996b), " 'Playing the Champion': The Role of Disputation in the Jesuit Mission," *The Reckoned Expense,* McCoog, ed. (Woodbridge, Suffolk, Boydell Press);

--------- (1994), *English and Welsh Jesuits,* 1555-1650, 2 vols. (Catholic Record Society nos. 74-75).

McDonald, James H. and Nancy Pollard Brown (eds.) (1967), *The Poems of Robert Southwell* (Oxford).

McGrath, Patrick (1967), *Papists and Puritans under Elizabeth I* (London).

Milward, Peter (1977). *Religious Controversies of the Elizabethan Age: A Survey of Printed Sources*, (University of Nebraska Press).

------- (1973), *Shakespeare's Religious Background,* (Bloomington).

------- (2005), *Shakespeare the Papist* (Naples, Fla.).

Motley, John Lothrop (1888), *History of the United Netherlands: From the Death of William the Silent to the Twelve Years' Truce*, (1888).

Munro, Lucy (2026), "A Man of Property," *Times Literary Supplement*, April 17, 2026.

Murdin, William (ed) (1759), *A Collection of State Papers relating to ... the reign of Elizabeth* (London).

N

Neale, John Ernest (1957), *Elizabeth I and Her Parliaments, 1584-1601* (London).

Newdigate, C.A. (1931),"A New Chapter in the Life of B. Robert Southwell, S.J.", *The Month* 157: 246-54.

Nicholl, Charles (1992), *The Reckoning*: *The Murder of Christopher Marlowe*, (London: Jonathan Cape).

------- (2008), *The Lodger Shakespeare: His Life on Silver Street.*

Nicholls, Mark, (1991), *Investigating Gunpowder Plot* (Manchester).

------- (1995a), "Sir Walter Ralegh's Treason: A Prosecution Document." *English Historical Review* 110:902-924.

-------- (1995b), "Treason's Reward: The Punishment of Conspirators in the Bye Plot of 1603," *The Historical Journal* 38/4:821-42.

------- (1995c), "Two Winchester Trials: The Prosecution of Henry Brooke, Lord Cobham, and Thomas Lord Grey of Wilton, 1603," *Institute of Historical Research*, 68: 26-48.

Nichols, John (1827), *The Progresses and Public Processions of Queen Elizabeth* (London).

Nungezer, Edwin (1929), *A Dictionary of Actors* (New Haven, CT).

P

Parker, Geoffrey (1972),*The Army of Flanders and the Spanish Road 1567-1659* (Cambridge).

------- (1998), *The Grand Strategy of Philip II* (New Haven).

------- (1979), *Spain and the Netherlands, 1559-1659* (Short Hills, NJ).

Parmelee, Lisa Ferraro (1994). "Printers, Patrons, Readers, and Spies: Importation of French Propaganda in Late Elizabethan England," *Sixteenth Century Journal*, 25: 853-72.

Parmiter, Geoffrey de C. (1975), "Plowden, Englefield and Sandford: I," *Recusant History* 13:159-177.

------- (1977), "Plowden, Englefield and Sandford: II," *Recusant History* 14:9-25.

Persons, Robert (1582), Epistle *of the Persecution of Catholics in England.*

------- (1602), *A Manifestation of the Great Folly.*

Petti, Anthony G. (ed.) (1959), *The Letters and Despatches of Richard Verstegan*, (London, Catholic Record Society no. 52).

------- (1957), *A Study of the Life and Writings of Richard Verstegan* (c. 1550–1640), (thesis, London University).

------- (1963). "A Bibliography of the writings of Richard Verstegan (c. 1550-1641)," *Recusant History* 7: 82-103.

------- (1958), "Peter Philips, composer and organist, 1561-1628," *Recusant History* 4: 48-60.

Pollen, John Hungerford (1916), *The Institution of the Archpriest Blackwell* (London).

------- & W. MacMahon (eds.) (1919), *The Ven. Philip Howard Earl of Arundel 1557-1595* (London, Catholic Record Society no. 21).

--------- (1903a), "The Accession of King James I," *The Month* 101: 572-85.

--------- (1903b), "The Question of Elizabeth's Successor," *The Month* 101: 517-32.

--------- (1904), "Dr. William Gifford in 1586," *The Month* 103:243-56, 348-66.

--------- (1914) "Introduction," *Campion's Ten Reasons* (London), 1-29.

--------- (1908), *Unpublished Documents relating to the English Martyrs* (London, Catholic Record Society no. 5).

------- (1922), Pollen, *Mary Queen of Scots and the Babington Plot,* (Edinburgh).

Pritchard, Arnold (1979), *Catholic Loyalism in Elizabethan England* (Chapel Hill, University of North Carolina Press).

Q

Questier, Michael (2006) *Catholicism and Community in Early Modern England,* (Cambridge).

------- (1997), "Loyalty, Religion and State Power in Early Modern England: English Romanism and the Jacobean Oath of Allegiance," *The Historical Journal*, 40/2 (1997), 311-329.

R

Rawson, Maud Stepney (1911), *Penelope Rich and Her Circle* (London, 1911),

Read, Conyers (1925). *Mr. Secretary Walsingham and the Policy of Queen Elizabeth.* 3 vols. (Oxford: Clarendon Press).

Reif, Sister Mary Richard, *Philosophy in Some Early Seventeenth Century Scholastic Textbooks* (Ph.D. dissertation, St. Louis University, 1962).

Renold, Penelope (1967), *Letters of William Allen and Richard Barret, 1572 – 1598* (London, Catholic Record Society no. 58).

--------- (1958). *The Wisbech Stirs* (London, Catholic Record Society no. 51).

Riggs, David (1989), *Ben Jonson* (Harvard).

--------- (2004), *The World of Christopher Marlowe* (London).

Riis, Jacob A. (1901), "Hamlet's Castle," Century Magazine, lxi. 391.

Rollins, Hyder Edward (1931 ed.), *The Phoenix Nest* (Cambridge, Mass.).

Rowse, A. L. (1965), *Times, Persons, Places* (London, Macmillan).

--------- (1964), *Christopher Marlowe: His Life and Work* (NY: Harper & Row).

Ryland, J. W. (1922), *Records of Rowington* (Oxford).

S

Sawyer, Edmund (ed.), (1725), [Ralph Winwood], *Memorials of Affairs of State in the Reigns of Queen Elizabeth and King James* I, 3 vols. (London),

Schmitt, Charles B. (1983). *John Case and Aristotelianism in Renaissance England,* (Montreal and Kingston, 1983).

Schoenbaum, Samuel (1975), *William Shakespeare: A Documentary Life,* (Oxford, 1975).

--------- (1991), *Shakespeare's Lives*, (Oxford).

Schrickx, Willem (1986), *Foreign Envoys and Traveling Players in the Age of Shakespeare and Jonson* (Gent).

Simpson, Richard (1867), *Edmund Campion: A Biography*, (London).

------- (1899), and H. S. Bowden, *The Religion of Shakespeare* (London).

Smith, Alan Gordon (1936), *The Babington Plot* (London).

Sorlien, Robert Parker (1976), *The Diary of John Manningham of the Middle Temple 1602-1603* (Hanover, N.H.).

Southern, A. C. (1950), *Elizabethan Recusant Prose, 1559-1582* (London).

Southwell, Robert (1953), *An Humble Supplication to Her Majestie*, R.C. Bald (ed.) (Cambridge).

Spedding, James, Robert L. Ellis, and Douglas D. Heath (1857-74), *The Works of Francis Bacon* (London, Longman).

Spedding, James (ed.) (1861), *Letters and Life of Francis Bacon*, 2 vols. (London).

Strachey, Lytton (1928), *Elizabeth and Essex* (New York).

Strong, Roy (1977), *The Cult of Elizabeth: Elizabethan Portraiture and Pageantry* (London, Thames & Hudson).

Sullivan, Mary, *Court Masques of James I* (1913).

T

Taunton, Ethelred L. (1901), *The History of the Jesuits in England, 1580- 1773*

Taylor, Gary (Editor), et al., (2016), *The New Oxford Shakespeare: Modern Critical Edition* (Oxford).

------- (2003), 'The Cultural Politics of Maybe', in *Theatre and Religion: Lancastrian Shakespeare*, edited by R. Dutton, A. Findlay and R. Wilson (Manchester, 2003), pp. 242-58.

------- (1989), *Reinventing Shakespeare*, (New York).

Teague, Frances (1998), "Jonson and the Gunpowder Plot," *Ben Jonson Journal* 5: 249-252.

Thoms, William J. "Was Shakespeare ever a Soldier?" *Three Notelets on Shakespeare* (1865).

Thornbury, Walter (1873), *Old and New London: A Narrative of its History, its People, and its Places*, 3 vols. (London).

Tierney, M. A. *Dodd's Church History of England*, 5 vols. (London, 1839-43).

Tighe, William Joseph, (1984) *The Gentlemen Pensioners in Elizabethan Politics and Government* (unpublished PhD thesis, Cambridge University, 1984).

Trappes-Lomax, T.B. (1951), "The Englefields and their contribution to the survival of the faith in Berkshire, Wiltshire, Hampshire and Leicestershire," *Biographical Studies* (*Recusant History*), 2: 131-148.

Treggiari, Susan, (1969) "The Freedmen of Cicero," *Greece & Rome*, 2nd Ser., Vol. 16 pp. 195-204.

Trimble, W. R. (1964), *The Catholic Laity in Elizabethan England* (Belknap,1964).

U

Ungerer, Gustav (1976), *A Spaniard in Elizabethan England: The Correspondence of Antonio Perz's Exile,* 2 vols. (London, Tamesis Books).

Vickers, Brian (1996), *Francis Bacon: A Critical Edition of the Major Works* (Oxford UP).

------- (2002) *Shakespeare, Co-Author* (Oxford University Press).

------- (2007) "Incomplete Shakespeare: Or, Denying Coauthorship in "1 Henry VI" *Shakespeare Quarterly*, pp. 311-352

W

Wadsworth, James (1629), *The English Spanish Pilgrim* (London).

Walsham, Alexandra (1999), *Providence in Early Modern England* (Oxford University Press).

------- (1993), *Church Papists: Catholicism, Conformity and Confessional Polemic in Early Modern England* (Woodbridge, Royal Historical Society, Boydell Press).

Ward, G.R.M. (ed.) (1840), *The Statutes of Magdalen College Oxford Now First Translated and Published* (Oxford and London).

Waugh, Evelyn (1961), *Edmund Campion, Jesuit and Martyr* (London).

Wells, Stanley, Taylor et al (1997), *William Shakespeare: A Textual Companion,* (Norton).

Wernham, R. B. (1976), "Christopher Marlowe at Flushing in 1592," *English Historical Review* 91: 344-5.

------- (1987), "Queen Elizabeth I, Emperor Rudolph II and Archduke Ernest," in E. I. Kouri & Tom Scott (eds.), *Politics and Society in Reformation Europe* (Macmillan, 1987), 437-52.

------- (1994), *The Return of the Armadas: The Last Years of the Elizabethan War Against Spain 1595-1603* (Oxford).

Wilcox, John (1941), "Putting Jaques into 'As You Like It'," *Modern Language Review* 36: 388-394.

Wilkie, Vanessa (2023), *A Woman of Influence: The Spectacular Rise of Alice Spencer in Tudor England.*

Williams, Franklin B. "An Initiation into Initials", *Studies in Bibliography*, ix (1957), 163-78.

Wilson, Derek (2007), *Sir Francis Walsingham: A Courtier in an Age of Terror* (London).

Wilson, Ian (1993), *Shakespeare, The Evidence: Unlocking the Mysteries of the Man and his Work* (London: Headline).

Wilson, Richard (2004), *Secret Shakespeare* (Manchester).

Wilson, Thomas (1936), 'The state of England anno dom. 1600', ed. F. J. Fisher, *Camden miscellany, XVI*, CS, 3rd ser., 52 (London).

Winkler, Elizabeth (2023), *Shakespeare Was a Woman and Other Heresies* (New York).

Wood, Anthony à (1691), *Athenae Oxonienses* (revised ed. Bliss, 1815-20).

Wood, Michael (2003), *Shakespeare.*

Woodfield, Denis B. (1973) *Surreptitious Printing in England, 1550-1640* (New York: Bibliographical Society of America, 1973).

Wright, Thomas, *Queen Elizabeth and Her Times*, II, pp. 266-69 (London, 1838).

Y

Yates, Frances A. (1964), *Giordano Bruno and the Hermetic Tradition* (London, Routledge & Kegan Paul).

------- (1934). *John Florio: the life of an Italian in Shakespeare's England* (Cambridge 1934).

Index

G

H

T

U

V

W

www.ingramcontent.com/pod-product-compliance
Lightning Source LLC
Chambersburg PA
CBHW051546030726
47592CB00001B/154

9781964075112